Royal Fright

G J Bellamy

ISBN: 9798304276412

This publication is a work of fiction. All names, characters and events in this publication, other than those clearly in the public domain, are fictitious and any resemblance to real persons, living or dead, or actual events is purely coincidental.

Copyright © 2024 by G J Bellamy. All rights reserved.

The moral right of the author has been asserted.

No part of this publication may be reproduced, stored in a retrieval system, or transmitted in any form or by any means, without the prior express written permission of the publisher.

G J Bellamy

gjbellamy.com

Cast of Characters

Family & Friends
Sophie Burgoyne / Phoebe King
Lady Shelling (Elizabeth Burgoyne) - Auntie Bessie
Ada McMahon / Nancy Carmichael - Sophie's friend
Flora Dane / Gladys Walton - Sophie's long-time friend
Archie Drysdale - Sophie's second cousin

The Agency
Miss Jones, typist and office manageress
Elizabeth Banks, researcher and office helper
Douglas Broadbent-Wicks, footman and spy

The Royal Family
King George V (Georgie)
Queen Mary (May)
Queen Alexandra (Alix)
Prince Edward (David)
Prince Albert (Bertie)
Princess Mary
Prince Henry
(Prince George does not appear)

Lud's Gang
Mr Healy, the planner
John Godfery, the manager
Barrett, blackmailer
Lefty Watts, thug

Arthur Morrish, Healy's manservant
Others — James Mitchell, Mateo, Gustav, Old Davey, Lottie Bradley, Teddy Moss.

Scotland Yard and Government Departments
Superintendent of Special Duties (Inspector) Penrose
Detective Sergeant Gowers, CID
Ralph 'Sinjin' Yardley, Foreign Office agent
Maxwell Handley, Palace official

Prologue

King Lud may have been the first king of London, and his statue stands in Fleet Street. Some say he never existed and is purely a myth. Those who believe him to have been an actual living man say that he founded and fortified London before the Romans invaded Britain — and that was a very long time ago. Whatever might be the truth of the matter, by 1921 another King Lud had appeared and had become a byword for the perpetration of any unsolved cases of nefariousness, especially in the capital city. If a serious crime occurs, and there is no clear suspect, one officer or another will inevitably quip, "King Lud must have done it."

It all started in 1911, at the time of the fabulous Festival of Empire at The Crystal Palace. Among the events to be held was the Pageant of London, a dramatization accompanied by music composed by such leading lights as Vaughan Williams and Gustav Holtz. Before the opening night, someone had the temerity to deface dozens of the colourful posters for the pageant. Whoever did it, for the police never did find him, simply pasted a smaller white poster with bold printed lettering over the advertisement. Its message was short and enigmatic: London Belongs To Me — King Lud.

The expression of outrage in several newspapers reached astronomical heights, fueled in one journal by a letter to the editor from someone purporting to be King Lud, the instigator of the furor. Some respondents then accused journalists of having concocted the letter in order to sell more newspapers, others declared the letter to be the work of a lunatic. The substance of the letter was as follows:– 'King Lud' explained that *he* was the rightful King of London. The Saxe-Coburg and Gothas (which is how the writer referred to the Royal Family) were foreign interlopers who had stolen his birthright.

After a few days, the blaze of indignation burned out and was all but forgotten, except for one interesting and peculiar change in the vernacular. Whereas in the past, especially in political or journalistic circles, a group of individuals may have been called Luddites, afterwards, anyone found to be particularly irritating was quickly labelled 'a King Lud.' The term even appeared in headlines connected with other matters.

Over the next few years, the name of King Lud came to be associated with darker exploits and, as with the original ancient king, he was generally considered part man and part myth.

The Suffragettes had been carrying out a widespread bombing campaign, which lasted two years. Towards the end of their efforts, in June 1914, someone detonated a bomb under the Coronation Chair in Westminster Abbey. The shrapnel of nuts and bolts narrowly missed some bystanders, but severely damaged the chair, while the blast itself caused a great deal of panic. Although everyone assigned this outrage to the Suffragettes, a brief note found at the scene pointed in a different direction.

> This chair is rightfully mine. If I cannot sit in it,
> neither shall your descendants.
> King Lud

Although reported upon widely, at the time the authorities believed the note, obviously intended for King George, to be merely an opportunistic move made by a deranged person who was not the individual who had planted the bomb. However, within the next few months, the situation had changed. An armed gang successfully hit a bank, a jeweller's, and a van carrying a payroll. With obvious good planning and comparative ease, this gang eluded the police, who had neither clues nor suspects. It was galling for the detectives that, on each occasion, one of the gang members had said to someone at the scene, "This is for King Lud." The police had no way of knowing if it had been spoken in jest or in earnest.

A claim as startling and lurid as that could hardly be suppressed, but the kernel of truth was soon amplified and much embellished, until it spread like wildfire through the East End of London, because that was where all three incidents had occurred. Seemingly overnight, King Lud became a household name, and almost a source of pride, which naturally led to much speculation about his identity. Soon, every unsolved murder or other criminal deed was being ascribed to this ethereal parvenu. He became an instantaneous legend, and the legend, even as war broke out in France, solidified in the common knowledge as if it were known fact!

This, then, is the myth that prevails and is embedded in the subconscious of hundreds of thousands of Londoners — King Lud is an evil genius, a lurking, dark and untouchable magician, a spirit who comes and goes at will to cause death, destruction, disappearances, and the loss of valuables. Yet is there a real person behind the myth? And, if so, how came he by such an extraordinary name?

Chapter 1

Mr Healy

December 1920

They called him Mr Healy, but that was not his name. At the far end of a large upper-storey room, arranged and specifically lit like an art gallery, and where the windows were bricked up, Healy copied old architectural drawings while seated at a wide Georgian desk — part of an office area. On the desktop, a pair of small lamps revealed a litter of plans and schematics in the otherwise gloomy space. Spotlights picked out on the walls the exquisite paintings by famous artists and, in much the same way, the desk lamps isolated the work of Healy's hands, leaving the rest of him in semi-darkness. Taken at a glance, his soft, manicured, middle-aged hands seemed to operate by themselves — putting on a performance in the light by creating an arresting display of swift, precise artistry, generating line, form, and meaning in ink upon paper. Discernable in the faint glow beyond the desktop, Healy's tailored jacket was open, revealing a discreet tie and a glowing white shirtfront, while his head and shoulders suggested only a grey shape against the grey wall behind him.

Three men came up the stairs at the other end of the room. They filed in silently to take their seats, which were positioned opposite Healy's desk. On the middle chair now sat a man wearing a rough jacket and trousers, which were far from new, and identified him as a labourer or artisan. A slender shaft of light from a small overhead lamp picked him out from the gloom. He balanced a small, stiff leather bag on his knees and fiddled with the handles. The light bothered his eyes, requiring he turn his head. To one side of him was a tall man sitting upright, while on the other, another man lounged easily.

Healy put away his drafting implements. Then he carefully rolled up the original drawings he had copied and slid the tube into a long, narrow canvas bag.

"These drawings are in their correct order." He looked at his watch, and then said to the artisan, "It is now 2:00 a.m. Can you return them to the museum before they are missed?"

"Ahh…" The man glanced towards the shorter of the two other men with him before looking back. "Yes, sir." He spoke with a heavy Italian accent.

"I understand your hesitation. The agreement was to pay you fifty pounds to bring me the drawings, but I will pay you an additional fifty to put them back in their proper place." He held up the canvas bag.

The Italian smiled and nodded, then went forward to take the bag.

"Excellent… Godfrey," he addressed the man sitting easily, who now, being thus addressed, also sat upright. "You and Morrish can drive the gentleman to the museum. After he completes the task, you shall settle his account. I won't need either of you after that."

"Very good, Mr Healy," said Godfrey.

He arose and touched the Italian on the arm. The three men filed out in silence.

When they had gone, Healy returned to his copies of the drawings. Working with a ruler, a pair of compasses, a pen, and a notebook, he worked unceasingly, often consulting maps, sometimes pacing, but always absorbed in his work. It was almost six when he finished and cleared his desk, putting all his work into a safe. He slotted in his notecase a single slip of paper upon which were listed the things he intended to do.

He descended the stairs and, three floors below in the ground-floor hall, met the tall man named Morrish, who was holding a fur-collared coat at the ready.

"My dear fellow, you needn't have waited up." There was an agreeable, almost affectionate quality in Healy's voice as he put on his coat.

"Well, if you're in the house and awake, Mr Healy, then so am I." He spoke with a deep voice. The homely and rather shabbily dressed manservant took from the hall table a bowler hat, gloves, and a scarf.

"Such devotion. I value it greatly. And our visitor?"

"In the river." He handed the items one by one to his master.

"An unfortunate necessity, because we can't be too careful with this job. It is tremendously important." He put on his hat. "Good morning."

"Good morning, sir. And please be careful. It was snowing earlier and, although I cleared the steps, they might be a bit icy. The streets may be as well."

"Then I'll be careful, as you suggest. Oh, didn't I give you fifty pounds earlier?" he asked just before putting on his gloves.

"You did, sir. I put it back in the petty cash box."

"Tidily done, as always. I'll just make a note." Healy took out a small book and a gold propelling pencil. In a precise hand, he jotted down the information, then paused. "We're coming up to Christmas." He stared at Morrish. "It's come a little early for you, Morrish. Take a hundred and fifty from the box." Healy made an entry in his book.

"That's very kind of you, sir. Indeed, it is. Mrs Morrish will be overwhelmed by your generosity. And a merry Christmas to you, too, sir, if it's not too early for me to say."

"Of course not." Healey smiled. "Far be it from me to meddle in your finances," he said, becoming confidentially playful, "but buy her something nice."

"Normally, we're great savers, but I'll give that some serious thought... May I be so bold as to ask a question?" They moved to the front door.

"Yes, what is it?"

"Will there be any more like tonight's?"

"More than likely... Consider it a certainty. Why do you ask?"

"Well, sir, I was just wondering. You see, I weighted tonight's gentleman, but I'd rather the river took 'em downstream after a high tide, otherwise we'd have 'em all planted in the one spot, so to speak. If they bob, I'd prefer 'em to be far away when found. The problem, sir, is like this. I'm not familiar with the tides and they are a-changing every single day."

"I appreciate your difficulty and agree with your proposal. Tidal information is published in the newspapers, but you'll be better served by purchasing a tide-table for London Bridge." Healy smiled.

"I'll do that very thing, sir. And thank you once again."

Morrish opened the door. Healey went out into the raw, chill air. It was still dark and the small, gently falling snowflakes added to the slush. He walked away from the stark lonely building — an end-of-row townhouse that had lost its immediate neighbour and still bore the scars of its former attachment. With its windows heavily curtained or, as they were on the top floor, bricked up, 12 Crescent was a withdrawn and brooding house, disfigured and unfriendly, where no light entered during the day, and none escaped at night.

Chapter 2

Behind Guildhall

Early May 1921

Directly behind old Guildhall there is a vile alley that leads nowhere. It lost its name centuries ago. In old times, the place was larger and simply known as Backyard. It had been lively enough, what with stables, a blacksmith, a baker, and small, dark shops, with smaller, darker, overcrowded rooms above. Back then, it was the communal well that vitalized the place. They used to say the stream twenty feet beneath the flagstones was the Walbrook River and that the water from it was as sweet as if it came fresh from a mountain stream. That notion lasted until an ostler threw in a bucket for water and pulled up in it a human skull. The inhabitants left off using the well for a while, and this was at about the time of Anne Askew's trial in the Great Hall. They do say that when Lady Jane Grey had her trial a few years later, another skull came up in the bucket. The same happened again for Thomas Cranmer's trial — so they say. After that, they covered the well and the not-so-sweet water of the Walbrook flowed unmolested down to the Thames.

The buildings around the alley had burnt to the ground in the Great Fire. Guildhall was nearly lost, too. Afterwards, new structures were raised, but these were offices to serve Guildhall or warehouses — all busy enough during the day but deserted at night, except for the few who called the place home. The alley remained and later became a dead-end with the location of the well lost.

Nowadays, the windows that overlook the alley are opaque with the grimy patina of weather and smoke. No one looks through them anyway because there is nothing of interest to be seen. If someone could look, they might catch sight of Old Davey shuffling from his tiny cottage. Every morning at eight, he begins his day's work of keeping the Guildhall front courtyard swept. What an onlooker could never see just before daybreak on any given day of the week were several burdened men entering Old Davey's cottage.

In the dark of an early May morning, three newcomers crowded inside the decrepit cottage, which was wretchedly furnished, although clean, and lit by a single lantern. The men laid down their burdens, which were mainly short, newly cut planks. The first transaction was Old Davey being paid his two shillings for the day, which he gladly accepted from a man named Lefty. Next, Davey detached the stove's chimney. Then between them and by using two short pieces of wood, they carried the lit stove to one side. Davey scrambled to attach an extra length of metal chimney to prevent his cottage from filling with smoke. Underneath where the stove had stood was a metal plate, which they removed. Beneath that were two flagstones that they readily pried up with crowbars. Once everything was out of the way, one man got down into the opening and descended a ladder. It was the old well which, many years ago, had run dry when the river Walbrook had changed course. At the bottom, he threw a switch and lights came on below, the power for which the electricity company unknowingly supplied gratis. A second man descended the ladder. Davey and the third man first passed down the planks. When that was finished, they replaced the flagstones, plate, and stove.

"Rather you than me," said Davey in a gravel voice, pointing with his thumb to the underground passage. He was a gruff man, bearded and dirty. He pulled up a chair to the stove.

"You got yer florin, so shut it," said Lefty, who was a big scowling man. "The less you know, the healthier it is."

"Oh, I'll keep quiet all right. But you'd never get me going down there in that little hole… Want some breakfast?" Davey took down a skillet from a nail, preparatory to frizzling some eggs and bread.

"I ate already. I'll see you later."

"See you, then."

After he had closed the front door, Davey put lard in the skillet and set it atop the stove to heat.

Down below, the two men had to stoop while laboriously moving the planks along through a recently dug, low tunnel. This part was roofed and shored up with planks similar to those they carried, and it ran for twenty feet until it branched. To their left, the old riverbed continued on and from somewhere along that dank passage, they could hear the flowing water of the Walbrook. To their right were six narrow steps, and these they ascended, bent over to pass through a narrow gap at the top. This brought them into an altogether different tunnel — sufficiently open for them to stand upright and walk normally. The string of bulbs revealed the large medieval foundation stones of Guildhall on their right while the men faced south. In a shadowy opening let into the foundation wall, stairs lay behind a rusted, locked gate. These once led up to the Guildhall crypt, but they were now strewn with rubble and the passage sealed off by blocks of stone. To the tunnel's left were the foundations of another building that had completely gone to ruin. The uneven, mismatched stones of Saxon builders rested upon and filled in earlier Roman foundation work. In a few places overhead, the tunnel roof curved and was made of brick but, more often, wooden beams soaked in pitch held back the weight of the earth above. Pale new wood marked a few places where rotten beams had collapsed.

This ancient, dusty tunnel, this forgotten underground passage — mostly dry but damp in places — had not been used for a very long time. Northwards, the zig-zagging passage ran for fifty yards to the George Hotel, but the old entrance to that building's cellars was bricked up. Southwards, the passage connected with other, smaller tunnels, but most of them had collapsed.

The two men now carried their planks with ease. Away from Guildhall, they passed by a long curving section of Roman wall. Occasionally they saw Catholic crosses and Latin inscriptions which sometimes overlay Hebrew script — signs suggesting that at various times people in peril had used the tunnel as a hiding place or way of escape.

"Where's Raoul today?" Mateo the Portuguese broke the silence with his guttural English.

"I don't know," said James Mitchell.

"More work for us, but we go slower without him." After several more paces, Mateo asked, "What we do, huh?"

"I've told you before," James answered in perfect English, "it's dangerous to ask questions."

"Why, Jimmy? Just you and me here."

"Leave off, old boy. Do the work, get paid, and go home to your family."

"You answer same every time... We're friends, yes?"

"Yes."

"Friends trust each other."

"As your friend, I'm doing you an immense favour by telling you to drop it completely."

"But I wanna know."

"Be quiet... For goodness' sake, talk about the weather or anything else."

"It's hot up there and cool down here... Tell me little bit. Very small. Is it a bank or a jeweller's? Must be something like that."

"Ask Lefty."

"No, not him! He's bad."

"Then drop the subject and stay safe."

"But it's only us. I say nothing, you say nothing."

This final, weak appeal went unanswered, and they walked on southwards, towards Old Jewry. Before reaching there, however, they turned eastward into a smaller tunnel beneath Coleman Street. This section was wet and water dripped through the arched brickwork overhead. It was not a sewer as such, but it certainly smelled like one, and it was unlit because lightbulbs could not survive the damp conditions. Ahead, the tunnel opened up into a bell-shaped and obviously man-made cavern. Six feet below their feet ran the somewhat loathsome and dark Walbrook river. Its level was lower than usual on account of the recent dry weather. Fifteen feet above them was a circular grating set in concrete. It was still dark now, and no light filtered through this hole as it would later. It vented into the basement of an unknown building. All they knew was that they must be quiet here because there was sometimes movement in the basement above. So, with great care, and out of sight of the grating, they extended long planks across the river. Slowly, they shifted the day's supplies from the precarious shelf that was the bank they were on to the far side. In the dark gloom, they shuffled along the planks using lanterns turned down low. Before them was a skull perched on a mound of soil waiting to be dumped in the river when the water level rose again. In its meanderings, the Walbrook had scoured out an old burial site, depositing a few bones along the way, before washing the rest into the Thames.

Once clear of the river, they proceeded with greater ease. Along this section, the new repairs were more numerous, and it was dry enough that the lightbulbs did not blow. Finally, they reached the newest tunnel, which headed south once more. It was low-roofed and, after a while, it squeezed between the foundation walls of the church of St Margaret Lothbury and the building next to it. Here, the men were only twelve feet below ground level but, once past those walls, the tunnel dived deep beneath a sewer pipe and underground public conveniences before rising again.

They reached the tunnel's face. Mateo arranged his tools and a sack to kneel on, while James, sitting further back, sat down by the bellows with its long tube which was to supply fresh air. Later, they would take turns at digging, working the bellows, removing the soil, and shoring up the tunnel.

"All set?" asked James.

"Yes, all set, my friend." He had tied a handkerchief across his face.

Mateo crossed himself before spitting on his calloused hands. Taking up a short-handled pickaxe, he selected a spot on the tunnel face. He drove the pick home. James began working the bellows' lever with a steady rhythm. Their long day underground had begun and would not end until the sun went down.

Chapter 3

A Hint of Great Danger

Thursday 19 May 1921

All the world comes to the London Dock — the orient, represented by spices and tea, the Caribbean by exotic fruit, Canada by timber, the Argentine by beef, the Baltic by herring, Egypt by cotton, Kenya by coffee and cocoa — the list is endless. What goes out through London Dock are finished goods — clothing, boots, machinery, cars, soap, tools, and many other things besides. Then, among the exports, there is the occasional and exceptional one; a floating dead body to be sucked out to sea by the tidal Thames, and sent wherever nature decides it should go.

Wapping Basin — the entrance to the docks proper — was lined with waiting freighters. On a section of quay between the stern of one large vessel and the bow of a smaller one, a corpse lay on a square of canvas. Two Scotland Yard detectives examined the body which had been hauled out of the water less than an hour earlier.

Inspector Morton spoke to one of several nearby constables. "Have them move back." The constable began asking the small crowd of dockhands and seamen to give more room.

"Broken neck... same as the others," said Gowers, staring down at the body. He pushed back his bowler hat and squatted on his haunches.

"Hasn't been in the water long," said Inspector Morton.

"No, sir. No more than a few hours... Nothing in his pockets... He's got tattoos." Gowers had pulled up a sleeve of the man's jacket. "Hello, he's Catholic. Here's a cross with a bit of Latin."

"Going by his complexion, he's from the Mediterranean. About forty, and capable-looking. Who broke his neck, then?"

"A gorilla, I should think." Gowers searched the interior of the man's jacket. "No maker's label."

"We can't do anymore here, so let's get him in the van. Hopefully, the police surgeon will find something."

Morton scanned the crowd and those further away. He could see no one behaving oddly. Gowers stood up and motioned to a couple of orderlies with a stretcher.

"Third in two months," said Gowers to Morton. "All unidentified foreign seamen with broken necks and thrown in the river."

"This is the first corpse in the Basin," said Morton. "The other two were outside." He paused with a sour expression on his face. "Has to be the same business as the others."

"Looks that way, sir."

Morton scanned the surroundings. "There are no lamps hereabouts... There'd be the ship lights, but this part between the freighters would still be in darkness sure enough."

"Are you thinking they were all done around here, and the tide took the others out when the locks were open?"

The body was put on the stretcher and taken to the waiting van.

"Around here somewhere. You see, we're near the outer locks, but still inside the Basin. I reckon someone got sloppy and meant to do the job outside the locks and by the river."

"Looks as though he put up a bit of a fight," said Gowers. "See here, where his knuckles are scraped?"

"Hmm. Maybe he was jumped by the river but escaped, getting as far as here."

"A gang, then?"

"We'll see. If he was murdered aboard a ship, we'll have a chance to identify him once we show the photographs to the ship's officers, but if he wandered in here to meet someone or the murderer followed him, we've got no hope. Now, with the other two, they may have been dumped in the river outside the locks."

Gowers looked towards the river and watched four barges being pulled by a tugboat. He turned towards Morton. "And with three of them killed the same way, none of them look like accidents anymore. Not one of them slipped, broke his neck, and ended up in the water."

"Right, let's try this big freighter first." Morton looked up and there were three deckhands leaning on the rail looking down at him. "It won't be any of them," he said wryly to his companion.

The two detectives walked over to the midship gangway and climbed aboard.

It took several days for the detectives to get a break in the case. At first, they interviewed countless ship's officers, dock workers, and others while showing photographs of the three men who had died. They had gone to nearby boarding houses, shops, pubs, and association halls. Early on Monday morning, they started on missions close to the docks. At the Foreign Workers' Relief Mission on Neptune Street — an old, unattractive small building wedged in among towering, unadorned brick warehouses — Sergeant Gowers met Pastor Clarkson, a man in his late thirties. He did not need his dog collar and dark suit to identify him as a cleric. He was the personification of mildness, and no wayward soul would ever feel condemned in his presence. The soft-spoken pastor had curly, almost fluffy, hair, while his pink, fresh complexion and innocent blue eyes gave the impression he was an oversized infant rather than a grown man.

"How may I help you, Sergeant?" he asked after Gowers had introduced himself. They were standing in a tiny front office. A short corridor with doors to other rooms led to a large open space filled with six rows of five beds. There was a pervasive smell — a blend of cabbage, human occupation, and ammonia.

"We're conducting enquiries into the murders of these three gentlemen." Gowers took the photographs from an envelope and handed them to Pastor Clarkson. "Unfortunately, Pastor, we don't know their identities."

"How terribly distressing. Such wickedness. Are these the men taken from the river?"

"They are."

"I had heard of two of them, but I didn't know there was a third. Dear, dear me."

He looked at the photographs, pausing over the third.

"I know this man."

"You do? A resident of yours?"

"Yes. His name is Raoul Martin, from southern France. Is he dead then?"

"I'm afraid so. What can you tell me about him?"

"Well, he said he was a merchant seaman throughout the war and, um, let me see, he arrived here a fortnight ago. Mr Martin was having difficulty finding permanent work and came to us. And to think he's gone. It's so sad."

"Yes, it is... Would you mind telling me what it is you do here?"

"Of course not. We provide food and shelter for newly arrived foreign nationals who can't find work. There really is no support for them, otherwise. Typically, they don't know anyone and, without work, their little reserves of money are soon exhausted, so they end up here. We help them find employment and support them as best we can until they do. Then we also assist them in finding lodgings. You see, we desperately need the beds, because we're always so busy."

"I imagine you are." Gowers was writing in his notebook. "Could you spell his last name, please?"

"It's the French pronunciation of Martin."

"Oh, is that so? Funny that, eh? I daresay *we* sound peculiar to *them*, as well. I take it Raoul Martin was unable to find work, then?"

"As far as I know, he never mentioned that he had found any before he left suddenly on Sunday evening. I wasn't here at the time, so I'll have to ask the volunteers who were."

"It would be very helpful if you would let me know. He didn't happen to leave a forwarding address?"

"Well, no, he didn't. We believed Mr Martin was returning that night because he left some of his things behind."

"Might I see them, please?"

"Of course, Sergeant. If you would kindly follow me this way." They started for the back of the hall and the pastor continued with an explanation. "We don't normally keep belongings. Our flock is expected to take their possessions when they leave." He paused before adding, "You should understand, Sergeant, that among those who come here are what one might call people in desperate circumstances. They have come to Britain to start a new life." He smiled awkwardly.

"Because things got too hot for them in their own country?" queried Gowers.

"Um, yes. One could put it like that, but we prefer to be optimistic about the future, rather than pessimistic about the past. Who knows what temptation may have lain in a person's path? A moment of weakness, and they are ruined forever... Before you decide I might be somewhat simple-minded over this point, let me assure you I am well aware of the depths of depravity into which a person may sink. What we strive to do here is to provide the right help, encouragement, and spiritual guidance, so that these otherwise lost souls may regain their dignity. Allow me to further assure you that among those staying here, those experiencing such moral difficulties are a small minority. Here we are."

He reached into a pocket and produced a large bunch of keys. The door in front of them had two sturdy locks.

"These locks won't keep the best of them out, but they certainly slow them down." He smiled and then opened the door. "We don't keep valuables on the premises for the simple reason we don't have any."

"Now that's the best deterrent against theft," said Gowers.

"How true. Yet even mere trifles are a great temptation to a few of our friends. You must remember, they have nothing."

"Indeed, sir. This minority of criminals — are they still active?"

"Sergeant, I would be much obliged if you would refrain from using such language while here. However, to answer your question, a minority undoubtedly was once in that class, but now no longer operate in it. Of that, I am certain."

He switched on the light. Occupying what he had expected to be the only free space on the cluttered floor of the small room was a rocking horse with a broken rail.

"Not again," said Pastor Clarkson as he stared at the object.

"You take in women and children, too?"

"Yes. They are housed upstairs. We look after the children during the day while the mothers and older girls are out seeking work."

"That must be hard for them when they don't speak the language."

"Naturally, it is. However, in the evenings, we teach English to all our residents. It's quite amazing the aptitude some of them have." The pastor took down a stained canvas duffel bag from a nearby pile.

"But don't they all come from different countries? How do you manage that?"

"Out of the kindness of their hearts, several who have applied to the mission in the past return to help their compatriots to learn English. It is most rewarding to see such enthusiasm. Any evening you care to drop in, you will hear Russian, German, Dutch, Italian, Danish, Norwegian, and more. At present, we have a Somalian gentleman staying who, besides his own language, knows only a smattering of Spanish. He's our first from Somalia and, although we're making progress, he's proving to be a bit of a challenge." Clarkson smiled.

"Thank you for explaining that. Ah, may I?" Gowers put his hand out for the duffel bag.

"I'm sorry...? Oh, yes, of course. What can I be thinking about?

The pastor handed over the bag. Sergeant Gowers rummaged through it but stopped upon noticing a piece of paper. He unfolded the sheet, which was a printed pamphlet with notes written on the back.

"I don't want to take up any more of your time," said Gowers abruptly. "I'll have to take this to the Yard. It's evidence, you see. I'll give you a receipt for the duffel bag and contents. Looks like old clothes and papers mostly, but it will have to be gone through properly, considering the circumstances." He began writing out the receipt.

"That's quite all right. I don't suppose any next of kin would know to come here. Raoul was not with us for very long, so his family may have been ignorant of his whereabouts."

"Don't you obtain details from your, um, customers?"

"We don't think of them as customers as such. They are more like our friends. Beyond examining their passports, we never enquire into their background. All we know is what they volunteer to tell us."

"Very nice of you... There is something else. Do any subversive elements try to get at your friends?"

"Subversive? How do you mean?"

"Well, are there any organizations with extreme views operating in your mission?"

"Not at all. The street gangs give us a wide berth. Frequently, there is pamphleteering, but that has always been the case. It comes and goes. Recently, someone has been rather clever, and they've translated several of their pamphlets into French, German, Spanish, and Italian."

"Is that so? Rather cheeky of them. What sort of thing do they say?"

"I suppose they are after the foreign seamen — there are many dwelling near the docks, although not so many as there used to be because of the new immigration requirements. Often the tracts contain extreme socialist views. Sometimes they are Communist and pro Russian, but those types are rarer these days. Of late, there have been some vitriolic anti-monarchy tracts, outlining how the monarchy should be removed. Actually, now that I think about it, it is this type that has been translated. I can't understand the mind that feels it necessary to generate and publicize such hateful and untruthful rhetoric."

"Do any of your friends here at the mission discuss such things?"

"Oh, never. At least, I have never heard them doing so. Is this important, Sergeant?"

"It may have nothing to do with Mr Martin's death, but it's a fact that he fell in with the wrong company at sometime or other. So, we have to keep an open mind and explore all possibilities."

"Yes, I can see that."

"What sort of chap was he?"

"Like many of our friends, somewhat insular and quiet, although his English was quite good. He was helpful on the occasions when we were short-staffed. As I mentioned, he was not here for very long, so I didn't get to know him particularly well. In our few, brief conversations together, I always found him to be pleasant... It's amusing, really. Being a clergyman, many people I meet, especially so here, are not quite sure how to behave towards me. Typically, they are polite, respectful, and moderately distrustful of me." He smiled and became conspiratorial. "I invariably have to win their confidence and dispel the deeply held notion I'm trying to convert them to a new religion." He chuckled, and the years that the serious subject matter had added fell away so that he looked like a child again.

"I can appreciate that." Gowers became brisk. "I must go now. Thank you very much for your help. I'll be back soon, no doubt."

Clarkson relocked the door, and they returned to the entrance. They said goodbye. Gowers hurried away to find a taxi to get back to the Yard as soon as he could. All he knew was that in Martin's duffel bag was the most astonishing and disturbing thing he had ever read.

It was Tuesday morning, 24th of May 1921. Sophie Burgoyne arose very early and ate her breakfast alone at White Lyon Yard because her Aunt Bessie never came down before ten. The young woman wanted to make the most of the day for several reasons. After she was satisfied that the business of Burgoyne's Agency was proceeding smoothly, and after she had dealt with the inevitable troubling issues which occurred daily, such as supplies running short, awkward customers, and so forth, she could then devote herself entirely to the more satisfying prospect of buying what was needed to re-decorate the office. Her grand vision of how the office should look was under the budgetary constraint of what she could afford. Unfortunately, there was a mismatch between the two. The office needed repainting — that was a must, but perhaps there might be money left over for a new rug to dress up the reception area. This morning, she would find out, or so she believed.

Often, things do not go as planned. This Tuesday was one of those days. A typist handed in her resignation, and the maid who was to come in to finish her training for a dinner engagement on Thursday never arrived. This meant Sophie had to scramble, spending the first part of the morning looking for replacements. The rest of the morning was taken away from her by an urgent telephone call from Scotland Yard. Superintendent Penrose summoned her, and she could detect the urgency in his usually placid voice. She ended up spending the day being rapidly briefed in meetings with the police, Home Office, and Foreign Office, and all thought of paint pots and pretty rugs evaporated. There was, it appeared, going to be a serious attempt made upon the lives of the Royal Family.

Early Wednesday morning, Ada McMahon and Flora Dane met Sophie in her office.

"What's come up that's so urgent?" asked Flora. "I'm trying out for a part in a new play this afternoon."

"Cancel it," said Sophie.

"Just like that? Good parts are scarcer than... Do you know, there *isn't* anything scarcer than a good part?"

"I'm sorry, but the situation demands that you cancel."

"Something exciting, is it? Murder at the manor? Homicide at the Hall? Spies in the Spinney or Agents in the um, the um, oh, Abbey?"

"How about Bombs at Buckingham Palace!"

"Blimey," said Ada.

"You're not pulling our legs, are you?"

"I wish I were. You can add to that, Stilettos at Sandringham, Automatics at Ascot, and Booby Traps at Balmoral."

"It must be that the pressure of running your own business has sent you off your head," said Flora. "I always knew it would happen."

"Ha-ha, not funny at all. This is extremely serious. Yesterday, I was in meetings all day with the HO, FO, and Yard. Many government departments are involved, and they want us, meaning we three and Mr Broadbent-Wicks, to be in attendance on the Royal Family wherever they go. You see, King George has been receiving death threats by post. They were all intercepted by secretaries, except for the most recent letter, which was left... on his bedroom pillow!"

"Oh, good grief!" exclaimed Flora.

There was a long, incredulous silence.

"If the King goes overseas, miss, do we go an' all?" asked Ada at last.

"No. We shall only be present for public engagements, visits in the British Isles, and while the family is at home."

"At Buckingham Palace?" asked Flora.

"Or even Balmoral or Windsor Castle. Their actual home is York Cottage on the Sandringham Estate. Apparently, the place is like a rabbit warren and quite overcrowded because the King, Queen, and five children live there. I was told that the King loves it because it was the house he grew up in, but Queen Mary is not so partial to it."

"But Sandringham is huge, or so I thought," said Flora.

"Well, yes, it is. But Queen Alexandra has a life interest in Sandringham House and *won't* move out."

"So, there's one aged royal in the big house," said Flora, "and there are seven others crammed into a tiny cottage? I suppose it's not your ordinary cottage, but still. That sounds peculiar to me."

"I thought they all lived in Buckingham Palace," said Ada. "Do you mean we won't be going there?"

"It all depends on the King's duties. We'll get a look inside on Friday, when we must present ourselves for training."

"Training? How long is this mission?" asked Flora.

"It lasts indefinitely — while the threat continues."

"Um, Miss? I hate to bring this up, but we've got a big dinner booked for this Friday."

"We're not doing it. Staff from the Royal Household will fill in for us. How about that? I'll explain now why we must drop everything at once."

"Please, do," said Flora.

"The government is aware of a small radical group who, through political reforms, is intent upon the abolition of the monarchy. They have so far confined themselves to agitation through speeches and the distribution of pamphlets. Although ardent, there are few of them, and they are having difficulties attracting people to their cause. These anti-monarchists are well known and the police do not consider them to be dangerous. More recently, however, propaganda of a violent nature has surfaced in London and the authorities have yet to discover who is publishing it. They could be a splinter group from the original set or another organization entirely."

There was a soft knock on the door.

"Come in," called Sophie.

"Excuse me for disturbing you, Miss Burgoyne," said Elizabeth Banks, the receptionist, chief researcher, and car mechanic for Burgoyne's Agency. She closed the door quietly behind her. She lowered her voice. "Superintendent Penrose just telephoned to say, 'It's all on.'"

"Thank you, Elizabeth."

She inclined her head and left the office as quietly as she had entered.

Flora and Ada looked at each other and then at Sophie.

"Don't keep us in suspense," said Flora.

"I won't. For this mission, we're not actually to serve, as such, but will busy ourselves sufficiently to give the impression that we are servants while in the dining room at meals. At all other times, we will be near at hand to the Royal Family, whether they are walking in the grounds or at meetings. At public events, we will constantly be in their vicinity."

"Miss?" Ada put up her hand. "There's only four of us and there's a load of them. How can we watch 'em all?"

"As the threat could be described as the destruction of the Royal Family as an institution, the principal targets are obviously King George and Queen Mary, Edward, the Prince of Wales, Prince Albert, Princess Mary, and the princes Henry and George. They were advised to confine themselves to York Cottage for the moment, but they must attend public engagements at some point."

"What if they all have public engagements on the same day?" asked Flora.

"We'll work it out at the time. We're not the only ones involved in this security action."

"Then, we're not like bodyguards, are we, miss?"

Sophie laughed. "Not exactly. Our purpose is to watch for suspicious behaviour among the staff and any others who might come into close contact with a royal personage. We are also to be on the lookout for suspicious packages — anything which could contain a bomb."

"A bomb!" exclaimed Ada.

"I'll run off screaming if I suspect a bomb is anywhere nearby," said Flora. "The Royal Family will just have to follow my lead."

"I don't like the sound of this, miss. A bomb is not a very nice thing."

"No, it isn't," agreed Flora. "How do you know they're going to be blown up?"

"Well, we don't know that for certain, of course, but there has been an interesting development following on from the death threats, which establishes it as the primary potential method. Last week, Inspector Morton and Sergeant Gowers were investigating a murder at the London Docks."

"I read about that," said Ada. "He was the third foreigner dumped in the Thames this year."

"That's true," said Sophie. "What I'm about to say has yet to be publicized, because the police don't want to alert the murderer. So, you mustn't repeat any of this to anyone. Scotland Yard contacted the French police. They sent the fingerprints and photographs of the dead man to the Sûreté Nationale in Paris, where they positively identified him. Here, he was known as Raoul Martin, but that was an alias. His real name was Paul Floquet, and he was wanted by the Sûreté because he had robbed a large bank. Before the war, he worked on the Rove Tunnel in France, where he became proficient in handling explosives. The war intervened, and he was conscripted before the tunnel was finished. Afterwards, and unable to get his old job back, he turned to crime by joining a gang. He used his skills to blow open several bank safes. Although the gang's last raid was successful, the police caught them shortly afterwards, with only Floquet narrowly avoiding arrest. This was about two months ago. He left the country and became a merchant seaman. About three weeks ago, he arrived in England using a fake passport. Before I go further, shall we have some tea? This is thirsty work."

"Good idea," said Flora, who got up. "I'll put the kettle on, but don't you dare say another word until I return."

"I'll get the tray ready, miss, and bring some biscuits," said Ada, who also left.

Sophie knew very well that they were going to have a private discussion about the mission.

When they were all settled with their tea, Sophie resumed her story telling.

"Raoul Martin entered England and found a place to stay at the Foreign Workers' Relief Mission. Of interest is that he left the ship and immediately went straight to the mission.

Now, I wasn't aware of this, but you can't just do that these days. He should have registered an address with the passport officials and reported to the police, but he didn't do either, and yet his passport was franked. Something funny went on there and the Home Office is looking into it. Lord Laneford was very put out about it."

"Do you mean to say Sidney is involved in this?" asked Flora. "He didn't say a single word about it to me!"

"Operational secrecy."

"That's the sort of thing *he* would say."

"Be fair. This has only just all come to the fore."

"I shan't be fair to him. But never mind that now. Please continue."

"The conclusion drawn is that someone here arranged for Raoul Martin to come to Britain. That is a significant point to remember. He was murdered a week ago and identified yesterday. The big news is that, among his possessions left at the mission, there was one of the anti-monarchist tracts of the worst kind. A death-to-them-all type of thing. On the back of it were three detailed sketches of time bombs! I have been informed that they are all quite viable and demonstrate a high level of expertise. Two were using alarm clocks as timers, and one, a smaller one, relied upon acid eating through metal to detonate the dynamite. It was suggested that this particular device was suitable for a car bomb."

"I don't like the ideas of bombs, miss. They're cowardly and horrible, that they are. But don't it mean, if the bomb-maker's dead, there's nothing to worry about?"

"Unfortunately, no. You see, each sketch was numbered ranging from five to seven. That means there were at least four more designs on other sheets. There were also some technical notes in French with added English comments written in another hand. The comment for the car bomb said, 'Timer too risky for an attempt in the Mall.'"

"That's the road which leads directly to Buckingham Palace," said Flora.

"Yes, it is. Another note said a loudly ticking alarm clock might become noticeable during a large dinner in a stateroom."

"Blimey," said Ada.

"The HO, FO, and Yard were forthcoming with the details for once," said Flora.

"I think it's because they're all a bit rattled."

"Can't blame them for that. I feel a bit rattled, too."

"Flora, are you sure you want to do this?"

"Oh, absolutely! I'm not missing out on a chance to hobnob with the royals, even if it results in my untimely demise."

"What rubbish," said Sophie, who smiled. "You'll want to know what we're to be paid, of course. Let me tell you, it got *extremely* awkward when I brought up the subject. There were all these decisive men, yet not one of them had given a moment's thought to our remuneration. Then, Archie — oh, I really could have kicked him — he volunteered that I had a Foreign Office salary. That made the negotiations so much harder! Anyway, after a great deal of hemming, hawing, and general willingness to shirk, the Home Office, quite sensibly and generously, I thought, agreed to pay Burgoyne's an excellent rate. I got it in writing, too. You will each receive two pounds ten per day or part thereof. I always attach that last clause so that they don't take advantage and get half a day for nothing."

"Did Sidney sign it?" asked Flora.

"Yes, he did."

"Good old Sid. I won't tell him off now. He has completely redeemed himself."

"Do you call him Sid?" asked Sophie.

"He doesn't care for the name but, unfortunately, that's how I think of him. I only use it when he's being annoying."

"But he's so nice," said Ada.

"Not a hundred percent of the time, he isn't... But then, he's never been *that* bad. On occasion, he obstinately argues against some of my little ideas."

"Ah, glad to hear it's no more than that," said Sophie. "Now for our itinerary. This Friday we will go to the Palace for training, then on Saturday, we shall travel to Sandringham. Hopefully, Mr Broadbent-Wicks will join us."

"That's marvellous," said Flora.

"How's he doing?" asked Ada.

"Much better, so Nick tells me. He's cleaning windows again. That's why he couldn't be present for this meeting."

"Glad to hear he's back on his feet," said Flora.

"Yes. Now for tomorrow, the work will be different. This is a stop-gap measure until the police can make other arrangements. Flora and I will be at the Foreign Workers' Relief Mission, while you, Ada, will work at a tea stand inside the dock gates. All of us shall keep a lookout for suspicious characters."

"Hold on," said Flora. "The royals won't be on the docks or at the mission. What's all this about?"

"The police suspect foreign criminals are being recruited and brought in through the London Docks. They wish to keep the area under surveillance. We will be there temporarily — just for the day. The tea stand overlooks the main gate where a newly arrived criminal is likely to meet a contact. Similarly, with Raoul Martin having stayed at the mission, it is likely such establishments are being used as a way of hiding the criminals who have entered illegally."

"So," mused Ada, "someone's bringing in foreign criminals and, if their face don't fit, they're doing them in?" She sounded thoroughly disgusted.

"That's absolutely awful," said Flora.

"Regrettably, that seems to be what's happening. The police are renewing their enquiries in the two unidentified victim cases. If they find any further similarities with Martin's arrival and use of a mission, then it may prove the point." She paused, waiting for further comments. "Let's discuss a few of the minor details. But first, are there any questions?"

"What exactly do you mean by indefinitely, miss?" asked Ada.

"Usually, it's not knowing when a time period will end, depending on the setting. For us, it means until the threat is past, and that, in turn, could mean this work continues for weeks or even months."

"Thank you, miss. Two pounds ten a day... *indefinitely*." She gave a sigh of satisfaction.

"What a beautiful word it is," said Flora.

"I'd say," said Ada.

They were all smiling now.

"Furthermore," continued Sophie, "we must go at once to Mrs Green's for new outfits. We can't wear our maid's dresses at Buckingham Palace."

"This gets better and better," said Flora.

"Doesn't it?" said Sophie. "We'll meet there at one and BW will join us. I'm trusting that Mrs Green has a contact who can tailor a good suit for him before Saturday."

Chapter 4

Lessons

Mrs Green's establishment sells high-quality garments at very low prices, but only if you are in her exclusive members-only club. This arrangement is unusual for a business situated above the shops of Brick Lane and comes about because Mrs Green sells expensive ladieswear to West End shops and must accept returns, but on the strict condition she not sell the garments to the public. The prospect of high-end clothes at discount prices made the agents happy to meet there — almost deliriously so. They all arrived promptly and, while Ada and Flora were busy choosing suitable dresses for themselves, Sophie spoke to the proprietor about a suit for Broadbent-Wicks, who stood at her side.

"I wish I knew what you were up to," said the short, well-dressed, energetic Mrs Green as they stood outside her cramped office, "but there, you'll not tell me. Buckingham Palace... And all three of you!?" She turned to BW. "Excuse me, I should say four, of course."

"Don't worry about that, Mrs Green. People often forget about me."

"Do they?" She gave him a puzzled look. "For a quality suit to be made as quickly as you need it, there's only Morrie At-the-corner."

"Um, which corner?" asked Sophie.

"That's his nickname. He started out on a stall at the crossroads selling second-hand clothes. Now he has a shop three doors down. You probably passed it."

"Oh, I see."

"I'd better telephone him first — to tell him you're coming." She sped into her office and dialled his number.

"Hello, Morrie? It's Evie."

"Evie! So nice to hear from you... What do you want?" The older voice on the other end was firm, yet possessed a hint of weariness.

"I have some very good customers here. Gentiles, but like mishpucha to me. A young gentleman needs a suit yesterday. Dark grey, lightweight worsted. He's going to Buckingham Palace, and it must be ready by Friday."

"Buckingham Palace! What's he doing in Brick Lane?"

"He wants a good suit for a good price. Your best price, Morrie."

"Best price already, and in such a big rush! It doesn't matter that I live on thin soup and stale bread, I must give your customer my best price. Would he like my shop, too? Ah, I'll give it to him if he wants it."

"I'm only asking for a favour."

"What a blessing it is to have friends."

"I'm sending him over now."

"Sure, sure, send everyone over. Why not?"

"Thank you, Morrie."

"Evie, the next time you want a favour, do me one — call somebody else."

Mrs Green replaced the receiver.

"He'll see you right away."

Sophie walked with BW downstairs.

"Here's the money for the suit." She gave him several notes. "Get a receipt and only say you have to work at the Palace for a few days because of meetings."

"Righty-ho. No mention of bombs and what-not."

"Correct. Mention nothing more about the mission than what I've stated. Not a word. None."

"I'll just chit-chat with the fellow about the weather. And thank you, in advance, for the suit, Miss Burgoyne. Totally spiffing of you, don't you know?"

"I'm glad you're pleased. If we finish first, we'll come to you. Otherwise, come back here."

"Got it. Toodley-pip."

BW found the shop and entered, setting a bell in wild motion. He stood in a small, gloomy showroom crammed to the ceiling with suits hanging from three tiers of rails.

"Good afternoon, sir. Are you looking for anything in particular?" A white-haired man in his sixties stepped forward, staring at the visitor over his horn-rimmed glasses. He was wearing a striped shirt with a tape measure draped around his neck.

"Good afternoon, Mr, er, At-the-corner. Mrs Green sent me over to get togged out for the jolly old Palace."

"So you're the one. Just call me Morrie, if you please."

"Hello, Morrie. My name's Broadbent-Wicks, but you can call me BW." He stepped forward and, to the tailor's surprise, shook hands.

"Nice to meet you. Please remove your jacket so I can take your measurements." Morrie whipped the tape measure from off his shoulders.

"Absolutely. How much do you think the suit will be?"

"Don't worry about the price, BW."

"I wasn't worried, exactly. Just curious."

"We'll come to all that later... So, what takes you to Buckingham Palace?" Morrie busied himself, jotting down a number after each of the many measurements.

"A bus, I should think." BW roared with laughter. "No, I'm only going there to do some work. Sounds like a lot of mooching about, mostly."

"Is that so? And what type of work do you do?"

"This and that, you know, but I usually clean windows."

Morrie stood back and straightened up to stare. "You're going to clean the Palace windows in a suit!?"

"I doubt they'll have me doing that. It was this way, Morrie. I got Shanghaied into delivering messages for some fellows who are having a meeting there. No idea what it's all about, but at least I'll get to see the King at close quarters."

"There is that... It's supposed to be beautiful inside."

"Yes... Here, Morrie. You're Jewish, aren't you?"

The tailor stiffened, but BW did not notice.

"What I've always wondered is why you chaps have Saturday as your day off and not Sunday, like the rest of us."

"Because the Torah commands us to do so."

"Torah?"

"The first five books of the bible are what we call Torah."

"I didn't know that. And there's a commandment in there somewhere?"

"It's one of the ten commandments."

"Oh, those! Of course, *they're* in there. But surely *that* one refers to Sunday."

"No, you're *wrong*, if you don't mind me saying. The commandment says we must keep the *seventh* day holy. Sunday is the *first* day of the week."

"I never knew that, either." BW was silent, a concentrated look furrowing his brow. "Then why did Christians choose Sunday?"

"You're asking me? How should I know?" Morrie shrugged.

"I must delve into this matter... I say, Morrie, you can probably help me understand a few things about being Jewish. What exactly is lox? I've heard of it, and if I were to guess, I'd have said it was some type of hair tonic."

Morrie smiled, then patiently explained it was salmon. Then BW asked his next question — one of many.

An hour later, BW returned to Mrs Green's establishment. While going upstairs, he met all three agents who, having said goodbye, were descending, excitedly exclaiming what marvellous purchases they had made.

"How did it go at the tailor's?" asked Sophie.

"Miss Burgoyne, Morrie is such a splendid chap. We chin-wagged the whole time like old friends, and he taught me some Yiddish. Anyway, he says he'll get them working on the schmutter, sorry, the suit, and it will be ready Friday morning. He only charged six pounds. Morrie said he was losing money at that price, but when I asked how much, he replied he was only kibbitzing. I knew he was joking because, afterwards, he included two shirts and a tie in the price, and said I should come back soon."

"Six pounds? That seems very reasonable for a tailored suit… What is his quality like, though? I'm relying upon Mrs Green's judgment in this."

"He had many suits at different prices. The ones he showed me, which he said were his best, looked all right, but then I'm not very clever about such things."

"We must hope for the best," said Sophie.

Walking in the street, the agents began the slow progress of leaving noisy Brick Lane — slow because of the crowds of people milling about the stalls. They had not got very far, when Sophie stopped and turned to say to the others,

"Does anyone know how to make a time bomb?"

"No, miss," said Ada.

Broadbent-Wicks shook his head.

"They're mentioned in stories," said Flora, "but they don't explain how they work. Why do you ask?"

"Well, there's a watch repair place right there." She pointed to a hole-in-the-wall shop. "I wondered if they would know."

"That's doubtful. I don't think they would make bombs," said Flora. "Bomb-making only goes on in the back rooms of secret hideouts. That place hardly looks like an anarchist's establishment."

"I know." Sophie started whispering, "But if we're to prevent the Royal Family from being blown up, we should know what a time bomb looks like. I mean, what do we look for? How big is the standard bomb?"

"Reckon they'd come in all sizes, miss," said Ada. "Like dresses — small, medium, and large."

"Yes, I suppose they would. We really should take this opportunity to go in and find out what they know. Whatever it is, it must be more than our combined knowledge on the subject."

"We can't go in together, miss, or they'll think we're only there to nick stuff." said Ada.

"I'll go in alone," said Flora, excitedly. "My watch is running really slow, and they can take a look at it. Then I'll pump them for information."

"What will you say?" asked Sophie.

"I'll think of something," she replied. "Would you be so kind as to hold these for me?" Flora held out her shopping bags for BW to take.

"My pleasure, Miss Dane."

"Thank you. Hopefully, I shan't be long, so walk ahead and I'll catch you up."

The others moved away to look at the wares displayed on nearby stalls, while Flora entered the diminutive shop.

"Good afternoon, Madam," said the proprietor, who arose from working at a bench behind the counter. All the merchandise was in glass cases except for the larger clocks hanging on the walls or standing on shelves. A subtle, ticking cacophony filled the air, underlying the dominant sounds of the larger, more sonorous clocks. Flora noticed that every timepiece told the correct time. The shop was dim except for the bright pool of light created by a lamp where the man worked. He was about fifty, with close-cropped, wiry, grizzled hair, and wearing spectacles, a tan apron, and a skullcap. As he was in his shirtsleeves, he put on his jacket to serve Flora.

"Good afternoon. It's Miss, actually. I was passing by, and remembered my watch has been running slow of late. I thought I'd pop in to see if you could mend it."

"Let me see the vatch."

"Of course." Flora undid the leather strap and handed the watch to him over the counter.

He stared at the dial, then held it to his ear.

"It might only need a clean. I need to open it. You permit?"

"Please, go right ahead."

He went to the bench and, using a tiny strip of metal, deftly pried off the back of the case. Next, he screwed a jeweller's loupe into his left eye and peered inside. The effort to hold the magnifier in place made him grimace, as if he found Flora's watch disgusting. After a few seconds, he returned to the counter with the magnifier still in place, which Flora, inwardly, found highly amusing.

"Your movement is vorn. But there's some type of grease inside. Did you oil it?" he asked in disbelief.

"No. I wouldn't know how, anyway. Surely, wouldn't a spot of oil make it go faster?"

"That's not how a timepiece works. So, how did the grease get inside? It's all around the stem... Take a look."

With effortless dexterity, he slid a piece of cushioned velvet across the countertop, placed a magnifying glass and the watch on it, switching on and repositioning a lamp before she could answer.

"Where am I looking...? I see it... Oh, I know what that is! A few months ago, I dropped my watch in a pot of cold cream. I'm an actress and I was in a Shakespearean play when I nearly forgot to take off my watch." Flora laughed. "I fumbled it... See where it stained the strap as well?"

"Ah."

"Speaking of plays, I absolutely need your expert opinion on something. How does one make a time-bomb?"

Without moving his head, the watchmender let the loupe fall from his eye to be caught in an open palm. "Bomb!?" He enunciated the second b. "I sell and repair vatches and clacks. I don't know anything about such a thing."

"Well, in a way, I'm glad to hear that. As an actress, I'm in a new and rather exciting upcoming play... I'm the leading lady." She imparted the fact with a certain amount of coyness. "We were doing a reading — that's where we sit with scripts to read our parts out loud — and the subject of time-bombs, quite naturally, arose. You see, the play is a thriller about an assassination. Now, during the play, there will be a trunk to the left of the stage, only the side facing the audience has been cut away to reveal a huge bomb with a large clock attached to it. All throughout the play, and even in the intermission, a spotlight on the clockface reveals the precious time ticking away. The audience sees it, while we on the stage are unaware of the bomb's existence and yet the monstrous device is in the room with us. There it is, steadily counting down the final moments of our lives. At midnight the bomb goes off... Or, does it!? When first the curtain opens, the clock shows ten. Naturally, as time elapses, the dreadful tension builds and builds until it becomes almost unbearable for the audience."

"Vouldn't you hear the ticking on the stage?"

"That's what *we* all said. Do you have any suggestions on how to quieten it?"

"I don't know... You could insulate the trunk to make it soundproof."

"Splendid idea! I knew I'd come to the right place. But what really puzzled us more than anything, and no one could come up with a decent answer, was how does the clock actually set off the dynamite? Do you know?"

"Ehh... I should think an electrical charge is needed for detonation. There's a detonator, you understand, and that explodes first vhich then sets off the dynamite."

"This is fascinating. What happens next?"

"Everything goes ka-boom... But your problem is with the clack. Nothing must go inside the case or it will foul the mechanism... I think I have it. Reach me down that alarm clack."

"What, this one?" She pointed to a large, white-faced, nickel-plated Big Ben.

The watchmender nodded. He took the clock from her and opened it up.

"Listen... See?" He held it towards her ear. "This is a quiet movement, perfect for a bomb. Now, if a vire is attached here," he pointed to the hammer, "and another one here," he pointed to the bell, "then, when the alarm rings, everything goes ka-boom. I don't know so much about electricity. You need batteries and maybe a condenser, I don't know. But you could modify the hammer action so that it only strikes once, and when it hits the bell, it closes the circuit. Then the electrical current flows to the detonator." He scratched his chin, then wagged a knowing finger. "You'd have no more than twelve hours to set off the bomb. And don't no one go knocking the clack or it's goodbye. So, I think, the big timepiece in the trunk should look like this one — a Big Ben."

"Only it would need to be larger, of course, for the audience to see it clearly. A stagehand will put something together... Thank you very much for your most professional help."

"Don't mention it. But tell me something. Vhat happens when the stage clock goes off?"

"You wouldn't believe it, but I can't give away the ending. You'll have to come and see the play when it's in production."

"I think I might do that. Vhat's it called?"

"Umm... A Race Against Time."

"That's a good name. And your name is?"

"Miss Gladys Walton."

"Miss Valton, to return to business... Your vatch — I'm sorry to say it's no good. Does it have a sentimental value?"

"Not really. What do you mean, it's no good?"

"The movement's vorn, and it needs a new balance staff. I can fix it, but that costs a lot. This is not a high-quality movement and the case — it's nice, but... Economically speaking, you're better off buying a new or a good used vatch. Take a look if you don't believe me. You'll see what I'm saying."

Flora looked at her watch through the magnifying glass and nodded when he pointed out the defects with a tiny screwdriver.

"Economically speaking, do you have anything that's cheap, looks very expensive, and lasts forever?"

"Ha! Such a timepiece shall never be made. How much do you vant to spend?"

Flora puffed her cheeks. "I hadn't expected this... Two pounds?"

In the next instant, a velvet-lined tray containing three dozen ladies' watches of every description appeared on the counter.

"Everything here is thirty shillings to five pounds."

"Ooh, I like that one." Flora smiled. "It looks like a sixpence."

"You have a good taste — it's the best piece on the tray. That's a Union Horlogère. Silver case and band, with a fine

Swiss Alpina movement. It's used, but in perfect condition. Sadly, the price is five pounds."

"Oh, it would be. Which ones are two pounds or under?"

"All the bottom row and this one." He unclipped a gold-plated watch and held it up for her to inspect. "Mechanically speaking, in your price range, this one is the best."

Flora studied it. "It's not bad…" She draped it over her wrist. "No… Fashionably speaking, I don't think it suits me. Could I just try on the sixpence watch?"

"Certainly."

He handed her the watch. She thought it looked perfect on her wrist, and she smiled as she listened to it ticking.

"It's lovely, but far too expensive for me."

"A vatch like this, you should think of as an investment. It is best quality and vill last for years. Treat it with care by having it professionally cleaned. Allow me to show you something." From the workbench, he picked up a slim gold hunter pocket watch. He opened it to show her the face.

"Made in 1820," he said with pride.

"How beautiful! And it looks so modern."

"The thin case and silver secondary dials do that. This vatch is a Breguet. My grandfather bought it from the factory the day it vas finished… from Père Breguet himself! Miss Valton, that vas one hundred and one years ago! And yet this piece only loses 4 or 5 seconds a day. Of course, I maintain it, as did my father."

"It's beautiful."

"Thank you, yes, it is. I show you this only because, if you take care of it, that Union Horlogère vill last you just as long. And may you live in good health another hundred years to enjoy it."

"You tempt me, Mr…?"

"Markovitz."

"Mr Markovitz, but five pounds is too much, and I don't really like anything else on the tray half as much as the sixpence watch."

"I can do a little something about the price… Ehh, you can have it for three pounds, fifteen shillings."

"This is so difficult... It's such a shame, but that's still too much for me, although I'm sorely, sorely tempted."

"How much money do you have on you?"

"Oh, um, less than three pounds; I'd have to count it up."

"Count it, Miss Valton, count it."

Flora took out her notes and coins.

"Two pounds, seventeen shillings and ninepence."

"Then this is the bargain. You take the vatch and keep the ninepence to get home. I can't, I just can't go any lower. I'm so sorry."

"Oh, please don't apologize. You've bent over backwards for me... All right, it's a bargain, Mr Markovitz."

"You won't regret your decision, Miss Valton. It's a beautiful timepiece." He spoke while clearing everything away.

With the business concluded and a promise made to return with the watch for a future cleaning, Flora rushed from the shop to catch up with her friends, who were now outside the market area waiting by a wall.

"Look! Look at this lovely watch I bought!" She pointed to her wrist.

"Now, that is nice," said Ada. "I'd like one like that. How much was it?"

"Two pounds, seventeen."

"That's a lot of money," said Ada.

"I know, but it's a very, very good make. He wanted five pounds originally. I said I couldn't afford it, then he took all my money and gave me the watch, so how could I refuse?"

"It reminds me of a sixpence," said BW.

"That's what I said to Mr Markovitz."

"I must say, it is beautiful," said Sophie. "Did you happen to learn anything, by chance?"

"Yes!" Flora made sure no strangers were nearby. "It's very easy, really. All you need is a Big Ben alarm clock, a battery, two wires, a detonator, and some sticks of dynamite. Next, you take the back off the clock, fiddle with the hammer that strikes the bell, attach some wires somewhere and have them go to a condenser, although Mr Markovitz was unsure about that part. When the alarm goes off and the hammer strikes the bell, the electricity goes to the detonator and then everything goes ka-boom. He said to handle the clock carefully so that it doesn't go off ahead of time."

"He said all that?" asked Sophie.

"Yes. I told him it was for a play…" She repeated the explanation she had given to the watchmender. "Thinking about it, it's a jolly good idea for a play. I really should have a bash at writing it."

"Does the alarm clock method work on any size of bomb?" asked Sophie.

"I should think so," said Flora. "He also mentioned that the clock could be placed in an insulated container so that one couldn't hear it ticking."

"That's rather devious and such a nuisance, should this maniac do that. I'd been relying on our being able to hear the clock while we were searching for bombs."

"If anyone puts themselves to all that trouble," said Ada, "they'll be right tricky about disguising what the bomb looks like, an' all."

"You mean they'd make it look like something ordinary?"

"They could put a large one in a trunk, as Miss Walton suggests," said BW. "That's enough to blow up a house, I should think."

"A small one could be disguised as a parcel," said Ada.

"And a middle-sized one could fit in a drawer or a bread bin," said Flora.

"Good grief. Buckingham Palace is so vast!" said Sophie. "They could hide a bomb anywhere!"

"Then there's Sandringham, too," said Flora.

"And Windsor Castle," said Ada.

"Don't forget Balmoral," said BW. "I wouldn't mind going to Scotland."

"Then all we can do is hope the authorities have everything under control, because *we* certainly can't search all those places."

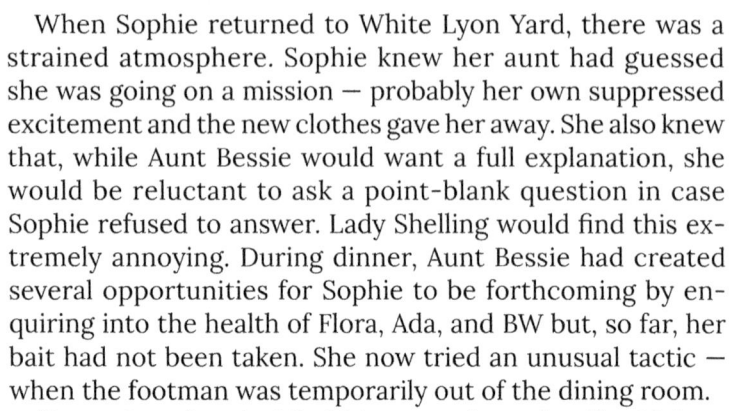

When Sophie returned to White Lyon Yard, there was a strained atmosphere. Sophie knew her aunt had guessed she was going on a mission — probably her own suppressed excitement and the new clothes gave her away. She also knew that, while Aunt Bessie would want a full explanation, she would be reluctant to ask a point-blank question in case Sophie refused to answer. Lady Shelling would find this extremely annoying. During dinner, Aunt Bessie had created several opportunities for Sophie to be forthcoming by enquiring into the health of Flora, Ada, and BW but, so far, her bait had not been taken. She now tried an unusual tactic — when the footman was temporarily out of the dining room.

"I wonder what Archibald is up to these days!" said Aunt Bessie. "He's so terribly busy, I know. And, of course, his important and secret work is vital to the nation." She paused. "I should think it must be a great burden on him."

"What is, Auntie?"

"His work... All those secrets, and plans, and goodness knows what... A terrible burden on the poor fellow."

"I can't tell you, because it's hush-hush."

"Oh, do forgive me. I didn't mean... I hadn't meant to pry or anything like that." With a sweet simplicity that was altogether foreign to Aunt Bessie, she then said, "Are you going on a mission, then?"

"Yes, and I mustn't speak of it to anyone. We are all under the strictest prohibition."

"Of course, you are... I wonder who you can mean by 'we', Sophie dear? If you told me that much, it wouldn't really be giving anything away, would it?"

"Just by stating there is a mission, I have given too much away already..." Hawkins, the butler, silently entered the room.

"Do you think we'll hear the results of the Irish elections tomorrow?" Sophie asked nonchalantly.

"I'm sure we shall," replied Aunt Bessie. "Whatever the outcome, I sincerely hope there is an end to the fighting."

"As do I. Elizabeth and I were discussing it the other day, and I came away quite saddened by the fact that Ireland has been divided in two."

"Yes. I think part of the issue, perhaps the largest and most obvious part, is that once the Home Rule movement became established, the British Government failed to act quickly to accommodate its demands. Had they done so, a reasonable settlement could have been reached. Instead, we had the Easter Rising, and now this current and quite awful situation. But there, perhaps the election results will stop the violence, and peace shall return."

They finished dinner and adjourned to the drawing room for coffee. Aunt Bessie dismissed Hawkins after he had served them. He shut the door quietly behind him.

"You were saying?" asked Aunt Bessie, almost immediately.

"I'm not supposed to say *anything*, Auntie. Unfortunately, and I mean this very sincerely, you cannot be involved in the mission this time, even though I would value your assistance."

"Is it a big operation?" asked Aunt Bessie.

"What I'm about to say is all I can tell you and is in the strictest of confidence! The mission involves the Royal Family and it may go on for an extended period of time."

"The Royal Family! Then it has to be critical... Is that all?"

"Yes."

"You're going to Buckingham Palace, I take it. That's the reason for your buying two smart new dresses."

"How do you know they're smart? You haven't even seen them."

"I questioned Mary."

"You've been spying on me."

"Naturally, and you're in no position to say anything because *you're always* spying on people."

"That's my job — for the country, but you're spying on family for, for..."

"Oh, here we go again. Sophie, before you say anything regrettable, you should first get your priorities in their correct order. I am your aunt. You are staying at my house. Mary is my servant, whom I pay. You know very well that I am the soul of discretion. Being aware of these things, you should have rightly concluded that it is a great discourtesy to me personally when you decide what it is you will or will not say. If I ask you a question, you are duty-bound to answer it."

"No, I'm not. I am always grateful for your hospitality, and mindful of your unstinting generosity but, in this matter, I'm duty-bound and under the Official Secrets Act to not say anything to anyone about the mission."

"Utter nonsense. I wouldn't repeat a word of it."

"What about your friends at the Regent's Hotel tearooms and Dot Callan?"

Aunt Bessie paused, moving forward slightly in her seat to better answer the question. "Of course, I wouldn't tell anyone at the Regent's Hotel."

"And Dot Callan? She's coming to stay next month."

"I decline to answer such a pointed question. The very idea of it... That you should suspect..."

"You know you'd tell her everything, so save yourself the embarrassment and just admit it."

"I'll do no such thing. It is entirely useless my trying to have a normal conversation with you, when all I'm doing is taking an interest in your work. I'm deeply offended... I may as well retire for the night."

"Before you go, Auntie," said Sophie innocently. "I was wondering if you knew of anyone with inside knowledge of the Royal Household."

Aunt Bessie stared at her niece. "Did you do all of that deliberately?"

"No. Did you?"

"It was only a simple enquiry on my part. But let us set aside the unfortunate episode. I presume you wish to know about the Royal Family."

"Yes. I know a little from what I read in the newspapers, but I can't quite grasp what they are like individually."

"They are the same as any other family except they live in the hothouse of public scrutiny. Everything they do, or don't do, is subject to comment. King George has just the right character for a monarch. He's quiet, calm, conscientious; a navy man — no scandal has ever been linked to his name. In the early nineties, he proposed to Princess Marie of Edinburgh — met her while he was stationed in Malta, but she rejected him on the advice of her family. We all know that was her mother's doing. Grand Duchess Maria Alexandrovna simply could not stand the thought of being ranked lower than Queen Alexandra, who was of lower birth. It's all quite childish, really. Still, as she died last year and, as many of the Romanovs were murdered on Lenin's orders, I mustn't be uncharitable."

"Marie did become Queen Consort of Romania."

"Ah, true. She dodged marrying a minor British royal who, because his brother died young, became the next king. I believe she is happily married to Ferdinand, and is quite devoted to Romania, but I wonder if she has any regrets over missing the British crown."

"I'm sure she loves her husband and has no regrets."

"And I'm equally sure, Sophie, that the thought of her missing out on becoming the British Queen Consort because she listened to her mother has crossed her mind more than once."

Sophie smiled. "You're probably right."

"Queen Mary, when she was Princess Victoria Mary of Teck, was favoured by Queen Victoria as a suitable candidate for marriage. Mary dropped her first name on becoming the Queen Consort — quite rightly so, I thought. Originally, she was engaged to Prince Albert, her second cousin, but he died early in '92. By July '93, she was walking up the aisle with his brother, Prince George. There were some unkind comments made about that, but I think they fell in love during the period of mourning over brother Albert. As Mary already had Queen Victoria's backing, and George only needed a push, we believe the situation was discreetly resolved to everyone's satisfaction."

"The King and Queen are second cousins once removed, aren't they?"

"That's right, dear. Ring the bell for sherry."

Sophie did as her aunt requested.

"We know Mary is a bit of a tartar, but she is staunchly devoted to the King and quite tireless in her work, particularly for charities. They call her May at home, and she loathes York Cottage, while Queen Alexandra occupies the big house."

"I wondered about that."

"Don't we all? Alexandra can be quite difficult, too. She's hung on to some crown jewels that she positively refuses to give back, and she and Mary have had their differences in the past. No one knows if they've had words over the house, but it wouldn't surprise me if they had, and there must certainly be a little coolness between them because of it. Of more significance is, have May and George had words? They could live anywhere they please. We know Mary loved Marlborough House, and there's Kensington Palace, and Buckingham Palace, of course. It's virtually uninhabited. Makes one think, doesn't it?"

"It does, indeed."

Hawkins came in and served them sherry. They waited until he had left.

"You said it would last for 'an extended period of time'. How long might that be?"

"We don't know."

"This is all very irritatin', Sophie. How am I supposed to help if you don't provide some guidance? I know enough to talk for hours."

"What you have said so far is very helpful. Do you know anything about the children?"

"The children — are they all in some type of danger?"

"I'm not permitted to say."

"Ah, I see, I see. The problem with the children is that they are not quite old enough to have made major decisions or mistakes, so there are fewer stories doing the rounds. This makes their characters more difficult to define. I'll speak of

Princess Mary first. She is twenty-three and, by all accounts, a quiet, generous person much devoted to good works."

"She's now the honorary president of the Girl Guides."

"So, she is, and makes an excellent model for the girls of Great Britain. It is rumoured, and this is not widely known but comes from a very reliable source, that Harry Lascelles has taken an interest in her."

"Is that so? I don't believe I know who he is."

"Viscount Lascelles, next in line to be Earl of Harewood. Entertainin' type — a war hero, intelligent, fifteen years her senior and looks every minute of it, but has more than enough money to keep her in the style to which she is accustomed. I've entered him into the book I opened last year. He's recently taken the lead in the Princess Mary Matrimonial Stakes. Betting is very tepid at present, because there's a wide field. I already have him down at five to one and, with a clear favourite, the odds will shorten. So, while you're hanging about the Royal Family, keep an eye out for Harry, and report back to me if you spot him."

"I can't believe you're doing this. It's the Royal Family, Auntie!"

"Don't chide me, gel. It's just a little hobby of mine, and my friends appreciate the trouble I take."

"You called him Harry. Do you know him?"

"Oh, yes — known him for years. I've asked him to dine here next month. Getting a clear favourite will help with the betting so that I can make a profit and not lose my chemise. And I also want Dot's opinion on his chances — she has a good eye for winners... You can join us for dinner, if you wish."

"Well, I'm in two minds about that, but thank you for the invitation. In the current circumstances, the decision to join your dinner party may not rest with me."

"I understand, but be warned. Seating is limited, so decide soon. Now, concerning the princes. I know very little about Henry or George. Albert, or Bertie as they call him, must be twenty-five now, and he's a shy, retirin' sort. Stutters when he's nervous. Despite that, several years ago, he got involved with a married woman named Sheila Chisholm. She's married to Lord Loughborough. Fortunately, his father made him see reason, and that affair came to an end. Now the really interestin' thing about all that is this. She was good friends with the Dudley-Ward woman, the one who's having an affair with Prince Edward, next in line to the throne. Her husband seems to tolerate the situation. So, there you have it — two married women, friends, having affairs with two princes, brothers. They even went around together for a while — thoroughly shocking behaviour."

"What is the matter with them all?"

"I really don't know. A marriage can breakdown for a variety of reasons, and the thought of divorce is anathema to most, but, for some, the notoriety of an affair is in itself an attraction. How any of them thought they could keep such things secret is beyond me. Therefore, we must deduce they behaved as they pleased, knowing the attention would come."

"I don't know how I'm going to face Prince Edward if I meet him."

"You'll do what we all do — examine him as though he were a rare species, and then wonder why everyone fusses over his good looks when he's only quite ordinary and self-centred. For quality of character, he cannot hold a candle to his sister Mary's glowing example... and yet a mention of his name in a polo match gets him on the front page, while her welfare work gets pushed to the back."

"But he did some excellent work during the war, and he will be the next king."

"Despite those things, it is apparent he puts self-interest above the realm." She sipped her sherry. "It should be said, he may mature and change but, as things stand, he will make a poor king and an appalling head of the Church of England."

Sophie reflected for some moments.

"Do you know you've given me an idea?"

"Yes, what is it?"

"I can't tell you."

"Sophie!"

"No, wait, wait... From the little I've said, what do you imagine is going on?"

"That there has been some sort of death threat made against the Royal Family."

"What if it were directed against specific individuals? Whom would you choose?"

"King George... and the heirs."

"Supposing it's only Edward they're after? It could be that they particularly don't want him to become king."

"If I knew more, I could comment."

"Sorry, Auntie... What puzzles me most is why a warning was sent in the first place? If one were to contemplate an assassination, surely one wouldn't warn the victim?"

Chapter 5

12 Crescent

12 Crescent is the last in a semi-circle of fine Georgian townhouses built in 1770, two hundred yards from the Tower of London. When they were first sold to wealthy merchants, there were still fields nearby and these substantial properties could be seen to advantage from a distance. Now, number twelve is virtually invisible beyond fifty yards in any direction. All around the area, prosperous London burgeoned, folding Crescent within itself like an amoeba. Fenchurch Street Station had been built close by, and soot from the many trains had by now turned the brickwork of Crescent black. A sprawling goods depot two streets over had caused the area to go into a general decline as unfettered trade poured in. Then, when an underground line was built, it needed to run directly under the road of Crescent, making it necessary to tear down numbers nine, ten, and eleven to create a railway cutting leading out from the tunnel. That left eight properties in the original curving row and orphaned number 12 so that it now stood unattached and by itself.

By standing at the wall above the open, below ground-level tracks and looking up, the scars and holes of number twelve's former attachment are noticeable even beneath the thick, black grime deposited when the underground trains used to burn coal. The disfigured brickwork suggests the building is incurably diseased. Because of the gap and the stains and the marks, number twelve is a leper house, isolated and shunned by its companion houses who have drawn back, as it were, as if they feared catching the contagion of dereliction; for the solitary, gaunt house seems derelict, yet it is not.

As if in response to its outcast status, 12 Crescent has effectually turned its face away in shame from the rest of Crescent. The attic windows are boarded up, the top floor windows are bricked up, and every other window heavily curtained. Together, these combine to make number twelve a sightless and altogether unwelcoming house. None of the neighbours go near it, and only the milkman, postman, grocer, and gas meter reader knock on the door because they must.

A married couple are the caretakers. Outside, they clean only the ground-floor windows, steps, railings, and the brass work about the front door. The woodwork has not been painted in years. The name on the old, highly polished brass name plate says 'The Rt. Hon. James, Lord Godfrey, Tea Importer,' but that plate is old, and no such business has operated from the house since well before the old queen died. As far as anyone knows, the property still belongs to the Godfrey family, but Sir James' title, a life peerage, had lapsed when he died and that was almost forty years ago.

The night of Wednesday, eighth of June, the badly lit Crescent was deserted. A little before ten, a van pulled up in front of isolated number twelve. Three men got out. One of them wore a light-coloured suit and supervised the other two as they removed a large packing case from the back of the van. With difficulty in carrying the awkward, heavy case, they approached the door, which opened before they knocked. The group entered the house, someone closed the door behind them, and the van drove off.

In the wide hall, nothing had changed since before Sir James had died. The furniture, decoration, and rugs had all been his. In fact, the only difference in the elegant hallway between the height of the Victorian era and 1921, were the six people now congregated there. None of them looked as though they belonged.

"Hello, Mrs Morrish, how's tricks?" The lively man in the light suit lifted his trilby, then set it down on the hall table. He was of medium height, had a fleshy face, wore several gold rings, and oiled his short, dark curly hair.

"I don't know about no tricks, Mr Barrett, but life's tolerable." She was a small, depressed, slovenly dressed woman in her late thirties. "You boys'll want tea. Kettle's already on, so I'll go and make it." She made it sound as though this was the last tea she would brew before she died, and that her death was imminent.

"Thank you, lovey," said Barrett, smiling. Turning to one of the two men already in the hall, he asked, quietly and peculiarly, as though not wanting to disturb anyone, anywhere, "Mr Godfrey's in, is he?"

"Upstairs, 'course," replied a powerful, intimidating man named Lefty Watts. "Hope you've brought him something very nice."

"Oh, like that, is it?" Barrett winked. "I gotcha." He addressed the two men still holding the packing case, "Come on, you two. Get that case upstairs and don't go knocking nothing over."

"We won't, but it's bloody heavy, boss."

"Then shut up and get a move on."

The vibration of a passing underground train made itself felt for some seconds.

Lefty Watts led the way upstairs, and the two men behind him struggled to carry the awkwardly sized case.

"You all right, Arthur?" asked Barrett.

Standing silently, watching, almost forgotten, and out of everyone's way was Arthur Morrish, caretaker. He was six feet six inches tall, about forty, and you could tell immediately there was something wrong with him.

"Are there any more for me?" He had an incredibly deep voice.

"Not at the moment, Arthur. You've been busy enough lately, don't you reckon?"

"S'pose... Just askin'... *You're* nice to me, but I don't like *him*." He pointed upstairs.

"You mean Lefty?"

Morrish nodded.

"Has he been mouthy to you again? Want me to have a word with him?"

Morris shrugged. "If you like."

"Don't take it to heart, you know what I mean?"

"Yeah... If you don't stop him, I will."

"Come on. Mr Godfrey wouldn't like to hear of you taking against his man, so we have to knock it off. He wouldn't like a disturbance, you know."

It was some moments before Morrish answered.

"Well... you're right. I ain't said nothing to Mr Godfrey, nor yet to Mr Healy. I don't want to trouble either gentleman. See what you can do... Thank you, Mr Barrett."

"That's all right, Arthur. It'll all be fine... Is Mr Healy here tonight, as well?"

The caretaker nodded. Then, barely making a sound, he moved slowly away along the hall to the back. Barrett watched him, then mounted the stairs.

Two flights up, there was a single room — an open, white-walled space occupying the entire floor. Despite the heavy curtains keeping out all light, the interior could be well lit by multiple arrays of lights, except most of them were switched off at present. There were overhead lights, groups of spotlights on slender pillars, and lamps over the pictures which hung on the walls. A panel of switches sitting on a huge, eight-foot-wide desk facing the stairs controlled all the lights. The desk stood in the centre of the room and at the intersection of four long red runners, which stretched across a wooden floor stained the darkest of browns.

Seen in profile from the landing, John Walter Godfrey, about thirty, wore glasses and stood leaning against one end of the desk. With fashionable negligence, he kept his evening jacket buttoned and his hands thrust into his trouser pockets. He watched as the two men before him pried open the packing case with a crowbar.

"Gently, boys, gently," he cooed to them. "There's no hurry."

Lefty Watts set up a display easel between the wall and the packing case. Godfrey lazily reached back to switch on a spotlight.

"Bring it forward a foot," said John Godfrey.

"Yes, Mr Godfrey," replied Lefty, who moved the easel until it was under the light.

"Hello, Barrett," said the lounging younger man, acknowledging the presence of Lefty's companion.

"Good evening, Mr Godfrey." He approached to stand near him.

They waited in silence, until Godfrey spoke again, saying,

"Put the small ones up first."

He took up a pad and pen. The nib hovered over the paper. Lefty placed a small watercolour on the easel. Godfrey stared at it briefly, then jotted down some numbers and a description. "Next," he called. He repeated the routine for five more paintings — three of them oils — writing after he had looked at each of them. "Now the large one."

The two men carefully set the canvas in place. It was a biblical scene of the magi visiting the infant Jesus in the stable. Godfrey stepped onto the red runner and slowly advanced towards the canvas, stopping several times to view the painting from different angles.

"I don't think so," he said, shaking his head when he was very close. "No." He took out a magnifying glass and bent down to examine the paint surface in several key places, darting suddenly to each different section. While peering, he said to himself more than to those around him, "No... I do not see the hand of the master."

"But it is a Rembrandt," said Barrett. "I mean, that's what we were told... Are you saying it's a fake, then?"

Godfrey straightened up. "It is not a fake, as you put it, but neither is it a Rembrandt. Undoubtedly, this painting is of his circle... probably a student of his, a good one, who could emulate Rembrandt's style with some facility, but it lacks the vigour and grace I expected to find. Undoubtedly, it is a copy of a lost Rembrandt painting... Such a pity it's not the original."

"That knocks the value down, dunnit?"

"It does, indeed." Godfrey laughed. "I know you were expecting thousands. Sadly, it is only worth… two hundred… and that's generous."

"That's a real hard blow," replied Barrett. "Still, we'll have better luck next time."

"I like your spirit. The information I received was inaccurate, and I apologize for that. Did your men have any trouble getting in?"

"No, it was easy enough, and they got away clean. They're going to be disappointed, though."

"Yes… Yes, I can see that. I'll tell you what I'll do. I'll take the painting, of course, and I'll have someone fix it up to make it… more *saleable*. We'll get rid of it in an overseas market, pass it off as a Rembrandt. If, and I mean *if*, we get a good price, there'll be some more money for you and your boys."

"That's very fair, considering everything, Mr Godfrey. So, the bloke who wanted it, he won't want this one?"

Godfrey smiled. "No. He's a connoisseur and collects only the best. He pays very well to get what he wants, but he won't want this."

"Oh, I see. How much does it all come to, then?"

Godfrey leaned forward to whisper so that only Barrett could hear him. "Four hundred and sixty."

Barrett nodded slowly. "That's decent money, anyway."

"Excuse me," said one of the men by the packing case, "but there's another paintin' in the box."

"Hold it up, then," said Godfrey.

The man did as instructed.

"Well, well, and what do we have here?" Godfrey stepped forward to examine the small, dirty canvas in its heavy battered frame. He used his magnifier again. After a minute, he stepped back and smiled. "Someone has a good eye. That's a Nicolas Poussin. Did you also get this from the address I gave you?"

"Yes, Mr Godfrey, they all came from the same place. When they broke into the attics, one of them spotted that picture leaning against a wall. He thought that as it looked so old, it must be valuable."

"Ha! Splendid! He was perfectly right, so give that man something extra. This little gem has *doubled* your money."

"Is that so?" said Barrett, better pleased with this unexpected turn of events — especially after the disappointment with the Rembrandt.

"Yes. Have your men take the packing case away and I'll give you your cash."

Some minutes later, when the men had left, Godfrey sat himself behind the grand desk. Lefty Watts and Barrett sat down opposite.

"How far has the tunnel progressed?" asked Godfrey.

"It's going nicely," replied Lefty. "There's about thirty yards to go and the digging's easier. Jimmy says they've run up against another basement and can go round it rather than under it."

From a drawer in the desk, Godfrey took out a thick pile of detailed architectural drawings and hand-drawn maps — some of them ancient. He sifted through to find the map he sought. Then, using a ruler, he calculated a distance.

"It's closer to fifty yards of tunnelling left because of the basement being in the way. Have you inspected the tunnel recently?"

"I went down at the beginning of the week," said Lefty, "so Jimmy's estimate sounded about right."

"I see. Call them off for tomorrow morning. There must be no more digging during daylight hours. Start them at ten tomorrow night, and they'll work until, mmm... six, but no later. Have them work over the weekend, too."

"Why's that, Mr Godfrey?" asked Barrett.

"It's simple. We can't have anyone hearing noises from the tunnel. Should someone in that basement hear pickaxes, it would naturally arouse suspicion. However, we must keep up the pace. Have you another man for us?"

"Yes, and there'll be a second man in a couple of days, but one is all ready to go."

"Then put him on tomorrow night. We must keep going, despite the shorter hours."

"There's a bit of a problem with that," said Lefty. "You know they used to chuck the dirt in the Walbrook River? Well, the level's gone down so far, it's not being carried away anymore, so they can't use it. Jimmy reckons if they do, they'd block the river, and the tunnel would flood."

"Is that what he said?" Godfrey showed surprise and then was silent for some moments. "I'll visit the diggings in the morning to see for myself." He looked searchingly from one man to the other. "Is the team ready?"

"It is," said Lefty. "They all want to know what the job is, though."

"I'm sure they do. Remind them of the consequences of asking questions and talking."

"I will," said Lefty.

"Barrett?"

"The equipment and transportation are ready. Just say the word, Mr Godfrey."

"Good. Then, depending upon what I discover tomorrow, the night of Saturday, 11th of June should still be on… It's quite exciting in a way."

"I'd say it is," said Barrett. "Can't believe we're doing it."

Godfrey smiled. "Lefty? Do you care to comment?"

"There's a lot of danger, and we've never done anything this big before, but I *know* we'll bring it off."

"Yes, I'm certain of that, because failure cannot be tolerated." He stood up. "Right, gentlemen, I'll bid you goodnight and go up to see Mr Healy."

Chapter 6

London Docks

On Thursday morning, there was the usual crowd outside the main gate of London Docks. By arrangement with Scotland Yard, a Port of London Authority constable allowed Ada to enter the London Docks at 5:30 a.m. She showed him her paper, and he merely waved her on. To identify themselves, everyone else going in at the docks held out a brass tally — an oval disk stamped with their name and number, which permitted them to work in the dockyards. If they worked, they handed it in and received it back when they were paid.

The docks were busy morning, noon, and night. Ships crowded in the river, waiting either for high tide before they could enter the docks or, for the smaller vessel, to allow the lightermen to load or unload the cargo into barges. London Docks was only one part of the massive area where a hundred thousand men handled sixty thousand ships a year, and every family for miles around had a relative or two who worked there.

The permanent men — the stevedores, lightermen, and many others — had secure employment, but there was a vast pool of temporary workers also needed. These had to fight for work. It was a struggle to get a brass tally but, even then, it only got a man within the gates. Next came the free-for-all around the men standing on boxes who gave out the daily work tickets. Usually, there were more men than tickets, so it was good to be known as a hard worker or to know the man on the box or to have paid him a little something. Concerning this last, there was a definite limit to how often it would meet with success, because against this unfairness there was in place the self-correcting mechanism of desperation. The one giving out the tickets somehow had to get home after work, during which journey a few aggrieved, idle workers — hard men with no other recourse — could and would take out their despairing displeasure upon the greedy miscreant.

The dock area was vast. Ships lined the quays where derricks and cranes were already in motion even at this early hour. Indeed, they had not really stopped during the night because there had been a high tide at two in the morning, and the next would be at three in the afternoon.

Ada walked quickly, going around the loading areas, and passing the two detectives with whom she would be working. They had stationed themselves by the leg of the nearest crane. This great crane was unloading sacks of potatoes, and gracefully swung each net load onto the dock to the waiting gang of men in shirtsleeves and coarse trousers, heavy boots, and flat caps. The crane landed the potatoes, and Ada saw the men unhook the net with their brown, calloused hands, and quickly carry away the heavy sacks while the hook receded. She glanced along the row of massive cranes that could move on their tracks. They were all in motion, dark against the pale morning light. As she passed by the nearest crane, she nodded to a detective who gave her a reply of equal subtlety.

She soon came to the tea stand where she was to work. It was a long wooden shed, built against a warehouse wall, from which projected a tin roof to protect the open-sided counter wall of the stand as well as the customers who stood at that counter. This was the place to get tea. It never closed, was always busy, and was a natural meeting place.

"Good morning," said Ada to the middle-aged woman in a white apron and bonnet who had opened the narrow side door at the end of the shed in answer to Ada's knock.

"Mornin'." She stepped outside, closing the door behind her so as not to be overheard. "You the one from the police?"

"That's right. I'm Nancy Carmichael. Are you Mrs Dicksie?"

"I am... So, what's this all abaht? I was told it was foreigners gettin' in illegal."

"That's all they told me, an' all. I'm only here for the day, 'cause the regular girl can't start 'til tomorrow."

"Oh, I see. What I don't get is how you'll stop the illegals while you're pourin' tea?"

"I'm an observer, I am. 'Cause the tea counter's raised up, I can see a lot more people than a bloke on the ground — an' there's all the customers in front of me, of course. If I see a foreigner meet an English bloke, an' I think they look dodgy, I give the nod to a copper — I mean, another copper — who's wearing plain clothes. He'll go after them if I give him the signal."

"And you make sure you let *him* do that, or you'll get yourself knifed! Some people'll stop at nuffin'."

"Ain't that the truth?"

"Oh, yes. So, we better get you started. I'll show you wot you'll be doin'. Come through here."

"Right. Are you always this busy?"

"Busy? This ain't nuffin'. Just you wait 'til the 'ooter goes, then you'll know what busy means."

Mrs Dicksie showed Ada the ropes. Now wearing a large, white apron, Ada was instructed in the various jobs of the tea counter operation. During the early part of the morning, she acted as a relief worker to the existing staff, except for washing the mugs, which would have meant Ada having her back to the area in front of the stand. While on the front line, she had little leisure time to watch the constantly shifting patterns of movement. Workers, officials, seamen of every nationality, and liner passengers constantly entered or left London Docks. Some stopped for coffee, the uninspiring sandwiches, or for sticky buns, but the majority stopped for a mug of tea. To put it bluntly, it was a literal tea-slinging operation. The strong, dark liquid, dispensed from an urn standing in a battery of four, was already in the thick, chipped and worn mug before a customer asked for it. Most drank the beverage the same way — with a little milk and sugar — and, as most had the prices by heart and the right coin in hand, the queue was processed with alacrity, yet there were always more people joining the end of the line.

"Hold on a mo. Don't I know you?" said a quite personable young man to Ada as she slid a mug across the counter towards him with one hand and slid his money laid on the counter away from him with the other.

"No, you don't!" said Ada, using the appropriate amount of savagery East London women employ when rebuffing an unwanted advance.

"I'm sure I know you from somewhere. It'll come to me."

"You're holding up the line," said Ada.

"All right, then. How about this? We'll go to a nice pub after work. What d'ya say?"

Ada raised her voice. "With you!? I've seen better things crawling out of cheese!"

This produced smiles within the tea stand and laughing and jeering along the queue.

"It's your loss," said he, maintaining his dignity while leaving.

A ship from the far east must have recently docked, because a crowd of seamen wearing loose turbans and the light, cotton working garb of India walked towards the main gate. They talked excitedly among themselves. Ada glanced at them frequently because they looked so different. All the morning, she had been noticing the different clothing styles of the various nations and could now even identify some of them. Dutchmen and Germans had been quite easy for her, particularly as some had stopped for a 'kaffe'. West Indians were different to the Africans, but she had not the knowledge to identify either more precisely than that. As for all the other European nations, she could only broadly categorize them as northern or southern. It helped her that all nationalities tended to appear in batches — released from their work onboard after a ship came in, or returning to work just prior to sailing.

The detectives loitering opposite the tea stand had to change position because the crane they stood near was now moving along its rails to access a different hold on the ship. Ada had yet to signal to them about a suspect, and they, for their part, had seen no one worth investigating. It was as they moved that a swarthy, stocky man carrying a duffel bag walked past the tea stand to be intercepted by an English working-class man approaching from the opposite direction. Ada saw them speak briefly. Then the Englishman turned about and the two walked together for a moment towards the docks' entrance, where identification papers and landing passes were liable to be checked. As they neared the gate, the Englishman fell a few steps behind. Ada immediately caught the attention of a detective, but could not convey by signal what had happened. She pointed, trying to indicate to him that the targets were walking separately. Both detectives began following, but she was sure they had not understood her frantic message.

"Can I have my tea, love?" asked the puzzled customer in front of her.

"Sorry about that. I just saw me uncle waving."

She handed over a mug and then called Mrs Dicksie over.

"What's the matter?" she asked.

"I've got to follow a geezer," urgently whispered Ada.

"Go on, then. I'll take over 'ere. You be careful!"

Ada rushed to leave the tea stand, removing her apron as she went.

Outside the crowded area in front, she saw it had gone as she had feared. The detectives were questioning the swarthy man, but the other was just passing through the entrance.

She neared the detectives and shouted, "There was two of 'em!" She continued walking. One detective broke away to catch up with her.

"I tried telling you there was an English bloke, an' all. Hanging back he was."

"What did he look like?" asked the detective.

"Ordinary... a docker, average height, about thirty. He's just gone out."

The detective ran ahead, and Ada hurried to keep up with him. Together, they rushed to the gate and stopped in the middle of the road.

Outside, the street was moderately busy, and the detective immediately spotted a man hurrying along the gutter. The man furtively looked back and made eye contact. Despite the detective waving him back, the man broke into a run. The detective gave chase, losing his cap in the process.

Ada moved to the pavement and followed them at a walk. Just ahead of her, she noticed a new and expensive car pull away from the kerb. She stopped to wonder what such a vehicle was doing there among the parked lorries and carts, and so she memorized its registration number. Then she heard the dockyard hooter sound, which made her decide to leave the chase to the detective. Ada returned to the tea stand and there discovered the true meaning of the word busy.

Lefty Watts and a young man named Eddie entered the newsagent's on the corner of a depressing little street. No one else was there, so Eddie locked the door behind them. The old man behind the counter was nervous.

"Mr Bigelow, do you have my two quid?" demanded Lefty.

"It's here, Mr Watts. I'm ever so sorry about last week's misunderstanding. I was..."

"I don't need a song and dance, just the cash."

Bigelow handed him the money.

"Your wife. Is she talkative?" He leaned on the counter so that his face came menacingly close to the shopkeeper.

"No, not at all. She won't say a word."

Lefty lowered his voice. "That's good, because we don't want any accidents, now do we?"

"Honestly, she won't say a thing."

"Yeah, for your sake, I hope you're right. Otherwise, you'll be a widower, and that would be very sad. What flowers does she like? You know, just in case."

"She won't talk."

"Glad to hear it." Lefty stood up straight. "So, see here. I'm a reasonable man. Last week was a mistake and now you've made good, so I won't charge the extra five shillings that you, by rights, should pay me. You're in business, and you know about expenses. When someone doesn't pay, it messes up my bookkeeping something awful. I can't have poor Eddie here going hungry, can I?"

"It won't happen again, I promise."

"That's all right, then. Eddie'll come round as usual next week. Now, Bigelow, you play straight with me, and we're like family. But, if anyone thinks they can get out of payin', well, they're wrong. My rates are low, my service is good, and you've never had any trouble, but if anyone mucks me about, then it's a question of honour. I've a reputation to maintain and so I must. I mean, I'm literally forced to make an example of someone." He paused. "Don't you be that one, Bigelow. Eddie, unlock the door, a customer wants to come in. We mustn't interfere with the man's trade."

Lefty and Eddie were walking away from the newsagent's shop when a chauffeur-driven car pulled up. Barrett opened a back window."

"What's the matter?" asked Lefty.

"A right bloody mess. I can't get back to my garage. The coppers were waiting at the docks. They saw the car and I need to hide it."

"Are they after *you*?" asked Lefty.

"No, but it's all gone south. They got one of my boys, and they'll get the bent passport bloke if they haven't got him already."

"Eddie, carry on with the round. I've got to go somewhere with Mr Barrett."

Lefty got in the back and gave the driver an address.

"Godfrey won't like this," said Lefty.

"Tell me about it."

"Will your man grass?"

"No, he's all right."

"They saw your car?"

"Some nosey little cow took down the number. Wasn't even in uniform, so how could I know she was with the rozzers?"

"They're getting clever. Is it registered in your name?"

"Yes. What do I do? I just bought it."

"I can get that sorted out for not much money, so don't worry."

"Do whatever you have to do."

"I'll get the registration fixed up, the car painted another colour, and sell it up north before you know it. It'll cost you, but you'll have peace of mind. First off, you go to your local nick to report the car stolen from your garage. That way, when they pay you a visit, you can show you weren't involved."

"That's a good idea... What a day! I never go down the docks as a rule. The only reason I was there was because Godfrey urgently wanted men for the tunnel... How's that going?"

"We're getting close, but the extra help is needed to finish on time... What are you going to do after this one?"

"Retire for a bit. Blackmail pays, but it's hard finding the right targets with enough money to make a squeeze worthwhile. Still, Mr Healy's kept me busy of late. How about you?"

"I'm getting right out so I can travel. I'll make Eddie a partner, and he'll run my businesses for me while I'm abroad."

"That makes sense... What do you reckon of Mr Healy, who doesn't like to show his face?"

"He's clever, and he's planned this job carefully, so we're going to be rich. That's all I need to know."

"I wonder who he is really, though."

"Does it matter? I'll say this much. Godfrey's scared of him."

"I noticed that, and it makes me wonder why. He acts like a servant around him."

"We all do that."

"That's true." He spoke to the driver. "Here, drop us at the corner and we'll get a taxi to the cop shop. Lefty is taking the car."

"Oh, but don't forget," said Lefty as the car came to a halt, "before you do anything, go to break the padlock off the garage doors first. The coppers like that sort of evidence."

"I'll have to clear some stuff out, the sort I don't want the coppers seeing. What a day."

Earlier in the morning, just after the last overnight resident at the Foreign Workers' Relief Mission had breakfasted before sallying forth into the world, Sophie and Flora made a start on changing the linens of the thirty beds in the now unoccupied dormitory.

"I hope none of them have anything catching," said Flora, as she stripped a sheet from a mattress.

"For our sakes or theirs?" said Sophie, who was using a long-shafted window opener to open the topmost of the grimy windows. "It's very smelly in here."

"Bad smells can be endured; deadly diseases can't."

"Pshaw! Pastor Clarkson mentioned earlier that a doctor visits once a week, and no one reported themselves sick this morning, so I think we're safe." She opened the last of the windows and turned, holding the pole upright as if it were a spear. "We'll do the floors before putting on the fresh sheets."

"The windows need cleaning."

"And the lavatories."

"I'm not doing the lavatories."

"There are two, so we'll do one each." Sophie began stripping a bed. "We don't have a ladder, so we'll leave the windows."

"Sophie, when I signed on for this operation, there was no mention of w.c. cleaning."

"There was no mention, because no one told *me*. When asked to work at this mission, I imagined we would do nothing more than ladle soup into the bowls of the grateful, smiling recipients, while keeping an eagle eye out for suspicious behaviour."

"None of them looked particularly grateful at breakfast and, although I smiled, no one smiled back. I felt like a grinning idiot."

"No more than did I. Still, we'll be cheerful even if they're not."

"Why aren't they more cheerful?" asked Flora.

"Probably because their lives are in a muddle."

"Down on their luck and in a foreign country? Yes, I can see how it can't be easy for them."

They worked steadily through the morning and got everything done. At midday, Pastor Clarkson returned.

"Hello... It's only me!" he called from the entrance before walking to the dormitory.

The lavatories now sparkled, and Flora had just finished polishing the floor.

"My, Miss Walton, that floor certainly looks splendid," he said in a bright voice. "We don't usually polish it, though... We once had an accident. A gentleman slipped over and hurt himself."

Sophie heard what he had said while returning from further back in the building.

"We didn't know... Surely, everyone knows how to walk on a polished floor?" she asked.

"I'm certain they do, Miss King, but we can't risk our friends injuring themselves."

"I can't *un*-polish it," said Flora.

"Of course, you can't. I'm sure it will be all right just for today. The beds look excellent... And you've cleaned everything so well... I hope you've left something for Mr Jorgensen to do."

"Mr Jorgensen?" queried Sophie.

"Yes. He's our cleaner and comes in daily. He'll be here soon. Didn't I mention him to you?"

"No, you did not," said Flora. She glanced at Sophie.

"That's a pity," said Sophie. "We also cleaned the lavatories."

"Oh, he will be pleased he can forego that task. As you can imagine, indeed, as you must now know, such work is a tiresome chore, but it must be done. Nevertheless, I am tremendously impressed by your zeal."

"We're always zealous," said Flora, "and occasionally over-zealous." She shot another look at Sophie.

"It is a pity you're only here for the day," said the Pastor.

"Yes, I'm afraid we must busy ourselves somewhere else," said Flora.

"I have been wondering," Clarkson hesitated. "About your work among our friends. Did you, perhaps, notice anything?"

"No, we haven't so far," answered Sophie.

"As I said earlier, there have been no unusual characters lurking about since the necessity for this observation work was first mentioned to me. But then, I'm not entirely sure I would be the best person for such a job. I tend to see the best in people and would put down any hint of malicious behaviour to an idiosyncrasy or a minor indisposition or something of that nature."

"Because we work for the police," said Sophie, "and are actively seeking evidence of criminal behaviour, we must take the completely opposite approach."

"Then I'd make such a dreadful policeman." The pastor laughed. "A very poor judge, too. Undoubtedly, I would be overly sympathetic to the plight of the accused."

"And what of the victims, Pastor?" asked Sophie.

"Naturally, one has solicitude for them because of what they have undergone. But, I usually find, in the inevitable rush to judgment, the accused has committed a crime simply because he or she must do so to survive."

"I can understand there being mitigating circumstances in certain cases, but where does one draw the line? Anyone can tell a hard-luck story — even a hardened criminal."

"Some will, of course. Yet a man who steals a pair of boots because he has none is hardly in the same category, Miss King, as the man who viciously attacks someone in the street to steal money. Yet even *he* may have some urgent reason for his action, however weak a reason it may seem to others."

"Then, wouldn't it be fair to say that you have already drawn a line?"

"Yes, I suppose I have... Ah, I hear the greengrocer knocking at the side door. Excuse me one moment."

When he was out of earshot, Flora said,

"He's so wishy-washy. If he were a judge, he'd let everyone off."

"Probably... Sorry about the lavatories."

"Oh, don't worry about that, although it is really unforgivable of you. The question now is, what shall we do next?"

While they were discussing their options, a roughly dressed merchant seaman entered the dormitory. He looked a little lost.

"Good morning," said Sophie.

"Guden tag," replied the Dutchman. "My name Molenaar. I here for bed tonight."

"Are you?" said Flora. "Wait here a moment, please. I'll fetch someone who can help you."

"Ya, I wait."

Flora left to find Pastor Clarkson. Sophie smiled at the man and then excused herself to go to the front door. Although she carefully looked up and down the street, she saw no one who might have brought the Dutchman to the mission, so she returned inside.

The Pastor returned with Jorgensen the cleaner and introduced him to Sophie and Flora. Jorgensen volunteered to make some tea. Clarkson then addressed the newcomer, Molenaar, in a mixture of English and common Dutch words. With elaborate simplicity, he explained to the grateful, smiling man how the mission functioned, reassuring him several times that he would get a dinner and a bed for the night.

"Sophie," whispered Flora, as the two of them deliberately and slowly remade a bed, "he's rather pale for a sailor."

"Yes... Perhaps he's a stoker or an engineer who works below decks."

"That could be. Did you see anyone outside?"

"No. The street was almost empty." She glanced towards the pastor. "He's examining the man's passport… I suppose he has to do that."

"It looks newish to me," said Flora. "What do you think?"

"Very interesting. If he's here illegally, he's not going to tell anyone, and certainly not us. We'll watch him, though."

"We're only here until seven when the volunteers resume their duties."

"We'll report our suspicions to the woman police constable and leave it at that."

"It is a peculiar juxtaposition," whispered Flora more quietly, "cleaning lavatories one day and off to the Palace the next. Now *that's* a dynamic social calendar."

Sophie gave a short laugh. "At least we're adaptable to circumstances. It's lunchtime, so let's find a restaurant."

"There's supposed to be a good fish and chip shop on Cable Street. It's not very far."

They stepped out into what should have been quiet little Neptune Road only to see a police car, with a constable standing on each running board, lurch around the corner and pull up with a screech outside the mission. Sergeant Gowers got out and ran towards to Sophie.

"Miss King. Is there a man named Jorgensen inside?"

"Yes, he's the cleaner. He's just arrived."

"Thank you. Stay here, please." He then spoke to the driver and a constable. "You two, round the back."

The car sped away, while Gowers and two constables rushed inside.

"This is so unfair," said Flora. "I want to see what's going on."

"So do I, but Sergeant Gowers was rather exercised… Perhaps we could just take a little peek."

"That's right. We shan't get in the way at all."

They quietly returned inside and heard stamping and shouts. When they reached the dormitory door, Jorgensen was on the floor stunned and groaning, Sergeant Gowers was sucking his knuckles, while a young constable with a bleeding nose was holding a handkerchief to it. Molenaar had run out of the back door, only to be caught.

"Either block the punch or duck," said Gowers. "Don't just stand there looking pretty or you'll get walloped every time." He turned to Pastor Clarkson, who was motionless, blank-faced, and open-mouthed. "Do you have any smelling salts handy, Pastor Clarkson?"

"Er, yes… Did you have to hit him so brutally?"

"Well, I only hit him the once, because he started hitting us, as you probably noticed. I tried to caution him, and he lashed out, so he left me no choice. That's what we call obstructing an officer, which is a criminal offense, I might add."

"Oh. I'll find the salts for the poor man."

"And if you could find something for the poor constable here, that would be very nice of you, too." Under his breath, Gowers muttered, "I don't think." He turned back to the constable. "You all right, son? Let's have a look at it… Does it wiggle?"

"No, sarge."

"Then it's not broken."

"Allow me to assist," said Flora, who came forward with cloths and a basin of water.

Gowers turned at her approach. He then noticed Sophie examining Jorgensen.

"He's coming round," she said.

"Please, Miss King, he's dangerous. I'd be much obliged if you could fetch the constable down from upstairs."

"I'll go at once." Sophie hurried off.

Gowers had to take the prisoners to the station. Before he left, he explained matters, including Ada's involvement, to Sophie and Flora. First off was that a passport officer was under arrest. The foreign man whom Ada had spotted had proved to be a Spaniard, who volunteered the information that he was on his way to the mission and let slip that Jorgensen was his contact. He did not, however, know anything about the dockworker who had walked with him to the gate. The Spaniard maintained the man had only given him directions to the mission. The unknown man had escaped the pursuing detective.

Over their fish and chips lunch, which they ate while sitting on a nearby wall, Sophie and Flora discussed what had happened. They concluded that whoever was running the operation would now be forced to close it down, and wondered what effect that might have.

Chapter 7

Buckingham Palace

When the grumbling taxi driver picked up four passengers near Burgoyne's Agency, he said he feared for his springs seeing as such a great weight was to be placed upon them. By their exchanged looks, Ada, Flora, and Sophie, once crammed inside the rickety machine, signalled to each other that the man was to be considered odious but that it was far too early in the morning for a row. Broadbent-Wicks seemed to have missed or ignored the implied insult, because he chose to chat to the man in the driver's seat through the partition window.

"Don't go through the front gates of Buckingham Palace. I mean, it would be top hole if you did, because we could wave at people and all that, but I don't think the sentries would like it. We have to use the side entrance in Buckingham Gate."

"I know where to go, guv."

"I'm sure you do. Have you ever been inside?"

"Who, me? I should think not." He shifted the gears.

"Would you like to go inside?"

"What? You mean you can get me in?"

"Oh, no. What I meant was, would you *like* to go inside?"

"I dunno... S'pose. It'd be nice to see the Royals up close. I saw 'em from a distance once..." Another car whizzed in front. "Oi!" shouted the cabbie while shaking his fist. "Who does that geezer think he is? Cuttin' in front like that. I've a good mind to..."

"I say, no language, please," said BW. "There are ladies present."

"That's right, guv, and I'm sorry, but did you see that git?"

"Yes, and I sympathize completely, but we are gentlemen and shall behave as such."

"I know all about that, and it won't 'appen again." The driver changed gears. "It's the war that dunnit. Ever since, there's been no bloomin' courtesy on the roads. It's all gone down 'ill along with everything else."

"I don't drive, so I have no opinion. But I would say, on the whole, life is wonderful."

"You would?"

"Oh, yes."

"Now you can say that guv, 'cause you're wearing a nice whistle and are orf to shake hands with the King."

"I doubt that will happen… What's a whistle?"

"Whistle and flute, suit… Your'n is Saville Row, I bet. Must 'ave cost a packet."

"No, it's Brick Lane and was quite reasonable."

"Is that right? 'Ow much?"

"Six pounds."

"That's all? I mean, it's a lot of money to me, an' more than I'd ever spend, but not for what you got. Where did you get it from?"

"From Morrie's."

"Morrie — don't know 'im. But I'll remember for the next gent who's on abaht tailors."

"Do you really think it's in the same class as a Saville Row?"

"Well, I ain't an expert, but I see a fair few well-dressed gents, and your whistle is as good as any of ther'n."

"What's your name?"

"Alf."

"Alf, you are positively a diamond in the rough."

"Knock it orf, guv'nor, you're makin' me blush."

A car travelling in the opposite direction began to creep towards the median.

"What's that geezer doing?" asked BW

"Wandering over the line, while looking for a number. 'Ere, watch this, guv."

The cabbie suddenly bellowed at the top of his voice and squeezed the horn's bulb repeatedly. The other driver was terrorized and wrenched the steering wheel to return to his side of the road.

"See 'im jump?" Alf was laughing.

"Serves him right." BW gave Alf a friendly tap on the shoulder. "Here, what do you have to do to become a taxi driver?"

"Well, you 'ave to 'ave The Knowledge to get your license. That's knowing every street in a six-mile radius of Charing Cross and, guv, let me tell ya, there are thousands of 'em."

"You have all that lot stuffed in your brain?"

"Oh, yes, indeed. And it's a well-known fact that a cab driver's brain is bigger than other people's because of it."

"Good grief... So, if I became a cab driver, my brain would grow?"

"That's right."

"Tell me more."

They kept themselves, and the ladies in the back, entertained with the subject until Alf applied the brakes sharply upon entering Buckingham Gate. The taxi veered hard to the left, squealing as it slowed because, as Alf unabashedly explained when they had stopped, "The brakes need seein' to."

The secret agents had been told to enter the Palace through a side door in Old Equerry's Court. What they found inside was an area for work and, although clean and well-appointed, it contained nothing of the splendour yet to be seen throughout the rest of the building. A Palace official wearing a dark blue uniform sat at a table in a vestibule with lists and clipboards. Standing behind him was a police constable.

"Good morning," said Sophie. "My name's King. We are here to see Mr Maxwell Handley."

The official greeted them, asked for all their names, and consulted his lists, while the constable stared accusingly at each agent in turn with the painfully obvious assumption that they were probably carrying concealed explosive devices.

"Everything's in order," said the official. "I'll ring Mr Handley and tell him you've arrived."

He did as he said. While they waited, other visitors entered, and the agents moved out of their way.

Sophie had met Handley before, during the meetings which had brought Burgoyne's into the operation. She remembered him to be a short man, reserved, soft-spoken yet with a deep voice, a pleasant manner, a fine head of black curling hair, and an innocuous, ruddy face. Taken altogether, he was quite handsome in profile and from some angles, but not so much from others. So, she received quite a shock when the impeccably dressed man shot into the vestibule at great speed, while fussing volubly in a high-pitched voice.

"Oh, a thousand, thousand pardons, my dear Miss King! What can you possibly think of me for leaving you stranded here for so long?"

"Good morning, Mr Handley. Please don't concern yourself. We've only been here three or four minutes."

"Even a second is far, far too long when I had hoped to be here waiting for you. Never mind, never mind! Onwards and upwards, as I always say."

"Do you really?" asked Broadbent-Wicks.

"It is an excellent motto to live by," he replied earnestly.

They went through the elaborately formal introductions, during which they learned that, when Mr Handley was in London, he was the Assistant Coroner of the Verge, as well as being the Second Deputy Assistant Yeoman to the Wine Cellar. He also implied he had other offices at other places.

"Now, if you would be so kind…" He gestured for them to precede him out of the vestibule. "We can get started on your induction as we go."

Handley, having moved to their head, passed quickly through a maze of minor corridors and up some stairs while telling them that, although the King was in residence, the agents would not be meeting any of the Royal Family until tomorrow when they assumed their duties at Sandringham.

Once the party was in the high-ceilinged corridors of the Palace proper, it became evident why Handley walked so quickly. The passages were long — not just ordinarily long, but immensely, expensively, and quite shockingly long. Upon entry, the awe-inspiring vista of tall windows, mirrors, soft illumination, large paintings, console tables bearing objets d'art, and the long, thick, deep red carpet immediately slowed the agents and Handley soon noticed he was losing his followers.

"You're new, of course, and it takes some getting used to."
"Can I ask a question please, sir?" asked Ada.
"Yes, of course."
"Who keeps the carpet looking so nice?"
"Oh, my goodness, Miss Carmichael, there's a veritable army of servants who attend to such things."
"I bet there is an' all... Sorry, sir."
"Not at all." He turned to a nearby door. "We'll use this room." He opened the door and motioned them inside. "Ah, Miss King. Might I have a word with you?"
"Yes, Mr Handley."
They remained outside while the others entered.
"Miss King, are your staff aware of the... network?"
His voice had returned to how she remembered it in the meetings, and she could not prevent her eyebrows from shooting up. She answered,
"To a limited extent. If you wish to speak of the operation, you may do so freely, because they are all most trustworthy."
"Excellent... Do you have a question?"
"Um..."
"My voice?"
"Yes."
"It's an involved story but, to put it succinctly, I must be annoying so that both the Lord Chamberlain and the Lord Steward, each of whom believes I work for the other chap, will not promote or fire me. You see, they aren't in the network, so they must be kept in the dark as to why I'm here. This will come as no surprise, but I don't really do any official

work. All the offices I'm supposed to fulfil are mere sinecures and are actually purely fictitious."

"Now I comprehend. Well, up to a point, anyway. How many offices are involved?"

"Seven, and they are dependent upon where I am. At Windsor, for example, I am the Second Assistant Marker of the Swans. At Balmoral it's bagpipes, Sandringham it's pheasants, and so on and so forth. These were all created as a pretext for me to be near the King, only he is unaware that I'm in the network. Also, because of such proximity, it is vital I be an irritant to Queen Mary."

"Why must you irritate Queen Mary?"

"It so happens that I'm rather good at calligraphy. In a thoughtless moment, I semi-illuminated a rather dull message dictated by the Lord Chamberlain when he was in a hurry, and I wasn't. I delivered the embellished note to the King. Unfortunately, Queen Mary saw my handiwork and was impressed enough to question me with a view to my becoming a private secretary — not a position I aspire to. The King was present, so I had to think quickly. In knowing that she likes a calm, dignified atmosphere at all times, my hasty plan was to act in a way she found upsetting. The trouble is, I've had to keep up the pretence, and the voice, ever since. A side effect is people often shake their heads when they see me coming."

"Why not tell the King and Queen the truth?"

"Because he would be annoyed if he thought he was being watched."

"Aren't you watching him?"

"In a way, I am, but my main purpose is to observe those who approach him, in case they mean harm. That includes the staff."

"Oh. Then, did it come as a surprise when a death threat was left on the King's pillow?"

"It was a thorough-going shock, let me tell you. There had been no hint of the like before. However, on that score, there have since been developments. A maid went missing and, despite exhaustive enquiries, she has completely vanished.

Naturally, such a suspicious occurrence has been linked to the death threat." He looked at his watch. "I had better explain the intricacies of the mission because, in twenty minutes, I'm supposed to deliver you to Sir Frederick Tunstall-Green. He's in charge of Etiquette and it just doesn't do to keep him waiting."

In the luxurious sitting room, Handley succinctly outlined the duties the agents were to perform around the Royal Family. They were to check rooms for explosive devices, prevent unknown individuals from approaching, and remove the family to safety if there were a threat of any kind. Otherwise, the agents were to observe and report anything suspicious. He handed Sophie a list of the police officers in charge at each of the royal residences. They then sped to their next meeting, which was at the other end of the Palace.

Rather than go through the Central Block at the back, Mr Handley and Burgoyne's Agency bolted along the empty Principal Corridor at a speed almost suitable for a hundred-yard dash. This passage lay behind the rooms of the Palace's more famous eastern side. To their left was a view of The Quadrangle, around which the building was arranged. Most of the doors were closed on the right, but they got the briefest of glimpses into the Balcony Room and the Chinese Luncheon Room. It was as though they had been running through an Aladdin's Cave, or a museum, and were left only with the single impression that they had missed out upon seeing a lot of interesting, rare, and costly things.

When Mr Handley guided Burgoyne's to Sir Frederick's office door, he unceremoniously ushered them into the small room, then promptly disappeared without introducing anyone.

"Oh... I wanted a word with Handley," musically murmured Sir Frederick.

The baronet was seated at his desk, looking his elegant best in a morning suit. About fifty, he was the epitome of all that a courtier should be — distinguished, intelligent, polished. What he looked like paled in comparison to what he sounded like because, to put it plainly, the gods, or at least one of them anyway, had touched his tongue. Sir Frederick spoke, not with the voice of an angel, but with the same virtuosic skill as a violinist such as Paganini or Vivaldi commanded. Vibrato, sostenuto, staccato, trills, and all the other artifices that a musician could employ to deliver an impassioned performance were present in Sir Fredrick Tunstall-Green's voice. Often these effects were employed in a single sentence, sometimes within a single word. The agents stared at him blankly, awaiting his next utterance.

"Are you from Burgoyne's Agency?" he enquired as he stood up.

Never had Sophie heard her name performed in such an oddly melodic fashion, and she found it bewitching. It was as if the direction and gyrations of the sound he brought forth were as follows: his tenor voice rose slightly, clear and beautiful, on the B, before a descent as rapid as if thrown from a cliff on one side of a valley. This is where the UR became noticeably breathy and intimate. The G proved to be the transitional point, quite trampoline-like, because now his voice soared up the opposite cliff but with a slight tremolo effect on the OYNE, which sound suggested a plucked wire spring. He slowed at the ' before coming to rest on a quite ordinary S. Naturally, this word fitted perfectly with the cadence and rhythm of the whole sentence.

"Er... yes, sir," said Sophie.

"Good. What are your names?"

She hesitated for a moment, and then did the introductions.

"My name is Sir Frederick Tunstall-Green. I shall impart to you the basic requirements for your conduct in the presence of majesty. The time allotted for today's instruction will, of course, be inadequate for your proper training. Nevertheless, we shall proceed and see what may be accomplished.

"To begin. There are, within the Royal Household, four classes of servant. First are the courtiers. These are all gentlemen and ladies of rank. Should you find it necessary to speak to such a person, you shall first ascertain their name and title, then address them in the proper manner, which I shall explain in a few moments."

He spoke at great length and, although much of it was interesting, his performance had a numbing effect on his audience. No matter how hard each of them tried to focus on what was said, they became mesmerized by how he spoke.

"Never shall you precede majesty…" The rest was lost to them.

"If you wish to attract the attention of the King, or the Queen, or the…" The list was very long, and they missed the various nuances.

"If the King is conversing with a foreign ambassador…"

It was here, after half an hour, that it became apparent that Sir Frederick had no understanding of their mission or duties. He was delivering a set speech of unknown length that could easily include everything there was to know. There had been several side excursions already which had taken in such things as top hats, twenty-one-gun salutes, sudden indispositions, and garden parties — each a glorious vocal performance but, when unrelentingly delivered without pause, the aggregate became an exhausting ordeal for the silent agents standing to attention. As the voice washed over them, they could not take it in at all and it threatened to unseat their sanity.

"At breakfast — indeed, and at other times, too — you may encounter the Royal Parrot."

For some reason, the sudden mention of a parrot almost caused an outbreak of laughter among the wilting agents who heroically managed to contain themselves.

"In the absence of the appropriate attending servant, you may be called upon or, rather, it will naturally come to your attention that the Royal Bowl must be presented at the table. This is quite usual…"

Bowl is such a simple word, except when it issues from the mouth of Sir Frederick. He enunciated it with such lavishness that it became either a three- or five-syllable word depending where one cared to demarcate the intricate sound. He fully intended to say bowl. They all heard his highly extended and nuanced version of the word but heard him say bowel. Not any ordinary bowel, mind you, but a royal one. Uncomfortable thoughts arose in their minds.

"Excuse me, sir," said Broadbent-Wicks.

"Yes?" said Sir Frederick, annoyed at being interrupted at the forty-minute mark of his soliloquy.

"What is a Royal Bowel exactly? And, goodness me," BW laughed, "should we really be putting it on the table?"

Under normal circumstances, Sophie could have anticipated BW's question and forestalled it. Now, she realized, as one awakening from a stupor, that an avoidable incident had already occurred and got away from her.

"We'll discuss this later," she said, but it was too late.

"What is the matter with you?" asked Sir Frederick.

"Er, nothing, sir," said BW. "You said bowel, and I wondered where we would get it from."

"Don't be ridiculous. I said bowl."

This delivery produced the same result, only it was less mellifluous this time.

"There you are, sir. You said it again."

"Are you saying bowl?" asked Flora.

"Of course, I am. Are you all imbeciles?"

"Absolutely not, sir," said BW. "Then am I right in thinking you were trying to say bowl after all? That makes much more sense. I suppose it's for the parrot. What goes in the bowl, sir?"

"This is intolerable. Such impertinence! Get out. All of you, get out. You have not heard the last of this!"

Sophie suddenly found her voice. "We have done nothing amiss for you to adopt such an insulting manner. Etiquette! You can't even pronounce the word properly."

"Don't you dare bandy words with me..."

"My advice to you, Sir Frederick, is to have elocution lessons. Language is used for communication, or have you misplaced that concept? Come on, we're leaving."

The agents began filing out.

"I shall report this transaction to the appropriate authorities."

"Don't be too long-winded when you do." She smiled and then closed the door behind her.

"Are we in trouble, miss?" asked Ada, when they were well away from the office.

"A little… I cannot imagine that he will say nothing!"

"I bet he doesn't explain it verbatim," said Flora. "How could he?" She laughed.

"I really shouldn't have lost my temper."

"Well, I'd say you was wonderful, miss, an' he deserved it, goin' on and on like that. He sent me cross-eyed."

"That didn't happen to me," said BW. "Although I found him difficult to follow. Quite distracting, really."

"Does anyone remember anything he said?"

"Don't walk in front of the Royals," said Ada. "But we knew that already."

"I must have gone into a trance," said Flora, "but what did he say about finding out someone's title before addressing them?"

"Who knows?" said Sophie. "However, although it would be right to find out to whom one is speaking before doing so, there is a simple workaround in a pinch. It's unlikely we'll meet any dukes or marquesses. Therefore, we shall address anyone we approach as if they are an earl or a countess. In doing so, we are safe, because if they are lower ranked, they won't jib at the sudden elevation. Conversely, if we addressed a noble by a lower rank, then we'd hear all about it."

"That is pure genius, Miss King," said BW.

"Not really, BW. Are we all clear on how to address the Royal Family at least?"

Ada gave a small preparatory cough. "King and Queen was Majesty first, then Sir or Sire or Ma'am rhymes with jam afterwards. The others were Royal Highnesses first and then the same again afterwards."

"You should have been our instructor," said Sophie, smiling.

"We have a difficulty there," said Flora. "He didn't enunciate either of those two words correctly and they were different to each other. He said, and I quote as nearly as possible, 'Mahhyeahum rrrhymes whhithh jaaah-um.'"

"Well, blow me down," said BW. "That sounded just like him, including shooting up and down the jolly old scale."

Flora curtsied.

"Ah!" said Sophie. "I see the problem now. Did he intend for us to say Ma'am the way he said jam or the way everyone else says it?"

"I don't know if this helps, miss, but I've heard married ladies called m'm, marm, mom, mum, madam, and madame. One old butler used to just say mm, 'cause he was close to nodding off all the time."

"Phonetically speaking," began Flora, "I think it should be mahm as in marmalade, with no emphasis on the r, of course."

Ada put up her hand and Flora answered.

"Phonetics refer to how words sound as opposed to how they're written."

"Thank you, Gladys. I had wondered about that. So there's a word for it an' all. You learn something new every day."

"Right, we'll call her ma'am, which rhymes with jam, and then we'll see...," she consulted the list Handley had given her, "Inspector Maddox. If he has nothing specific for us to do, we shall search for bombs. That way we can explore the Palace properly while working." She smiled. "However, we must be careful not to be seen by the Royal Family until tomorrow when we are to be presented."

It was fortunate they went to see Inspector Maddox, because he had a packet for them from Superintendent Penrose, which included passes into all Royal Households.

In the tunnel below the streets of London, work was continuing at a quickened pace, but only at night. At this time of the morning, the crew was finishing up because any work at the face might be overheard.

"Psst, Jimmy. A moment, huh?" said Mateo, putting a hand on his friend's arm as they moved along.

"Yes?"

"Let them go on."

Two other men were in front, shuffling along the airless passage. They waited a moment for them to get far enough ahead.

"We're near the end, yes?"

Jimmy nodded.

"Then what happens?"

Jimmy shrugged.

Mateo drew a thumb across his neck. "That's what happens to us."

"You don't know that."

"I don't trust the boss. Me, I was a criminal. You never were. They gave me a chance because the police wanted me in Portugal. Bring your family, they said, and you'll have safe work in England. I was desperate, so I agreed. You and I have been here longest. Six men have been down here with us, and one by one, poof, they disappear into the river, then reappear, but only in the newspapers."

"You think that, too?"

"Yes. We foreigners work in the tunnel because we can't get work anywhere else, then we go in the river when we cause trouble for them. I knew as soon as I saw the second one in the newspaper. The only reason I survive is because of you, my friend, who always says, don't ask questions. The ones who have gone — they asked. Then they vanish into the river."

"It seems likely. I've also connected the two."

"But Jimmy, tell me two things. Why are you here? How do we get out alive?"

"They have a hold over me. Not only personally, but also involving my family... I can't explain any more than that."

"I understand, because I'm scared for my family as well. If I die, it will be bad for them. Anyway... I don't *wanna* die. So, what we gonna do?"

"I think we only have a few more days tunnelling left... The new fellows, what do you make of them?"

"They don't talk much. The little Frenchie, he has a tattoo on his arm from the prison. I know, because I've seen the same before. The Norwegian, I don't know about. Could be helpful. He looks tough."

"Yes, he does. If we're to do something, we would need their help." He was silent for a moment. "I had actually resigned myself to being killed when the work finished." He laughed without humour. "By that, my family would be safe, so there was some value to losing my life. I've had to do everything they say, so it has become my habit not to think of escaping their clutches... I've taken to ignoring the obvious for my own sanity."

"Ah... Who is the big man in all this?"

"I don't know. I've only dealt with Godfrey."

"Yes, I met Godfrey before, and again when he visited last week. He does not get his hands dirty, that one. Lefty is the big danger. He will bring men and kill us in this tunnel. All of us. They are after something big, yes? When they get it, they don't need us no more."

Jimmy slowly nodded his head. "Tomorrow. We'll come up with a plan tomorrow. If we all work together, I think there may be a way of doing this so that no one dies."

"Good. Come on, we go now, or someone will be suspicious."

Chapter 8

Royal Train

The Royal Train was ready to depart St Pancras Station and travel non-stop to Wolferton Station, it being the nearest to the Sandringham Estate in Norfolk. The usual waving crowd was much reduced today, and a notable police presence kept at a distance such onlookers as there were. A persistent reporter tried, and failed, to get a comment from Sophie as she and the other agents approached the platform gate.

The agents showed their passes to the ticket collector, who sent them to a table on the platform. While an official was inspecting the documents, including a note signed by the Lord Chamberlain allowing them to board the train, a detective scrutinized them, and another man searched their suitcases. They were then directed to sit in the last carriage of the train. As this was immediately before them, they only had a distant view of the Royal Carriages, their varnished teak gleaming in the morning sunlight.

The carriage was already nearly full, with others still entering. The occupants were mostly men and, as they were of a similar age and stature, Sophie assumed they were additional security personnel being sent to Sandringham. Many looked like policemen out of uniform and in their best clothes. It soon became apparent that there was a class distinction between the agents and the rest of the passengers.

"Miss," whispered Ada, leaning forward, "I think we've all just shot up into the upper class."

"What makes you say that?"

"No one's sittin' near us. One bloke squeezed in between two others when I've got a three-seat bench to meself. He saw it an' all. Do I look like a duchess or something?"

"Absolutely you do."

They laughed.

"It's funny, ain't it? Just a change o' clothes makes all the difference."

"Mrs Green did us proud. Really, her dresses are up to the standard of the courtiers. So, we're dressed for first class, but travelling third."

"That's right, miss. I've got a lovely dress for Sunday. Beautiful it is. I'd never thought for a moment, not for one bloomin' moment, I'd ever have anything like it."

"Fun, isn't it?"

"I'd say. Now we're on the Royal Train — even if they did stick us in an ordinary carriage. What a lark."

There was some commotion outside, followed by a surge of passengers to the platform side windows.

"They're here!" said Flora.

"Where?" said BW, putting his newspaper aside.

The agents stood up to look but were too late because all the windows were blocked by other passengers. After a minute or two, everyone returned to their seats.

"We should be off presently," said Sophie.

Soon, whistles blew, and the train lurched into motion.

Later, Sophie took a moment to study her companions. BW was devouring the content of the Times. Flora was gazing out of the window, a novel in her lap. Ada was reading the Tatler and looking at the photographs containing nobility in case she might meet them. Flora turned and saw that Sophie was scrutinizing her staff.

"Anything the matter?" she asked.

"No, nothing," said Sophie. "I was just wondering if anyone had any thoughts on the case, but you all looked so comfortable I didn't like to ask."

"I think the police are mishandling it," said BW.

"Come closer and lower your voice. What makes you say that?"

"Well, it was funny how we could toddle around the Palace for hours, where there was barely a soul in sight, and never be questioned."

"I thought it odd, too," said Flora.

"But they were watching all the entrances," said Ada. "Then there was all them coppers in the Central Block with the Royal Family. You couldn't pass that lot to get at the King without being stopped."

"I agree totally, Miss Carmichael. But we were practising looking for bombs. Supposing we were planting one instead? No one challenged us."

"That's an interesting point, BW," said Sophie. "We *could* have planted a small time bomb. Had we known where everything was in advance, we could have hidden even a very large one without being seen."

"We'd have to get it past the officers at the entrances."

"Do you know, we might have?" said Sophie. "If each of us carried a part, then we could have assembled it inside. They didn't search us, after all."

"I should think not!" said Flora. "We are respectable agents. But, to return to your point, we would have had to know that they wouldn't search us before trying to sneak a bomb past them."

"Are we sure it's a bomb they'll use?" asked BW.

"The drawings, you may recall," said Sophie.

"Dashed peculiar leaving them lying about like that. Do you think it's a gag?"

"Murders, explosive devices, and death threats — I think not."

"What if these criminal johnnies are trying to mislead us?"

"To cover up what, exactly? What can be worse than the assassination of the head of state and his family?"

"No good asking me, Miss King. It was only a thought."

"It's not a bad theory, though. It opens up possibilities. In a similar vein, I puzzle over why these people sent a death threat to the King rather than carrying out the attack. By that warning, they put the authorities on the alert, which only makes a real attempt so much harder."

"Somebody showing off, do you think?" asked Flora. "Do criminals show off, though?"

"Not when they're on a job," said Ada. "They might boast about it after. However, through a brother, I know of a twerp who boasted beforehand — Larry the Mouth. He lives two streets over and is a burglar. Down the local, he kept telling everyone that he could burgle any house in London and get away clean. Now, to be fair, he was a busy fella in his line of business, an' has never been nicked for anything. Larry also likes a drink, he does.

"Some fellas at the local challenged him to burgle this house that everyone said couldn't be turned over. It had broken glass on top of the wall and a big dog roamin' the grounds. Larry had downed a few, so he got all worked up over maintainin' his honour. Said he'd burgle that house and prove it by bringing to the pub anything they cared to mention, so that when they saw the burglary reported in the papers, they'd know it was him who'd done the impossible. Someone said, 'How about the kitchen sink?" so Larry said, 'You're on.'"

"Why would he steal a kitchen sink?" asked BW.

"He was showing off to the others, of course," said Sophie. "Try not to interrupt, please. We want to hear what happened. Go on, Nancy."

"Well, it was about a fortnight later when he had a go at the house. How he got in was never explained, but he'd got past the bits of glass and the barbed wire, and given the dog something to make him go bye-byes. The report of the burglary appeared in the newspaper. It said a sink and some silver plate had been taken.

"After that, Larry goes on the missing list for a week. Finally, he shows up at the pub with crutches and a cast on his leg, and no sink. He reckons he was taking a shortcut across Tower Hamlets Cemetery, which is a big place with a low fence, and he fell down into an open grave in the dark. Broke his leg, he did. Larry couldn't get out, and so there he was, six feet under with the sink and the stolen silver."

"What did he do?" asked Flora.

"The only thing he *could* do when you think about it. He buried everything in the side of the grave. Said it took him all night using his bare 'ands, and he was in agonies 'cause of his leg. The next day, about ten, they start turning up for the burial. Turns out it was for a retired police sergeant, and there's Larry in the grave looking up at a ring of uniforms staring down at him. So, he gave 'em a story about being drunk and they believed it. He got taken to the doctor's, and they buried their old sergeant in with the sink and the silver. It could all be true, but Larry's a bit slippery, although they reckoned he *had* burgled the house. Afterwards, they called him Old Resurrection for a while."

"Good grief," said Sophie. "Pride goeth before a fall."

"Literally," said Flora.

"He wouldn't go back for the sink, would he?" asked BW.

"No, he wouldn't," said Ada. "I think he learned his lesson."

"What's interesting about that story," said Sophie, "is that the police had a criminal at their mercy but, being oblivious, let him go." She paused for a moment. "I wish I knew how they were conducting the case. Mr Handley said that a maid has gone missing from Buckingham Palace."

"I hope she's not become another drowning in the river," said Flora.

"They can't find her, so it is possible. It's all very troubling, but perhaps only a coincidence."

The train slowed as it approached a level crossing. Ada got up to look out of the window. Three children had clambered onto a gate and were waving at the Royal Train. Ada waved back.

"Only a level crossing," she said. "You all right, miss?"

"Oh, I'm terribly anxious about all of this... It's not knowing what the police are doing."

"They're doing all they can, I think."

"Yes, I know they will. But supposing we're dealing with someone like Larry the Mouth. Someone who is showing off or playing a game out of sheer bravado. Such behaviour makes everything so uncertain."

"True," said Flora. "If we had some idea who it is, we could dig a pit and he would fall in it."

"A trap, you mean. The trouble is that we have no idea what he will do next... If anything."

"Whoever it is," said Ada, "must have changed his plans, since he can't bring in the illegals anymore."

They were still discussing the matter when the train entered a cutting before a tunnel.

"Look!" shouted a man. He stood up and pointed. Everyone looked out of the windows.

Stretched out on the slope were two white bedsheets weighted down at the corners. Upon them, painted in large crude black letters, were the words:

NEVER RETURN TO LONDON.

No one spoke inside the carriage until they entered the tunnel, then everyone began at once. It was outrageous! they exclaimed in various ways, raising their voices above the increased din of the train being in the tunnel. The perpetrators were the vilest human specimens ever known and, if only hands could be laid upon them, they would get their just desserts. When the train was in the open again, many of the men discovered they were being overly loud, and the carriage settled down into an embarrassed, sullen, bad temper.

"Phoebe." Flora tapped Sophie on the knee. "Those sheets were new. They still had the crisp fold lines in them, so they hadn't been washed."

"So they were. Then someone purchased sheets just to paint on them?"

"They have money. Anyone else would paint on old sheets and keep the new for use. It's your Larry the Mouth-like fellow again." Flora was nodding her head.

"He's not *my* fellow, but I believe you're right. What a strange threat, though. Obviously, it was directed at the King. He can't possibly stay away from London, so why even say it? And what will happen should he return?"

"It's the sort of nonsense meant to get under one's skin, if you let it," said Flora. "From the few things we know, we can deduce that the enemy has money, is bold, paints poorly, although a minion probably did that for him, and passes off vagueness as being deeply psychological. I don't believe I know anyone like that, particularly the money part. But I *do* know an artist who paints poorly."

"You're taking it very calmly," said Sophie.

"I refuse to be frightened by bedsheets, and the inane message does nothing to make the threat any more serious than it was before. It was you who suggested wonkiness about the death threats sent in advance. I now concur. It's been all show and no substance so far. Will it come to anything? I've no idea, but I hope it doesn't."

"What do you think about this? The bedsheet message obviously can't be well-intentioned and, therefore, cannot be taken as a friendly warning. That means there might be great danger at Sandringham, because the message is to put everyone off their guard. That means the safest place for the King is back in London. But, if we take the message at face value, as a warning, the safest place is Sandringham or anywhere outside of London. Why even deliver it, and in such an extraordinary way?"

"Which is it?"

"I don't know, but I have a feeling there's more to come."

"Undoubtedly, but I don't believe there'll be a bomb at Sandringham."

"That's good," said BW. "Makes you wonder why the blighter's even bothering." Having said that, he went back to reading his paper.

At Wolferton Station, a fleet of vehicles was drawn up awaiting the Royal Family and retinue. As today's retinue was so numerous, local vehicles had been pressed into service.

After the King's party had exited the front carriages of the train — which the agents had missed completely because they were in the last carriage and there were so many people in the way — they went outside to find a conveyance. Individuals had not been assigned to any of the sundry vehicles. Selection, therefore, was determined by lining up in a queue and allowing chance to select the vehicle. When the four-wheeled covered cart of Follett's Bakery pulled by an old grey horse stopped in front of the agents, the women of Burgoyne's looked at their dresses and quailed. Follett himself, dressed in his Sunday best, saw the alarm on their faces. He climbed down, talking all the while in his slow, lilting Norfolk drawl.

"Don't you be afeared, my ladies. I ain't carryin' no flour, an' it be as clean as a whistle inside. Your bootiful dresses'll suffer no damage. And your suit, sir, my lord, er, yes, loikewise."

"Thank you for your assurance. Is it Mr Follett?" queried Sophie.

"That's roight, your ladyship. No harm shall befall you and your party, I promise. Lily, here, is the best of horses. Quiet and goes noicely through the rough parts, and I won't let her do otherwise, and she don't want to anyways. Allow me to help you in. The back door's easiest. I've nailed some crates to the floor and put cushions on 'em, and covered 'em with clean sacks which the wife washed only yesterday." He then became nervous. "Would you... would you happen to be a duchess?"

Sophie imagined the speculative domestic conversations full of expectation that must have occurred leading up to this awkward moment.

"No, I'm only a countess."

"A countess! My word. Please, take my arm, and let me help you up. Clean as a whistle, it is, as you can see, my lady... Is that what I should say?"

"Yes, Mr Follett."

"Oh, good."

He helped Flora and Ada to climb in. Then came Broadbent-Wicks, who put the luggage on board.

"Do you need help, my lord?"

"No, I can manage, thank you."

"I hope you don't moind my askin', but would you be the count? Or is it an earl?"

BW saw Sophie shaking her head vigorously.

"Ah, no. I'm just a friend of the Royal Family."

"Oh. All the same, it's a great honour for me to have you a-sitting in my cart."

BW got in and, without further ado, Follett shut the door, climbed onto his perch, and they set off. The estate was only a couple of miles away, which was just as well because, although it was a good road, the agents could feel all the bumps.

Sandringham is where the Royal Family finds peace. The monarchy discharges its duties at Buckingham Palace and elsewhere, but Sandringham is its home. The estate, a huge tract of Norfolk land close to the sea, has entire villages within its boundaries. Near to the house are complexes of buildings devoted to farming, horses, and the administration of the estate. The land is flat but varied — there is as much forest as there is arable land. Throughout everything, there can be seen the touches of studied attention to detail of successive monarchs. The improvements made were for the comfort of themselves and their guests, yet equally important, was that the expansion and refurbishing of the working estate caused it to become the leading industry in the area. The local people have benefitted in numerous ways by having the King as their employer. A horse stud, pheasantries, domestic work, building and repairs, forestry, gardening — these centres of activity introduced by the Royal Family bring the local population a measure of prosperity beyond that which ordinary farming alone could provide. Over time, the family and the people have become intertwined.

Follett's Bakery cart was stopped at the gate by infantry in khaki and was only allowed through after uniformed police and detectives had questioned everyone and searched the cart. When the cart moved on, a constable sat next to Follett, directing him.

"I know the way to the house," said Follett. "I deliver bread sometimes, when they're in a pinch."

"I 'ave to accompany you, sir, 'cause it's the rules," said the London constable.

"What's goin' on, then?"

"Can't say. Not allowed, you see."

"Sometimes, there are too many rules. You can't say anythin'?"

"Sorry. Instructions was, everythin' by the book or you'll 'ave it thrown at you. It's the King, see. All gotta be done proper."

"Ahh."

"I'll tell you this much, though. We're up 'ere until further notice. 'Ow about that?"

"Excuse me, constable," said Sophie from the back. "Who is in charge of security?"

"Oh, er..."

"She's a countess, an' you have to say my lady," said Follett quietly.

"Sorry, my lady. I didn't know. Um, I don't know his name, but he's an army captain. Got a lot of ribbons an' all that."

"Thank you. One more thing. Where shall I find him?"

"I couldn't say, my lady. He was about earlier, then he disappeared when the King showed up. Which suits us, 'cause he's a pain... An army type, you might say. Very loud."

"One of those, is he?"

"That's right." The constable laughed nervously.

The horse jogged on.

They passed by some clean white tents pitched in orderly rows on sun-scorched grass. The entire country was going through a prolonged dry spell and Sandringham was as much afflicted as anywhere else. The constable directed Follett to stop outside a pavilion. Whether army, police, or civilian, this was the place to be assigned a billet. Follett departed after a hearty farewell, and Sophie left a tip on the driver's seat to save any fuss, certain that Mr Follett would have declined the money and have been embarrassed in doing so.

The agents queued with their luggage, and they felt very much out of place. The open side of the pavilion revealed two corporals seated at tables and checking names against lists and issuing dockets. One table had a sign saying, 'Police', the other sign said, 'Civilians'. It was a slow process. When a man received a docket, he then went to draw his blanket and proceed to his assigned tent.

"This doesn't look good," said Flora, as they shuffled forward. "They're all men here."

"There has to have been a mistake," said Sophie, who compressed her lips in anticipation of the coming battle.

The confrontation went more or less as she had expected. Sophie presented at the Civilian table and stated she was Phoebe King. The corporal had already gaped at her because she was a woman and an extremely well-dressed one at that.

"You're not on my list," he said at last.

"Perhaps we are on the police list."

"That's possible." He called to his companion. "Here, Harry. Got a P. King there?"

"Wot? Like the Chinese place?" He looked up smiling, saw Sophie glowering at him, and so stopped. "I'll 'ave a look." A few moments later, he announced that she was on the list and should join the police queue.

"It is likely," said Sophie calmly, "that you will find three other names on your police list that should also not be there."

"You're not police?" said an incredulous Harry.

"Are you civilians?" asked the other corporal.

"No." When she began speaking, the queues took an interest because of the delay. "Undoubtedly, you have a chain of command…" She stopped because a sergeant had come over to investigate the hold up.

"What's going on 'ere, then?"

"This lady says she's not a civilian and not police, but she's on the police list. There's four of them like it, she says."

The sergeant glanced at the other agents, then returned his gaze to Sophie. It was apparent that he had no idea what to do.

"Might I suggest you take us to your commanding officer?"

"Yes, that might be an idea," he said. "If you'd kindly step into the pavilion, the lads can continue processing."

An apologetic lieutenant was then brought into the dilemma.

"Clearly, there has been a mistake... ah..."

"Miss King."

"Miss King. Are you visitors, by chance?"

"No. We have work to do here."

She showed him the warrants and he read them.

"Yes... Still, if you could possibly explain what this work is, perhaps I could set things straight."

"Unfortunately, I cannot tell you what our duties are. My suggestion is that you take us to your commanding officer."

"Ah, the CO, eh? Tricky that."

"There is nothing tricky about it, lieutenant. It is simple expediency."

"Yes, very likely. Could you wait here one moment?"

"No, we cannot. As I said, we have work to do, and this unconscionable delay is setting us behind. If I do not see your CO immediately, I must go elsewhere to have the matter resolved. I apologize for being insistent, lieutenant, but we do not have all day."

"Ah, right, right... Yes. The CO is in Sandringham House... I should think he's finished his lunch by now."

"Does that mean he will be in a good mood?"

"Do you know him?"

"No, not even his name."

"Captain Purvis."

"Thank you. Let's get on, shall we?"

During the walk to the house, the lieutenant was pleasant, continued to be apologetic, and explained what the army was doing on the estate. He guided the agents to the new wing of Sandringham House. Sophie had the others remain outside on the gravel while she went inside to see Captain Purvis. She waited in a corridor while the lieutenant entered a room. As he opened and then closed the door, she heard men talking and laughing and could detect cigar smoke. She sniffed, certain the reek carried alcohol fumes. The door opened again.

"I'll see you at the stables in, say, an hour?"

The captain spoke to others in the room in a clear voice with a lazy drawl. He was tall, about thirty, with a small moustache, and wearing a smart uniform bearing a handful of medal ribbon bars. He smiled briefly at Sophie and then said,

"Good afternoon, Miss King. What seems to be the problem?"

Sophie returned the greeting and explained how her staff could not be expected to live in a tent, not only because they were unprepared for such an eventuality, but also because it would interfere with their ability to carry out their work. He listened patiently, but she sensed his rising hostility, principally because his jaw muscles had tensed.

"If you would explain what it is you are here to do, then perhaps we can see our way clear."

"I'm sorry, but I'm not at liberty to be specific. I would have thought the warrants issued by the Lord Chamberlain permitting us to attend the Royal Family would have been sufficient."

"That's all well and good and allows you on the estate but, at present, I'm in charge of security, and I cannot imagine a good reason for your being here. If you refuse to explain yourself, you may as well go back to London and have your superior contact me in the proper manner. Then I shall decide. Who is your superior?"

"Before I answer, I'd have thought you would have been informed of our coming prior to our arrival."

"Have I been informed?" he wondered out loud. "Laneford, was it?"

"Yes, Lord Laneford. So, he wrote to you, did he?"

"Yes. Said something about female employees mixing in with the servants, I believe. The general idea seemed to be to provide an additional layer of security... Oh, that's right! He mentioned your name. I thought it sounded familiar."

"And you took no action or made no preparation?"

"Totally unnecessary. We have the situation under full control and the last thing we want is untrained individuals disturbing the King and getting in the way. Now, as a courtesy, and if convenient, you may stay on the estate tonight and return to London tomorrow. Although, it will mean your sleeping in a tent. We're tight for room, and that's all that can be offered." He smiled again.

Among her churning thoughts, Sophie might have been angry had not the hollowness of disappointment edged it out. There was no one to whom she could appeal this final decision. Of one thing she was certain: Captain Purvis had dissembled and played a game with her, but she did not know why.

"You have not heard the last of this," said Sophie, who spun on her heel and left before he could give a supercilious and patronizing reply.

Outside, she delivered the bad news to her friends, and they took turns expressing their outrage and disgust at the captain's behaviour. Having said all that there was to say, they now had to decide if they should stay or go.

While they deliberated, a nearby gardener pushing a wheelbarrow came towards them. The way the agents were standing, only Sophie could see the bearded man in stained corduroy trousers, shirtsleeves, and an old open waistcoat missing its buttons. She could not see his face properly because he wore a weather-stained broad-brimmed hat pulled low. When a few yards away, he looked up to stare at her, winked, then subtly nodded, suggesting she follow him.

Sophie almost squeaked in surprise. The gardener was Ralph 'Sinjin' Yardley, whom, one day, she might marry. The others had not noticed the signal. Sophie picked up her suitcase.

"We'll go that way," she said, pointing in the direction the gardener was taking.

"Why?" asked Flora. "We either have to find a tent or someone to take us to the station."

"We're not leaving. Come on." She walked away.

Ada and Flora exchanged puzzled looks, then followed suit.

"Hurry up, BW," said Ada.

He was gazing at the extensive East Front of Sandringham House. "Are we off somewhere?" He picked up his case and followed. "The house is so big, I'm sure they could squeeze us in if we asked."

"Queen Alexandra lives there, not the King."

"So, I understand… I say, do you think she gets lonely all by herself?"

"I doubt it," said Flora. "I'm sure she has many visitors."

"Yes, but it can't be the same since her husband died… I don't know why, but I feel very sorry for her. It would be dreadful if she wandered about the place all on her own."

"Let's hope she doesn't," said Ada.

They caught up with Sophie as she turned a corner. Their path between flowerbeds was directly beneath a row of windows on the new wing's eastern side. After a few paces, Flora asked,

"Are we following that gardener?"

"Yes," said Sophie. "It's Sinjin."

"I would ask what he's doing here and why are we following him, but I think I can work it out. He doesn't want us to be seen talking to him?"

"That's right."

"The gardener's name is Sinjin?" asked BW. "How could you possibly know that, Miss King?"

"He's one of us. However, we must take no notice of him."

"Righty-ho. I'll ignore the chap. Not that I had been paying him much attention before now."

They passed by a courtyard of buildings, which contained the working departments of the house. There followed another connected building. Trees and bushes stood opposite, screening the more unseemly parts of Sandringham House from the private road through the estate. A pair of high double-doors stood open.

"A fire-engine? Here?" said Flora. "Who would have thought?"

"I doubt there's a shinier one in the whole of Britain," said Ada.

They went around the corner to find another collection of offices, with Yardley beyond them and approaching a row of four small cottages. It was much quieter here and not overlooked. Sophie quickened her pace.

Yardley paused outside the fourth cottage and pointed, then moved around to its side. The agents proceeded to enter the little house.

"This looks nice... Is this for us, miss?" asked Ada.

"I believe so."

As the group of four came into the small parlour, Yardley knocked on the side window. Sophie opened it immediately and looked questioningly into the eyes of Sinjin.

"Lovely to see you, dear," he said, smiling. He laid his hand on hers as it rested on the sill.

"And very nice to see you, too. What on earth is going on?"

"We only got word this morning that Purvis was cutting up rough about your being here. As you were travelling, we couldn't contact you. I'm here doing the rounds, as usual, but I couldn't approach you in the queue without giving the game away."

"*Why* is that dreadful man cutting up rough?"

"I don't know him but, according to Handley, who arrived last night, Purvis is ambitious. He wants a senior job at court and tries at every opportunity to be of service to the King. He sees your being here as interference with his plans for advancement. You may have noticed by the royal cypher on his uniform that he is already an Equerry. Laneford only knew of his being put in charge of security yesterday. Sent him a telegram, and the blighter didn't reply, so Laneford telephoned him this morning. That ended in a row."

"Lord Laneford argued with him? I can't believe it."

"Well, he did. Purvis is of no use to us, so keep out of his way. Handley, however, is a great organizer. He got this workman's cottage for you on short notice."

"I shall thank him when I see him."

"I must go... I wish I could stay." He squeezed her hand gently.

She smiled. "You look very dirty, Sinjin."

"Well, miss," he said in a country accent, "you moight say that's a credit to me. Shows what an 'ard workin' fellow I be."

"Passable, but it's not a Norfolk accent."

"I tried, I really did, but it sounded awful. I must go... York Cottage is that way, about three hundred yards." He pointed south. "The family is in residence but, as far as we know, the place hasn't been searched for explosive devices, because Purvis didn't think it was necessary. We're all certain you will do your best under the circumstances. Goodbye."

Chapter 9

Trouble at Work

York Cottage on the Sandringham Estate is reminiscent of, although certainly larger than, a prosperous suburban doctor's house. A wedding gift from his father, King George V himself described his beloved home as 'three merrie England pubs joined together.' In the past, it was used for the overflow of male guests visiting the estate and appropriately named Bachelor's Cottage. Because it was not originally set up as a family home, the rooms were on the small side, particularly the reception rooms, and with some bedrooms almost cabin-like. This constriction suited King George V because, unlike his father, Edward, he preferred not to entertain guests within his private domain.

While approaching York Cottage through parkland with a lake on their right, the agents thought the house attractive and prettily situated. However, it took time for them to find the right entrance and the house was larger than it first appeared. Inside, they waited in a narrow corridor while a footman went to find the steward, to whom, once found, Sophie explained matters. In the crushed space, she showed him her warrant, and expressed the urgency for searching the house — if that had not already been done. He accepted her authority, in part because she was, as were the rest of the agents, so extraordinarily well dressed — down to her freshest pair of gloves.

According to the now slightly alarmed steward, no search had been performed. He sent a footman to find the Equerry on duty. The Equerry came, expressed a moderate amount of alarm, and invited Sophie to follow him upstairs to the private office of the King's Personal Secretary, Baron Stamfordham. They ascended the narrow, winding staircase to enter a corridor of even narrower proportions. Here, the Equerry knocked on the door of a room with a row of three chairs outside. From within, the Personal Secretary called out, "Enter!" When the door opened, Sophie learned that the office was, in fact, also the man's bedroom. The door shut. She could hear what they were saying, so she moved a few paces away. The door opened. The seventy-one-year-old Personal Secretary came out flustered, his white soup-strainer moustache bristling, and asked the same questions they had all asked. He examined the warrants before returning them to Sophie. He swallowed and then said to the Equerry,

"I'll inform the King. If you'd be so kind as to get things under way with the minimum of disruption. The absolute minimum. Excuse me, Miss King."

Baron Stamfordham hurried away. Sophie and the Equerry, a former naval officer, decided how best to conduct a thorough search of the King's home and, within minutes, half a dozen footmen and pages were assisting the agents as they began systematically going through the rooms, starting on the top floor and working their way down. The King's household staff wore their anxiety on their faces, while Sophie struggled to keep hers hidden. She grasped that, should they not find a bomb, and the household should have been unduly unsettled for no real reason, someone was going to be blamed for the inconvenience. She was already on thin ice because Captain Purvis, himself an Equerry, had earlier thrown her off the estate. Looked at from a certain angle, her actions were indefensible. Would the King — they were bound to tell him — see her behaviour from that same unflattering angle? She considered for a moment. Of course, he would — Purvis would make certain of it.

Many of the rooms were congested with bric-à-brac that offered a myriad of places to conceal an explosive device. Some rooms were in use, requiring time and patience to explain the situation to the occupants, many of whom quickly became disgruntled. The agents found that the early use of the word 'bomb' worked wonders in persuading someone, even the most obstinate, to leave a room. However, there was one titled lady-in-waiting who was not so easily convinced or shifted. In her case, they summoned the Equerry to employ the appropriate manner when extending an invitation for her to leave the building in case it blew up.

Soon, there were more people outside than in. Those on the outside formed cliques, according to their various ranks and classes, and all were muttering darkly in their different ways. As the house cleared, the pace of the search picked up, and even long-dead Prince Albert-Victor's bedroom was unlocked and inspected, only to find that it was exactly how he had left it.

Sophie had just searched all the rooms that gave off from a short ground-floor passageway and was now plagued with a deepening sense of personal doom. There was nothing left for her to search except what was probably a cupboard. She looked at her watch, then heard Flora call her.

"Are you hiding?"

"Yes," said Sophie. "I don't think I can face them."

"We did the right thing. In fact, we were under instruction to search, and I think we did it rather well."

"No one's going to see it like that. Look at the trouble we've had so far with Sir Frederick Tunstall-Green and Captain Purvis. Now rate our chances."

"Oh, they're pretty low, I should say, but not non-existent."

"Miss!" called Ada as she approached. BW was with her. "We didn't find nothing."

"I suppose that's a good thing," said Sophie. "Did you see anything of the Royal Family?"

"No, miss. They must be outside."

"I expect they are."

"Do you know, I love this house," said BW. "Reminds me of home, only it's at least ten times bigger… What are we all doing down *here*? Hiding?"

"Phoebe doesn't want to face the brickbats outside," said Flora.

"Ah," said BW. "Not to worry, Miss King, because it had to be done, and I think most people entered into the spirit of the thing. And what is a brickbat, anyway?"

"I've got a cousin who's a brickie," said Ada. "He said it was 'alf-a-brick, but only the old geezers use the word."

"So, whether insults are hurled or actual half-bricks," said Flora, "we shall all stand or fall together."

"Thank you for that comforting thought. We might as well get it over with… Ooh, I must just search this first."

She opened the small door to what she thought was the cupboard, but found it was, in fact, an entrance to a narrow conservatory running along the side of the house. Sophie froze. They all froze because, turned in their direction, were six pairs of royal eyes. Four of the owners sat near the door in wicker chairs while two princes stood together further away. If there were any doubt about whether their entire conversation in the passageway had been overheard, the smirk on the face of Prince Edward, or David as the family called him, completely dispelled all uncertainty.

The silence lasted several seconds, and Sophie had a hundred different thoughts and impressions rush through her mind, among which were: My face is hot. Prince Albert is embarrassed, too. Queen Mary must have had ginger hair when she was younger. A prince is missing, so who is the tall one? Edward is the centre of attention. Princess Mary looks friendly. The King seems patient. I must address him properly.

"Your majesty," said Sophie, gracefully curtsying before the King.

Behind her, BW bowed, while Ada and Flora bobbed.

No royal person seemed inclined to speak. The King continued to look at Sophie. Impeccably groomed and dressed, his kindly, fatherly face seemed tired or, rather, that he had been tired in the past and his face had permanently recorded the fact. Despite that, his pale blue eyes were alive. It was evident he expected Sophie to continue speaking and explain matters, her presence — everything. While she struggled to find the correct form for speaking before the King has spoken, Ada, much like a ventriloquist, whispered, "I 'ear two clocks ticking, miss."

A second longer, and Sophie heard them — a loud tick and a quieter one.

"Sir, forgive me for speaking first." She spoke urgently. "How many clocks are there in the room?"

In answer, King George simply pointed to a mantel clock over the fireplace. Then said,

"There's another over there, but it doesn't work." He pointed towards a large wooden bracket clock standing on its own shelf. By way of explanation, he enigmatically added, "It was a gift."

"It's ticking now, sir," said Albert, with a slight stutter.

"Is it?" asked Sophie, sounding appalled. "I'm dreadfully sorry, sir," she said, speaking to the King, "but I must ask you to leave the conservatory... All of you, your Majesties and Highnesses."

"Why are you making such a fuss over a clock?" asked Queen Mary in a frozen hauteur.

"Because Mama," said Edward, "this young lady believes there may be a *bomb* inside that clock. She doesn't wish for us to be blown to pieces, and so is doing us a kindness."

"On occasion, David, I detect a cruel streak in your manner."

The King sighed heavily, but over what was not apparent. "Come, my dear, we shall leave." He arose from his chair. "Bertie, help your sister." To the Queen again, he said, "We don't want to get in the way, now do we?"

"Very well." She took his hand and stood up.

The family did not rush from the conservatory; rather, it assembled itself first before going out to the garden. Seeing an appropriate open gap to weave through, Sophie rushed over to the bracket clock and put her ear to it. Flora joined her.

"It's ticking," whispered Sophie, "but it's showing the wrong time."

"Sounds like a Big Ben alarm clock to me."

"You can tell the difference?"

"I've been trained by an expert."

Sophie laughed out loud because of her anxiety. "Oh, come off it. How can you take this so lightly?"

"The same as you."

"But I'm a bag of nerves."

"Well, you don't look it."

"I suppose that's something."

As the King was leaving, he stopped for a moment to catch the eye of Prince Henry. When he had, he nodded towards Sophie and Flora. Henry nodded his assent and went to them.

"Excuse me," he said deferentially. "May I be of assistance?"

"Thank you, your Highness," said Sophie. "That is so kind of you, but…"

"Your Highness," said Flora, "what Miss King is trying to say is that we have the situation under control. I have some training and know what to do."

Sophie looked at her friend in utter astonishment, which she struggled to quash.

"That's reassuring," said Henry. He enunciated the letter r in an unusual way. "By the by, that clock has a glass back, so you can see all the works without opening it."

"That's convenient," said Flora. "Let's have a look, shall we?"

She carefully swivelled the clock round on its shelf.

"Good grief!" said Sophie when she saw the alarm clock with wires attached to dynamite. Two waxed paper cylinders, about eight inches long, were standing upright in the corners.

"We must have this removed," said the Prince.

"Excuse me, sir," said Sophie. "Nancy! BW! Get everyone well away and bring the army and the police." BW and Ada hastened away.

"There's no real hurry," said Flora. "See this? They set the alarm hand for twelve, but the main clock says it's ten forty-five, which is the wrong time, of course, but it means we're safe for over an hour."

"Ah, interesting," said Prince Henry. "I have an idea. Shall I throw it in the lake?"

"That's a good idea, sir," said Flora.

"No, we can't do that, I'm afraid, sir," said Sophie. "The police will want to examine everything for fingerprints."

"That's true," said Henry, emphasizing his agreement with a well-manicured index finger.

"We already have a clue."

"Do we?" asked Flora.

"Yes. The time. Whoever set the alarm must have done so at…" Sophie looked at her watch. "It's almost three now and I'm on Sandringham time. Deducting ten and three-quarter hours from three means they set it at… four forty-five."

"That's good, but I disagree," said Flora. "When setting any alarm, should the hands be too close to the alarm time, then the silly thing is liable to go off by itself, and you have to go all the way round again. It's very tiresome when it does that."

"You're right, of course. Let's suppose the time was showing one o'clock when they set the alarm. The time elapsed then is nine and three-quarter hours, so it was set at approximately five forty-five." She looked at the Prince. "Sir, who would have been here then, other than the servants?"

"Hmm, we weren't present, of course, but no one in particular whom I can recall. Just the servants, as you suggest."

"Ah, good. My next question is this, what happens in this conservatory in an hour and a quarter's time?"

"At four, we have tea, which lasts about forty-five minutes at the most. On a nice day, such as today, we have it in here. We were only in the conservatory early today because they sent us. Really, they should have sent us anywhere *but* here."

"That's very interesting. Who sent you?"

"Stamfordham, the King's Personal Secretary."

"Thank you, sir. Would you know if he travelled on the train with you?"

"He did, actually. Surely you don't suspect him?"

"No, not at all, sir. I simply wanted to exclude him from suspicion. The police will want to question everyone the same way."

The Prince nodded.

"Shall I defuse the bomb?" asked Flora.

"Absolutely not." Sophie was astounded.

"Ladies, I believe it is time for us to retire. I cannot leave unless you do. As there is no more to be done, may I suggest the garden?"

"Yes, sir," replied Sophie. "But we must caution the army about preserving fingerprints for the police. Miss Walton, please wait outside for their approach. I'll station myself somewhere safe inside and intercept them if they enter the house that way."

"An excellent plan. Shall we, Miss Walton?" He swept a hand towards the garden door.

During the shambling effort of removing the Royal Family and others to safety, the army disposing of the bomb, and the police taking charge of the evidence while a crowd of tut-tutting servants and long-faced courtiers observed the proceedings from a distance, Sophie instructed BW to become friendly with the detective whom she had noticed taking fingerprints in the conservatory. By late afternoon, the detective was in a tent examining the evidence while BW stooped to look over his shoulder.

"What unit did you say you're with?" asked the detective as he took off the last of the prints from the clock case.

"Penrose's," said BW, peering right over the detective's shoulder, fixedly studying the prints. "I say, that lot's a bit of a mess."

"Isn't it? These will only be servant dabs, but it must be done... I know of Penrose, you mentioned him before. What I meant was, what's the name of your unit?"

"It hasn't got one. Don't tell a soul, but it's a sort of casual 'as needed' arrangement. I get a call then hare off hither and yon."

"What do you do the rest of the time?"

"Can't say. It's all terribly hush-hush, and I've said more than I should."

"And you're definitely not Special Branch?"

"Scout's honour and all that, although I was only ever a cub."

The detective shook his head. "This is yet another case of the more I find out, the less I know."

"I'm like that with practically everything... Are you certain there were no fingerprints on the note?"

"Clean. Everything was clean. He must think himself right funny — planting a dummy bomb in the King's home."

"Yes, but those dynamite sticks would have fooled me. Are you sure they're all right?"

"They're just empty tubes. Have a look. That explosives bloke from the army reckons the beggar who made up the timer is an expert, and it's lucky for everyone it wasn't real and that your lot found it."

"Just doing our job."

"Right. Can you imagine what would have happened otherwise? Don't bear thinking about."

"I can't bring myself to think of it, either, and they're such a decent sort of family as well... May I look at the note again?"

"Help yourself, but don't go walking off with it. The brass haven't studied it yet."

"I'll jot it down, then."

He borrowed the detective's pen to copy the badly handwritten note which read:

> The genuine article is at the Palace.
> Stay away to save yourself.

"It's a pity the note doesn't say more, although the message seems straightforward enough to me," said BW.

"Does it? You never know, it might be in code. Do you ever do that kind of stuff?"

"No, I've never been trained. I'm sure it's very interesting, but you have to have the right head for it and be good at mathematics and that sort of thing."

"Yes… Analytical, I think you mean… Are you going to the pub in Dersingham tonight?"

"Unfortunately, I'm on duty at the house. I have to stand about while everyone's eating to make sure no fanatical types put them off their feed."

The detective turned to him.

"Well, you've got the suit for it, don't you? When I first saw you, I thought you were a diplomat or one of them 'Equerries' floating about the place. Where did you get it?"

"Morrie's of Brick Lane. He's such a splendid chap and very reasonable."

"I go to Brick Lane sometimes. I'll look him up."

"Do so. You won't regret it. Tell him BW sent you… I suppose I should leave and let you get on. Did the inspector say anything?"

"He thinks it's an inside job. Someone on the estate set it early in the morning… Here, I'll tell you something for nothing. That army captain is hopping mad, because the bomb was planted right under his nose, so to speak, while his troops were here. He's out looking for blood."

"Meaning what?"

"C'mon, BW, use your noggin. He'll shift the blame as soon as the enquiry is under way. A stuck-up career bloke like that won't take the responsibility, so he'll find someone to blame. He'll say it was the fault of the police, but that won't help him none. We weren't here, and he knows it."

"Neither were we."

"Then you're in the clear — unless he lies, of course."

"But he's an officer!"

"He's also a member of the human race, so he doesn't get an exemption. If I were you, I'd watch myself. You and your lot being in the shadows, like, well, you'd be just perfect as scapegoats. You know what I mean?"

"I believe we're on solid ground, but I'll take your warning to heart."

"Do that, BW, and I hope I'm wrong. Now, should you get away early, come down the pub."

Chapter 10

Dinner and afterwards

Because the dinner was being held at Sandringham House, there was much discussion about how it should proceed according to protocol. Queen Alexandra had her own Master of the Household while the Deputy Master of the King's Household had travelled to Sandringham. These two august persons had a conversation in which the question of Burgoyne's Agency arose. Both men searched through their accumulated experiences, but neither of them could find an instance where servants were meant to be idle in a dining room where royal personages were present.

"What about during the war?" asked QA's MH.

"No, not once," replied KG's DMH. "In fact, the palace staff had to be trimmed after so many had gone to the front, so none stood idle!"

The gentlemen were standing in the dining room — a sombre place of dark wood panelling and large Spanish tapestries

"It was the same here. In fact, it has never been the same since that rotten business in Gallipoli."

"Of course, dear fellow — the King's Own Rifle… Only two survivors, weren't there?"

"That's right. The entire company was from this area."

"How sad, indeed. Naturally, you must have recovered afterwards."

"Oh, we did, but it has never been the same since," said QA's MH. "Returning to the present, the problem is, where do we put them? They don't intend to just stand there, do they?"

"I wish I could say, but I haven't met them. I understand their manners are good, they're well-dressed, and have already met the King. We must also bear in mind that they found that bomb and, although it was fake, they didn't know it at the time. That shows they are resourceful."

"True, but finding a bomb is hardly of significance here... Three women and a man... A dining room is a very different situation and, you must remember, this dérangement has only just been sprung on me."

"Most regrettable," said KG's DMH. "Please accept my apology. I, myself, only found out today when I received a peremptory note from the Home Office."

"The Home Office! How abominable."

"I agree, but to the question. Do we treat them purely as servants during dinner? Or do we allow them every latitude in their action, which will be tantamount to their virtual autonomy while in the proximity of their majesties?"

"Although an important question, it is, in its way, one we are considering too late." He then said hollowly. "The police have been here. They actually entered the house and searched all the rooms and corridors."

"You have my deepest sympathy."

"To see their great big boots marking the Queen's carpets... Language fails me in describing such degradation."

"A distressing ordeal — I commiserate with you," said KG's DMH. "Perhaps, if we jointly held an interview with these persons, we may discover that they do not wear boots. Hopefully, we can persuade them to keep a suitably respectful distance from their majesties."

"It is vital we speak to them. Where are these people now?"

"Oh, I don't know."

QA's MH put a hand to his brow. "This is quite dreadful. What can I say to Her Majesty?" He referred to Alexandra. "I must forewarn her in case she notices female servants in the room."

"You'll think of something, dear chap."

"But she's so difficult these days."

"Then may I make a modest suggestion?" asked KG's DMH.

"Certainly."

"If you have a Chinese or some other style of mobile screen, perhaps you can put these so-called agents behind it, thus minimizing the likelihood of them interfering with anyone's digestion."

"You are so kind. That is an excellent idea."

"That is an excellent idea," said Sophie to Broadbent-Wicks, "because they'll never accept female servants in the dining room. Let's go there now and see what we're up against." They left the hall, proceeding south.

"The Royals like their corridors long and beautiful," said Ada.

"Don't they just," said Flora.

A Siamese cat joined them as if he were an old friend.

"Where did you come from, hmm?" asked Sophie.

"He seems to know where we're going," said Flora.

"Siamese are renowned for their intelligence."

"I've never seen a moggy with blue eyes before," said Ada.

"Puss," called BW. The cat mewed loudly.

"He's a noisy boy," said Ada.

They reached the dining room just as the Masters of Households were leaving.

"Ah!" exclaimed QA's MH. "Don't let him in!"

In an undignified lurch, he pushed his companion aside to leap for the doorknob. Upon reaching it, he slammed the door shut just in time. The thwarted cat stalked about in front of the double doors, screaming in annoyance.

"Be quiet," he said, snapping at the cat, who hissed back at him.

Becoming aware he had an audience attending him, QA's MH resumed his dignified manner.

"I say," said BW, "you two don't get along together, what?"

"No." He instantly noticed BW was attired in clothes of a quality suitable for a peer. "The cat is highly perverse. It jumps on the table unless kept from the room. May I help you, sir?"

"Oh, that's rather spiffing, but don't trouble yourself. We'll just whizz round the old dining room and have a gander, don't you know?"

Sophie interjected before BW could say anything else.

"Allow me to introduce ourselves. My name is Miss King. We are here at the behest of the authorities to help ensure the continuing security of the Royal Family."

"Miss King? My name's Willard, the Master of the Household, and this is Sir Geoffrey Fortescue, Deputy Master of the King's Household. How fortuitous it is that you have arrived." She spoke so well it had heartened him, although he cast a wary glance at BW. He also looked to Ada and Flora but could as yet form no opinion about them. Then he looked down at the cat, who glared back. "Unfortunately, we can't get in at the moment."

"Perhaps he's hungry," said BW. "What's his name?"

"Fosco."

"Oh, after Count Fosco," said Flora.

"Who's that?" asked Ada.

"From Wilkie Collins' A Woman in White," answered Flora.

"He was the most dreadful villain," said Sophie. "But now let us concentrate on how to get in the room without the feline Fosco."

"The lady-in-waiting has charge of him," said Willard, "but she will be fully occupied with her Majesty at present."

"Would some food tempt him away, sir?" asked Ada. "I could fetch some from the kitchen."

"It is possible…"

"I should go," said Sir Geoffrey. "I believe everything may run smoothly now." He smiled and nodded goodbyes to everyone, then left at a smart pace.

"Fosco," said Ada cheerfully. "Come on Fossy, let's go to the kitchen, shall we? I'll find you something nice to eat."

For a second, the cat considered the alternatives of sitting outside a shut door or following someone who was making the right type of cooing noises.

"Thank goodness," said Willard, when the cat trotted after Ada.

Once safely inside, they discussed the upcoming dinner.

"I'm not sure I like the idea of a screen," said Sophie. "Our idea is that Mr Broadbent-Wicks would be the only one of us present. Throughout the meal, he would stand by the door the footmen use and act as a doorman. In that way, he has a function while keeping everything under observation."

"Oh... Oh, I see. Yes, that sounds like a suitable arrangement. What about the rest of you, though?"

"One of us shall be outside the dining room, just in case. Two of us shall search the White Drawing Room and the Grand Saloon before the family enters."

"But the police searched them earlier."

"Indeed, but until *they* catch this maniac, *we* must take every care. We shall search the rooms, beginning with the dining room."

"I totally agree with you about the level of care." He smiled wanly. "I should leave you to your work." The QA's MH disappeared with alacrity, making it apparent that he did not care for bombs.

While the dining room was impressive, it was not overly cheerful; dark wooden panelling, a dark ceiling, and carved columns imparted a profound but sombre air and although a series of large Spanish tapestries by Goya added colour, there was little delicacy to them. The heavy wooden furniture was ponderous, yet well-crafted, and added to the solid feel of the room. The agents began opening drawers and cabinets and looked under the table, which was set for twenty-four.

Ada returned from feeding Fosco. "They've set the table very nice, miss," said Ada, a note of pride creeping into her voice. "But they've done it no better than what we would 'ave."

"Does that please you?" asked Sophie.

"It does." She smiled. "You see, I always thought royal servants would be the best. But now I know... Well, I don't like to say anymore, miss."

"There you are, Nancy. You're the best, too."

"Oh, go on, miss... You are an' all, then."

Sophie laughed this time. "We shan't mention this to anyone... I had to straighten a fork." They laughed together.

"No bombs here, as far as I can see," announced Broadbent-Wicks.

"What about secret cupboards or passages?" asked Flora.

"I sincerely hope there aren't any," said Sophie. "We'll have to ask, though, just to make sure."

After the search, Ada remained behind to guard the dining room while the rest returned to York Cottage. From there, they would accompany the Royal Family when they departed for dinner at the house.

Twenty-four sat at table and seven of them were royal persons. There could have been eight, but Prince George was in Scotland. The other seventeen were courtiers. Together, the group ate decorously, talked quietly, and left in good order. Throughout the two-hour ordeal, BW stood as one immobilized, as if afflicted by a nasty-minded mythical god or some rare Amazonian poison, moving only to hold the door open for servants. He did, however, manage to attract the attention of two of the diners. Queen Alexandra, seated in the middle of the table with her son opposite, had no recollection of the smartly dressed BW and, at first, it puzzled her why a guest should choose to stand in the corner by the door. When he opened the door, she assumed he was a servant and so BW passed from her mind. Captain Purvis noticed him, though, and became annoyed. He was sure BW was not one of Queen Alexandra's staff, knew he was not army, and almost certainly not a policeman. His calculations led him to believe that he must belong to Miss King's following, and so he hated him. The staring idiot was how he thought of BW, and guessed he was one of those who had found the bomb — the fake, inconsequential bomb — which was more practical joke than actual threat when he considered it. However, that discovery made him, Captain Purvis, King's Equerry, look bad — and to be shown up by someone he had already thrown off the estate was both galling and smacked of incompetence on his part. So disconcerted was he by his thoughts, Purvis noticeably missed laughing at one of the King's mild quips — something he always did at every opportunity.

The dinner ended, and the ladies retired to the White Drawing Room. Queen Alexandra's touch was evident throughout this, the prettiest and most exquisitely detailed of Sandringham's rooms, and if there were any doubt as to her authorship, her glorious portrait by Hughes dating to 1902 hung over the unlit fireplace to confirm the fact. In the painting, she wore a silk, steely-blue gown with voluminous white and puffy engageantes sleeves. Seated to one side of the fireplace, it was clear Queen Alexandra herself had changed a great deal when compared to the portrait above her, yet she was undeniably the same woman, albeit frailer and with a carefully made-up face. Queen Mary sat in the chair on the opposite side of the fireplace. The Queen Mother and the Queen Consort both wore splendid Edwardian-style formal dresses with high collars and long sleeves. Neither had taken a step towards adopting any of the newly emerging fashions.

"I could not help but notice the little frog again," said Queen Mary loudly because Alexandra was hard of hearing.

"What frog is that, May?" asked Queen Alexandra in an equally loud voice.

"The one in the cabinet with the ruby eyes. Simply charming. It is always a delight to see it."

"I know which one you mean... That frog is my favourite."

They had got the frog out of the way, and now could talk of other things. The frog was emblematic of a much larger outstanding issue between the two women. Mary, or May, liked jewellery and expensive bibelots. So did Alexandra. May believed that if she dropped hints often enough, Alexandra would either gift the frog as compensation for the jewels that should have come to her when Georgie became king or else give her the jewels themselves. Through the metaphor of the frog, Mary alluded to the issue and presented an avenue of righting a wrong. Alexandra, with her conscience untroubled, dodged the offer yet again. So that was that.

"Am I to understand," said Alexandra, "that someone placed a bomb in the Cottage?"

"Yes. It was a dummy bomb accompanied by a silly note."

"So, if it couldn't go off, why did they put it there? And who put it there?"

"I can't answer you. No one seems to know." Mary looked irritated.

"This is quite unsettling. Strangers wandering around the estate while the army is here? I don't see how that's possible."

"Well, they did, but it's no use asking anyone, because they never give you a proper answer."

"I remember my warning you about the wall of silence before you married Georgie. They only ever tell you what *they* think you should know. Then they look one right in the eye, utter inane blandishments, while expecting one to sluge en kamel."

"Trapped by convention, aren't we?"

"Quite so. Today, it has come to my notice that there are a quantity of inexplicable people standing about in my house. There was a gentleman in a corner at dinner, and now there are two ladies in here not wearing evening dress. One's by the door and the other by the pillar. Do you know who they are?"

"I know *of* them. There is a fourth somewhere about, and there could be many more. They are the ones who found the bomb."

"Oh?" Alexandra stared first at Flora and then at Sophie. "While everyone's talking, let us question them."

With a slight yet abrupt gesture, she beckoned them over. Sophie and Flora exchanged surprised looks and then did as bidden. They reached the two queens and first they curtsied to Queen Mary, murmuring, "Your Majesty," then they turned to Queen Alexandra and similarly murmured, "Your Majesty."

"Who are you and why are you in my house?" Alexandra asked Flora the question.

"My name is Gladys Walton, ma'am, and the government requested I assist in protecting the Royal Family."

"And you are?"

"I am Phoebe King, ma'am."

Alexandra gave Sophie a searching look.

"We understand you found a pretend bomb. Who put it in York Cottage, do you know?"

"Unfortunately, we don't as yet," said Sophie. "The police are investigating, and it is bound to take them a while before they discover the perpetrator — hopefully sooner, rather than later."

"Aha!" said Mary. "You're not from the police, then, are you?"

"No, ma'am, we are not."

"Who sent you?" asked Alexandra.

"We cannot say with any specificity, your Majesty."

"You can't say?"

"This is what they *all* do when they want to fob you off," said Mary. "It is impossible to get a straight answer from any of them."

"To explain, your Majesty," said Sophie, "we are under oath to be evasive because we are, in fact, secret agents employed by the government."

Silence prevailed for some seconds, and Queen looked unto Queen, and agent looked unto agent, before the Queens turned their attention to the agents again.

"If it pleases your Majesties," said Sophie, "I have ventured to tell you this in the strictest of confidences. No one must know."

Queen Mary smiled. "Of course, they shan't."

"That being the case," said Alexandra, leaning forward, "what *can* you tell us?"

"It seems," began Sophie, "although it is not entirely certain, that there is a connection between aliens entering through the London Docks, the murders of several of those aliens, and the threats against the Royal Family."

"No!" said Mary, aghast.

"Would that be those drownings?" asked Alexandra, intensely interested.

"Yes, ma'am," said Sophie. "A criminal gang was using at least one charitable mission as a safe place to hide the aliens."

"And at least one of the murdered aliens was a known criminal," said Flora. "The French authorities wanted him for robbery, and he was an expert with explosives."

"Ah-ha!" exclaimed Mary. "Then do you mean to say...?"

"Yes, ma'am. The threat is real, but there's something peculiar about the messages."

"One moment," said Alexandra. "How do you come to know all of this?"

"Ma'am," began Sophie, "we are, as I mentioned, agents — lowly ones. However, we do not or cannot turn off our brains. Instead, as anyone does, we try to make sense of what we see before us. As I'm sure your Majesty can appreciate, the gentlemen often leave us in the dark, which means we must provide our own illumination."

"Is that so?" Alexandra was now smiling. "How enterprising... Do you know, Miss King, you remind me of someone, only I can't think who it is at present... It will come to me, though."

"How considerable is the danger to ourselves?" asked Mary.

"That is a hard question to answer, ma'am. The potential danger is real, yet the threats, in themselves, seem designed to fulfil a purpose. That purpose appears to be to keep the Royal Family away from London. If murderous intent were really involved, why give the warnings? A true assassin does not warn. Whoever is behind this scheme has an ulterior motive, possibly unconnected with yourselves, and which has yet to be discovered."

"Is that what you think? said Mary. "Then, should we return to London, what can we expect?"

"More threats, ma'am, probably some kind of demonstration, but beyond that, we don't know. We should acknowledge that the perpetrator has considerable reach, and so every precaution must be taken."

"I see. No matter what, the King has to return to London soon, and I shall go with him while the children remain here."

"Quite proper," said Alexandra. "May, do you ever experience déjà vu?"

"Rarely... I had a profound touch of it once, long ago, while riding a horse. Why do you ask?"

"Well, I don't say I'm having it now, but there is a definite familiarity about all of this. Do you recall that King Lud business?"

"Naturally, I do... Oh, yes. I see your point — the direct communication to the King by that individual. I say direct, when really it was most absurd. Yes, it *is* similar."

Alexandra could see the agents were unfamiliar with what had gone on before and so she explained the white posters at the pageant, the note accompanying the bomb in the Abbey, and the letter sent to the newspaper by someone calling himself King Lud.

"That is *most* interesting, your Majesty," said Sophie.

"Taking everything together," said Flora, "it all points to a man who believes he is the king of London."

"How could anyone believe that?" asked Mary, adding, "Unless they were insane."

"Insane or not, he's acting upon his beliefs with determination," said Alexandra. She abruptly announced, "That is all for now, Miss King and Miss Walton. Thank you for your frank responses."

"Yes, thank you," said Mary.

Sophie and Flora curtsied and departed.

"The King shall join us shortly," said Mary. "Should we say anything?"

"It might be unwise to trouble him with any of this. Some of what they said might contradict what his advisors are telling him, and then you will never hear the last of it."

"I shan't utter a word, then."

"They are both rather attractive and intelligent women," said Alexandra, "and you have four sons... Beware."

"I *know* and am already extremely vigilant in the matter. I'll have Georgie speak to the boys if developments threaten."

"I don't mean to be tiresome, but Miss King reminds me of someone — I just can't think of whom."

Chapter 11

Making friends and enemies

The Great Saloon had remained the same since the day it was first furnished when Edward VII had virtually installed a gentleman's club in his home — and it was a very comfortable place at that. The proportions of the room were those of a baronial hall, and the lofty ceiling was easily high enough to mitigate the post-prandial cigar smoke of fifty men. This evening, there were only twelve gentlemen present and several of them did not smoke.

Broadbent-Wicks stood in an unfrequented corner beneath the minstrels' gallery to keep watch over the courtiers. Supposing they were all right and none of them presented a threat, he surveyed the room. Once more, his eyes swept across the Turkey rugs, travelling over the cluttered desk where the mother-in-law's-tongue stood, around the red-flock wallpapered wall, heavy wooden ornamentation, paintings, and numerous hunting trophies, up to the beamed ceiling, then down the massive chandelier of glowing globes. His gaze was next, yet again, arrested by the large pair of ebony statues, each supporting the largest artificial bouquet of shrubbery imaginable in which, he was rapidly convincing himself, a bomb might easily be concealed. He had helped search the rest of the room but, without a ladder, could not examine the monstrous bouquets. The longer he stood where he was, the more certainly he knew an evil device lay within them.

While performing his comprehensive scan, the gaze of another rested on BW. Captain Purvis could not fathom what the young man was doing. Whatever it was, it irritated him. BW's very existence irritated the officer. It had to happen eventually — in the process of time, BW's ever travelling eyes locked with the captain's unwavering glare. BW smiled, pointed to himself questioningly, and then went over.

"Did you want me for something, sir?" asked BW quietly.

"What do you think you're doing here?" hissed Purvis.

"I am guarding the King, the Princes, the guests, and, of course, yourself, sir."

"Leave the room."

"Oh, no. I mustn't."

"I said leave the room. Do so, immediately."

"No, can't be done, sir. I'm under orders to stay put and guard the King, the Princes…"

"Don't be stupid. Leave now or I shall have you removed."

"Under normal circumstances, sir, I'd be happy to oblige, because standing about doing nothing is not all it's cracked up to be…"

"Stop talking. I suppose Miss King is your superior officer?"

"Oh, yes. Although she's not actually an officer, she is very much a leader. You met her earlier, I believe. I must say that she is…"

Captain Purvis's face took on a concentrated expression such as when one happily reaches for a slice of orange but unwittingly pops in a slice of lemon. Where the conversation would have ended, they did not discover because the King spoke.

"Gentlemen! It is time we rejoined the ladies."

Thwarted, the captain stalked off to almost flounce out of the room. There he encountered Ada monitoring the corridor. Assuming correctly who she must be, which goaded him with a fresh surge of annoyance, he turned away from the drawing room and hurtled towards the north corridor.

The Saloon emptied and, as the last few were leaving, BW moved forward slowly, studying the nearest bouquet from different angles.

"Is anything the matter?" asked Prince Edward, tarrying behind after noticing BW's erratic behaviour.

"I'm not sure, your Highness."

"Do you believe there's a bomb in there?" He pointed to the statue.

"Well, I *was* wondering, sir."

They both began slowly circling a statue and searching the dramatic bouquet. They then proceeded to the second statue.

"I can't see anything," said Edward.

"Neither can I, sir... Oh, hold on. Yes, I can. There's a piece of paper."

"Where?" Edward looked to where BW was pointing. "Look at that."

"Would you know where to find a ladder?" asked BW.

"Er, no, not off-hand. Stables, perhaps?"

"Hm. How about this, sir? Why don't I give you a leg up? I have gloves I can put on."

"Yes, we'll do that."

BW put on his gloves, interlaced his fingers, and the Prince of Wales placed a royal foot in BW's hands. The hoist, accompanied by grunts, was a vigorous one, causing the bouquet to shudder.

"We'd better be careful," said Edward while wobbling, steadying himself with one hand against the wall and clutching a reed-like leaf on a wire stem with the other. The wobbling motion subsided.

"That's better," said Edward. "Goodness, it's dusty... It's a small envelope and I can just reach it."

"Be careful, your Highness, if you please," said BW, feeling the strain.

"Yes, yes."

"Handle it by the corners, sir."

"Why?"

"Fingerprints."

"Ah, clever of you... One moment... I've nearly got it... Yes! Lower away."

"Aye, aye, your Highness."

"Very droll."

Back on the floor, the prince held the envelope by a corner while brushing with the other hand at some dust on his jacket. When he had finished, he read the superscription.

"It's addressed to Mr Saxe-Coburg and Gotha." He looked up. "It's that swine again... What do we do with it?"

"Give it to the police, sir." Edward handed the envelope to BW. "Although I must add, Miss King would appreciate knowing of its existence. She's in the White Drawing Room, and I'm not allowed in unless it is a dire emergency. She was most emphatic about that, sir. Doesn't want too many of us on view at any given moment in case you find us disturbing."

"Well, you trot it along to the police, while I inform the intrepid and most considerate Miss King. What's your name, by the way?"

"Broadbent-Wicks, sir, but my friends call me BW."

"You really are quite original. Very well, BW, my sporting fellow, let us be about our business."

Prince Edward paused to turn on the threshold on his way out. "Seeing as we're so chummy, tell me something. Who's your tailor?"

"That would be Morrie of Brick Lane, sir."

"Morrie of Brick Lane." Edward repeated the phrase slowly, deliberately, then smiled and left the room.

Sophie did not exactly shoot out of the drawing room, but she moved at a fair clip.

"BW!" she called, seeing him further along the south corridor. She picked up her skirts and ran.

"I say, Miss King, you're dashed quick on your pins."

"Never mind that. What have you and Prince Edward been up to?"

"We found this letter wedged among the flowers that the statue's holding in the Saloon. They're not real flowers; more like assorted shrubbery constructed of painted wire and tin. They don't keep them very clean — his Highness said so." He held out the envelope for her to see.

"Hold still." She read the inscription. "It will be more of the same inside, no doubt. I'll come with you to see the detective."

"Oh, I say, that's rather spiffing of you."

"Spiffing? What on earth can you mean?"

"Well, the detective is at a pub in Dersingham, and Prince Edward told me to trot along to see him. Now you're coming, too, so isn't that just *splendid*!?" He beamed at her.

"Neither you nor I are meeting detectives in public houses tonight! Don't be silly, BW. That letter stays here. She reached out a gloved hand. Broadbent-Wicks gave her the envelope. "Thank you. I shall find a detective here in the house." She looked him in the eye. "I must commend you for finding this." She waved the letter. "What distresses me is that not only did you give the prince a leg up, but he also now refers to you as BW. I can well imagine how that came to pass. Mr Broadbent-Wicks, you have over-stepped the mark by becoming too familiar with him. Good grief, he will be the King one day, and you've got him calling you BW?"

"It just came out, don't you know? But he's a friendly chap, Miss King, and didn't seem to mind."

"Very lucky for you he didn't. Supposing he *had* minded? What then? We could have all been removed from Sandringham, and we already have an enemy here."

"Ah-ha! That's what the detective was saying. He thinks Captain Purvis will blame us should he get hauled over the coals at an enquiry."

"Why would he do that?"

"Because he's a member of the human race. At least, that's what the detective said. It seemed to make sense at the time. Anyway, I can verify that the captain doesn't like us because I spoke to him."

Sophie sighed. "What did he say?"

"Not a great deal because he was like a needle stuck in a groove. Basically, he wanted me to leave the Saloon. For my part, I firmly and, I believe, politely refused his offer. Then his face scrunched up as if I'd punched him on the hooter, although that hadn't even crossed my mind. Just as he was about to explode, the King spoke, so he didn't."

"The King heard your conversation?" Sophie looked alarmed.

"I don't see how he could have, as he was over at the other side of the room. He only announced that it was time everyone buzzed off to join the ladies in the drawing room and the captain buzzed first. Ha! Purvis darted off like an angry wasp. Do you know he bounces when he walks? It wouldn't surprise me if he suffers from headaches."

"He certainly sees us as a headache," said Sophie. "Right, you patrol this corridor, because Nancy must stay in the drawing room for now. I understand the Royal Family won't be much longer because they like to both retire and rise early."

"What are *we* doing overnight, Miss King? Sitting outside their bedrooms?"

"No, the police will take over the night watch — we can't keep going around the clock."

Sophie left, heading for the north corridor. She really wanted to open the letter, and it had occurred to her to deliver it to the King, but she knew the missive would only disturb his evening for no good reason. Instead, she would seek the detectives on duty, and believed she might find them in the Equerries' Room, which was as good a place to start as any. To get there, she had to pass an entrance to the library, so looked in there first.

After opening the door quietly so as not to disturb anyone, she peered in. Two women — ladies-in-waiting, she presumed — were talking quietly at a table in a corner. They did not look up, neither did the gentleman reading a book by the fireplace. She shut the door again with a question in mind. What was Sir Frederick Tunstall-Green doing at Sandringham House? Why was the 'Bowl Man' here? She could not think why he, of all the King's staff, should be present. Sophie tried to remember his title but realized it had never been given because Maxwell Handley had very carefully avoided Sir Frederick at Buckingham Palace.

She opened the door to the Equerries' Room. This was also decked out like a club, still grand and with the same high ceiling as the Saloon, but of smaller dimensions. An old gentleman dozed in an armchair, his feet resting on an ottoman, with a half-finished glass of port, and some cheese and digestive biscuits on the side-table next to him. Around a large desk sat a group consisting of Archie Drysdale, Lord Laneford, Superintendent Penrose, and Maxwell Handley, all dressed in evening clothes, and another man completely dressed in black — black jersey, trousers, and boots, black gloves, black woollen cap, with grease paint smeared in a jagged pattern on his face. He was drinking a whisky — as they all were — and if it had not been for one little yellow curl escaping from under his cap, Sophie might not have recognized Sinjin.

"Well, if it isn't Miss King," said Superintendent Penrose, rising. The others rose, too. Handley bowed slightly.

"I hope I'm not disturbing you."

"Far from it, Miss King," said Sinjin, putting his glass down. "Indeed, you are most welcome. Would you care for something to drink?"

"No, thank you."

"You have caught us mid-celebration, as it were. They have just made Archie an equerry."

"Have they?" Sophie was delighted. "Congratulations."

"Thank you," said Archie. "The honour is not, I hasten to add, merited. It is purely a matter of political expediency."

"Such delicacy. Such modesty." Sinjin sighed. "It does us proud that our boy got the push he so deserves."

"Yes, indeed," said Laneford. "Whatever the reason, he was undoubtedly, undeniably, and unimpeachably the best man for the job, and he also happened to be handy."

"Hear, hear," said Penrose. "King's Equerry will go on your record, and that's all anyone ever needs to know. Don't forget to have the letter framed and hung on the wall so that you can point it out to visitors."

"Ha! I like that," said Sinjin. "Sadly, Miss King, august gentlemen, and Mr Drysdale, King's Equerry — just rolls off the tongue, doesn't it? — I must bid you all adieu. Several gentlemen of my acquaintance are patiently awaiting my return among the trees. Goodnight."

The others returned him a good night.

With that, Sinjin picked up his rifle and revolver in its holster on a cartridge belt and left the room, giving Sophie an affectionate little wave as he closed the door behind him. She, blushing faintly, gave a little wave back.

After the conversation had become more general, Sophie gave Superintendent Penrose the envelope and explained how BW had found it. Penrose immediately left to have it and its contents analyzed. Archie took Sophie to one side, and she reported the activities of the day.

"Excellent work in finding the device at the Cottage," he said.

"Thank you. Now, tell me. Why did they make you an equerry?"

"There was a dreadful stink over jurisdiction, mostly incited by Captain Purvis. He got on to His Majesty's Body Guard of the Honourable Corps of Gentlemen at Arms, who became vocal in their opposition to the Home Office being involved in the Royal Family's security. The matter spread until literally everyone was involved. The Palace and Whitehall were barely being civil to each other while seeking a compromise. It so happens I am acquainted with several of the Gentleman at Arms and, because I work for the Foreign Office, they deemed me sufficiently neutral to be put in charge of any building where the King is present, while everything else at Sandringham remains under Captain Purvis's control. He was here, and in a foul mood, not ten minutes before you arrived. His mood worsened when I showed him my authority. I thought he was going to burst into tears."

"The whole thing is ridiculous."

"You'll get no arguments from me there. It is extraordinary how otherwise intelligent men have wasted so much time. We, however, shall not be like them. I'd be obliged if you would state your opinion about what the deuce is going on."

"All of it — murders included?"

"The whole bally lot, my dear Soap."

"To begin with, there is a Mr X behind it all. He is a violent and sinister man. I can't see him clearly... Good grief, I'm sounding like a gypsy fortune teller. I know nothing about him except that he must exist. He has his men bring in foreigners, who may all be criminals but certainly some of them are. I can't understand what they're doing, either. At some point, Mr X has them murdered because either they are causing problems, or else they are no longer useful to him. Paul Floquet, the explosives expert, is the only verified example of this. The murders are all committed the same way — a broken neck, and the body thrown in the Thames. X is obviously a vile and ghastly creature, surrounded by servile wicked beasts who do this kind of work for money. Therefore, X has plenty of money and power. He runs a criminal organization. We know this because of the illegal alien-smuggling operation. There were at least three people involved in that venture. By the way, what happened there?"

"The foreign gentleman they arrested was forthcoming. He said he was contacted in Spain with the offer of a new start in Britain. The local man who approached him and arranged everything was a fellow countryman and a known criminal. This establishes that your Mr X has a working relationship with a criminal organization in Spain. From the information so far gleaned from the passport control officer named Mason, X has similar relationships with criminals in several countries."

"Does he know who Mr X is?"

"We don't believe he does. He has not been as helpful as we would like and refuses to identify any other alien who has entered with a forged passport. The fact that Mason received money regularly to rubber stamp forged passports is a given, and a moderately healthy balance in his bank book reveals the operation has been running for a good six months. The police also discovered, without his volunteering, that he leads a rather indelicate life, for which, we believe, he was being blackmailed by X. His wife knew nothing about it."

"Oh dear. There is always someone else being hurt, isn't there? One never quite reckons the unseen victims."

"It is often the case. Please continue."

"Yes, I must be quick because of the return to York Cottage."

Archie looked at his watch. "You have eleven minutes precisely. Everything the King does is in accordance with a schedule, and he, and those who have the care of him, are extremely punctual. I didn't know this until a few hours ago."

"Neither did I until now... What you said makes me think X's organization must be large, because it also includes blackmail. I assume that requires some level of expertise to bring off successfully. Also, one doesn't just wake up one morning and think to oneself, 'I'll bring in some illegal aliens. Who do I know on the continent?' Therefore, X has a known reputation in the underworld."

"Very good, Soap. Go on."

"Shh, don't interrupt or I'll lose my place." She smiled as she spoke. "So, there he is — X, sitting atop his Empire of Evil, and he conceives a master plan; a brilliant coup that shall shake the world to its foundation. That's how *he* sees it, not me. I think he's just another malevolent oaf like the rest of these arch-criminal types. All of that constitutes part one."

"You have eight minutes left."

"Thank you. Part two is so completely different that it is hard to credit that the same person is behind it. All we have is the very tenuous thread of time bombs. Indeed, had not a fake bomb been planted at York Cottage, the theory of an assassination by explosion may have been discarded. What *do* we have? There is a man, probably Mr X, who is trying to scare the Royal Family into staying away from London. How has he conducted the recent campaign to accomplish this? By sending peculiar messages. The letter left on the King's pillow was different. It threatened death and destruction. Afterwards, a maid disappeared. Did she pen that note while under instruction? It appears to me..."

"Sorry to interrupt. The note *was* in the maid's handwriting. It was compared to a sample retained in the files when she requested a leave of absence. Furthermore, the maid was not who she claimed to be, so we don't know who she was after all."

"Then she must have been one of the gang. There you are. The plot thickens, does it not?"

"Yes, and it has now achieved the consistency of a watery soup."

"Philistine, but you prove my point. That message was all 'death to the monarchy.' Every message since has been 'stay away from London if you know what's good for you.' It all makes me think that something is going on at Buckingham Palace at this moment. My suspicion is that a large, well-concealed bomb is being installed so that, when the Royal Family returns, they will all be killed in a dreadful blast."

"The Palace is being guarded against just such an eventuality."

"Oh, is it? Bang goes my theory. I wasn't that pleased with it, anyway." She put a hand to her brow. "I really don't think X intends killing the King. Surely, he would have tried by now instead of just sending aggravating messages. I mean, that bed sheet message... It was effective, but childish in its way. All show and no substance, if you see what I mean."

"I follow you. There are several opinions on the situation, but they all agree on these few points. We assume the messages contain substantive threats and the Royal Family is in actual danger. We cannot do otherwise because the risk is too great to allow for mistakes. The King cannot hide and will return to London. X knows this. If X does nothing, his bluff will have been called and, when it all comes out in the press, he will then become an object of ridicule. X knows this, too. It is reasonable to assume that he has something planned that is on a large scale. If it is the destruction of the Royal Family, then everything he has done so far is sheer bravado — the actions of a vain and pompous man. These actions are not the same as found in your part one. The hallmarks there are careful planning and secrecy. Are those same elements found in part two? Most certainly they are. It requires organization to place a fake bomb in York Cottage and put the note in the Saloon. Also, it means that whoever did those things is very close to the King or otherwise thoroughly familiar with his habits."

"That's what worries me," said Sophie.

"Mr Handley is working on that part. Laneford requested he draw up a timetable of everyone's movements around Sandringham over the last three days. Three and a half minutes left."

"But we haven't finished," said Sophie.

"We could spend another hour, so I'll end with this summing up of what we've said so far. X has planned something big. We don't know what it is. It may involve the King."

"I suppose that's the best that can be said at present. I must go. Good night."

"Good night. I believe it will be a peaceful one."

Queen Alexandra was restless in bed. For an hour she had tried to sleep, ever turning to find a more comfortable position, but to no avail. Lying on her back, she opened her eyes to stare up at the canopy overhead, its pattern hidden in the darkness. She thought she might as well get up, only she would give it a few more seconds... a minute at most. Alexandra dozed; welcome sleep had arrived. Then she sat bolt upright, and exclaimed to the darkness,

"Bessie Burgoyne!"

After having identified Sophie's aunt, Lady Shelling, from the distant past, the smiling Alexandra folded her hands on the coverlet and slept peacefully for the rest of the night.

In far away London, beneath the streets at the tunnel's face, the roof caved in without warning.

"Jimmy!" screamed Mateo in the dust-filled darkness. He scrabbled rapidly at the mound of earth with his hands, desperate to uncover some part of his friend. Behind him in the cramped space, a Norwegian named Gustav toiled to move the loose soil further along. Fifty feet back, where the lights were still on, little André, a Frenchman, pumped the air bellows like a fiend.

They laboured frantically — sweating, breathing hard, grit in their throats and eyes. Half a minute passed. Mateo found a leg and now knew in which direction to burrow.

"Help me," he rasped.

The Gustav crawled forward.

"Give me your hand."

In the dark, Mateo guided it to Jimmy's foot.

"I got him."

"Pull!"

They grunted as they strained. Jimmy shifted.

"Again!"

He came free from the mound and more dry dirt fell from the roof like sand falling through an hourglass.

Jimmy choked and spat earth from his mouth. Then he was sick.

"That's it," said Mateo. "Get it all out."

"Thanks…"

"For what? You did the same for me last week. This was worse, though."

"You saved my life." Jimmy started laughing. "It's only polite to say thank you. You, too, Gustav. I owe you."

"Save it. All I know is this," said Gustav. "None of us dies on this stinking job and, when it's over, we all walk away — no matter what it takes. Come on. Let's get out before there's another fall."

"You're right. We need more planks to shore up everything good," said Mateo. "Can you manage, Jimmy?"

"Yes, mother."

"Now I know you're all right. Next time, I leave you in the dirt longer, then you won't be so funny."

"Had you been another thirty seconds, I wouldn't be here… I don't know how earthworms cope with eating their way through soil."

That death had brushed past them and been so close made all the men laugh loudly.

Chapter 12

A serious turn of events

According to Sandringham Time, a convention introduced by Edward VII, the meal began at 8:30 a.m. on Sunday, which meant it was 8:00 a.m. for the rest of the country. The breakfast room at York Cottage is not small by any standard, but it becomes minute when six royal persons attempt to sit at the same table at the same time. Add footmen and other servants and it almost becomes unbearable. The King likes it, however, because the cramped conditions remind him of his halcyon days in the Royal Navy. Queen Mary was never in the Royal Navy and so she does not see things quite the same way.

Speaking of the Royal Navy, when Georgie was a midshipman on HMS Bacchante, the corvette put in at Port Said. There he acquired an African Grey parrot and named her Charlotte — why, nobody knows. From then on, she became his constant companion. So that everyone could be as snug as they could possibly be, Charlotte also breakfasts with the family.

"Where's the Cap'n?" enquired Charlotte at 8:25 a.m. just before anyone had descended.

"Captain?" responded Broadbent-Wicks, who had been warily eyeing the parrot on its perch.

"Where's the Cap'n?"

"You already said that. Do you mean Captain Purvis?"

"God save the King!"

"Oh! You must mean King George. It's funny your calling him Captain. *I'm* required to say 'your majesty' or 'sire.' How do you get away with it? Silly me, you're a parrot, aren't you? You probably take all kinds of liberties. What's your name, by the way?" The bird did not answer. Instead, she put her head to one side to study her questioner. "Would you like some brekkie? Seeds, I mean."

"Charlotte!" announced the parrot.

"A-ha! So, you accept bribes, do you?" BW stepped towards Charlotte and opened the jar of hulled sunflower seeds standing on the table. "This is just between you and me, so don't go squawking to anyone." BW laughed. "Oh dear, that's so funny... Here you go. Three, that's your lot for now." Charlotte pecked a seed from his hand and BW gently stroked her head. "You seem like a good girl... Charlotte, allow me to introduce myself. My name's Broadbent-Wicks, but you can call me BW." There was a noise outside the room. "Quick. Polish off the seeds, then as you were."

BW returned to his unobtrusive position in a corner. The King entered. Charlotte called out, "Hello, Cap'n" and flew across the room to perch on his shoulder.

St. Mary Magdalene's Church is on the estate and only a quarter mile distant from the big house. York Cottage is further away. The cloudless Norfolk morning was an extra brilliant blue because of the nearby sea, and it beckoned with promise and a warmth tempered by a gentle breeze. The Royal Family decided they would walk to church. Usually, the family went as a group, accompanied only by a few friends, for a quiet, contemplative amble to the house of worship. Today, a company of soldiers — in khaki and armed with rifles — was split equally into a bellowing, gravel-crunching vanguard and a rearguard intent at all costs upon guarding their majesties and highnesses. Not to miss out, half a dozen of the Honourable Corps of Gentlemen at Arms, with ceremonial swords and wearing cocked hats, formed an actual bodyguard fore and aft of the family. The police had constables stationed along the route, and four Scotland Yard detectives were closer to the King than the bodyguard. Yet nearer was a clutch of equerries in their Sunday best, except for Captain Purvis, who wore his smartest uniform. These attended the Princes. Closer still was Archie Drysdale, Equerry and FO representative, who talked separately with Prince Edward. Closest of all to the King was Lord Laneford of the HO. He and the King discussed cricket, pheasants, fly-fishing, and the dry weather — the latter made apparent by the burnt lawns and tired gardens they passed. Competing parties had debated vigorously over all the various positions of proximity to the King's person. Captain Purvis had envisioned a much different arrangement with himself placed next to the King, which is why he now wore a sour expression, and glowered occasionally at Lord Laneford.

Within a separate cordon, Ada walked ahead of the two Queens while Sophie walked immediately behind them and they could hear everything they said. The Queens carried parasols and yet again were talking loudly. Alexandra had a noticeable limp.

"How is your leg holding up, Alix?" asked Mary.

"It doesn't pain me, and the exercise is beneficial," replied Alexandra.

"Good... I don't understand why our going to church must be turned into a parade. It is so unnecessary."

"Well, perhaps. But you must remember my situation. I don't get about like I used to. So, for me to see all the boys marching is rather a treat."

"But we're only going to church. What do they think will happen?"

"Nothing. Nothing can happen with them here. I sincerely hope Canon Rowland doesn't have a heart attack when he sees us coming... May, I have a question and I don't wish to trouble Georgie with it... Not yet, anyway. Why is it you and he have those young people guarding you — four of them, I think you said? Nobody's guarding me. Not even one. Am I no longer worth the trouble because I'm old?"

"That isn't it at all. The maniac Lud is intent upon wiping out the royal line, so they say."

"Then he has miscalculated, because there are many more heirs than are present here. What about guarding them? Are they doing that?"

"No one has advised me of such." Mary turned to Sophie. "Miss King. Please join us."

Sophie hurried forward.

"Your Majesty."

"Queen Alexandra wishes to know if the more distant heirs to the throne are also under close protection."

"Your Majesty," said Sophie to Alexandra. "I don't believe they are, but I cannot say with any certainty."

"Can you find out for me? Also, when can I expect my personal bodyguard? I'm sure you could be assigned to me."

"Me, ma'am?"

"Yes, you. If I'm not mistaken, Bessie Burgoyne is a relative of yours."

"Your Majesty... I don't know how to request this..."

"Don't forget," interjected Mary and addressing Alexandra, "that Miss King is a secret agent, which makes her sensitive about certain names."

"I understand... That must mean I'm right!" Alexandra laughed. "See what you can do about arranging your transfer."

"I will mention it, ma'am."

"Thank you, Miss King," said Mary

Sophie retired to the rear. Alexandra spoke to Mary.

"What do you think Lud hopes to gain by all his activities?"

"When Georgie and I were discussing it, we agreed Lud acts as though he has a real claim to the title of King of London — not that there is any such title. I said that the claim obviously arises from a disordered and deluded mind. Georgie thinks the fellow is intelligent and, therefore, must have some small basis in fact — documents, perhaps a genealogy, supporting the idea."

"There are no documents from two thousand years ago. There are very few before the Domesday Book. Lud cannot have proof of his claim, whatever it is he thinks he has. It could be he has one of those histories concocted centuries later. They contain some facts, but the writer fills in the blanks or embellishes those parts he agrees with while excluding others."

"That must have been what Georgie meant. He also said Lud is not claiming a right to the throne, he's claiming a right to control London."

"He can claim all he wants," said Alexandra, "but it's impossible it be given to him... When are you returning to London?"

"Tomorrow afternoon. There was some talk of delaying the return for longer."

Just then, two men came running towards the front of the column. Sophie recognized the lieutenant from the day before. The other wore a morning suit. They reached the King's party, and the column stopped. She saw Archie, Lord Laneford, and several others speaking to them. The lieutenant then went to speak to Captain Purvis.

"I know it," said Queen Mary. "Something dreadful has happened."

Sophie eased her way out of the column and hurried to join the conference. She stayed for a minute and spoke to Archie. After that, the King received the message. The messenger went back to the house while everyone else returned to their places in the column. The procession resumed its march. Sophie came back and hurriedly whispered to Ada. Queen Mary waved to them, and they drew near.

"Well?" asked the Queen of Sophie, ignoring Ada's curtesy.

"There has been an attack at the Palace. A grenade exploded in the grounds by the wall. No one was hurt and there was only a little damage. They found a terse note near the scene advising the King to stay at Sandringham."

Queen Mary received this in silence.

"Wasn't a note found in my house last night?" asked Alexandra.

"There was. That was a longer message, and it stated emphatically that the King and his family would suffer no harm while staying at Sandringham."

Alexandra made a noise that was almost a snort.

"Did the King say anything?" asked Mary.

"Yes, ma'am. His Majesty intends returning to the Palace today."

"I thought he would… He has many pressing engagements."

"What's your name?" Alexandra asked Ada.

"Me, your Majesty?" said Ada, caught off guard. "Nancy Carmichael."

"Speak up or come closer. I can't hear you."

Ada moved closer to Queen Alexandra. "I'm Nancy Carmichael, your Majesty."

"What do you know about this bomb business?"

"No more than Miss King does, ma'am. But I know what I'd like to do to the bloke who's behind it all."

Alexandra studied her for a moment. "And what would that be?"

"I'd wring his scrawny neck, I would an' all."

"You can only do that after I've had my turn," said Alexandra. "How dare he put everyone to such inconvenience?"

"I don't know, ma'am. It don't make no sense, or I can't make no sense of it, anyhow."

"I'd like to know what he thinks he's playing at. Superficially, it seems absurd. But fundamentally, there must be a reason."

"It has to be something big, ma'am. And if he wants the Royal Family to stay away from London, then he's up to something *in* London."

"I wonder," said Sophie.

"What do you wonder?" asked Mary.

"Excuse me for speaking out, ma'am. It's just everything seems over-elaborate and foolish."

"But the grenade?" said Mary. "You could hardly consider that to be foolish."

"That's what I'm wondering about. The horrors of an explosion are not to be minimized but, setting it aside so as not to cloud one's thoughts, what do we have? Just one more message harping on the same theme. The grenade adds drama, but it did no damage except to some bushes, which leads me to believe Mr X… I'm terribly sorry, ma'am."

"No, please continue. You refer to him as Mr X, I take it?"

"Yes, ma'am. In my estimation, he has unwittingly betrayed a weakness, because the explosion did no real damage. For example, blowing up the Palace gates or a reception room would have been impressive. Throwing a grenade over a wall is more of a show, and unconsciously demonstrates his organization has limitations. Mr X couldn't get inside the Palace, which may mean he has no agent there or no one capable of getting in while the Palace is guarded."

"Then what is his ultimate aim?"

"I believe he has achieved it, ma'am," said Sophie. "X has been successful in tying up useful resources. We are all looking in one direction, while he works, unmolested by those same resources, elsewhere."

"I suppose in due course we shall learn what it is," said Queen Mary resignedly.

The column arrived at the church.

Mr Healy had dressed as a working man in his best summer clothes, as if he were on his way to church or walking out with a lady friend. He waited among several others at a bus stop at Marble Arch. The late morning sun revealed him to be in his forties, above the average height, with a round, mild, ordinary face. He had a cornflower in his buttonhole, and he held a small posy of them.

A bus slowed, and a thirty-year-old working-class woman in a pretty frock alighted with assurance before the bus had stopped.

"There he is," she said loudly and with obvious pleasure. She swept up to Mr Healy, immediately kissed him, and put her arm through his.

"Hello," said Healy. "You're looking lovely."

"An' you can say that as often as you please, dearie... Are those flowers for me?"

"Of course." He gave her the posy. "I'd look silly if I'd bought them for myself." Healy did not sound working-class.

They began walking away, silent until there was no chance of their being overheard.

"Where are we going?" asked the woman, her voice becoming educated after a few steps. "A walk around Hyde Park?"

"Yes. I thought we'd stroll about for a while, take out a punt on the Serpentine, and then get something to eat later."

"Suits me... Is something the matter? I haven't seen much in the papers."

"Neither can anyone, because they are suppressing the reports. However, tomorrow, you shall see something. A grenade in the back garden is not something the press, or the Palace, can easily ignore."

She laughed. "I don't suppose they can... I know you're tremendously busy, but have you given me a thought? Are the police still searching?"

"Lottie, they have sought, and could not find, so you are safe, as I promised you would be."

"That's what I love about you — your certainty."

"Which, as I've said before, rests on careful planning."

"You make it sound so easy. It was a bore keeping up the pretense at the Palace, and a relief to get away. At least it worked... How is the tunnel coming along?"

"There have been setbacks. However, everything will be ready for next weekend as scheduled."

"And afterwards? What about us?"

"A quiet period, during which I shall retire. I explained where and when you fit in, so there is no need for you to concern yourself."

"You aren't very romantic."

"Which you knew from the outset. Lottie, we are out in public on a sunny day. Let us enjoy the simple pursuits available to us."

"Then I'll call you Bob. You'll be a plumber out with his sweetheart, and we'll get along swell with plenty of billing and cooing."

He smiled and shyly said, "Don't overdo it."

"Relax, my sweet Bob. Dressed like that, no one will ever guess who you really are."

After the service in little St Mary Magadelene's with its exquisite chancel and painted roof interior, the Royal Family returned home. This journey seemed more relaxed than before. Early on, Sophie noticed BW walking by the side of Princess Mary. Later, she could hear them both talking and laughing — particularly BW — which she found aggravating but could do nothing about. Ahead of her, the queens were quiet. As they neared the big house, Sophie saw a tall, thin man waiting on the terrace. Suddenly, Princess Mary came to her mother's side and whispered something that Sophie did not catch.

"I'll ask," said Queen Mary. "Alix. Harry Lascelles is here. Can you give him lunch?"

"Viscount Lascelles...?" Alexandra leaned forward, and turned towards Princess Mary to smile and say,

"Yes, my dear. Leave it to me."

"Thank you, Grandmama."

Sophie could not miss the look of relief and gratitude the princess returned to Alexandra. She wondered what Aunt Bessie would make of this snippet of information.

The hitherto leisurely pace of life at Sandringham disappeared and York Cottage suddenly became like an ant hill recently poked with a stick. The King was leaving a full day before his expected departure in deliberate defiance of the threats. This meant the legion of staff swooped into efficient and decorous action earlier than expected. Concern soon arose over the exact time the Royal Train would be ready. The Railway promised it for six o'clock today if the four royal carriages alone were sufficient. Should additional ordinary carriages be required, then the Royal Train could be ready to run before the rush hour at four-thirty-five in the morning, or at ten-seventeen — after the rush hour. This dilemma produced hectic communication throughout the cottage until it was finally decided — the King would go today.

As difficult as that was, it was as nothing when compared to the next dilemma. Senior courtiers gnashed their teeth as they considered who was to travel with the King. From the available gallon of important persons and key staff there had to be poured just the select right quantity into the pint pot of a train, without there being a drop too much lest their Majesties were inconvenienced. Fortunately, their Highnesses were remaining at Sandringham, so they were excluded from the delicate calculations. Neither were the secret agents considered, because their names did not appear on any official lists. The crisis point for the agents came during the informal embarkation at Wolferton Station.

The station is charming, sleepy, and very small. Over the years, it has seen the arrivals and departures of many Royal Trains. This fine Sunday it was crowded as it had never been before, thanks to the presence of a company of soldiers, forty constables, and several dozen others who were present to protect their Majesties. The platform where the train waited was crowded and bustling right up until the King and Queen arrived.

Sophie and the others had travelled ahead of the royal party but could not get further than the gate because the ticket collector, aided by a courtier with a clipboard, had decided they were not proper persons to be on the train or platform at this time. Sophie succinctly pleaded her case. The refusal was firm. During the rising tension, two constables joined the fray and began asking questions. A soldier took a mild interest. As the conference was blocking the entrance, the constables began edging the luggage-laden agents to one side.

Sophie, who had been trying to remain calm to prevent a scene, said,

"This is intolerable! What is your name?"

"I decline to answer," said the man with the clipboard. "You are not on the list, you are not entering this station, and if you don't stop now, these constables will remove you."

"There is a mistake on your rotten list. We are to accompany their Majesties at all times. There wasn't room for us in the car, of course. So, we came on ahead…"

"A likely story and I don't wish to hear any more. Constables." He signalled to them.

"Move along, please…"

At that moment, Captain Purvis strode up and joined them.

"What's going on here?" he demanded.

"These persons…"

"Never mind. I know of this woman. She is a suffragette and possibly dangerous. They all are. Constables, arrest them."

"Oh, I say," said BW, "we're not suffragettes."

Just then, a limousine followed by two other cars arrived. The King and Queen got out, and the constables hesitated, not wishing to create a disturbance in front of the King. A clear path to the train opened spontaneously, and everyone turned to face the royal couple. King George and Queen Mary moved forward. From the second car came a footman carrying a tall birdcage covered by a cloth. The King noticed him and stopped to say, "Be careful."

Right behind Sophie, the man with the clipboard uttered a groan and hurriedly leafed through his pages. He found the place he sought and muttered, then began looking around frantically.

"What's the matter?" whispered Captain Purvis.

"No one told me about the parrot."

"So? Surely, you can put a parrot anywhere?"

"No, it goes in a special compartment by itself, accompanied by an attendant."

The Captain laughed.

"Would you be Captain Purvis?"

"Yes. Why?"

"I'm afraid you and your men will have to take a train tomorrow."

"What!"

The King, accompanied by his cage bearer, drew opposite the contentious group. From inside the cover, a little bird voice piped up.

"Call me BW."

The King stopped and turned his patient face to Broadbent-Wicks. When he spoke, every nearby ear strained to hear what he said.

"Are you BW?"

"I am, your Majesty."

"Then I wonder if you could do me a small service."

"Anything you care to name, sire."

The King's eyebrows rose a smidgen. "Would you be so kind as to accompany Charlotte on the journey? She becomes restive when travelling and she's been mentioning your name for the last hour."

"Oh, absolutely, sire. Charlotte's a lovely bird, so it will be my pleasure."

The King signalled to the footman who gave the cage to BW. Queen Mary now joined the little group, and she read the faces in the circle. A baffled ticket collector, two abashed constables, one grinning private, a red-faced captain, a stricken courtier holding a clipboard, Ada and Flora smiling, holding suitcases, and Sophie looking directly at her expectantly — she guessed there was a problem.

"Miss King, I was hoping to see you," said Mary. "I'd be obliged if you and your party would join us on the train."

"Thank you, your Majesty."

The Royal couple moved through the gate. Sophie turned to the courtier.

"Are we on your list now?"

The constables hurried off, and the private also made himself scarce.

"I'm dreadfully sorry for the oversight. If you would be so kind as to give me your names, I'll record them in the appropriate place."

Captain Purvis stormed off in a fine rage.

"How do you always do it?" asked Ada.

They were in a separate compartment for eight passengers, which was plush but plain.

"Do what?" answered BW, who was playing with Charlotte while she was in the cage.

"Get away with it."

"No, sorry, I'm not following."

"It's luck," said Flora.

"Ah... I know what you mean now. Things just happen and turn out for the best without my doing anything... As for luck, I feel extraordinarily lucky just to be alive."

Sophie smiled. "I'm sure Captain Purvis doesn't feel the same at present. He went positively purple." She took out a notepad and pen. "Reports, please."

"Not much today," said Flora. "However, I overheard the Princes Albert and Henry discussing Sir Frederick Tunstall-Green. He's stayed behind to give elocution and speech improvement lessons. As soon as Henry mentioned his name, Albert began stuttering badly."

"His stutter is barely noticeable when he talks to the family," said Sophie. "As soon as he's confronted with a stressful situation, he either goes quiet or speaks with difficulty."

"Poor bloke," said Ada. "Then Sir Frederick can't be an agent of King Lud, 'cause there's a reason for him being here."

"It seems so. I became suspicious when I saw him, but he's cleared now. Those poor princes — I pity them having to listen to him all day long."

"They're going about it in completely the wrong way," said Flora. "My advice would be for Albert to take up amateur dramatics. In learning a part, he would know exactly what to say and when to say it, which would build up his confidence. I'm certain acting would train him to get over his nerves — if he stuck to it."

"That sounds like a sensible plan. Perhaps he's already tried, though. Let's move on, shall we? BW?"

"I don't have anything. I intercepted a servant carrying a paper bag near Princess Mary, but there was only a pair of Queen Alexandra's old shoes in it. She sends them off to a charity... Makes you think, doesn't it? Some dear impoverished lady, without two brass farthings to her name, will suddenly be dancing about in the Queen's old clogs without ever knowing it. There really should be an inscription inside them to buck her up. Queen Alexandra stood here... That's not very good. Queen Alexandra's foot graced this shoe. Yes, that's much better. What do you think, Miss King?"

"I am wondering how far someone can possibly diverge from giving an eyewitness report."

"A bit off topic, what? Shan't happen again... Would you like another seed, old girl?" He held one for the parrot to take. "Do you know Charlotte's well over forty? She's twice as old as I am. Now, if anyone had asked me, not that they're likely to, I would have said she was about three... five at the most."

"Nancy?"

"Nothing useful for the case, miss. The staff don't like us, though. I could see it in their eyes, so I think we should expect the same at Buckingham Palace."

"They were a bit offish. Why do you think that is?"

"It's simple, if you work it out. We're not guests or titled or nothing, so they're not goin' to serve us, are they, miss? If we're not servin', an' they don't know what we're doin', then they think we're just staff, and should be pulling our weight with the rest. They think we're mumpers."

"I beg your pardon," said Sophie.

"Oh, er, a mumper is like this. If there are four blokes standing at the bar an' they're each buying a round of drinks, before it comes to the mumper's go, he suddenly shoots off saying he's got to meet someone urgent. He does that so's he don't have to pay out nothing."

"I've never heard of such a thing."

"It's a well-known phenomenon within the acting profession," said Flora. "Although it's looked upon by those actors who have money as a type of charitable work for their less fortunate brethren and sistren. How do your four blokes in the pub settle it?"

"They'd set him up, I should think. As soon as he appears next time, they'd tell him it's his turn or else. He then buys the round or gets out of the pub quick. After that, I don't know what happens. The mumper probably goes somewhere else."

"Do you mean to say," said Sophie in her most shocked voice, "that they think of us in that way?"

"Yes, miss."

"This is... dreadful."

"Don't let it worry you, Phoebe," said Flora. "It hadn't crossed my mind, but what difference does it make, after all?"

"It means we must be the subject of gossip in the servants' hall."

"We'd be that, anyway, because we're outsiders," said Ada.

"Also," added Flora, "we had no time or opportunity to talk to anyone, therefore they never discovered how wonderful we are."

Sophie laughed despite herself. "We will *make* the time at the Palace; otherwise, I don't think I could bear it."

The parrot started acting up. "Just a moment," said BW. "Charlotte, put that in your beak and crunch it... Overall, what do you think is going on, Miss King?"

"Yes, we haven't discussed the case, miss, an' we should."

"I cannot speak with any certainty, but I feel sure that all this with the Royal Family is a blind for something else. Mr X has been active in the past with all that King Lud business I told you about. He has reactivated it now. He can never be a king over London, because he would have to show his face. As soon as he did that, he would be arrested. So, what does he hope to achieve? I'd say he has achieved his objective, which is getting everyone riled up and concerned over the Royal Family's safety. Do you agree?"

"That sounds spot on, Miss King," said BW.

"I agree," said Ada. "I think he's goin' to nick something. You see, if it was just murder, he'd have done it, 'cause he's not shy about that, as them poor illegals could tell you if they could only speak from the grave. If he was goin' to blow up something, he'd have done that an' all, otherwise why would he *hang* about? No reason whatsoever. No. Instead, he's workin' on a big burglary, he is, and he has to take the time to do it proper, or has to go slow, or something has to turn up first — I don't know what, exactly."

"Hah!" exclaimed Sophie. "He's going to steal the royal art collection! That's why he wants everyone out of Buckingham Palace!"

"I should think that's it," said Flora. "What about the crown jewels, though?"

"Yes! Those, too. This is very, very good. I believe we're getting somewhere. As soon as we're off the train, I'll telephone everyone. Well done, Nancy and Flora."

"Where's the Cap'n?" inquired Charlotte.

Chapter 13

Monday with the Royals

It was late Sunday evening at Buckingham Palace and Sir Geoffrey Fortescue, Deputy Master of the King's Household, could finally remove his jacket and slip his shoes off to put his feet up while lying on the couch in his office. After an exhausting and stressfully tedious day and with the monarchy now safely tucked up in bed, he could relax and drink his whisky and soda before retiring for the night. The couch was a two-seater while he was a full three-seater in length, but he managed to get comfortable. Later, he would go to bed, but he wanted to laze for a moment while the trials and tribulations of the day dissolved and slipped away.

Sir Geoffrey loosened his cravat, sipped his nightcap appreciatively, then, setting the glass aside, laid his grizzled, close-cropped head on the cushion. He stared up at the ceiling and calmly wondered if he would be blown up. He considered the precautions that had been taken. Pairs of constables patrolled the corridors, detectives were at every entrance, a detachment of guards was stationed near the bedrooms of both the King and the Queen. A footman stood watch in every room the Royal Family used as well as every principal room. Then there were the police and soldiers outside, patrolling the grounds. Surely, they were all safe? Sir Geoffrey Fortescue was really too comfortable to be too worried... or was it the other way around? He was not at all worried, and that's why he felt so comfortable? Stretched out full length, with his legs dangling over the arm, he smiled while unconsciously wiggling his toes inside his perfectly gartered socks.

Someone knocked on the door. Sir Geoffrey supposed it was a page, messenger, or footman, and so he reluctantly answered from the couch.

"Enter."

Sophie opened the door. Shocked, she hurriedly said, "I'm terribly sorry," before closing it again.

"Miss King! Wait a moment!" Sir Geoffrey fumbled for shoes and jacket but forgot to put his cravat straight. He opened the door to find all four secret agents in the corridor with their suitcases. Despite looking dishevelled by Palace standards and smelling of scotch, Sir Geoffrey Fortescue was dignified, nonetheless.

"No one notified me you were staying at the Palace. You are staying, I take it?"

"If we may, that would be most kind of you," said Sophie. "It's necessary for us to be close to the King at all times, so sleeping elsewhere is not really an option."

"I can appreciate that. Please, follow me, and I'll have someone show you to your rooms. This way, if you please."

They walked for some seconds in silence, then both Sophie and Sir Geoffrey spoke at once — she deferred.

"All I was simply going to ask is, would you mind telling me what it is you do?"

"Certainly. Our primary task is to search and make safe any room before the King or Queen enters. After that, we remain to observe people for any suspicious behaviour when they approach their majesties."

"I thought it was that sort of thing. But what about the Princes and Princess?"

"Others are now watching them. That was decided when we four were instructed to return to London."

"Ah... I understand these messages that have been discovered only warn the King to stay away from London."

"Yes, Sir Geoffrey, they do."

"Very odd. I fail to see what these persons hope to accomplish. I met an acquaintance, and he categorically stated that none of the fringe political groups are involved."

"Did he say who he thought it might be?"

"No, he didn't. What we are most concerned about is the relative ease with which this man, or group, can approach their majesties... Here we are."

"It is most disturbing," agreed Sophie.

"In the extreme."

They stopped outside a room. Sir Geoffrey knocked and, when the door opened, he explained the situation to an assistant.

"Mr Forbes will arrange everything for you, Miss King. I bid you all good night."

Within half an hour, every agent had a separate room. These were guest bedrooms — modest ones — used primarily for the accommodation of senior servants accompanying distinguished visitors.

When one stays at the Palace and is not a guest, visiting dignitary, or staff member, one discovers that there is a void, a sizeable lacuna, among the massive quantity of established protocols. In the early morning, the secret agents were floating weightlessly in that lacuna. Nobody quite knew what to do with the agents or even how to address them because they were, from the Palace's point of view, unpigeonholeable. Because of this, a definite line of demarcation soon became apparent among the respondents to almost all the agents' questions. In general, any staff member who was doing royal physical work, such as cleaning, carrying, or even standing still, returned a blank stare to the simplest enquiry, followed by the statement, "I'm sorry, I don't know." On the other hand, those who did royal mental work furrowed their brows or rubbed their brows or did something with their brows, anyway, in the hope of stimulating the brain to produce a response. What they were really doing was employing delaying tactics while groping for an answer, as the following succession of thoughts ran through their minds: 'Who is this person? Why is she asking me that? Dash it all, I have more important things to do than be bothered with this now.' Then, once the brow stimulation had jump-started all available acuity, words issued from the royal mental worker's mouth such as "Sir John will know." The smile of successfully shifted responsibility then appeared while any remaining furrows vanished. Invariably, Sir John (or whoever) was at the other end of the Palace, was never in his office, and, if found, most decidedly did not know and was surprised and disgusted that it even be thought that he should know.

The agents decided that two of them would be on duty with the King and Queen during waking hours. Broadbent-Wicks exclusively attended the King and was present for all meals. King George liked BW, mainly because his parrot liked BW. Queen Mary put up with BW because she had to. What she found particularly irritating was the officious way in which BW stopped every footman entering the room in order to lift the silver, domed lid from the dish being carried to search for explosives in the food they were about to serve to the family. The footmen did not appreciate this behaviour, either, but they could say nothing — no one could. The Royal Household now had a Yeoman of the Silver Dome without ever having requested there be one.

The other two agents searched rooms, interviewed policemen, detectives, staff, and soldiers to find out what they knew. By mid-morning, they had not learned or found anything.

"Nothing out there," said Ada, as she returned from the balcony.

"And nothing in here," said Flora, as she finished the interior of the balcony room. "Why don't we stand on the balcony and wave to passersby?"

Ada giggled. "You're not serious, are you?"

"Semi-serious. I think it would be nice for the people and buck them up. They would tell their friends and family they had seen someone important but didn't know who it was."

"With all the rozzers about, someone'd see us, and we'd get caught."

"Very likely."

"You're getting bored, you are."

"Yes, and it's almost to the point that I wish we'd find a real bomb."

"No. You don't mean that."

"Not yet, but I'm getting there. I think Phoebe might be right, and there are no active Lud agents in the Palace."

"I'm not so sure. There was someone at Sandringham, 'cause they left a bomb in the cottage and a message in the big house."

Maxwell Handley breezed into the room, speaking as he walked. "Dear me, you've been very hard to track down. Good morning." Ada and Flora returned his greeting. "The police detectives are interviewing everyone close to their majesties, which naturally now includes you. I have informed Miss King, and she asked that you be interviewed first, then Miss King and Mr Broadbent-Wicks will go after you relieve them."

"Oh," said Flora. "Would the detectives be at the other end of the Palace? Most things are."

"They would indeed. They are in the ground floor service area — the first office around the corner from the Ballroom. I suggested to Miss King you answer their questions fully, but invoke the Official Secrets Act for anything sensitive."

"How do we do that, Mr Handley?" asked Ada.

"You simply refuse to answer troublesome questions, stating that you are duty-bound *not* to respond because it is a subject that comes under the Official Secrets Act. Subsequently, you can just say 'The Act' to anything you don't want to answer — it saves everyone's time. Then they'll stop bothering you... I'm sorry, I must fly. I have a hundred things to do." He then breezed out of the room.

"His saying that," said Flora, "is like discovering a fundamental law of the universe but with no idea what to do with it."

They left the Balcony Room to get their interviews out of the way.

"I reckon there's a lot of people who'd like to know about this... S'posin' there was a drunk being what they call disorderly — decently dressed, mind you — and a copper stops him and asks for his name and address. If the bloke says, 'The Act' when asked, would he get away with it?"

"I doubt it works in a general way, otherwise the police would be powerless. It probably states within the act the circumstances under which it can be used."

"I knew what I thought he meant sounded too good to be true."

They arrived outside the office that the detectives were using and would have knocked, but there was an envelope pinned to the door. The typewritten addressee was Georgie Saxe-Coburg & Gotha, Esq.

"We've gone and found something now, haven't we?" said Ada.

"The detectives can't know of it," said Flora. She knocked on the door.

"Come in!" called a man in the room.

"No! You come out. It's vital that you do."

"What did you say?"

"Come out. You must see something!"

A chair scraped on the wooden floor. An unamused detective opened the door.

"Ladies, you don't need an invitation to come in."

Flora pointed to the envelope and said, "Another one for the collection." The detective stared at it.

"Who put that there?"

"Don't touch it!" called Detective Sergeant Gowers, getting up from his chair with alacrity. "Put your gloves on."

"Of course, sarge."

"And be careful with the tack. There might be something on it."

With his gloves now on, the detective unpinned the envelope and brought it over to Gowers' desk. Flora and Ada entered the room and shut the door.

"Hello, Sergeant," said Ada.

The other detective looked at her quizzically.

"Hello... Make yourself scarce," said Gowers to the detective, who obliged.

When the door was closed, they greeted each other less formally.

"I shouldn't talk about a brother officer, but that fella drives me mad. Talks all the time. Also, he said something about my football team that I didn't care for. Now, down to business. I must fingerprint the envelope first before opening it. Do you ladies have a moment?"

"We'd be happy to wait as long as we can watch," said Flora.

"There's no hurry," said Ada, "because if the bloke's left a note, he ain't left a bomb, has he?"

"I wish I could be so certain," said Gowers. "Make yourselves comfortable, ladies."

"Oh, isn't he the nicest policeman ever?" said Flora.

Gowers looked at her steadily. "I recall the last time you buttered me up and, if I'm correct, you were both in a lot of trouble. Anything going on I should know about?" He began unpacking his fingerprinting kit.

"Absolutely nothing, we swear," said Flora.

"That makes me even more suspicious."

"We're as pure as the driven snow."

"Glad to hear it. Now, if you'd be so kind as to write factual statements about your trip to Sandringham, I'd be much obliged. Pen and paper's on the other desk. The facts only, please... about what you were doing and when... Leave out the bomb, though. Put that on a separate sheet."

"That was my best part," said Flora.

"It can't go in. Just say you were in the conservatory when the bomb was found... What I would also appreciate is if one of you ladies would be so kind as to ring the bell, so we can have some tea."

"You've got yourself set up nice," said Ada, who got up to push the button on the wall.

"Well, you take it when you can find it, don't you? Also ask for cake and biscuits when the footman comes."

Gowers worked efficiently. Ada and Flora wrote, and instructed the footman when he arrived. The tea came just as Gowers finished.

"What is the report on the note, Sergeant?" asked Flora.

"No one opened the door for twenty minutes prior to your arrival. The tack's been wiped clean, and the envelope and sheet have been handled with gloves. The envelope is slightly creased from being carried in a pocket, although the note is otherwise crisp, except for the single fold. There's no signature and everything's typewritten — an Olivetti, I believe."

"I'm impressed," said Flora.

"I'm not," said Gowers. "I hate to think how many typewriters there are in the Palace, and now they all have to be tested — Olivetti or not."

"You poor thing," said Ada. "They must be all over the place."

"I'm sure they are," said Gowers, gloomily.

"There's a difference with this message, though," said Flora. "Here, I'll read it out.

'Georgie, you silly boy, I gave you several clear warnings, and you have ignored them all.

Now you force me to make an example of you, so expect your punishment in a few days' time.

Where do I send the wreath?' See? It's jocular and matey in a twisted way."

"Yes," agreed Gowers. "It has a different tone, all right."

"It sounds like a gag to me," said Ada. "But we've learned something, I think."

"What's that?" asked Gowers.

"Him calling the King a boy — only an older man would say that, so whoever sent the message must be a similar age to the King."

Gowers stroked his chin. "I think you might have something there, Miss Carmichael."

"He also berates like a teacher — except for the wreath, of course," said Flora.

"That's true, too," said Gowers.

"What happens now?" asked Ada.

"It's like this. Every message we get gives a small clue about our man."

"We call him Lud," said Flora. "May I make a copy of the note?"

"Go ahead," said Gowers. "So you've connected him to that stuff before the war. Very well. Lud is slowly giving himself away. If he would send us his next hundred messages, we could probably find out who he is. Except in this note, he threatens violence in a few days — within a week, say. At present, we have no chance of catching him. And here's the thing, he has the cheek to pin this letter on *my* door? Now I want to catch up with the fella for personal reasons."

"Do you think the King is in real danger?" asked Flora.

"Yes. Lud and his agents are capable of an assassination. They've demonstrated their ability to get close to the King often enough. If Lud is also behind the murders... need I say more? But why is he playing such a game?"

"Because he has another big project on the go, and this is all a blind. Miss King says so, and I agree."

"So do I," said Ada.

"You wouldn't happen to know what it is?"

"Anything but the King's murder. With this letter, though... Do you think something has changed?"

"I don't believe so, Miss Walton. Lud has always known the King would return here to work, so it follows he would have sent this note. If not today, then tomorrow. All he has to do is change 'a few days' to two days or whatever suits."

"Blimey," said Ada, "so there is an agent in the Palace."

"Right, and we don't know a thing about the actual plan."

"What's being done about it?" asked Flora.

"There are no real leads. Every detective in London is putting out feelers to see if anyone has something big on the go, but that's produced nothing so far. The army, who is having a bigger say in all of this than they should, is convinced

Lud is after the art treasures in one of the royal residences. They've sent a battalion to Hampton Court, and a couple of companies to each of the others."

"There were a lot of soldiers at Sandringham," said Flora.

"And they're still there," replied Gowers. "That's all largely a waste of time, in my opinion. No criminal gang would be after those art treasures because no one on the black market would touch anything stolen from the Royal Family. Also, it's an awful lot of tremendously risky work for a collector wanting to get his hands on a few pictures and statues, and why would he send the notes? I can't see anyone doing it — not your regular criminal types, anyway."

"Are you saying a collector *might* steal paintings from the royal collection?" asked Flora.

"They might, but it's highly unlikely... Although, there have been a few burglaries from posh houses in the recent past where expensive artwork was stolen. None of it has resurfaced."

"Was anyone caught?" asked Flora.

"Not as far as I know. They weren't my cases... I'd better ask about that." Gowers made an entry in his notebook.

"I don't understand," said Ada. "Why would a collector nick someone's paintings just to hang them on his own wall without ever bein' able to sell 'em? That's daft, that is. He could go to a gallery to see stuff like everyone else does."

"It happens — rarely though — because some collectors are quite mad about owning things, and they just have to have them."

"Oh... What happened about that car? I took its number and I ain't heard nothin' since."

"Apparently, it was stolen, which is highly convenient. The chap who owns it should be in prison, and an illegal alien operation is just about up his street. However, he went and reported his car missing about the same time you saw it at the docks." Gowers nodded significantly.

"A coincidence?" asked Flora.

"No, not him. He must have known he'd been spotted, knew trouble would come, so did something about it. We can't prove anything now, except we're sure he was involved in the scheme. That's all shut down, by the way."

"Can't somebody investigate him?" asked Ada.

"I should hope they are, but I'm not involved, so I can't tell you anything more than what's been reported... I'm not even supposed to tell you that much."

"Thank you for telling us what you can. We appreciate it," said Flora. She looked at her watch and got up. "It's time we relieved the others."

The King was at his desk in his study. Charlotte was preening herself on her perch. BW was standing immobile by the door. It was peaceful. Baron Stamfordham, Personal Secretary, carrying a red leather document case, entered as noiselessly as was humanly possible. He glanced with irritation at BW and held up the case, saying,

"Good morning, your majesty." He approached the King.

"Morning, Arthur." He set down his pen.

"I have brought several important documents for your signature."

"Let's have them," said the King. "Anything interesting?"

"No, sir. They are merely routine. I have appended notes where appropriate."

"Thank you."

Stamfordham took three important-looking documents from the case. He went to a cabinet and brought back the Great Seal of the Realm.

"I have also brought some correspondence, which I shall leave for you to peruse at your leisure, sir. There is also one matter that requires a decision."

"Oh, yes?"

"Prime Minister Lloyd George telephoned..."

"Not him again!" squawked Charlotte.

The Personal Secretary looked aghast at the parrot and then, with his face brought under control, he turned to the King, who was intently studying BW, who was still staring into space.

"What does he want?" said the King, returning his attention to the documents.

"He is desirous of coming to the Palace this afternoon for a private meeting with your majesty. He declined to say what it was about."

"I see. Am I not busy this afternoon?"

"Unfortunately, no, sir."

"Then I had better see him at three. In here will do." He glanced at BW and then lowered his voice to his secretary. "Come and get me out at three-thirty — without fail."

"Yes, sir."

King George finished signing the documents. Stamfordham sealed them and returned the papers to the red case. "Is there anything else, your majesty?"

"I don't think so."

Stamfordham left the study.

King George stared at the young man by the door. Charlotte took flight and landed on the desk.

"BW, I sincerely hope that anything heard while you are in this house shall not be repeated outside."

"I won't say a word to anyone, your majesty. I promise to button my lips."

"Good... It so happens that I respect Lloyd George... for the most part. He, like many politicians, talks at length and says little. It is the habit of the House of Commons, and he, like the rest of them, seems unable to set aside the custom in ordinary conversation."

"Shiver me timbers," said Charlotte. She put her head on one side. "Button my lips."

The King gave her some seeds.

"That's the ticket," said Charlotte. "Call me BW."

"She says that all the time now."

"Honestly, sire, I didn't teach her to say it," said BW.

"I know you didn't. She'll pick up a phrase that pleases her, having heard it only once, but something one wants her to say, she stubbornly refuses to repeat. Don't you, you little pirate?"

"Stow it, Cap'n."

"Do you know Charlotte's the only person who answers me back?"

King George and BW laughed.

Since breakfast, Sophie had been standing in the Music Room while Queen Mary wrote letters. At ten thirty, Lady Eva Dugdale visited the Queen and an awkward silence arose.

"Miss King is guarding me," said Mary in explanation of Sophie's presence.

"I couldn't help but notice the police and soldiers, as have the papers, who are having a field day. So, it's all true, then, is it May?"

"Yes, Eva. I shall tell you about it in a moment."

"Thank you. About the, um, other matter…"

"Miss King," said Mary. "I understand your duty keeps you in this room, but I need to discuss something in private with Lady Dugdale for about twenty minutes. Please leave, and inform the footman to admit no one, except the King, of course. Would that be suitable?"

"Yes, ma'am, that is suitable."

Sophie curtsied and left, conveying Mary's instruction to the footman outside.

She was glad to walk after having stood for so long. As she was in the operational area of the Palace there were many people about — courtiers and staff swiftly moving about their business, slowly walking constables, stationery footmen by doorways, and four-man teams of khaki-clad soldiers from the Coldstream Guards regiment in readiness at the ends of corridors. There was ample room for everyone, yet Sophie preferred to avoid them — all those people she did not know. She had twenty minutes to herself and, as she was close to the terrace, she felt a walk outside would be just the thing.

She studied the sky — cloudy, with no imminent chance of rain. The air was pleasantly warm. If Sophie thought she could find some solitude in the gardens, she was mistaken. Constables were stationed at intervals along the terrace while soldiers were dotted about the extensive park. Walking briskly, she said good morning to each constable she passed. She felt the rising of a fine, indescribable feeling, almost proprietorial, as she walked in the Palace grounds and having the right to be there. She felt as though she belonged to something vast and more important than herself, and it felt vaguely thrilling.

Not one to analyze her feelings to any great extent, Sophie turned her thoughts to the case, such as it was. She was finding it very unsatisfactory in that the true objective of the menace remained in obscurity. As for the amount of trouble it was causing — it was absurd in the extreme. The King, Queen, and immediate heirs to the throne were all alive and well, and yet it required such a tremendous effort to maintain their safety. "It can't last for much longer." Deciding talking to herself was an unhealthy habit to cultivate, she looked about to see if anyone had noticed. They hadn't. She stopped and wondered where all these people — all the solid policemen nearby and the speck-like soldiers in the distance — where would they all be now if Lud had not put them here?

Sophie often had ideas, and some of them were good. The thought that Lud had deliberately begun a process to set all these protective measures in place now seemed more luminous than before. Where her thought truly shone was in the realization that all the effort was for nothing and Lud had planned it that way. Should his objective be the death of the monarch, then he might achieve it despite all the king's horses and all the king's men. She turned to study the back of the building to consider how she would accomplish an assassination in the current situation. Two concrete ideas presented themselves, but these were not as important as her third. A branch of reasoning budded which, with a little help, might blossom. She marched back into the Palace.

Chapter 14

The enemies within

Ada and Flora were near the detectives' room when Sophie entered the corridor. She beckoned them and waited in a place where they would not be overheard.

"Is something wrong, miss?" asked Ada.

"No. It's just struck me that, if this case is ever to be closed, we need to get on with things."

"I agree," said Flora. "But you should know Lud sent another message about an hour ago."

"Yes, miss. And Sergeant Gowers is hopping mad 'cause it was pinned to his door. He's taken it personal."

"Really?"

They reported the incident and much of the subsequent conversation.

"I knew it!" said Sophie. "There's an agent here now, obviously, and Lud means for us to know this. He's not making a mistake. Lud intends for us, meaning everyone, to go haring off after the wrong things, and he wants us all fearful, suspicious, and dithering."

"How do you know that?" asked Flora.

"Because that's what's happening. All we can do is react to whatever Lud chooses to serve up."

"I can agree in principle," said Flora, "but he can't mean for us to search for and then find his agent."

"He means for us to search and maybe is unconcerned that we should find the agent. The note said a few days. Sergeant Gowers said within a week. All this will be over soon."

"Oh," said Flora in disappointment. "Did you just redefine indefinitely? I was hoping for a month's work, at least." She looked at her new watch. "I've already spent too much... It keeps excellent time, though. I love it, but I wouldn't have bought it if I'd known."

"It comes as a blow, miss," said Ada, "but we're here to do the job, no matter what."

"That's right," said Flora. "I'll keep a stiff upper lip, even though it's the lower one that keeps trembling."

Sophie smiled. "That's the spirit. First, we must clear the façade out of the way. Will there be an attack on the Royal Family, yes or no? As things stand, there is no conceivable way for Lud to mount an attack, but we must be sure we haven't overlooked anything. Gladys, you look after Queen Mary if her friend Lady Dugdale has left. I'll be back at two, so you can have lunch. Ada, I want you to find out all you can about secret passages and tunnels within the Palace. If there are any, ask if they're being guarded."

"Yes, miss."

"I'll telephone Archie and Superintendent Penrose to find out what they're up to."

"Is that all?" asked Flora. "There must be more."

"Lots. This is only the start of our campaign. Next, we shall set out to catch the agent and clear the rubbish out of the way. Then we're going after Lud."

"How is that even possible?"

"By answering the question, why must the Royal Family stay away from London? Let's get to it."

Queen Mary joined the King, and they went to lunch with some friends. Flora dutifully followed. BW, preceding the King, searched the room first, and then pronounced it safe to enter. He conducted himself with dignity, similar to that of Black Rod at the State Opening of Parliament. However, he came out again, stepping aside to allow the King's party to enter first, and then whispered to Flora, who was stationed by the door,

"I'm starving. I hope they're fast eaters, because I want my lunch. Have you had yours?"

"No. Now I'll be thinking of nothing but food."

"Oh, sorry... I had better find out what they're getting up to."

With that, he went in and shut the door. A minute later, Flora, who had not been feeling hungry at all, heard her stomach grumbling and sincerely hoped the nearby footman did not hear it. She moved a couple of steps further away and politely coughed to cover when the noises became raucous.

Ada asked five people, all staff busy with various tasks, if there were any secret passages in the Palace. With variations, they all replied that there were none. It took her that many attempts to realize what they were really saying was, 'I'm not allowed to discuss the matter.' To rectify the situation, she went looking for a specific type of footman. He had to be older, which could mean he had spent years in the Palace and knew all its secrets. If he was old enough, perhaps there was no possibility of further promotion in his future, so he might also be talkative. Ada knew footmen were not supposed to chat, but that did not stop them when they could get away with it. She found a likely candidate on duty by an entrance. Ada approached him when he wasn't busy and put on her friendliest voice.

"Excuse me, p'rhaps you could help. I'm Miss Carmichael from the Home Office, attending Queen Mary. Her majesty was wondering if anyone's guarding the secret passages."

"Was she?" He paused for several seconds. "Well, I should think so. There are only the two — hers and his."

He was a Londoner and eager to talk, which made it easier for Ada. She rapidly calculated what she could get away with.

"I've never been in them, of course, so I don't know where they lead. What's your name, so I can tell Queen Mary who it was who was being so helpful."

"Palmer, footman, as you can see. Hers goes from her private room to the White Drawing Room. His goes from his private room to another private room on the floor above. They use them to slip in and out when they don't want a fuss made."

"I see. All those rooms connected by passageways are being guarded, so that's all right then. But what about the tunnels, eh?"

"Oh, I don't know about them." He shook his head. "They might be guarded, they might not. I couldn't really tell you."

"How many are there?"

"Three in all. There's Tyburn Culvert, but it's bricked up, because the river used to flood the wine cellar it's in. Although, I think you could knock the bricks out easy enough. But it's smelly in that cellar and nobody likes it and, when you think about it, why would anyone want to use it?" He squared his shoulders. "Now, in the wine cellar next-door to that one, you'll find the tunnel that leads to St. James's Palace. They used it all the time before the war, but not so much these days. Can I say if it's guarded or not? No, I don't think I can."

"What about the third one?"

"That one goes out into the grounds at the back, but the building it connects with fell down years ago. I've never been in it, and I should think no one would want to, either."

"It might have collapsed," said Ada. "Where's the entrance for it?"

"Through a cupboard below the Throne Room... Look, somebody's coming, and it's been nice talking, but I ought to..."

"Thank you very much. I'll pass the information on, and she'll be very pleased, I'm sure."

"Oh, that's nice of you."

Ada hurried away to find Sergeant Gowers, who was still in the office. Others were present because interviews were being conducted. So, by looks and nods, she induced him to come out into the corridor.

"Sorry about that," said Ada. "I've no idea now who knows what about us."

"That's all right. Among the police present, I'm the only one in the know. So, is something the matter?"

"No, nothing. Miss King sent me to ask if the two secret passages and three tunnels have been searched and are they being guarded?"

Gowers was puzzled. "What secret passages?"

Ada then explained all she had learned from the footman.

"I only knew about the tunnel to St. James's Palace. They're a closed-mouth lot in this place. No one volunteers anything. Still, you found out. Do you want a job on the force?"

She just laughed.

"I'll send someone to check the tunnels but, as it's lunchtime and their majesties are busy, I'll examine the passages for myself. I like that sort of thing."

Ada left him, but it was a while before she caught up with Sophie again.

Archie was out when Sophie called from the Telephone Room, so she tried Superintendent Penrose. He could not tell her much, except he dropped a hint that Archie was busy with another case. Penrose said that both he and Lord Laneford were no longer directly involved in protecting the Royal Family, and that the oversight for the operation was by an august committee made up of courtiers, military personnel, and an Assistant Commissioner representing Scotland Yard. They would tell her nothing, because they had told him nothing. The only person, he suggested, who could provide limited help was Maxwell Handley. Perplexed, she hung up the receiver, understanding that the agency was on its own and should keep to its assigned duties.

She left the room and went for a walk to think things through. As it stood, her only hope was that the august committee had everything under control and progress was being made towards the apprehension of Lud and his confederates. Considering a committee now ran the show, she was sure they had not progressed very far because no one had yet asked her anything specific. She had still to see Sergeant Gowers, but that interview was only routine — everyone who had travelled with the King was being interviewed. No one was asking for her insights, observations, and certainly not her opinion. It was now abundantly clear that the committee was in charge and would proceed according to its lights and, whatever happened in the end, she would have to read it in the newspapers.

As far as the network was concerned, Burgoyne's Agency was on its own and was obviously expected to get on with it. *That's what they do*, she thought. She meant men in authority. *They never spell things out because they don't really know what to do themselves. Spying, clandestine operations, and subterfuge are the stock in trade, and the mode of operation is to pick the right person and let them get on with it.* She had heard several stories of the type where, during the war, a senior officer would informally say to a junior officer something akin to, 'Fancy a wander behind enemy lines? Fritz is planning something. Find out what it is, there's a good chap.' And that was it for preparation and guidance.

Men think differently. Sophie knew that. She wanted everything organized and spelled out, but that would not happen. She and her friends were guarding the Royal Family as a pretext for finding out who was at work against them in the Palace. As far as the network was concerned, the actions of the august committee did not factor into this matter. The committee would handle the mundane and obvious. She, on the other hand, was expected to be a good junior officer and find out, if she could, what was really going on. No one had told her anything or given her direction. Sophie considered the possibility that she might make a muddle of it all, which made her nervous.

Ultimately, she knew, the safety of the monarchy would only be complete once the threat against it was removed. It seemed it was expected of Burgoyne's, if practicable, to catch a Lud by the tail, and shout for help while hanging on. But how was this to be done? Then she saw the answer with clarity. The undefined mission was to find any Lud agents in the Palace. There had been a maid in the past, but she left, and there was now another agent present. She knew that, because the envelope pinned to the door proved it. The network would want Burgoyne's Agency to apprehend the envelope-pinning Lud agent. Failure to capture this person would reflect on their abilities. If they made a grievous error, trouble would follow. That's how it would fall out should she go beyond her assigned duties. But what the network demanded was success and secrecy, and for her to take the risk. She halted by a window to watch soldiers in red-tunics and busbies marching in perfect formation across the Quadrangle. A sergeant shouted an order. She thought everything would be much less complicated if only someone would occasionally bark an order at *her*. Then she saw Maxwell Handley crossing the open space in the company of two men. She could see which entrance he was heading towards and decided she could catch him if she hurried.

Following a spy — a friendly one — was a novel experience. Sophie could study his mannerisms from a distance, which were fussy and exaggerated, and see how an actual spy maintained his cover. The two men with him were in their sixties and very well-dressed — senior office-holding courtiers. She did not know who or what they were, but noticed they were not in any kind of rush. They had eaten lunch together, she believed, and Handley endeavoured to keep them entertained on their way back to work. She could see this from the older men's conduct — a subtle inclination of the head or a measured laugh in response to Handley's comments. They were friendly and being politely indulgent. She followed. Each gentleman returned to one of a pair of adjacent offices. Sophie called Handley's attention before he sped away.

He turned, showing mock surprise upon seeing her. "Miss King... We can use this office. It's empty." He opened a door and waited for her to enter.

"Certainly."

Inside, he smiled and asked,

"Has anything happened?"

"There's been another message. It was rude and chiding, and someone had the audacity to tack it to the office door of the room the detectives are using."

"That's very daring. Did it say anything specific, or was it like the others?"

"It was unlike the others. It threatened some type of action in the next few days."

"Oh, dear. This sounds more serious... And what with the grenade, it seems we are about to reach a crisis point."

"It does, indeed."

"Thank you for informing me, Miss King."

"I thought you should know, but I also wanted to see you about something else. Do you have a moment? I know you're busy."

"Not too busy. What is it about?"

"It's difficult to phrase. As we're both within the network, and it's standard procedure not to tell another agent what one is doing, this conversation seems a little tricky. We both, I'm assuming, have similar objectives in this instance."

"Er, yes, you could say that."

"I just wish for some clarification on what my staff and I... Well, what are the limits as to what we can do? We're here to guard the Royal Family. Are we also to investigate or hunt down Lud's agent?"

"Lud?"

"Sorry, that's what we're calling him for the moment. It seemed more convenient than saying Mr X all the time."

"Ah... I can't say I'm placed to answer your query. I should think Penrose or Drysdale can better help you there. I can offer my opinion, if that's of any use."

"Please, do."

"It is usual, in my experience, to stick closely to one's mandate. It doesn't really do to go venturing off on one's own. You see, Laneford, Drysdale and the others have the situation under control. Naturally, I cannot explain everything I do. You must have some idea from our former discussions, but I obviously can't explain everything, and you're intelligent enough to realize that."

Sophie paused for a moment. "I see. Then I've probably been overthinking things."

"Easily done. We all do it. Now, should you suspect someone, that's a different matter. Do you have anyone in mind?"

"Oh, no. Not at all. If I had, I would have reported it already."

"Then don't be concerned, except if a suspect makes his or herself apparent to you. I would be much obliged that, if you do suspect someone, you would also inform me, so that I can take the appropriate steps in the Palace."

"Yes, of course… I apologize for troubling you."

"Think nothing of it. Now, if you'll excuse me, I have many things to do."

Sophie came away from the meeting feeling mildly irritated. She could not recall Maxwell Handley being put in charge of her part of the mission, but now he was acting as though he were. It was her fault, she decided. She had asked for his advice and, as some will do, he had given it in the manner of one wanting to take over. Furthermore, all her newfound determination was being stifled at the outset, and that did not sit well with her.

At two, Ada, Flora, and Sophie held a meeting in a corner of the empty White Drawing Room. Ada explained what she had found out about secret tunnels and passages. As one terminated where they presently were, they went looking.

"Here it is, miss. Behind this mirror." Ada opened a door with the mirror attached. The others came over to see it.

"It's rather posh," said Flora, who had switched on the light revealing wooden panelling and a long, hand-knotted Kazakh runner.

Sophie stepped inside to open another door, where she found a lavatory.

"They mustn't get caught short," said Ada, also peering in.

Flora entered and searched a small cupboard. "I can't do any more. I'm too faint with hunger. Can I go to lunch now, please?"

"I completely forgot about eating, and I haven't, either."

"I've had me lunch, miss. Shall I watch Queen Mary for you?"

"Yes, do. And tell BW to have his."

"He's eaten already," said Flora.

"When?"

"While I was outside, King George sent him away to have his lunch."

"He did!? Why did he do that?"

"Ah... I hadn't meant to say anything, and I don't know what was said, but the King, Queen, and their guests were all laughing heartily when BW exited smiling, bowing, and waving."

"Oh, no! Surely he wasn't really waving? He's going to give me a heart attack one day."

In an almost empty staff dining room, Sophie and Flora applied themselves to their lunches. They ate in silence for a minute.

"I spoke to Mr Handley," said Sophie. "He more or less told me to do what I've been told to do and let others worry about finding the agents."

"So, he treated you like a dimwit... Do you think, if we ask, we can get some more cauliflower cheese?"

"It's very good." Sophie turned towards the counter where the food was served. "They're putting everything away."

"Too late, then. We're not taking any notice of him, are we?"

"No, but his reaction brought me up short."

"You're getting old, dear. Time was when you would have punched him on the snout."

"I only did that once... And what do you mean, old? We're the same age."

"But our birthdays are coming up soon, and we'll be... No, I daren't utter such a dreadful number. It is far too hideous. Has your Aunt Bessie been on at you? I should imagine she has."

"You imagine correctly. 'You'll be twenty-four in two weeks, and you're not even engaged!' That was last week's rant, and she's unstoppable once she's started. It doesn't matter what I say, she goes on and on about when is he going to propose, as if it's all under my control and I can make Sinjin ask me to marry him whenever I like."

"You poor thing… I'm in suspended animation, just as you are. Sidney met the parents, and they all got on very well. Mother and Father now smile brightly whenever they see me because they are waiting for the momentous news, but are far too considerate to ask. I think I would prefer your aunt's nagging to their expectant looks. They're quite demoralizing in a way, because should anything go wrong, I'll worry about their disappointment. Can't win, can we?"

"No. Let's talk about something else, please."

"Here's something, then. What do you imagine this Lud agent looks like? I picture him with big moustaches, a top hat, a heavy cloak, and about to hurl a fizzing bomb."

"Ha! If only… What would a female bomber look like?"

"Oh, dark-haired — like me… with an intense fixed gaze — like this…"

"Stop it, you look demented."

"Hair pulled back severely, so… And add thin lips with a touch of cruelty."

"Someone will see you… Anyway, that's not a cruel mouth as much as a sign of indigestion."

"I need a mirror to do it properly." Flora returned her appearance to normal.

"Whoever we're up against must be hidden among… Let's see," she counted on her fingers, "the police, soldiers, staff, courtiers, officeholders, or visitors." She held up a thumb for the last. "We can discount visitors, because they wouldn't know where to find the detectives' room."

"That's good. It means we're down to about twenty-five hundred people to choose from. Aren't you double counting officeholders?"

"I consider those the ones who only occasionally come to the Palace for business."

"Hmm… The Luddite must be able to type. That would let off many people, but we don't know which ones."

"True. The decision to type the note, however, could only have been made from yesterday afternoon onwards in reaction to the King's return." Sophie took out her notebook and pencil. "The detectives were using the room last week..."

"Before you go any further," said Flora. "Today's message might have been prepared in advance."

"Possibly. Sergeant Gowers said the envelope was carried in a pocket — he couldn't say for how long, though... Here's something to consider. It was delivered mid-morning, while the interviews were in progress. Perhaps that was the earliest opportunity the Luddite agent had."

"Or, he may just have been being extremely sneaky. Had he delivered it the night before, he would have given himself away."

"How?"

"Well, I was thinking there would have been far fewer staff about yesterday."

"It doesn't help to narrow it down," said Sophie. "It's all just speculation."

Flora took out *her* notebook. "I made an exact copy of the note, if you'd like to examine it." She passed it across, open at the page. Sophie read and reread it.

"This note was dictated by a gentleman — I'm using the term loosely."

"Quite. Ada reckons Lud is about the same age as or older than King George because he called him a boy. That doesn't help with identifying his agent, though."

"No... The time limit mentioned in the note is perplexing, but it seems to me that we're all to be kept busy here while Lud is carrying out his actual plan elsewhere."

"I know you're convinced, but what on earth can it be to make Lud go to such lengths?"

"I can't even guess. All I am sure about is that Lud wants everyone around the King to be kept fully occupied, and for the King himself to stay out of London or be too afraid to leave the Palace."

"This business must certainly have disrupted his appointments schedule."

Sophie did not answer immediately. "His Personal Secretary, Baron Stamfordham, must know what meetings and ceremonies were cancelled or deferred."

"I should think so. If he doesn't, he can point us to someone who does."

"We'll see him at once."

It took two hours first to track down Baron Stamfordham and then to meet him, because he had been at various meetings with members of the august committee since lunch. Having been apprised earlier by his own secretary that two young ladies were anxious to see him about the King's schedule, it gave him time to consider the matter. Thus, when Sophie and Flora entered his office, he was fully prepared to refuse their requests, which he did immediately.

"Your zeal is to be commended," said Baron Stamfordham. "However, I have had many recent discussions with experts concerning this and other associated matters. The King's schedule — daily, weekly, etcetera — is, for the moment, a closely guarded secret... Allow me to finish." He held up a hand as Sophie tried to speak. "Therefore, as it is a secret, I cannot provide you with any information such as you request, and that is final."

"May I speak?" asked Sophie.

"Please."

"We, who are here to guard the King and the Queen, may not know his schedule in advance? We will know it eventually because we will travel with their majesties, but that wasn't what we came about..."

"I'm sorry. I don't wish to be abrupt, but I have duties to perform. Let me sum up the situation for you. Those in authority have instituted the highest possible level of protection for their majesties. Trained men from many services and departments are on duty around the clock. It may even be said that there is a great deal of redundancy in the security arrangements, because every precaution is being taken. Having said that, it is now unnecessary for you to continue on here."

"We're here to guard their majesties. Like everyone else. I should point out that it was we who discovered several notes and the fake bomb left by the enemy agents."

"Ah, but all those would have been found eventually."

"What if the bomb had been real?"

"It wasn't, so what is your point?"

"My point is, had it been real, and had we not been present, you would now be arranging funerals for the Royal Family."

"I grant you did good work in that instance. But now, we cannot see the justification for your presence in the Palace or, indeed, to accompany the King should he travel outside the Palace. The committee has put more permanent arrangements in place."

"I won't argue, but did our names happen to come up in any of these meetings?"

"Not individually, but as a unit, yes. That's all I shall say on that matter."

"Thank you, sir. We shan't trouble you any further."

"Good day, ladies. And you have my profound gratitude for all you have done."

Outside in the corridor, Sophie and Flora walked in a silence that bulged with feeling. Sophie broke it.

"Those snivelling rats!" she said in an intense whisper.

"That's a good one," said Flora. "How about glib and oily artists?"

"Yes! That's good, too. Those wretched creatures are going to bung us out!"

"I don't want to be bunged out; the pay's too good for one thing. And we really should get a bit further in the case if we can."

"I know... I don't understand it. Everyone seems to have deserted us. Where's Archie when he's needed? Then Superintendent Penrose said he was out of the picture and for us to talk to Mr Handley. When I spoke to him, he more or less said, mind your own business."

"Oh, well. We're getting sacked, whether we like it or not. I'm sure Baron Stamfordham will mention it at their next meeting to make sure — that is, if it hasn't *already* been voted on."

"Wait a minute… Wait a minute." Sophie stopped and, for a few moments, collected her thoughts.

"What is it?" asked Flora.

"Archie's missing… and Penrose knows nothing? That's all rubbish! Both know so much of what goes on it can only be deliberate on their part. I'd wager Archie has removed himself on purpose just so he doesn't have to sack us. The glib artist committee has already decided to get rid of us. Stamfordham couldn't say so, because he has no actual authority over us and is waiting for Archie to do the deed, but Archie is dodging getting the message."

"So Archie's hiding to keep the mission going a bit longer?"

"That's the assumption we will work under."

"Sooner or later, the bigwigs will chuck us out."

"I'm sure they will, but first they have to get off their backsides to do it."

"Sophie, I'm profoundly shocked. I've never heard you use such a word before."

"Sorry. That comes from staying with Auntie. You should hear her reading a newspaper sometimes. She bellows like anything when an article annoys her."

"I think you'll be exactly the same when you reach her age."

"No, I shan't. But enough of all that. We all need to meet to decide what we're doing next. I'll get Nancy. You fetch BW, tell him to stop whatever he's doing, and we'll rendezvous…" Sophie opened a nearby door. "…in here."

"Good choice. I suppose the Blue Drawing Room will be just about adequate for us," said Flora.

Chapter 15

On the run

They met in the Blue Drawing Room where Sophie explained the developments and how the committee wanted them to leave.

"That's a pity," said BW. "I'll miss Charlotte."

"Hold on a mo, miss," said Ada. "Who done us down?"

"The glib artist committee."

"No, I know that, miss. What I mean is, who put up our names to be done down?"

"Yes, that's right," agreed Flora. "Baron Stamfordham referred to us as a unit."

"A courtier, an officeholder, or someone from the army," said Sophie. "I don't think it would be the police or the Home Office."

"Oh, I see."

"What's the matter?" asked Sophie.

"Nothing, really. But it just crossed my mind the Lud agent might have had a hand in it."

"You mean he was at the meeting? Now, that's an interesting thought. I wish we had a list of attendees."

"The King won't know about the committee," said BW. "Nobody tells him anything unless they must."

"How did you discover that?"

"By observation. Would you like me to tell him about the committee's decision?" asked BW.

"Before we go any further, explain to me — how friendly are you with the King?"

"Ah. Yes. Before I answer, Miss King, am I in trouble again?"

"I shall reserve judgment, but I want a proper explanation."

"Righty-ho. I'd say that the King and I are quite chummy, but it's early days. I couldn't ask him to lend me a pound, for example — we're not that friendly. But when Charlotte attacked a footman, he told me to get the man out of the room because his nervousness was making her nervous. So, in a way, the King relies upon me for parrot-related things. As the King is devoted to Charlotte, I don't think I'm amiss in saying my standing with him is *pretty* rock-solid."

"Good grief," said Sophie. "Strange as it may seem, I draw comfort from your explanation."

"You're not angry? That's marvellous!"

"Who visited the King besides Stamfordham?"

"The Prime Minister, but that meeting didn't last very long. Some fellow named Michael, who brought in the afternoon post. I think he's an earl or higher. They chatted freely. There was another johnny from the kitchen who came to discuss a menu, and then there was Mr Handley."

"What was *he* doing seeing the King?"

"Let me see. He had a newspaper and wanted to talk about an article on the Bank of England. Apparently, the King was supposed to be there this week, but it's been put off until next Monday, so they chatted about that, and mentioned the Pearl Sword Ceremony. The King said it could be done at the Bank instead of Temple Bar. I had no idea what they were talking about."

"I don't, either," said Sophie.

"It's where the Lord Mayor of the City of London swears fealty to the King," said Flora. "He hands a sword to the King, who hands it back, and then they go off to lunch or a ribbon-cutting or whatever it is they're getting up to that day."

"Ah, thank you. Please continue, BW."

"Old Handley also delivered several notes, which he left for the King to read. The one they discussed was from the stables. It was about a mare they're expecting to foal any day now. It must have been a good report because they were both quite chipper, and the King said he would visit her this evening."

"So, he acts like a page?"

"I suppose so. However, on four occasions, actual pages delivered messages, but I haven't a clue what those were about."

"Is that everyone?"

"Um... yes."

"Surely that can't be right. His majesty is only informed of events by his Personal Secretary and what he learns from the newspapers? That bothers me because such control could easily be abused."

"Well, I've been with him all day, and the Personal Secretary never mentioned committees or anything that's been going on. As for the Prime Minister, he only wanted to talk about transport. The King explained afterwards, because they sent me out of the room, and, let me tell you, he's a bit miffed with Lloyd George. Said he can't stand the sound of his voice. The trouble stems from the war. At the outset, Lloyd George, who abstains and wanted everyone else to follow suit, persuaded the King that it would be a show of patriotic fervour and a demonstration of model behaviour if no alcohol were to be consumed in the Palace for the duration of the war. The King, in a moment of weakness he later came to regret, agreed to the Prime Minister's suggestion. Bullying and barracking were the terms he actually used.

"Now, this is where it all fell in a heap. The PM had told the King that the war would only last for a few months. But, sadly and unfortunately, the war went on for four years. Naturally, with the Palace being as dry as dust for all that time, the King blames the PM for putting him in an invidious position. He obviously wanted a pint, but couldn't go back on his word. What he gave me to understand is that, ever since, he hasn't trusted a single word Lloyd George has said. I mean, just think of it. If the King wanted to get a bit squiffy on the quiet, he'd have to hoof it up to Sandringham on the Royal Train to get away from the Prime Minister. That's a lot of bother to be put to just because your PM is untrustworthy and a teetotaller."

"Godfathers, he said all that?" said Ada.

"Mostly. The last part is my commentary."

"It's quite, quite remarkable," said Sophie in mild amazement.

"Not really, Miss King. He's probably lonely, and that's why we talk. I mean to say, who'd choose to live in a place this big? It's not exactly snug, is it? When I suggested he get some bicycles to get about, he thought it a practical idea, but a touch undignified for what was expected in the old Palace. You see, he's really two fellows rolled into one — the monarch and the chap who wants a simple bit of fun without fuss."

"Thank you," said Sophie, regaining her composure. "Let us get back to the case and our situation. Effective immediately, we shall cease searching for bombs and stay away from their majesties. We may have to change bedrooms so they can't find us. If they can't find us, they can't throw us out, and they can't confiscate our warrants. While we have them, we can get in and out of the Palace. It is my opinion that if they do not see us, they will believe we have already left. Out of sight, out of mind."

"We're going to sneak about Buckingham Palace even though we're personae non gratae?" asked Flora. "How absolutely ripping!"

"Yes. But we must find this blasted agent! There's only a matter of days before Lud's plan comes to fruition. We need to find and interrogate the agent, and we need clues! I don't trust that anyone else is investigating properly, so it's up to us now."

"What happens if they catch one of us?" asked Ada.

"If we're never together, they can only pick us off one by one, while the rest carry on. Our meeting place and rallying point will be... the Balcony Room. It is not in use at present, and we can hide on the balcony should someone approach the room."

"Then we can wave at the people," said Flora.

"We shall do no such thing," said Sophie. "Our meetings shall be every two hours, on the hour."

"What will we be doing?" asked BW.

"I'll come to that. First, let me say, I find it highly disturbing that the King is kept in the dark, but I doubt we can do anything about that under the circumstances," said Sophie. "Nancy, you brought up the possibility that the Lud agent is on the committee. They will all be men holding senior positions. Is it likely that one of them also types and put a note on the detectives' door?"

"No, they wouldn't, come to think of it, but they could get someone to do it for 'em."

"Yes, they could. That would point to there being two or more agents in the Palace. Whatever the case might be, we need to investigate the committee, and the only person who can help us is Sergeant Gowers."

"What about Maxwell Handley?" asked Flora. "I know he doesn't want us doing anything, but he'd have insights while Sergeant Gowers might not have anything useful."

"I could try him again, I suppose."

"I say, what's up with Handley?" asked BW. "Has he been rude to you?"

"Not rude, but obstructive. He doesn't want us looking for the agent."

"Gosh!" exclaimed Flora. "Do you realize what you just said?"

"Oh, dear. Surely not? I thought he was only being... That doesn't matter."

"You think he works for Lud?" asked Ada.

"Well, it is possible," replied Flora. "We've heard of double agents, so why not?"

"But this is awful," said Sophie. "He's one of *us*."

"What do we know about Handley?" began Flora. "People *we* know and trust implicitly trust him. But as far as the mission is concerned, he hasn't helped in the slightest. Instead, he's getting in the way. Now we find the committee is probably going to dismiss us. The Private Secretary will make sure of that, if he hasn't already. If we mention this to Handley, he'll say just do as you're told."

"It's funny," said Sophie. "Before I spoke to him, he was walking with two Palace officials — I don't know who they are — and it struck me how much gossip and intrigue there must be. A great deal, I should imagine. Looking at Handley in a different light, he is extraordinarily well placed for his network duties. He's talkative and busy all the time, but never stays in one spot and is always near the King. He could easily have approached someone on the committee to suggest we were no longer needed."

"I think that's what he did," said Ada. "And he was up at Sandringham the night before and would have known about the clock that didn't work in the conservatory."

"Yes, he would, and he would know when the family had tea."

"And he could have put the note in the statue's shrubbery," added BW.

"That, too... Dear me, I don't like this... What do we do?"

"Telephone Inspector Penrose," said Ada.

"Ask Sergeant Gowers to get a specimen of his handwriting to match it to the handwritten notes," said Flora. "Remember he prided himself on it when he told you that story about Queen Mary wanting him for a secretary?"

"That's very good. I'm sure he can type, too."

"He was chortling on about the Bank of England," said BW. "Can that have anything to do with it?"

"I don't see how," said Sophie. "Unless Lud intends robbing it."

"That's impossible, miss. There ain't a safer place in the country. Have you seen the walls round the place? And the soldiers guarding it?"

"I suppose you're right. Whatever Lud is going to do must be large scale, though. He brings in foreign criminals disguised as seamen. They're set to work and, when no longer useful, he has them murdered. Such ruthlessness serves a practical purpose. He doesn't want those men talking. He kills them to keep them silent, and he chose them because they don't know anyone here or they can't communicate in English. All that suggests they have worked on something before being removed. What can it be?"

"They robbed places, the blokes wanted their share, and Lud knocked 'em off to be rid of 'em. 'Cause they're foreigners, they won't be missed, so there won't be no trouble from relatives. The police will investigate but won't get very far unless they have a witness. There are no witnesses, so the investigations have gone nowhere, and Lud is safe. Double safe, 'cause it wouldn't be him wringing their necks and droppin' 'em in the drink, oh, no."

"That's a good explanation, but does it explain the threats against the Royal Family?"

"Er... no, miss. What about this? They're working on a building site, an' he's puttin' the foreigners in among the navvies... Oh, it won't work. Sorry."

"I think we're going about it all wrong," said Flora. "You wanted to know about the King's itinerary for the last little while. We get the first snippet about the King's visit to the Bank of England, and now it's been dismissed already. I say, all things seem to fit in with the theory that Lud is going to steal the gold from the Bank. That's a big enough venture to require all this mucking about with the Royal Family."

"There's a lot of gold in there," said Ada.

"Tons and tons of it," said Flora.

"How could they get all of it out?" asked Sophie. "They're not going to bring in lorries and calmly load up. Hundreds of people work there. There's a detachment of armed soldiers, as Nancy pointed out. How could he get past all of them?"

"Obviously, his use of foreign criminals is involved in that somehow!" said Flora, addressing Sophie, "because if one Briton blabbed, it would be all over. Therefore, it is readily deduced, the project requires a working, labouring type of criminal who speaks little or no English. Therefore again, manual labour must be involved, and the project is taking a long time, but is almost finished. That part is elementary, my dear Watson. The reason for the King staying away from the Bank of England until it's all over is more of a puzzler. A diversion, perhaps?"

"Are you now calling yourself Miss Watson, Miss King?" asked BW.

"Gladys was pretending to be Sherlock Holmes. As a humorous flourish."

"Sherlock Holmes? Elementary? Watson…? Ha! That is so funny, and I must remember it. Sorry, don't mind me. Please continue."

"Thank you. That scenario has merit, but evidence is required before the police would investigate. Let's start with what we can. Gladys, please see Sergeant Gowers and get as much information as you can about Maxwell Handley. Does he live in the Palace or leave at night? Also, any information on the committee members will be useful — who are they, what positions do they hold, etcetera?"

"Should I tell Sergeant Gowers everything?"

"Yes, including the Bank of England business. He may laugh, but the idea is better than nothing at all. Should we be wrong, it's still worth a try. BW, please find out…"

She stopped and put a finger to her lips because there was a noise outside the room. They all froze.

"Did you see them down that way?" asked a man in the corridor outside.

"I wouldn't still be looking for them if I had," said the other.

"Where could they have gone?"

"Dunno. I think they've left already. Nigel said the chap who was with the King had been missing for a good half hour before I arrived."

"They could be having dinner. We'll try there."

"Might as well."

They heard soft footfalls receding. Sophie nodded to Ada, who was nearest to the door. She opened it quietly and peered out.

"It's two footmen," she whispered.

"Right. We'll go to our rooms to get our things."

"Then what?" asked Flora.

"Find empty bedrooms on a different floor and move in. We could also go to that other dining room, the one the minor officials use. None of the footmen go in there."

"We'll never pull it off, miss," said Ada.

"Yes, we will," insisted Sophie. "Simply because we're present, expecting to be fed, everyone will assume we have a right to the dining room. BW, as I was about to say, please find out, as best you can, what the King's movements are this evening and tomorrow."

"Miss King, I'll try now, but he'll be dressing for dinner soon. I don't think I can get to see him until about ten tomorrow. Then I'll have to leg it before eleven or the Personal Secretary will catch me."

"Right," said Sophie. "Do try, anyway. Now, there's one last thing we should keep in mind. Should anyone ask for your passes, do not surrender them under any circumstances. We may have to leave, but we won't be able to get back in without them. Gladys, you find Sergeant Gowers, and I'll look after your things. We'll meet back here as soon as possible."

"Ooh. Don't forget my book in the bedside cabinet. Thank you."

Chapter 16

A shocking discovery

Flora discovered from Sergeant Gowers that Baron Stamfordham lived outside the Palace. He also told her where Handley's room was, because he lived in. Gowers asked why she wanted to know, and she explained everything.

"Get evidence, Miss Walton. If you don't have it, I can't help. It's as simple as that. If you're right, and Handley is as bent as you claim, then that's a nasty bit of business. Treason, you know?"

"Yes. We're in a bind because they want to chuck us out."

"I wish I could help, but..." He shrugged. "You'd better disappear now, and we never had this conversation. Good luck."

BW learned from a footman standing outside the King's chambers that the Personal Secretary usually visited his majesty after dinner around eight unless there was a reception.

Sophie and Ada got all the luggage out of the rooms and found an empty suite and a single bedroom for BW on the floor below. They hid all the cases in the single room and Ada locked the door by using a picklock.

When they reassembled in the Blue Drawing Room, their first order of business was an early dinner in a different dining room. In this other, more prestigious, quite large dining room, the wood-panelled and highly conservative surroundings made it club-like — a quiet cloister with full service. The agents chose a less prominent table, and a waiter approached them to explain the limited menu. They ordered and were soon whispering because the room seemed not to permit any more noise than that.

The agents quickly and quietly discussed their recent findings and resolved to search Handley's room as soon as they had finished eating. They had come early for dinner and had presumed Handley would dine a little later in yet another room — one reserved for courtiers and a higher echelon of staff. They were just finishing their main course when Maxwell Handley and a footman entered.

"Handley's here," whispered Flora, who saw him first.

From the corner of her eye, she observed Handley scanning the room, spot their table, then point and whisper to the footman. They approached the table. She thought it suspicious he should bring a footman.

"Good evening, ladies, sir," said Handley. "Please excuse the impertinence of my interrupting your dinner."

"Think nothing of it," said Sophie. "Would you care to join us, Mr Handley?"

"Just for a moment." He turned to the footman. "Wait outside, please." The footman bowed and left. Handley then pulled up a chair.

"You have been rather hard to find." He spoke in an amused tone.

"If we had known we were the subject of a search, we might have made it impossible."

"Oh, yes? Very good. I take your point... Miss King, unfortunately I am the bearer of a rather awkward message."

"I'm sorry to hear that."

"Yes. It concerns all of you."

"You want us to leave the Palace?"

"Very perceptive. I can assure you I have nothing to do with the decision. In fact, I petitioned strenuously against it but, sadly, to no avail. The committee, who is now in control of the security arrangements for the Palace, deemed your unit's proximity to the King at all times to be surplus to requirements."

"Mr Handley, I am surprised at you."

"Oh? In what way?"

"That you would think, even for a moment, that we would leave when we have Lud's agent within our reach."

"You do? Who is it?"

"You know the standing procedure — no discussion of any operational details. But the information has already been passed on and we await an answer. Until we receive a response, we are staying put. I suggest you go back to whoever it was who sent you to inform them of our intention."

"It doesn't work like that, Miss King."

"Yes, it does. Now, please leave our table, because I am very disappointed in you."

"What you may think of me is immaterial." There was an edge in his voice. "This is the Palace, you realize. You won't get away with defying those in authority. You must not cause any trouble here."

"Have you finished? Or would you like to stay for pudding?"

He got up. "This isn't over." He turned and left. Even his back looked annoyed.

"That footman's outside," whispered Ada, "but we can leave through the kitchens."

"Right! Let's go," said Sophie.

"What about pudding?" asked BW.

"None for us because we've been very naughty," said Flora. "Come along — we're about to be naughtier still."

The agents got out, threading their way through a kitchen staff too amazed to speak or stop them, and made their way to Handley's room, which was two floors and a long corridor away.

Upon arrival, they had to wait for a man to move out of sight before Ada could unlock the door. The others tried to screen her, but they were caught by a neighbour.

"Hello, that's Handley's room?" The elderly gentleman shuffled up and stopped to query each of them with a stare.

"That's right, sir," said Flora. "He wanted something fetched, but the lock seems to be broken. We thought wiggling it might help."

"He's locked out of his room, eh? Well, if you don't get it done tonight, he'll wait a month for the odd job man to turn up. The Palace is going to wrack and ruin. Shocking really. It's all very well overhaulin' the place every other decade, but what's needed is attention to the day-to-day stuff. For example, my light switch is loose, but can I get anyone to look at it? No!" He squinted at what Ada was doing. "I say, would you know anythin' about 'lectricity?"

"I'm terribly sorry..."

"Just my luck. Well, good evenin' to you. I wish you success."

"Thank you, sir," said Flora.

Ada got the door open, and she and Sophie entered. A large, well-appointed room, it functioned as a bedroom, sitting room, and office. Wardrobe, dressing table, chests of drawers, desk — they went through everything. They dragged suitcases from under the bed, scanned correspondence and diaries, and leafed through a pile of art reference books and periodicals.

"Handley likes opera," said Sophie, while reading his diary. "He doesn't seem to be romantically attached, and he frequently receives letters from his parents and an uncle named Bertram."

"His under garments costs a lot," said Ada. "They're all finest quality silk... How much does he earn?"

"Perhaps he's paid for every office he holds. That would soon add up. His shoes are handmade and all his clothes are from Saville Row, so he spends a lot on his appearance."

"I don't think he drinks heavy," said Ada, peering into the cupboard of the nightstand. "There's only an old brandy bottle with a dribble in it."

"His possessions are all rather featureless except for the art books and magazines. There are no documents... I suppose he's a spy, so all he has here is only to confirm his cover... If it is a cover. I think he's a courtier first... What I don't understand is if he's been living here for months, where are the little things that would show his personality?"

"P'rhaps he don't have a personality. Here's something, miss." Ada had retrieved a long envelope from the wastepaper basket. "If I was being suspicious, which I am, I'd say there was money in this once upon a time. A lot of money."

"Show me."

Sophie took it by a corner and examined the crumpled envelope before putting it in her notebook. "You may be right." She glanced at the fireplace. "Hello. Who's been burning paper?"

In an otherwise clean grate lay fragments of charred paper which had been stirred with a poker.

"Two pages, I should think. Nothing's readable, though."

"So, he got a packet of money and a letter?"

"And he burnt the letter, threw the envelope away, and put the money in his bank or his pocket or…"

"Somewhere in the room," said Ada. "We've looked in the normal places."

"Yes… Now, where would he put it?"

They were studying the room when the door opened. Flora put her head in.

"Excuse me, but please get a move on. People are giving us funny looks."

"Give them funny looks back. We're on to something."

"Good." Flora shut the door.

"Miss," Ada was by a wall-mounted mirror. "I noticed it was hanging wonky." She lifted a bottom corner and peered. "Something's behind it, that's why."

"Let me help you," said Sophie.

They took it down carefully. Secured by its own drawstring to screws in the frame was a large toiletries bag. Sophie opened it. Crammed inside were a small pistol in a holster, a tightly rolled canvas bag, and a small diary. She looked at Ada.

"We know he's a spy as we are," said Sophie. "He might need these things for a mission. What do you think?"

"All I know, miss, is that he's acting like he wants us gone, and that ain't right. We wouldn't be shoving him out like what he is us. That means he's up to something. We've got a Lud agent runnin' about the Palace, so I say it's him."

"I see the situation the same way. Oh, well. Here goes."

She carefully removed the bag so as not to disturb fingerprints, then they rehung the mirror. Sophie cast an eye over the room before leaving. It was tidy and as they had found it but, soon enough, Handley was bound to notice something amiss besides the missing toiletries bag. Ada relocked the door on the way out.

"Let's have it, then," said Gowers. They were using an empty office for the meeting. "Handley came to see me wanting to know where you are. He says you have to leave because awkward questions are being asked. Says his position is in jeopardy."

"That's just the type of thing he would say," said Flora.

"We believe he works for Lud," said Sophie. "This bag contains a pistol, a sum of money, and a notebook. He never mentioned to *us* about his being in jeopardy. He only stated that the committee wants us to leave."

"That's right," said BW. "And we missed pudding because of him. He had the cheek to interrupt our dinner."

"That's very serious," said Gowers with a chortle. "As a police officer, this is how it looks to me. You and he are having an argument over jurisdiction. Professional jealousy — I've seen it often enough at the Yard, and this looks no different."

"We may have evidence," said Sophie, "and we haven't been able to contact Superintendent Penrose yet."

"That's stolen property, as far as I'm concerned. So, I can't even touch it. As an officer, I advise you to return it. Now, privately, and as a member of this network myself, I might be inclined to examine the contents, but I've already telephoned Penrose. He's on his way to sort out your dispute. So, you might want to keep that thing out of sight until he arrives. You see, should Handley find out you've got it, and he makes a complaint, I'd have to arrest you as it stands. If I didn't, he could soon get another officer involved. I'm just warning you."

"Oh," said Sophie.

"I'll go back to the other office and, should I see him again, I won't mention Penrose is coming or that we've met… You could wait in here, couldn't you?"

Gowers smiled at them, then left.

An hour passed. During that time, the agents heard doors opening and closing and there had been a considerable amount of movement at one point. Gowers now opened the door to say,

"Miss King, please come to the other office and bring the bag with you."

Sophie received a shock when she arrived. Maxwell Handley was handcuffed and sitting slumped in a chair with downcast eyes. Superintendent Penrose was seated behind a desk and Archie Drysdale was lounging by a window, looking out. Both men stood up and greeted Sophie when she entered.

"You probably wonder how we arrived at this current state of affairs," said Archie. "Handley's a bit sulky at present, so I'll tell the tale. We have been, of course, looking for a Lud agent — is that the name we're using?" Penrose nodded. "Despite our vigilance, we had no sighting of him or her. Penrose and I had a chin wag discussing the virtues such an agent needed to possess and, after exhausting our limited intelligence, mine anyway, we eventually lighted upon the gentleman seated before you. Naturally, as he was one of us, we had to conclude he was above suspicion, even though he undeniably had just the sort of access an enemy agent would need. We dismissed him as a candidate, which left us no one at all to suspect.

"Lo and behold, things became clearer without our lifting a metaphorical finger. I and others found ourselves removed from all decision-making processes with the advent of the committee formed to secure all Royal Persons. As we were then at a loose end, we asked ourselves, why is this? And we answered, because Lud's agent is at work. Who knows of our existence? Only a few and, of all those here present, Handley was the best placed to bring it off.

"After that, we triangulated the two gentlemen known to be against us on the committee with any person who was likely to have their ear and was in a position to persuade them to go against us. Surprise, surprise, Handley's name cropped up again. He is friendly with both gentlemen. I spoke to one of them and you'll never guess what he said."

"Maxwell Handley put him up to it," said Sophie.

"Exactly! To continue. There was still the possibility that we were wrong, but we could in no way alert him to the fact we were watching him, so it had to be done discreetly. Had we warned you, a mistake may have been made and we could not afford to take the risk. That was how things stood. Then we hear he is actively trying to remove you and your associates from the Palace. Sergeant Gowers then telephoned and — here we are."

"But why is he handcuffed?" asked Sophie.

"Because I don't trust him," said Penrose. "He's under arrest for treason."

"You've made a dreadful mistake," said Handley.

"Apologies if we have," said Archie.

"My cover was in jeopardy."

"That's what you claim," said Penrose, "but you haven't demonstrated how that was possible. Anyway, I just don't believe you. So, who is Lud, and where can we find him?"

"I don't know."

"I believe you have something, Miss King." Penrose beckoned her forward.

"Yes." Sophie stepped up to the desk and carefully placed the bag on it. She then extracted the envelope from her notebook. "The envelope was in a wastepaper basket and there was a two-page note burned thoroughly in the grate. We found the bag behind a mirror."

"Thank you." Penrose donned some gloves and then delicately opened the bag and slid out the contents. "This looks interesting. Do you have a license for the pistol?" He began unrolling the canvas.

"No," said Handley.

"How much is here?"

"Four hundred pounds."

"That's a lot to have hanging behind a mirror."

"It's my money. I can do what I like with it."

"Gowers. Everything here needs to be fingerprinted. Every note, the pistol, and the envelope. You can take it all away."

"Yes, sir."

"Now what's in this here little book?" He used tweezers to open it and turn the pages. "Little books are always interesting... Look at that. There's my name, age, and home address... The names of my wife and children? You've gone too far, lad... Mr Drysdale, you're in here, too... Burgoyne's Agency..." Penrose glared at Handley over the top of the notebook. "Start talking now and make it good." He continued leafing through the pages.

"It was only a book for memos and pertinent facts."

"No. I'll tell you what this bag is. It's for when you got into trouble, you could make a bolt for it. But you don't earn this kind of money. Where'd it come from?"

"I'm good at saving. As to your other question — bolt from what? I have a secure position. In time, I would be promoted. I'm just waiting for the right offer. Those were just things I didn't want the cleaner to find."

"You liar. You have my children's names in your book. Do you think I'll believe any of your excuses?"

"Your career's over," said Archie, "but you know that. You can't even save your skin now. If I were you, old boy, I would give a full and frank confession. Should we find it useful, I'm sure something could be worked out. If not, I don't really fancy your chances. Any prison you care to name is so vastly different to living at Buckingham Palace. I doubt very much you will adapt to the life of a convict, especially when it's known you are a traitor. Great care shall be taken to ensure you go to one of the least desirable of prisons and, don't worry, your cellmates will be the most interesting ones. Now, the good Superintendent here is upset with you. Everyone is upset with you. You've tried our patience to the limit. Now's your chance to redeem yourself."

"I want a lawyer," said Handley.

Archie got up, went over to the door, and opened it.

"Miss King," said Penrose, "would you be so kind as to leave the room?"

"Yes, I will."

"What are you going to do?" asked Handley.

"Get answers to questions," said Penrose.

Sophie had never seen him to be so menacing.

"No... Don't leave, Miss King."

They all waited for him to speak again. Archie closed the door and Sophie resumed her seat.

"I'll explain everything," he said quietly, then licked his lips. With his decision, Handley had become less the courtier and more the frightened man. "I don't know if you'll believe me, but I swear, this is the truth." He paused before plunging on. "I have always had an interest in art. It is something of a passion with me. To be brief, I attend many art exhibitions and am widely known as an aficionado. About a year ago, I got speaking to a man named Forbes at a Bond Street gallery. He was very knowledgeable, and we discussed the slump in art prices. He then asked me if I knew of anyone who owned a French Impressionist painting and who might be interested in selling. I did, and I gave him the names of two people whom I knew at the Palace. Imagine my shock when, within a month, one of the paintings, along with other artwork, was stolen... Might I have some water?" Handley worked his lips again.

Archie went to the carafe on the desk and poured out a glassful. Sophie watched Handley take a few short sips and noticed beads of perspiration on his forehead.

"Thank you... I thought no more of it, believing it to be a coincidence. That all changed when I found an envelope slid under the door of my room. It contained seventy pounds, and a typewritten note which simply instructed me to be at the Lyons' Tea Rooms off Leicester Square that evening."

"Was it signed?" asked Penrose.

"No. It was from Forbes, though. I went, more out of curiosity than anything else, to find out why someone should give me such a sum of money. He met me and then explained that if I provided him with the names of people who owned high-value works of arts, I would receive more commissions... We rowed... Actually, I remonstrated, while he remained calm. He then produced an unaddressed letter for me to read. It stated that I was part of a criminal gang dealing in stolen art. Forbes said he would ensure the King got a copy. Well, I could see what he was up to, and decided to go to the police. I told him as much and left the seventy pounds he had sent me on the table. Then another man approached. He appeared to be a low criminal of the flashier type. He said there were witnesses in the tea room who would testify I willingly took the money, and that this wasn't the first time I had sold information, because I was a regular at that particular Lyons'. I then noticed several people staring at me, including a waitress."

"I'll need their descriptions, particularly of the second man who spoke to you," said Penrose. "Does Forbes have a first name?"

"He never gave one. I doubt it's his real name... After that, I complied with their requests, as I seemed to have no choice. I realized the network was in jeopardy as well as my career and... I panicked." He lifted his bound hands as if beseeching Penrose.

"What was their method of communication with you?"

"By typewritten notes put under my door. The envelopes sometimes included payments. The set up was that I would glean information from people in the Palace about who owned what in the way of valuable art. Every so often, I was expected to pass along such tips, as well as tidbits as to when the owner was next going abroad or out of town — things like that."

"How did you get the information to Forbes?"

"By handwritten letters posted to an accommodation address I can give you."

"So, they were gathering more and more evidence against you, and you fell for that?"

"I was trapped. I couldn't see what else to do."

Penrose and Archie exchanged glances. Sophie was mesmerized by the unfolding story.

"Right," said Penrose. "The Lud business. What part did you play in it?"

"Give me some assurances first."

"That depends on what you tell me…"

"But I've just explained how I was trapped and blackmailed by these people."

"Or you've just explained your involvement in an art theft ring that you've only decided to abandon because you're facing a charge of treason. It's a good story, but I don't know if any of it's true. Give me the lot or I'll proceed to take you into custody."

There was a long silence in which Handley visibly wilted under the threat. He spoke in a quieter voice.

"They made me leave the note and the fake bomb at Sandringham. It was I who pinned the note to the door here."

"The composition of the letters," said Archie. "Yours or theirs?"

"Theirs. The note today was given to me in the sealed envelope that Miss King found. I was the one who handwrote the notes at Sandringham. Those are the only ones where I was involved."

"Do they know about the network?" Archie continued.

"They haven't heard it from me if they do."

"So, why were our names in your book?"

"Not sure, really… For leverage, should anything go wrong. I was desperate and had precious little with which to fight back against them… And against you, should I be suspected of anything. I didn't know you were on to me."

"So, your attempt to get us out of the Palace," said Penrose, "was only you saving your own skin?"

"That's right. With everyone being under so much scrutiny, my chances of being caught increased. You must bear in mind that they might ask me to do something far worse. If they did, I was going to make a run for it… I'm sorry… Cowardly of me, wasn't it?"

Penrose stared at him. "What are Lud's plans?"

"I don't know. I've racked my brains, but I can't come up with anything."

"Forbes — is he Lud?"

"He could be, but I think not."

"What are these cryptic notes in the back of your book? They start around the middle."

"Information I've provided to Forbes about art. I can provide that information in full."

"Excuse us," said Archie. He smiled at Sophie, signalling they should leave.

Outside in the corridor, Sophie said,

"That was awful. How could he?"

"An unfortunate scene, but these things happen. In a way, I'm relieved that it's no worse than it is."

"What will happen now?"

"That depends on several things. Penrose is not in a good mood, as you might have noticed. However, we have a break in the case. It wouldn't do for us to scare our bird just now, so it's my guess that Handley will return to work as usual. It's just possible there are fingerprints on those banknotes. What is certain is that another Lud agent is at work in the Palace. Whoever delivers messages to Handley is probably only a low-level messenger, but it would be nice to follow such a one to see where he goes."

"Would you like us to do that?" asked Sophie in a bright tone.

Archie laughed. "Um, your presence in the Palace is rather awkward at the moment. Handley stirred up the committee, and they decided you're out. We will have to abide by that decision and keep the committee from knowing that Handley is one of Lud's agents. Consequently, Handley will be closely controlled from now on, but it must appear to Lud that Handley has not been discovered."

"Oh, dear. We're to go home, I take it?"

"Yes, Soap, I'm afraid you must. Be on standby for the next two days but, after that, your work will be finished."

"Do we get paid for being on standby?"

"No, not as a rule."

"No is not the right answer. Come on, Archie. Find us some work. You can't be casting us off when things are just getting interesting."

"I can't manufacture work out of thin air."

"Do try. We could do anything the other agents are doing. And, although I'm loath to sound our own trumpet, I think we've done rather well so far."

"I don't dispute that, but you aren't trained in the type of work likely to be required over the coming days. We have field agents for that."

"What is it they do that we can't?"

"A lot, but we shan't discuss the matter."

"Oh, very well. The others will be greatly disappointed."

"I fully understand. Perhaps I can get your pay extended for the next two days, but I can't promise anything. Finances are beyond my control."

They were about to part when a page, entering the corridor, saw them and approached.

"Excuse me, my lady," said the page to Sophie. "Do you know where I can find BW?"

"Yes. I supervise his work, so you can give me the message."

"His majesty wants BW to look after Charlotte for an hour. His majesty has been invited to attend a meeting, and the parrot is acting up."

"Thank you. Tell his majesty he is on his way and will be there shortly."

"My lady." The page bowed.

"I presume BW is Broadbent-Wicks," said Archie, both amused and puzzled. "How has he become both indispensable to and familiar with the King in such a short time?"

"He has an inexplicable knack for such things. I don't know how else to put it. Surely, he can't leave when the King is calling for him?"

"I will mention this, and it may tip the balances in your favour. For now, I bid you farewell, and wish you a pleasant evening. I, however, must now help defuse a very uninteresting and completely avoidable diplomatic row that's brewing. But there, people are so willful sometimes."

Sophie returned to the office where she sent BW on his errand and explained to Flora and Ada what had happened.

Chapter 17

A different point of view

There were no taxis waiting outside Buckingham Palace and, as the evening was pleasant, Sophie, Ada, and Flora walked along the Mall in the hopes of hailing one. Broadbent-Wicks was still in the Palace and was now, in fact, Warden of the Royal Parrot, although no one had uttered the title. King George had insisted that BW remain and had overruled his slightly irritated private secretary.

The three women walked along the pavement carrying their suitcases while keeping a watch for a passing empty taxi. As is usual, all the taxis were engaged, so they talked instead, becoming so engrossed that they failed to notice the four empty taxis that did pass by.

"I'm just glad that BW has been kept on," said Flora.

"I thought we'd get at least another week," said Ada. "All that lovely money... gone! Well, as they say, don't count your chickens before they're hatched."

"Counting chickens before hatching is the best part," said Flora. "That's when one can imagine all the lovely things one would have done had it come off... I think I'm going to cry."

"Archie may find us work," said Sophie. "The money's one thing, but I don't like being shut out of the case and not knowing. They won't tell us anything from now on... Good grief. I forgot to talk to Archie about that Bank of England business. I was so appalled by Handley's behaviour it completely slipped my mind. I'm sure Superintendent Penrose will have heard it from Sergeant Gowers."

"You can tell Archie tomorrow," said Flora. "Isn't it odd? Handley's behaved rottenly, and yet he'll be walking about as though nothing had happened. Will he be charged with *anything*?"

"Who can say? I mean, he was in an awkward spot, but he could have put it right at any time. So, why didn't he? He's not stupid."

"Because he wanted the money," said Ada. "We'd all refuse it, as most would, but not him."

"Penrose must know that."

"I'm sure he does, miss. So, he won't trust him proper. I mean, how can you? I suppose he's a double agent. Is that right, miss?"

"Yes."

"He's a triple agent, isn't he?" queried Flora. "No, a quadruple agent."

"No, a double agent. All spies would say he was a double agent."

"Quadruple. He works for himself, he works for the King, he works for the network, and he works for Lud. That's four."

"You're being too liberal with the term. His working for the King is his cover while working as an agent. Working for himself doesn't count."

"I concede the King and cover part, but he's working for himself, and that constitutes an agency in my book — network, Lud, and self. He's a triple agent."

"No one else will see it that way… but you have a point."

"Handley didn't mention nothing about the Bank of England, did he?" said Ada. "I reckon he'll keep it quiet 'cause he stands to make a lot of money."

"Are you suggesting he knows what Lud is doing?"

"Ah, yes, I am, miss. He's a bloke not to be trusted. He was on about visiting the Bank to the King, and that's something that's got to be looked into."

"Well, when I speak to Archie, I will definitely mention it."

"My left arm has definitely got longer," said Flora, as she changed hands to carry her suitcase.

Sophie turned and saw an empty taxi whizz past.

"Oh, we've missed that one... Why can one never find a cab?"

"If we stop," said Flora, "the cabbies will know we want a taxi."

They stopped and stood in a row at the kerb. Every passing cab was now full.

"We should visit the Bank of England," said Flora.

"With a view to breaking in?" Sophie laughed. "Very well. Do you want to come, Ada?"

"Yes, miss. I'd like to get rid of my suitcase, though. It's got heavier, that it has."

"Then why don't we do this? We'll go to Auntie's house and drop our things off there. I'll ask her to put you up for the night, and she'll be happy to say yes, because she'll be dying to know what we've been doing."

"That's all right by me, thank you, miss."

"Me, too, thanks," said Flora.

A sign confirming the rightness of their plan came in the shape of an empty cab pulling up in front of them without them signalling.

"Where to, ladies?"

"White Lyon Yard, please."

"Streuth, ain't that funny? I jus' dropped orf a fare from over that way. Hop in then, lovies, an' I'll get the cases."

Auntie Bessie was perfectly agreeable to Sophie's suggestions, adding that there would be a supper later. The agents loved her idea.

From White Lyon Yard south to the Bank of England was only a mile, and at half-past six the financial district of the City was truly winding down for the day. The pell-mell stampede of the rush hour had passed, with most of the workers having reached home, or well on their way there, by tram, bus, underground, train, bicycle, car or foot. The area still bustled, however, and the traffic was heavy in the six streets that met by the Bank.

Behind the high perimeter wall, the Bank of England is more like a Greek temple complex than a banking institution housed in the many buildings. Each little sector is devoted to a specific financial function, while they never admit the public to a majority of the buildings. Sir John Soane designed the Bank of England, but it was for him a long labour of love beginning in 1788 and which could only be said to have been finished in 1830. The Bank as a whole is of such reassuring and solid splendour that, just by looking at the place, one is readily convinced that here is an institution that can never fail. Indeed, the Bank of England is a byword amongst Britons as the epitome of safety and security.

A detachment of the King's Guard is always stationed within the wall, and there are officials stationed at the various gates and the front entrance on Threadneedle Street. With knowledge of these things, the agents came at the Bank from the eastern side and stopped at the corner of Lothbury and St. Bartholomew's Lane.

"I don't see how it's possible, miss," said Ada.

"Supposing they're only going to steal banknotes?" asked Flora. "They're a lot lighter and easier to deal with than gold... Sophie?"

"Sorry, I was just thinking of ladders and how to climb over the wall. You said banknotes... that's possible. I wonder where they keep them — and everything else, for that matter. It's a pity we don't have a map."

"Asking a porter won't help," said Ada. "Some of them blokes can be quite chatty, but they won't tell us that much."

"I suppose not. Our idea is that Lud is going to rob the Bank of England. We have no chance of working out how he proposes to accomplish such a feat until we have clues. All I can think is that Lud would want to know what is going on in and around the Bank right up until the robbery takes place.

Knowing how he operates, it is reasonable to assume he has agents inside. There could be a Handley equivalent working in the Bank. There may also be others, actual robbers, who are waiting for the right moment to spring into action. All this is hypothetical but, if we extend the theory, I think it reasonable to assume that he may have men watching on the outside."

"Watching for what?" asked Flora.

"I don't know… things."

"That's too vague. Do you mean like the soldiers coming and going? Shipments? Particular people arriving or leaving?"

"Yes, that's the sort of thing I meant. What I'm driving at is that if there's going to be a big robbery, then there must be a lot of criminals involved. Therefore, it follows, Lud would want to know what everyone is doing at any given moment, because he is not likely to trust them unreservedly. Murdering foreign criminals is a vile example of his distrust."

"It would be nice to walk along together," said Flora, "but if we are going to be proper spies, I suppose we go alone."

"Yes… Why don't we do this? We'll do a circuit of the Bank on the pavement opposite. Ada, you'll go first to identify anyone suspicious. Flora, you'll follow twenty yards behind or at least close enough to see a signal from Ada. Then you will slow or stop to keep that person under surveillance. I will then move up to take over Flora's position. So, Ada, please don't walk too fast or we'll make a muck of it. Should there be a second suspicious character, then it will be my turn to follow."

"And if there's a third, I take care of him?"

"Yes."

"For cover, I can search my handbag for change," said Flora. "That's good for at least ten minutes."

"I'll gaze at the architecture," said Sophie.

"If there's a shop, I'll have a look in the window," said Ada.

"You know, it's not fair really," said Flora. "Men can just read a newspaper or smoke, and get away with such lounging about in the street. We can't do either of those things."

"We'll manage somehow. Should you have to follow anyone out of the area, be circumspect."

"Er, miss?"

"Yes, of course. Circumspect means to be careful and prudent — not taking unnecessary risks."

"Thank you, miss. I thought it must be something like that."

In a staggered line on the opposite side of the road, they walked along Bartholomew Lane on the east side of the Bank — its least busy side. The massive, yet decorative, wall was so high that nothing of the buildings within was visible. Here, then, was the greatest bastion of Britain's wealth, and a classical quadrilateral citadel within the City within the county which is London. It is a proud, indomitable place, and dominates its surroundings where all the architecture is similar in execution or of the best design from its era. This, then, was the financial heart of the Empire.

While walking past the prosperous office buildings, Ada made a subtle sign. She carried her handbag in her left hand and raised her little finger to point left. She walked on. Flora stopped and positioned herself in such a way that the man Ada had identified could not easily see her without turning. He was a small man wearing a flat cap and leant against a pillar to stare at the finely columned wall opposite.

Sophie drew level, trying to act as naturally as possible, which suddenly became the hardest thing in the world for her to do. She got past him without tripping, despite her feeling as though her shoes had suddenly grown three sizes. *Every single time,* she told herself, *something like this happens, I always feel stupid and awkward.* Fortunately, when they had progressed to where they were opposite the Bank's main entrance on Threadneedle, Ada gave a second signal and Sophie had shaken off her malaise sufficiently to recognize it. She stopped, pretending to admire the tops of the columns.

As she turned, looking for an unobtrusive place to stand, she glimpsed the young man Ada had identified who was standing by a doorway with a bicycle. She had taken just two steps when a florid-faced businessman with whiskers came out of the entrance to thrust a large envelope into the young man's hand. Then he bid him, "As fast as you can." The young man hurried off on his bicycle. It was an ordinary transaction, after all. As she waited to cross the busy road, Flora caught up.

"What happened?" asked Flora.

"It was a waiting messenger with a bicycle."

"Mine was waiting for his sweetheart to finish work. As soon as she came out, they linked arms and went off chattering gaily."

"How nice," said Sophie.

The policeman stopped the traffic, which allowed them to cross. Traffic backed up in the intersection, and they had to weave around a packed bus to reach the other pavement. After crossing two more roads, they found Ada waiting on Lothbury. They told her what had happened, and she replied she had seen no more potential watchers.

"Would Lud have blokes in the street round here?" said Ada. "He's got to have money, so wouldn't he rent an office?"

"Definitely," said Sophie. They all looked up at the surrounding buildings. "Why would he, though? My idea was that he was timing the movements of guards or watching the front entrance to keep his men under surveillance... I don't think my idea is very good after all. It is impossible for us to enter all the offices surrounding the Bank, and the police would need more proof to undertake such a search. They won't act on what *we* have to say, even on the off-chance we're right."

"The idea *was* a little fluffy," said Flora, "but it's the best we have. Anyway, I think the premise is a good one." She looked at Ada.

"I know 'premise'," she said.

"If I were Lud," said Flora, "and my minions were working on robbing the Bank of England, I'd want to know when they so much as sneezed."

"So would I, but they're invisible to us because they're inside," said Sophie.

"Even so, Lud must know if they're working or not... Oh, I don't know."

"How about this?" said Ada. "Let's try one of the taller buildings. We'll see over the outside wall of the Bank and, if nothing else, it'll be an interesting view."

"There was an entrance to shared offices near the corner," said Sophie. "We'll try there."

They retraced their steps and passed through an entrance adorned with brass plates and small signs declaring the names and businesses of the occupants of the building. While the exterior had seemed quite magnificent, the irregular-shaped interior was clean but worn out with cracked plaster. It needed attention. The stairs and floors wanted polishing and light came only from dim electric bulbs or through grimy windows.

"We're not high enough," said Flora after glancing at the Bank's wall through the first available window.

They climbed another flight and encountered a man locking his office door for the night. He raised his hat and said, "Excuse me," to each agent as he passed.

The best view was from the top floor. Here, the top window was set in a decorative cupola, with a decaying plaster ceiling hiding the beams above. A fine dust lay on the floor.

"Look at all them footprints, miss," said Ada.

They stopped well short of the window to examine the wooden floor.

"Three men, I think," said Sophie. "One waited a while by the window and shuffled about two or three times, while a second walked on tiptoe to the window and back and was here only once. A third came and went, but stayed briefly."

"Today, I should imagine," said Flora. "There's orange peel stacked neatly in the corner of the window containing a stubbed-out cigarette end."

"So it is, an' all," said Ada. "I find that sort of behaviour disgusting."

A nearby door opened and closed with a bang in a corridor. They had heard a key turn in a lock. Someone burdened and breathing hard was now approaching. A cleaning woman emerged from the gloom. She shrieked, dropping her bucket, dustpan, and broom.

"You frightened the bleedin' life out of me, standin' there so quiet." She picked up her things.

"I'm sorry about that," said Sophie. "We wondered who was coming, and *you* gave *us* a bit of a start."

"Oh... Don't you go leaving no rubbish lying about, neither. We've got bins for that, you know. Why are you 'ere, anyway?"

"We wanted to look into the Bank," said Ada. "We're thinkin' of turnin' it over."

The cleaner now shrieked with laughter. "Come orf it! No one will ever do that. What you 'ere for, then?"

"Just for the view," said Sophie. "May I ask how often the apple cores are left?"

"I've got a lot of work to do."

"I'll pay you."

"Coo... How much?"

"Half-a-crown now, and another afterwards on the condition you answer all our questions."

"All right."

She put down her equipment and approached with her hand out while Sophie found the coin. When it was safely tucked in her pocket, the cleaner said,

"It's not every day, but around three days a week, some geezer is standin' by that winder eatin' a piece o' fruit. Apples, pears, or the odd banana — the little git leaves the core or the peel right in that... Oranges!" She pointed at the peel in the corner of the windowsill. "The little toe rag's now eatin' oranges! An' he's stuck a fag end in it!? What's the world comin' to, eh?"

"It's goin' down the plug'ole," said Ada.

"Too bleedin' right, it is... Where was I? Yes, three days a week, muggins here cleans up after the little whatsit. Don't know who it is... You're not police, are you?"

"No," said Sophie.

"That's all right, then. I can't understand why you're interested, but that's none of me business."

"Where's the dust coming from?" asked Flora.

"Ceiling. Every day, the traffic shakes plaster dust loose. Place is fallin' down an' the stingy basket what owns it won't do nothin'. All he needs is get the plasterer in, but not 'im, oh, no. He won't spend a farthing on account of tryin' to sell the place. The Bank ain't interested, though — he's asked them. Oh, yes. I bet he crawled on his 'ands and knees when he went to see 'em, 'cause that's the type he is — a bootlicker and a tightwad."

"Is that a day's worth of plaster dust?" asked Sophie.

"No, half a week's worth. I do it once a week. Nobody uses this part much, so what's the point of my cleanin' it daily, I ask you? If he can't be bothered, neither can I."

"Why would the Bank of England buy this building?"

"Really, that information's special, 'cause no one's s'posed to know abaht it."

"How do you come to know of it?"

"I keep me mouth shut an' me ears open, and that's all I'm sayin'."

"Our bargain was five shillings."

"That's true, but I didn't know you was interested in the special information. I thought you was interested in the apple cores and nothin' else."

"We might not be interested."

"That's for you to decide, not me — after you pay me."

"We'll come back to that in a moment," said Sophie. "I take it you haven't actually *seen* anyone at the window, but do you get the impression that they belong to any of these offices?"

"No. They've come in from outside, like you, 'cause he traipses the bleedin' dust 'alfway down the stairs, thank you very much... What do you mean 'they.' There's more than one of 'em?"

"You're wearing boots," said Sophie, "and you've left footprints, I believe."

"I walk on tiptoe when I pick up the rubbish."

"Ah! Then, discounting your prints, there are two other sets. The first is probably here daily, and the second only came once. Judging by your reaction, this is the first time a cigarette end has been left."

"An' the last, I 'ope. I'll tell the owner abaht this."

"No, please don't."

"You sure you're not police?"

"The police are not your enemy. If I were you, I wouldn't interfere with the men who stand at this window. They are up to no good and probably dangerous."

"I don't like this."

"None of us likes it. Now, this is what you're going to do. I'll give you a ten-shilling note, and it will be as if we were never here. You provide the information and then we leave. Under no circumstances will you tell the owner anything. Understood?"

"Yes, but..."

Sophie put up a hand. "In a week's time, I shall return to give you another ten shillings for simply keeping your mouth shut and your ears open."

"Ten shillings now, ten shillings later, an' I don't do nothin'?"

Sophie nodded and took out a note and gave it to her.

"Right, then. You say there are two blokes lookin' out the winder and one of 'em's reg'lar. The only reason they'd do that is 'cause the Bank is goin' to pull down all the buildings and put up new."

"They're doing what!? Are you absolutely sure?" asked Sophie.

"Oh, yes. He talks to his wife he does, an' she's stingier than he is. I listened at their office door one night and I'm not ashamed to admit it, 'cause I don't trust neither of 'em. They was talking about architects and surveyors for the new Bank, an' I knew it was true when I saw the surveyors in the street, 'cause they had those stick things and tripod things. They was goin' round outside the Bank and writing things down."

"When was this?" asked Sophie.

"October last year."

"Nothing of this has appeared in the newspapers," said Flora.

"I know. Nobody knows. The Bank reckons there'll be an outcry when everyone finds out, but don't ask me why, 'cause he never said. They're keeping the wall, though, and that's abaht it. It'll take years, an' they're gonna do it bit by bit, not all at once, like. That's what he said. How he found out in the first place, I don't know, but he come back after the meetin' with some directors knowin' more than when he went in — oh, yes. That was when I listened. They told him they'd keep his offer in mind but couldn't commit at present. So, he's still hopeful, but I reckon they'd brushed him off. His wife said as much and called him some names. She said they should have bought his silence by buying this building and he missed his chance. He told her to shut up, an' that's all I 'eard."

"Thank you," said Sophie.

"I can see some scaffolding," said Flora, craning her neck to look through the window.

"Would you sweep up the dust, please?" asked Sophie. "We don't want to mess up your floors."

"Yes."

"And leave the orange peel. We'll take that with us."

"Please yourself," said the cleaner.

After she had gone, the agents crowded around the window. Within the complex, they could see the top of a narrow scaffold tower that had been erected against the side of a building.

"This scene never varies except for whenever the raising of that scaffold occurred." Sophie paused for a moment. "Yet we have a man standing here watching most days of the week... What is he looking for?"

"What are *they* looking for?" said Flora. "Maybe the first fellow brought in the second fellow because he could now see the scaffold."

"Then the scaffold means something, but what?"

"If the King was going to be here this week," said Ada, "but his visit got put off 'til next week, then that scaffold might have something to do with that."

"A ground-breaking ceremony?" suggested Flora.

"Can't be," said Sophie. "There's no public fanfare. Pathé News cameras would be present, and we'd all know that the Bank of England was going to be rebuilt... Sounds like quite an overhaul... Ah! They might be moving the gold first!"

"That's a possibility," said Flora. "Where is it stored now?"

"We must find out." Sophie took an envelope from her handbag. "We'll return to White Lyon Yard, and I'll telephone Archie at his flat... What a nuisance. He won't be home. Superintendent Penrose, then." She carefully picked up the peel and the cigarette end as a whole and slid it into the envelope, which she then folded over to secure the contents. "Let's be off."

"What do we tell Lady Shelling?" asked Ada.

"Oh, everything. She'll enjoy all of this."

Chapter 18

Reasoning by the Ton

Supper at White Lyon Yard for the agents should have been a pleasant affair in pretty surroundings with good food over which eager, interesting ideas flowed freely. Instead, they had to listen to Lady Shelling shouting about what she would like said and done to the directors of the Bank of England. She was inventive, highly uncomplimentary, and attempted to reclassify them as a species into several phyla until she settled upon one that she found most suitable for her purpose.

"Those maggots should be kept in a deep, damp, mouldering pit, and never see the light of day again. How dare they!? How dare they tear down the Bank of England...? Because they are idiot maggots, that's why."

Aunt Bessie had, many years ago, accompanied her husband, Lord Shelling, to a quite delightful Bank luncheon at the invitation of several directors whom Shelling knew personally. Those directors were intelligent, gifted, graceful, and honourable, but they had all died or retired. By contrast, the current raft of sub-human directors was going to destroy the architectural gems of buildings and pull down her memories, and it was this that had set her off so explosively.

"Auntie," asked Sophie, believing the worst of the storm had passed, "where do they keep the gold?"

"What!?" She glowered at Sophie. "In a vault... That's a good place for *them*, too."

"Where is the vault, Auntie?"

"In the middle, off the Bullion Court... Do you know the bars look like ordinary bricks? They're much heavier, of course, and I recall being disappointed when seeing them. How they keep them doesn't help, and they're quite scruffy and dull. The bars are stacked on small carts... I was told there is half a ton and eighty thousand pounds to a cart. Well, I found that most surprisin'. The cart looked more valuable than the gold... I could do with a sherry after all this dreadful upset. We all could. Flora, be so kind as to ring for Hawkins."

"We don't see a way of anyone getting the gold out," said Sophie. "We wondered if they were after cash or bonds instead."

"The bonds and high denomination banknotes are traceable," said Aunt Bessie. "If you are correct about the Bank of England being the target, then such a sophisticated gang would only go for the gold. They can melt it down and sell it anywhere — not in any ordinary sense, but through international connections."

"Yes, they could."

Hawkins came in and Aunt Bessie gave him the nod to serve the sherry.

"They won't take all of it," said Aunt Bessie, "but enough to satisfy themselves, naturally. No matter how much they take, London's reputation as a safe, financial haven will be irretrievably wrecked. Hear that, Hawkins? Some bounder is after the gold in the Bank of England. What do you say?"

"I don't see how that is feasible, my Lady."

"Neither do we. If you think of something, pop back in and tell us."

"Yes, my Lady." He left soon after.

"Perhaps ruining London's reputation is Lud's real goal," said Flora

"Who can say? The police need to catch the fella to find out and, from what you say, they haven't got very far."

"Nor are they likely to," said Sophie. "I called Superintendent Penrose, but he had gone home, and Archie is on the missing list because a diplomatic row is developing."

"Only one? When I was a gel, we had at least three a month. Now that the press reports on everything so indiscriminately, our politicians are made cautious, which is the reason we'll lose our empire. But we shall not lose our gold, too. Nor the Bank of England! On that score, I shall start campaigning for their heads tomorrow."

"You can't, Auntie!"

"What do you mean, 'can't'? I shall!"

"No. You may write your letters and prepare your campaign, but you can only start when Lud has been defeated."

"Then you had better get on with it, my gel! What do you intend doing?"

"We're certain we only have a few days before they raid the Bank. So, first thing tomorrow, I'll speak to Archie and Superintendent Penrose. I left urgent messages, but without any details. Then, if they can't or won't do anything, the three of us shall go back to the office building next to the Bank. Should the man who watches and eats fruit turn up, we'll keep him under observation and follow him; if not, we have lost a day and are no further ahead."

"What if you lose him or he sees you?"

"We're sunk, but what else can we do? We're rather short on ideas or leads."

"I can see why," said Aunt Bessie. "Something you need to grasp is that the Bank of England is truly a fortress. The walls are six feet thick in places and it was built in a time when rioters might want to storm the Bank. The place is very defensible, as I saw for myself. Lud is certainly not coming over the wall, which only leaves subterfuge or a tunnel as the means of getting the gold out."

"Succinctly put, Auntie. I keep getting bogged down in details."

"Sidney knows many financiers," said Flora. "May I use your telephone, Lady Shelling?"

"Only if you call me Bessie from now on. I've known you for a dozen years or more, so you're old enough and, as you will be marrying a peer, you must acquire the easier habit in society."

"He and I are still a little way off from that," said Flora, who got up.

"If Laneford doesn't marry such a beautiful woman as you, he wants his head examined. He doesn't need a dowry, so don't worry. I enquired about him."

"Gosh," said Flora, in a rare state of confusion, and then bolted from the room into the safety of the hallway.

Aunt Bessie turned to Ada. "Are you getting married?"

"No, my Lady."

"Hm. You may also call me Bessie, but only if you feel comfortable doing so. I can appreciate the power of a lifetime's habit. Sophie insists on calling me Auntie as if she were still nine years old. Here we are, discussin' matters of national importance, and she calls me Auntie."

"I'm not changing, no matter what happens," said Sophie.

Aunt Bessie laughed, then asked, "Subterfuge or tunnel?"

"Tunnel," said Ada.

"I agree," said Sophie. "Subterfuge hardly allows for the foreign workingmen being brought so stealthily into the country."

Flora put her head around the door. "Would you mind if Sidney came over? He's very interested."

"By all means," said Aunt Bessie. "Does he want feeding?"

"No, he's had his dinner, thank you." She shut the door.

Lady Shelling resumed the conversation. "Tunnels, you said. From any point along the wall to the vault must be almost a hundred yards. Add the same distance from the wall to the starting point to disguise the fact they're tunnelling, and there you are."

Flora returned and took her seat. "He'll be here in fifteen minutes. This sounds more like it. They could be digging from the basement of a nearby building into the bank vault."

"Yes, that's good," said Sophie. "The police can check that by getting warrants or asking politely if they can search. What they might also investigate are any holes being dug near the scaffolding. Also, we should consider they might be tunnelling out of the Bank of England instead of in."

"That's a possibility," said Aunt Bessie. "Would any of you care for further refreshment?"

"Such as?" asked Sophie.

"I understand there is a chocolate cake for tomorrow. As it is nearly tomorrow, we can have it now with some tea."

"Ooh, lovely," said Sophie. "You must try some," she said to Ada and Flora, "Cook's cakes are exquisite."

As Ada rang the bell for Hawkins, she wondered if life for an East End girl from Poplar could ever be better.

"I hate to bring it up," said Ada as she sat down, "but there were some underground public lavatories in the middle of Lothbury. Those would be nearer than the basements."

"That's something to check on," said Sophie.

This scandalized Aunt Bessie. "Are you telling me you intend entering public conveniences?"

"Yes. We have no choice."

"You must never tell anyone."

"We'll try our utmost not to."

"It is simply dreadful that you should be forced into such extremity. However, as distasteful as this subject is, I foresee a difficulty. I'm sure you are aware that such facilities are divided into two sections. One section is naturally barred to you, and it is undoubtedly from that unmentionable place that a tunnel would be dug."

"We'll do what we can while keeping to our own side."

Aunt Bessie leaned forward towards Flora. "I strongly urge you not to mention this to Lord Laneford when he arrives. Gentlemen are so easily put off by low conversation."

Lord Laneford arrived promptly. He was formally introduced to Lady Shelling, whom he had briefly met once before, and he then informally, affectionately, and rather surprisingly for a gentleman of such conservative appearance, kissed Flora warmly on the cheek. Sophie and Ada exchanged knowing glances. Auntie Bessie had not seen the kiss.

He was soon sitting in the drawing room, sherry in hand, being regaled at length with the theory. He sat quietly, listening. When the Bank of England was mentioned, mild surprise flickered on his features for a moment, but he was otherwise attentive, sipping his drink. Flora watched him, because she loved him and, when he noticed, he returned her glance with a brief smile.

Eventually, the agents and Aunt Bessie ran out of things to say.

"First, I must just say this. Lady Shelling, your sherry is excellent. A Palo Cortado, is it?"

"Yes, it is." She smiled, gratified that he showed his appreciation.

"To the main point of the scheme. I initially felt the extraction of the bullion from the vault to be a virtually impossible undertaking. However, as I listened, you overcame several of my principal objections. The foreigners coming to grisly ends and the fabulous reward itself, should the plan be successful, ensure the venture's secrecy and warrant the expense it would incur. Again, the value of the objective means they can pay a large gang beyond its usual expectation. So, to dig a tunnel and have it remain a secret is certainly feasible under such conditions. The only actual impediment is my disbelief. You will think, why does Laneford disbelieve? My answer is because it is much more convenient than believing."

"Sidney," said Flora.

"I am not about to air *my* view, but explain what it is you are up against. To get the police involved is to get the Bank involved, and they will simply not believe you because you have no proof, except for some orange peel. Therefore, they will dismiss the idea. Should the most unlikely event occur that they *do* take you seriously, and believe what you say, the police will knock on all the doors round about and everyone would soon know why they are searching, including the press. The Bank does not want to appear in the press except on its own terms. Yes, they would be happy, relieved, and justified should the police actually find a tunnel. If they did not, the Bank would have to suffer the ignominious loss of prestige and reputation in the newspapers. The directors are cautious men. Despite that, they move millions around every day without a care. But a barracking headline in a newspaper would result in resignations or even some suicides, and that, I assure you, is no joke."

"What can we do then?" asked Sophie. "We're relying on the police getting involved at some point."

"Quite, but let us get down to practicalities, shall we? Please excuse me — I don't mean to be rude — but I believe I'm right in stating, Lady Shelling, that you are not in the network. So, I wonder how it is possible that you're holding a network meeting in your drawing room."

"Because I wheedled it out of my niece that she is a spy. Naturally, when she finally admitted it, I insisted upon helping her. That was some time ago. Lord Laneford, we barely know each other but, if you care to enquire, you will discover I am a person who keeps her word. I solemnly gave my word to Sophie that anything connected with her work would never be repeated by me. She trusts me sufficiently to confide in me. However, she never tells me everything, which is to her credit as far as you're concerned, but I find the habit most irritatin'."

Lord Laneford, who had listened attentively, now laughed. "Thank you for your candour, Lady Shelling."

"My friends call me Bessie."

"Well, Bessie, I sincerely hope to prove myself worthy of being considered your friend. My friends call me Sidney. May I proceed?"

"Yes, Sidney."

"Thank you. I shall now clear the other obstructions out of the way. In my position, I can only do so much because my authority limits me. I cannot send network agents to help, because they are all too busy as it is in protecting the Royal Family and others now have authority over them. You may not be aware of this, but we must often borrow agents from other departments and, in doing so, have to provide valid reasons to those who supervise them. Even if they agreed, which they won't at this present stage, those other departments would only replicate what the police would do and with the same result.

"Now, I have said I choose to disbelieve and that I cannot help, but this was only to set out the limitations imposed upon us. What you have discovered is worthy of thorough investigation, and I shall inform Drysdale and Penrose of my assessment and get their input. This is a Home Office matter, so you will work for and report to me. To facilitate that, my man Philpott will join you. I know he enjoyed working with you at Dredemere Castle, so I'm sure he will welcome this additional opportunity."

"Oh, that will be nice," said Sophie. "How is he keeping?"

"He's very well, I believe. I hope so, because I'm about to tell him he's going to be up all night. You ladies shall also be busy. I'm assuming, Bessie, you usually take no active part in operations?"

"No, I do not. I only undertake odd little bits of research and provide advice. Although I had to deal with some Russians once, as you might recall."

"And I'm sure your contribution is much appreciated." He then turned to Sophie. "Are you Miss King or Miss Burgoyne at present?"

"King, as we're on a mission — or two, so it seems."

"It does, rather. If it isn't too much of an inconvenience for you, we will go to the Bank of England tomorrow afternoon. I'm acquainted with a bank official who might be unofficially open to hearing the theory and will hopefully provide some insight into King George's visit. If we can, we shall investigate that scaffolding and see what they're up to. Would you be free to accompany me?"

"Oh, absolutely."

"Excellent. Let us now schedule the activities. Bessie, I wonder if I might trouble you for some paper. I have a pen."

They talked while night fell outside. By midnight, Lord Laneford had politely organized everyone — even Aunt

Bessie. Her task for tomorrow morning was to go to meet the Lord Mayor of the City of London, whom she knew personally, to find out if he was aware that the Bank of England intended to rebuild.

The immediate operation in the Bank's vicinity involved six people and three cars: Philpott and Sophie would travel in Rabbit, her Austin Twenty, Ada and Marsden, a footman, would go in Lady Shelling's ancient limousine, while Flora accompanied Laneford in his vehicle. The primary object was to survey the neighbouring streets to identify building sites, roadworks, derelict buildings, or anywhere there was a hole in the ground or a likely-looking entrance to a possible tunnel. Concerning the latter, Lord Laneford was also going to tackle the London Underground and the City of London's works department in the morning.

They soon set off for their assigned sectors. Marsden cheerfully joined the group because Lady Shelling, as communicated through Hawkins the butler, was going to put something extra in Marsden's next pay packet. He was also cheerful because Ada was pleasant company. What he really wanted, though, was to accompany Sophie, because he had for a long time believed her to be wonderful. Even though she occasionally did odd things and a lot of unnecessary running about, she was, to his mind, pretty much a paragon of everything good that could be named. As a realist, and as she seemed unobtainable, he sometimes consoled himself with the thought that no one could marry a woman like that. He was a bit fickle, though, because he also very much liked Mary, the housemaid. He drove around his sector, while Ada recorded items of interest. Often, they stopped to get out to examine narrow alleys and small courtyards into which the car would not fit. All the while, they were on the lookout for lookouts — suspicious characters who might be guarding the tunnel, if there were one. Marsden loudly declared it was all codswallop, he believing the Bank impregnable. Ada diplomatically kept quiet.

Sandy-haired, thirty-five-year-old Laneford was not fickle. He was besotted, yet still functional. Married before, his wife had died of influenza after only a month of marriage. His feelings for Flora were first kindled when he learned that her fiancé — Sophie's brother, Peter — had been killed during the last week of the war. That personal revelation had broken down his resolve not to remarry and spurred him to win, if it were possible, her heart and hand. A little later, they had started going about together. Dark, beautiful, fashionable Flora the actress actually enjoyed his company, which, to this very moment while driving through the empty streets, was an enigma to him. How could she be interested in such a dull chap as himself? One acquaintance had cautioned Laneford that she was probably after his title and money, but she was not like that, he had told himself. That acquaintance he quickly placed in the oaf class of person, vowing to cut him in future.

Laneford, however, did not understand how it was that Flora saw him. To her, he was kind, patient, tolerant, wise, and with an underlying streak of ever-present willingness to see the humour in things. In his way, Sidney was for her the perfect audience as well as a reliable certainty in an ever-changing world. She could be herself around him and he never minded. They quarrelled, sometimes, but it was only ever as a swiftly passing cloud on the otherwise perfect summer's day of their... friendship? When would he pop the question? If it was any other matter, she would tell him to get on with it, and he would.

"Sidney? Aren't we getting too far away from the bank?"

"Well, perhaps. But don't forget, dear, these chaps may have been tunnelling for some weeks or months. There's no telling how far they've dug, should that be the case."

"Don't say that... They couldn't possibly dig for a mile, could they?"

"I doubt it, but it is possible."

They turned a corner.

"Where are we going now?"

"Oh, we're just driving about looking for criminals."

"You're heading somewhere, aren't you?"

"Am I?"

He turned the car on to a small street.

"Lilypot Lane?" Flora smiled. "How charming. Come on, do tell. Why are we here?"

He brought the car to a standstill without answering. He waited a minute before he nervously said,

"Let's just stretch our legs, shall we?"

Flora, now quiet, also got out. They took a few steps and stopped on the pavement of the short street lined with townhouses. Laneford pointed across to number five.

"What do you think of that house?"

Puzzled, she looked at the early Georgian, pale-bricked, four-storied townhouse. It was on the plain side, but well-built, with steps down to a basement area. A streetlamp softly illuminated the first two floors, but everything above was hard to see properly in the dark.

"It's beautifully proportioned. I like the windows."

"A chap I know inherited the place and is selling because he doesn't have a use for it... As you know, I'm not fond of living at an hôtel."

"You were thinking of moving to a flat, though."

"I was, but I changed my mind. Now this house has come up for sale."

He lapsed into a momentary silence.

"Flora... You know that I love you and, I believe you return at least some part of my affection... Would you do me the inestimable honour of becoming my wife?"

There followed a moment of searching, 'can-it-be-true?' looks passing between them as certainty budded and blossomed in the half light of the streetlamp. Flora gave a barely audible affirmation, and they clung to each other. There followed a kiss, or kisses (it was hard to tell), of such intensity that it was a good job no one else was about, especially among their neighbours to be. Eventually, they remembered they were on a mission and so returned to the car to backtrack and resume writing things down. Amongst their operational discussions, Flora said she believed the phrase 'The Lanefords of Lilypot Lane' sounded like a storybook for five-year-olds, but, nonetheless, they were both extraordinarily happy that such a phrase could exist.

Sophie drove Rabbit while Philpott recorded details. Whenever they stopped, Philpott got out, produced a very large notebook and an army compass, and then, by the light of headlamps, wrote quickly and prodigiously. So much writing did he do in his tiny, cramped style that Sophie believed she must have driven past dozens of tunnelling criminals without noticing.

"What on earth are you writing?" she asked at the third such stop, where they got out of the car.

"Only the pertinent data, Miss King."

"Such as?"

"Many things, among which are the position of manhole covers and drain gratings relative to the Bank of England. I am including approximate distances and direction, rating them by ease of ingress."

"You are?"

"I would explain the subject more fully, but it would mean my mentioning the attributes and potentiality of, I'm sorry to say, sewers as a method of getting into the Bank to remove the gold. Please excuse my mentioning such a topic, Miss King."

"Yes, of course, but I think you should elaborate just this once. It is somewhat of an emergency, after all."

"Indeed, it is, Miss King. Very well. I contemplated how I would proceed with such a nefarious undertaking. To my mind, the most obvious way would be to utilize the already established system of large pipes, cannula-type lesser pipes, and other outlets installed by the City of London. It is difficult to be precise without engineering drawings, maps, etcetera, but when one considers the totality of the subterranean infrastructure, one can immediately visualize that as a set of predetermined pathways, built out of necessity, which can also lend itself to secret access to underground vaults such as the Bank possesses."

"I see what you mean."

"Thank you, Miss King. Through careful study, one can select an entry point in a less frequented or otherwise unnoticeable place. Upon entry, the structure is then followed to the next node, which will provide a more commodious means of progression. As these larger lines more or less follow the pattern of the streets above, one simply continues until the desired destination is reached. There, if the conditions are deemed to be restrictive, one may enlarge the existing structure until it attains the desired level of spaciousness."

"Are there not technical difficulties associated with that?"

"Yes, Miss King, but they are surmountable, and may even be unnecessary. Finally, at the terminus, a short passage must be tunnelled to bring one out of the system and to the wall of the vault. Such an operation requires only the most basic of tools, the determination to undertake such a venture, and, vitally important, the proper schematics."

"Good grief, what a frightful thought. Do you mean to say anyone could pop up anywhere? Even in private homes?"

"Oh, I don't believe so, Miss King. The system possesses an inherent drawback that would cause the majority to refrain from utilizing it. I believe only the insane or the most determined of criminals would consider such a venture."

"That makes it worse, if anything."

"I do apologize, but there is no way of disguising the possibility."

"I suppose not. Mr Philpott, let us now find a nice clean building site and hope Lud is using that instead."

"Yes, Miss King."

They got back in the car and resumed their survey. From that moment forward, Sophie noticed every manhole cover, becoming aware of just how alarmingly numerous they were.

The survey was expected to finish by 2:00 a.m. because it was conducted in only those streets lying within a limited distance of the Bank. Ada and Marsden finished ahead of time, and they waited at the rendezvous on Princes Street. The buses had stopped running and there was very little traffic. A few solitary pedestrians were about, some of them police officers. A constable stopped to ask what they were doing. However, Ada knew that by uttering the name 'Superintendent Penrose', any police officer would desist from bothering them, not daring to interfere in any of *his* inscrutable operations. After Ada spoke the magic words, the constable apologized for being a bother and moved on.

Flora and Laneford arrived fifteen minutes later, delayed because of all the things they had to discuss, including the case. They jointly decided to keep their news under wraps and release it at a more appropriate time. After an initial consultation, which revealed nobody had seen anything much in particular, the two sets of agents returned to their respective vehicles. Ada, however, was highly suspicious about Flora's effervescent behaviour and Laneford's tendency to smile, moon-faced, at nothing.

Sophie and Philpott stopped before entering Basinghall Street, north of the Guildhall. They would be late if they searched this area before meeting the others.

"I have two typing customers in this street," said Sophie. "I didn't realize there was such a concentration of businesses here."

The narrow road differed from the others they had searched. The area had blossomed during the nineteenth century into a hub of smaller banks, professional and investment offices, and halls for guilds and other associations. It may have been built in Georgian times and boomed in the Victorian era, but it had not lost all of its pre-Fire of London medieval structure. Sophie and Philpott faced walking into many poorly lit alleys and small courtyards to complete the survey.

"This will take at least half an hour," said Sophie.

Along the shadowy street, two men pushing an old hand cart were approaching Rabbit from the southern end of Basinghall. Sophie checked to see if they had sufficient room to get by the car. They had, but she was extremely concerned for her paintwork, and slid the window down.

"You can get past if you're careful."

"Comment, mademoiselle?" said the man, leaning forward to push the cart up the gentle incline.

"Sorry. I said be careful, please — faisez attention, s'il vous plaît, messieurs."

"We heard you the first time," said the other. He was a big man, surly and menacing.

Sophie was so taken aback by his rudeness that she stared, unable to think of a reply until they had gone.

"Did you hear what that man said?" she asked Philpott.

"I did, Miss King, and it was deplorable. But it is rather to be expected that men pushing a cart in the middle of the night will neither display good manners nor the refined sensibilities of gentlemen."

"I suppose so… The other man was French. Were they workmen from a building site, do you think? I noticed pieces of broken wood on the cart."

"It is a strong possibility, Miss King. Shall we follow them?"

"Not in Rabbit, we can't. They'd notice us straight away. We had better split up. You take the car and meet the others, but be quick. On the way, look out for potential tunnel entrances to see where those men might have come from."

"Surely, I should accompany you? It might be dangerous."

"I shall be extremely careful." She got out of the car. "They've taken the right-hand turn. See you soon."

Sophie hurried away, careful not to allow her footfalls to sound too loudly. Within a moment, she remembered she had not brought her torch or police whistle, which lack of foresight annoyed her.

After turning into the wider, better lit street of London Wall, she could see the men ahead and she moved quickly. They appeared as a mismatched pair of silhouettes against the lamplight — the smaller man in the road bent forward over the cart handles to take the strain of pushing, while the tall, burly man, with a hand in his pocket, walked nonchalantly along the pavement. Despite their ignorance of her presence a stone's throw behind them, Sophie had to be careful. A backwards glance by either and she would be noticed in the empty street, devoid of parked vehicles. As silently as she could, she rushed forward to a dark doorway. Just as she reached cover, the men disappeared into an alley. She ran after them.

While she prepared herself to look around the corner into the alley, loud crashes and bangs came from so close by it made her jump.

"Get in the back."

Recognizing the big man's voice, she slid away to the nearest entrance and hid in the recessed doorway. She heard a van's engine cough into life. Doors slammed — rear doors, she believed. Another door slammed, and then she heard the driver put the van into gear and rev the engine before letting out the clutch. The transmission whined and the vehicle lurched forward. She peeked, saw the dark van nosing out of the alley, and pulled her head back. After it turned onto London Wall, the van headed away from her, so she stepped out. It was a dark blue vehicle without markings. Sophie memorized the number plate. When it was a safe distance away, she walked into the alley where the van's pungent exhaust smoke remained visible in the still air. The alley was a short dead-end area of loading doors and dustbins. The cart was gone, and no lights showed from within the surrounding businesses. She calculated there had been at least three men — the foreigner pushing the cart, the rude man, and a driver. She put her hands on her hips and said to herself, "What on earth were they up to?"

When the three cars drove up Basinghall Street, Sophie was waiting for them at the same spot that she had got out of the car. She had already investigated several alleys but, afterwards, had given up all thought of going alone into dark areas, when she found three tramps bedded down for the night in a small court. One of them was awake and, as soon as he saw her, launched into an incoherent and argumentative conversation which awakened the others. She apologized for disturbing them and beat a hasty retreat.

The agents met and discussed their findings. Each pair of surveyors had found several potential tunnel sites, but these all needed to be checked during daylight hours. They decided to explore the hidden spaces around Basinghall. After hearing about the tramps, Laneford insisted that the men would investigate on foot while the women remained with the cars.

"Do we have to get up early, miss?" asked Ada, who had just stifled a yawn.

"No, not first thing. If we're ready by nine, that should be all right."

"That's good."

"I don't feel the slightest bit tired," said Flora.

"I do," said Sophie. "I'll ask Auntie if we can borrow Marsden tomorrow. He can inspect the men's conveniences while I search in the ladies'."

"Good idea," said Flora.

"So, I'll go with him, while you both watch for the man at the office window. After we've finished, I'll join you. Now, I can't think how we are going to accomplish this. We don't know what he looks like, so we need to see him in place first… Any ideas?"

"If there's a maid my size," said Ada, "I could borrow a dress and pretend I work in an office. All the clothes I have with me are too nice for standin' about. Yours both are an' all."

"You can borrow one of my dresses that I use on assignments," said Sophie. "I don't know how long this part of the operation will last, but you can stay at White Lyon Yard while it does."

"I need to go home and get some things," said Flora.

"Yes, you both shall need to… They're coming back."

Despite searching carefully, they had found no building or roadworks suited for a tunnelling operation. Only in front of the Guildhall did they find an area roped off using iron stands, but the work there had yet to commence.

Chapter 19

The hidden world

Aunt Bessie's home was within easy walking distance of the Bank of England. The agents were tired and looked it. Flora, who was usually very good at keeping secrets, had let slip just before they all went to bed the previous night that Lord Laneford and she were going to get married. This little bon-bon had started a tremendous amount of excited conversation and the young friends had hardly slept.

The next morning, on the other hand, Marsden was bright and cheerful. When he inspected the gentlemen's side of the conveniences, he did a thorough job, even unto putting his ear to the tiled walls in various places. Afterwards, he could honestly declare to Sophie that the gentlemen's lavatories were clear of any tunnelling operations.

Sophie felt downright peculiar inspecting lavatories, and she spent a great deal of time waiting and waiting and listening until no one else was present before entering another cubicle. She heard no sounds of digging, but only dull traffic noises, pedestrians walking on the small glass blocks overhead, vibrations from the occasional tube train, and a mysterious sound in the remotest cubicle. It was a whine that rose and fell as if a mechanical being was sleeping nearby. She never discovered what it was, but if there were ever a newspaper report stating that the Lothbury conveniences were haunted, she would readily believe it.

Having sent Marsden home, she dawdled in front of St. Margaret's, examining buildings, Sir John Soane's statue and the Bank's solid wall, hoping to notice something of interest. What she was really doing was thinking of Flora. Happy for her friend, and thrilled by her news, it was not long before Sophie was considering the changes that must occur. Would it mean a break-up in their partnership? She supposed it would, no matter how much she desired everything to remain as it was. It was then she realized she was annoyed — annoyed with Flora. Upon examining her uncharitable attitude, Sophie discovered she was a touch jealous of her friend, and was shocked that she entertained such a feeling. Deciding that being tired was probably a part of her problem and that unprofitably dwelling on the subject was not helping any, she went to find the others.

Flora and Ada had started off with a spot of tactical lurking about the office building. Now at nearly ten, with most workers safely at work, they stationed themselves on the floor below the top and awaited their quarry. When he went up, they would stealthily follow and observe. Easy — they thought. In practise, however, it was virtually impossible to do. Some clerks and secretaries were working at their desks, while others were flying about the passages and stairs. An insurance agency occupied two offices on either side of the corridor. The traffic between the two was incessant. When a woman, one who could not stay put for five minutes, awkwardly found them in the corridor for the third time and was obviously on the point of passing a remark, Ada and Flora decided they had endured enough. They descended a floor where Ada picked the lock of an office empty and bereft of any furnishings. Flora had the door cracked open and was eyeing the sliver of visible staircase. Ada was cupping her ear to listen at the walls of the adjacent rooms.

"The lefthand one might be empty," whispered Ada. "In the other, I can just hear someone typing, but it's very soft, so I think we'll be all right if we keep our voices down."

"That's good... Someone's coming." She closed the door in case the person entered their corridor.

The individual she heard stamped slowly up the stairs, almost as if trying to make as much noise as possible. This person reached the landing, and the noise ceased. In the silence, the agents looked at each other enquiringly. Then a woman called down from the floor above.

"Is that you, Mr Foster?"

"Yes, Miss Marney..." His breathing was short and laboured. "There you are."

"Can I assist you?"

"No, that's quite all right. I only need a moment to catch my breath. Is Graham in the office?"

"He's visiting new clients this morning..."

"Excellent... Sorry, am I in your way?"

"Nah, don't worry," said a newcomer who sounded like a working-class man. "Take your time."

"That's kind of you."

"If you don't mind my asking, was it a whiff of gas?"

"Yes. How'd you know?"

"We went through it at Ypres. Mortars, I was, and I lost a couple of mates 'cause we had rubbish gas masks. I still visit another mate to help him out, like."

"That's where I got mine. Hill 60?"

"Well, ain't that a turn up for the books? Same bloomin' gas attack, and what a rotten business it was an' all. Still gives me nightmares."

"You, too? If you don't mind my asking, how is your friend?"

"'Course he gets about slowly, but he's been better since he moved to the countryside to keep chickens. Has family in Kent, you see."

"Wise of him... Sorry, I mustn't keep you."

"I'm in no hurry, sir, but if I could just squeeze past — you must have been an officer."

"Yes, I was... a lifetime ago."

"Yeah, it's like that, ain't it, sir? Good luck to you."

"And the same to you."

The agents now heard the second man's lighter steps going up. A few seconds later, Mr Foster resumed his journey.

"Is that our man, do you think?" asked Flora.

"He might be," said Ada. "I'll go up an' have a look."
She was gone for only a minute.
"What's the matter?" asked Flora.
"The stairs creak something shocking, so I didn't even try the top floor. He'll hear me and there's nowhere to hide."
"Never mind. We'll watch for him coming down."
They waited, minute after minute, Flora with her eye to the crack in the door and Ada waiting anxiously behind her.
"Have you seen him?" asked Ada.
"I'd tell you if I had."
"I know. I'm impatient, that's all."
"Psst!" said Flora to Sophie, who had suddenly appeared on the landing. She came over.
"What are you doing in there?"
"Shh. Be quiet and come in."
Sophie entered. "Oh, it's empty."
"We had to let ourselves in, miss."
"You broke in?"
"Er... I wouldn't say that, miss. We didn't break nothing."
"What happens if we get caught?"
"I dunno, really, miss. Couldn't we say we're opening a typing agency?"
"Never mind all that," said Flora. "He's upstairs."
"Ah, is he? What does he look like?"
"We don't know, but he worked a mortar during the war, and he has a friend who was gassed at Hill 60."
"How can you possibly learn that and yet not know what he looks like?"
"We used our big ears, miss. He stopped to talk to a Mr Foster who's an insurance, um, he's something in insurance, anyway. Foster spoke nice and was an officer, but our bloke sounds about thirty, he's sure of himself, polite, definitely from the East End, and I think he has money, 'cause he never complained about not having any when he would have if he didn't in the hopes of touching Mr Foster for some. He's the sharp, mouthy type, he is an' all."
"Ah..."
"Shush, someone's coming," said Flora.

They could hear footsteps on the stairs.

"I think it's him," said Flora. "Light fawn jacket, bowler hat, open shirt, brown oxford bags, brown loafers, and he looks prosperous in the criminal style."

"There you are," whispered Ada, pleased with herself.

"You go after him," said Sophie. "I'll check to see if he left anything upstairs just to make sure, then I'll catch up with you." As soon as was practicable, the agents went their separate ways.

Sophie glanced through the window at the Bank. More scaffolding was being erected. An apple core lay in a corner of the windowsill. Sophie rushed downstairs and out of the building, only to find Flora waiting for her at the entrance.

"Where is he?" asked Sophie.

"We'd gone in different directions to find him. I couldn't see him anywhere, so I returned here and saw Nancy getting into a taxi. Presumably he had hailed one right away, so she followed him."

"She's gone after him, then. It is he, because he left an apple core. There was also a strong smell of Cologne up there... Good grief, I hope Nancy will be all right."

"Don't worry, of course she will."

"Yes... Right. Let's use the telephone at the Underground to alert the office and Auntie in case Nancy contacts them."

In the early afternoon, Lord Laneford arrived at White Lyon Yard to take Sophie to the Bank of England in his car. When they got there, they entered through the main entrance, where they were met by a tall man. The sober effect of formal bankers' attire of stiff collar, sombre tie, and dark suit was negated by the gentleman's lively eyes, mobile features, and pleasant manner.

"Sidney!" he called out and came towards them after disengaging from conversation with another gentleman.

"Hello. This is Miss King. Miss King, I want you to meet Mr Alex Fleming."

"Delighted to meet you, Miss King." Fleming *looked* delighted.

"I'm pleased to meet you. And thank you for sparing us the time. I'm sure you're a busy man."

"Don't mention it. We're not particularly busy at present — the office runs itself like a well-oiled machine, and I'm only present to apply a drop of oil when necessary."

"Unless there's a crisis," said Laneford, laughing.

"Yes! Then everything groans and shudders abominably. Fortunately, we haven't had one for a while, which makes me think one's due at any moment."

"What is it you do?" asked Sophie.

"I oversee the Consol's Office — government bonds, you know."

"Ah. That sounds very important."

Fleming smiled. "Shall we?" He stretched out a hand towards a corridor. "You can fill me in as we walk to the Coffee Room."

They crossed the Paved Court to enter the Bill Office. From there they entered a long, wide corridor and walked abreast, with Sophie in the middle. Daylight coming from the skylights made bright the classical halls and passages, and revealed the beauty of the stone and wood. Only a few people were about, which made it possible for them to speak freely.

"We have a theory," began Laneford. "There is an unknown gentleman to whom, for the sake of convenience, we are referring to as Lud. He has devised a plan to rob the Bank of England..."

"Sidney, surely not that hoary old chestnut?"

"Hear me out, and then decide," replied Laneford.

He continued, explaining the various strands and how they were interconnected, and was only part way through the explanation when they seated themselves in the well-worn leather chairs of the Coffee Room. Fleming recommended they try the coffee because it was excellent, so that was what they ordered from the waiter. By the time they were served, Laneford had finished and Fleming had not yet commented.

"Several things strike me." He spoke while stirring. "Had I heard this from another, I would have said the whole thing was too far-fetched. As it is you, and it isn't April the first, I must conclude you are persuaded that this is more than a strong possibility... Before I go any further, may I ask why Miss King is present?"

"She is a member of our network, and it is she and her associates who have discovered the connections."

"Ah, I see. Then Miss King, and I say this dispassionately, the connections, such as they are, seem tenuous to me. Foreigners being murdered, for example. Yes, I follow the logic of their being employed in some large-scale undertaking, but that it involves the Bank of England has not been demonstrated. Someone from a nearby building regularly observing what goes on inside our walls sounds odd, although the person can't see much, if anything."

"The scaffolding," said Sophie. "They can see that clearly. We also discovered that the Bank of England is going to be remodelled and wondered..."

"How do you know that?" He spoke sharply.

"Through a witness to a conversation."

"No one is supposed to know. That knowledge is limited to the directors."

"You're not a director," observed Laneford.

"Sidney, it is my job to know what goes on here... Like Miss King, there may have been a witness to a conversation somewhere along the line. I can't discuss it, but I can tell you this much. All of Soane's work is going, and they're intent upon building a hideous large block instead. They'll keep the walls, but not much more. The project will take at least a decade once started."

"That is a sacrilege," said Laneford.

"I quite agree, but the Bank is expanding its operations and will continue doing so. Some offices are badly cramped as it is. What choice is there?"

"So, it's been kept quiet because of a potential public backlash?"

"Correct. No one wishes it to be made public until it absolutely must be."

"What about the vaults?" asked Sophie.

"I really should not be getting into specifics... However, I understand they are being moved, expanded, and fortified."

"Fortified!" exclaimed Sophie. "When was this project first contemplated?"

"Almost a year ago, but the initial sketches weren't delivered until early December."

"Have the directors agreed to them?" asked Laneford.

"No, they're having a lot of changes made. There is a spat over whether the new building should have a mansard roof or a full floor with a flat roof. As for the vaults, I've heard nothing more, so I assume they're still going to be completely redone."

"Then all of Bullion Court, the Rotunda, and the Dividend Office, they're all going?"

"All of it. Remember, Sidney, you heard none of this from me."

"Of course."

"I shan't repeat anything, either," said Sophie.

"Thank you, Miss King." He sipped some coffee. "I suppose you would like to see the vaults."

"Yes, please," said Sophie. "And could we pass by the scaffolding just to see what is being done there?"

"I thought it was cleaning or something," said Fleming. "I don't think they're digging down if that's your line of reasoning, but we shall see."

"Have you heard anything about the King's visit?" asked Laneford.

"It's news to me, so I can't help you there."

They left the Coffee Room and, by a tortuous route, walked through areas ranging from the ordinary to several of such a surpassing, calm beauty that it made Sophie want to stop for a while to drink in the surroundings. They crossed one small Hellenic-style courtyard with a single sunlit corner where the pedestrians would have been better suited if they had worn chitons and cloaks. Sophie was astounded that parts of the Bank of England realized the same aura of antiquity as she had imbibed from the classical world engravings found in her picture books. Here was her childhood imagination made manifest, yet, she also learned, the citadel was slated for demolition. That anyone could contemplate such vandalism was both demoralizing and quite beyond her.

Several workmen were at work on the scaffolding, and Sophie could see they were making casts of mouldings and other stone decorations. Fleming questioned them briefly and discovered that two sets were being made. One was for an architect and a second set for King George. They left the men to their work.

"That's interesting," said Laneford. "The King must know of the plan to rebuild the Bank."

"I should think so," said Fleming, "although I always understood he was never much interested in architecture or even art."

"That was also my understanding. However, Queen Mary is very keen."

"A birthday gift?" suggested Fleming with a smile.

"Who knows?"

They entered Bullion Court. It was a compact open space, cleverly connected to other buildings and courts by archways and columned walkways. They passed a Beadle in his bicorn hat, heavy cloak, and carrying his massive staff. He was red-faced from being outside so often but also on account of the warm weather. The little party entered the Bullion Office and came to a heavy steel door, beyond which were stairs descending to the vaults.

It surprised Sophie how readily the bank's officers allowed the three of them to enter through the iron-barred gate, which served as the only entrance to the basement vaults. Fleming was evidently known to them, and she supposed they just accepted his authority as one of the Bank's principal managers.

The vaults, although large, were, to Sophie's mind, very ordinary, and were indeed of the same pattern to be found in thousands of churches or any old, large institutional building. The brick walls were whitewashed in a few sections, and a pervasive damp smell made her think that the Bank of England was absolutely indifferent as to how it treated its gold. There were dull bricks all over the place — some stacked, some loaded on movable, four-wheeled carts with heavy iron wheels. The vault with its incipient negligence was just as her Aunt Bessie had described it. The bullion did not look worth the trouble to steal.

"I know exactly what you're thinking," said Fleming. "What a disappointment it all is. David made golden shields and hung them in the House of Lebanon and Nebuchadnezzar made a golden idol. We at the Bank, however, treat gold like any common commodity, perhaps taking a *little* extra care. It is a store of wealth, and we like to keep it in its most readily transferrable form. It may interest you to know that it's not all ours. Some of it belongs to other governments and banks."

"I take it that mine is a common reaction," said Sophie. "May I pick up a bar?"

"I'll ask the gentleman."

After the quick conference with an officer, Sophie was permitted to pick one up. The man put a small mat on top of a nearby cart and placed a brick of gold on it. Sophie approached and picked it up using both hands.

"Good grief! It's so much heavier than it looks." She held it briefly, then set it down again.

"Yes, miss," said the officer, pleased by her surprise. "That's twenty-nine pounds, give or take. Despite their looks, we're careful how we handle them. The slightest scratch knocks down the value of a bar, and this gold is soft stuff, you know, because it's the purest to be found anywhere. Not like in jewellery where it's been alloyed with something to give it strength."

"That's very interesting, thank you."

"Happy to oblige, miss." He returned the bar to its place and went back to his position by the gate.

"Have you seen enough?" asked Fleming.

She had, but she believed if she stayed long enough, there would be a thumping at the walls until the point of a pickaxe broke through. "I'm concerned for the walls. Do we know how thick they are?"

"Looks like a double-brick wall to me," said Laneford. "Anything beyond that?"

"I couldn't tell you, and I'm not sure anyone knows." He mused for a moment. "I'll tell you where you could find out, and that's the Soane Museum. They have hundreds if not thousands of his drawings there, and many of them are of the Bank. I should imagine they include the diagrams for the vaults."

"Are there other vaults?" asked Sophie.

"Yes, but they're much smaller and contain silver, some other odds and ends, and records with which the Bank cannot part."

They left shortly afterwards, returning to where Laneford's car was parked. When they were inside and his chauffeur Philpott had got the car in motion, Sophie said,

"None of us mentioned it, but I believe we all realize that only someone with inside knowledge, a director, for example, could take advantage of the Bank's remodelling."

"Yes," said Laneford slowly. "I know several of them to speak to, and the inference is difficult for me to accept. You may not appreciate this but, among bankers, a professional rigour is expected in all financial dealings. There is a standard, or code, to which they adhere and it compels them as a group to treat those funds or assets they hold in trust for others as absolutely inviolable. If banks cannot be deemed trustworthy, they have nothing, for all banking transactions rest on a foundation of trust. Should a Bank of England director be involved in this plan, and it is inconceivable that there should be a group of them, he must either be a very singular person or a consummate actor."

"It disturbs you, doesn't it?"

"Profoundly, Miss King. As you know, I have a background in banking. For a director to steal from his own bank is the highest form of treachery, and he would do it knowing the degradation of reputation that is certain to follow. That we are considering the Bank of England makes the treachery even worse. It is an action against everyone in Britain! Sadly, I can see the possibility of such a plan, although I'm still finding it hard to believe."

"I know. More evidence is needed. I'm going to send someone to do research at the Soane Museum. Would you know where it is?"

"Yes. It's in Lincoln's Inn Fields, near Holborn Underground."

"Thank you. Hopefully, Miss Carmichael will have learned something by following that man." Sophie did not mention that she was worried about Ada's safety. "What do you think he gained by observing the scaffolding being erected?"

"That's a bit of a facer and I don't have an answer... Something I wondered about, though, is would Lud be perhaps wanting the King to visit the Bank after it has been robbed just to embarrass him?"

"He's been causing the King sufficient embarrassment as it is, so you may be right." The scaffolding question still did not sit well with her, and she felt she was missing some key point. Then an idea struck her. "What if the watcher has a confederate among those men on the scaffold? Perhaps he sends a signal."

"That's a possibility. What would he signal, Miss King?"

"I don't know... That no alarm has been raised, so that there has been no doubling of the guards or any other precautions taken... An all-clear signal."

"That is entirely plausible, Miss King. Whenever they break in, Lud would be anxious to know in advance that, in the vault, no trap awaits his men."

Sophie smiled because she was pleased with herself. "I wonder, then, how we should proceed. We have the observer, the possibility of a man on the scaffolding, and a director yet to be identified — when do we apprehend them?"

"It is a delicate problem. I'll work on finding the director. For the other two, I must consult with various people — the police need to be brought in at some point. The delicacy arises in wanting those three persons to lead us to the rest of their gang or organization."

"Is there a danger that they may actually break into the vault before we can do that?"

"Oh, yes. Time is limited; we know that from the note to the King. Whatever is planned is close to being completed. No one, save ourselves, is particularly interested in our theory."

"I thought Mr Fleming was quite open to the idea."

"I've known him for a long time. He was indulging me, because it cost him nothing. He thinks it possible, but highly unlikely. You will have noticed, Miss King, that he made no offer to pursue the matter. The reason for his hesitation is that should the theory prove to be false, he will have damaged his standing within the Bank. So certain am I of this that there was no need to ask him to be circumspect."

"What does he do?" asked Sophie.

"Without giving anything away, he reports upon the activities of foreign governments. If they buy our consols or move bullion into the Bank's safekeeping, then we can assume they are friendly towards us, or neutral at the very least. If they take out their bullion, or sell our government's notes, then we can investigate further and find out the reasons why. Fleming provides the network with such information, almost as it occurs. If he didn't, we would have to wait for the Bank's dense, interminable annual reports, which are published far too late for our purposes."

"There are worlds within worlds of which I know nothing," said Sophie. "Being at Buckingham Palace was also an eye opener... What has happened to Handley?"

"He's allowed to carry out his duties and is being closely watched. Drysdale is hoping Lud, or his agent, contacts Handley."

"You don't sound optimistic."

"None of us are. It's certain Handley has not told us the whole truth. Now, whether he is still working for Lud or is playing his own cards, we shall find out. As Drysdale said, we must first lull him into a false sense of security so that he can make a mistake."

"What if he jeopardizes our operation? It's fragile enough as it is."

"Miss King, if we controlled the situation, we would know exactly what to do. As we are still in the discovery stage, we must take risks. It is to be hoped that Handley will do something."

"Does he know this?"

Laneford smiled. "Who can tell?"

Chapter 20

In Search of a River

Laneford and Sophie entered the drawing room at White Lyon Yard to find Lady Shelling, Flora, Elizabeth, and Archie present. Lady Shelling had just finished recounting her and Elizabeth's morning activities, but happily summarized them again for Sophie because she could call the Lord Mayor of the City of London a nincompoop once more.

"It is my firm belief," she launched into it with gusto, "that his wearing all that regalia has gone to his head. He actually believes he is intelligent. I've known him since he was a boy, and he is not. Oh, no. It is quite beyond me that his father, a very capable businessman who used to do Shelling's printing, should produce offspring content to posture in front of mirrors. He was putting on his official robes while speaking to us... He barely gave us a civil answer. Isn't that right, Elizabeth?"

"Yes, Lady Shelling," said Elizabeth, who looked uncomfortable.

"The man has cloth ears and an empty head. He refused to countenance that there was even the remotest possibility of an attack on the Bank of England... He knew nothing about anything, of course. He didn't know the Bank of England is slated to be remodeled. It was like talking to a complete vacancy. We might as well have gone to Selfridges and spoken to a dummy in the shop window. And to think he's married and has children."

Sophie knew it was best to let her aunt wind herself down, and it was her drawing room after all. Ada entered at that moment, and Sophie breathed a sigh of relief. After the greetings, the others expected Ada to give her report. In the room full of well-spoken people, Ada swallowed, hoped she would not mess up her aitches, grammar, or pronunciation of difficult words, and launched forth, immediately in her full flow.

"I got in the taxi outside the office buildin' and said, follow that cab. I'd read that in a book once and never thought it would come in so handy. So, the bloke jogged along through the traffic with me right behind him. I was that worried about the fare the whole time, I was an' all. Anyway, it didn't come out too bad in the end — bad enough, though. The bloke went to 90 Wardour Street and walked straight into a nightclub. It's called The Egyptian Cat Club, which is a funny sort o' name, if you ask me.

"'Cross the road was an antique shop. It all looked like old clobber to me, but there you are. They had stuff out front, so I was lookin' over it, and I spotted a plate just like my Nan has. The owner had come out and was watching me, so I asked him how much it was. Do you know what he said? He said, 'Are you buying or selling?' So, I said, Do you see me carrying any plates? 'You're buying, are you, then?' he says. I said, No. I just want to know how much. He then said, 'That's a very rare and much sought-after pattern.' Well, I wanted to argue with him, but I thought I'd better not. But what a liar, eh? My Nan bought her set off a stall in Petticoat Lane after she was married. Factory seconds they were, but you couldn't find a fault in the whole lot. She and a friend had to get the set home by bus. A teacup got broken and none of us have ever heard the last of that, let me tell you."

"I find breakages highly disturbing, too," said Aunt Bessie.

"Aren't they just, my Lady?" said Ada. "But my Nan goes on and on about it because she thought the broken teacup was the sign of a broken marriage. She believed that all through her married life right up until Granddad died, so it was all rubbish in the end. What I think is, she paid money for the cup, never had the use of it, so it proper niggled her... Sorry, to go off like that."

"Never mind," said Sophie. "What did you discover?"

"I didn't think I'd have any luck with the antiques bloke, so I went next door. That was a furniture shop, and a porter was outside smoking. I asked him about The Egyptian Cat Club. He said they were raided once, and there's been some funny goings on there. He didn't say what they were, but he reckoned the place is run by criminals. I asked him if he knew the name of the owner, and he said it was Barrett, and I'd just missed him going in. I described the bloke who I'd followed from the Bank of England, and he said it sounded like him. So, the owner of the nightclub is the same bloke as who's watching the Bank of England."

"Well done!" said Sophie.

"Thank you, miss," said Ada. "The porter started asking awkward questions, so I gave him a shillin' and told him not to ask nothing more, so he shut up after that. I waited and walked about, pretending I belonged to the area. About an hour later, a taxi pulled up outside the nightclub. There wasn't another in sight, so I stepped across the road and hung about the entrance. Sure enough, Barrett come out and got in. 'Tower Hill,' he says and off they went. I couldn't follow, so I went up to Oxford Circus and got on the Tube."

"Excellent," said Archie. "Can you give us a description, please?"

"Yes, Mr Drysdale. He's about thirty-five and I'd say five feet ten inches tall. Hefty fella, well-dressed but not like a gentleman. He's all flash, but he's paid a pretty penny for it. Uses hair tonic and a lot of perfume. I was two or three yards away and he didn't half pong. It was sickly, it was."

"Perhaps he has a diseased liver," said Aunt Bessie. "I know of a gentleman who wears an inordinate amount of Cologne because he must."

"Maybe, my Lady. Barrett looked healthy enough, though. He's the sort who'll sit down at dinner and have seconds of everything, then have a supper later. I served a gentleman like that at a big function. Helped hisself something shocking every time I brought a serving dish to him."

"Was he a bishop?"

"I wasn't going to say, but it so happens he was, my Lady."

"That will be Beaky, the Bishop of Cirencester."

"That's right, an' all," said Ada.

"I've met him," said Laneford, "and observed something similar."

"He's a hopeless case, Sidney," said Aunt Bessie, "but he is also a very charitable man, full of the Christian virtues, save for the obvious one. I've always wondered what he does at Lent — struggles with the flesh, no doubt. But, to return to the main issue, what do we do now?"

They talked at length and came to several decisions. The major concern was that they were short on time and had no clear path forward, so they decided their best bet was to tackle the men in Basinghall Street that night. Philpott had been dispatched to follow up on the survey of building sites around the Bank, which Laneford said would keep him busy for the day. He was also to remain in the area around Guildhall.

The meeting in the drawing room broke up. Lady Shelling and Elizabeth were going to the Soane Museum. Lord Laneford, after a private conversation with Flora, departed to find Bank of England directors to question. Archie informed Sophie of two things: that BW had become more or less indispensable to the King for no apparent reason, and that the agents were continuing to be paid for their work. After that, he went to Scotland Yard to discuss matters with Superintendent Penrose. Marsden drove Ada to her home so that she could collect a change of clothes. Sophie telephoned the Agency only to discover that it was running perfectly well without her, although Miss Jones made it clear that Elizabeth must be back in the office tomorrow. After Sophie had hung up the receiver in the study, she and Flora were then left with nothing to do.

"Shall we go to the Bank or Tower Hill?" asked Flora.

"We have no idea what we're looking for at Tower Hill. The Bank is more promising. Besides, poor old Philpott is wandering about there on his own. We can walk; it isn't very far." They moved to the hall to get their things. "I doubt we'll find anything, but at least we're doing something. How preposterous can it get?" asked Sophie as she put on her hat and adjusted it, looking in the mirror. "The Bank's about to be robbed and nothing serious is being done to prevent it."

"Move over," said Flora, putting on her own hat, "or your aunt will find you guilty of posturing." Sophie made room. "It's ridiculous, I agree," continued Flora. "We could crack the case in a week or two, but that would be too late. However, won't it be frightful if it turns out we're all wrong?"

"I know. Every third thought of mine is, 'Supposing we've made a mistake?' Ah, well."

"Should we go armed?" asked Flora. "My blackjack pulls my pocket out of shape."

Sophie laughed. "We ought to. I'll get mine... Tell Hawkins we'll be out for a couple of hours."

While in her bedroom, Sophie slipped her automatic pistol named Freda into her handbag.

Sophie and Flora traipsed about the city. It was now four o'clock, and the streets were not busy. In the surrounding offices, city workers were rushing to get the day's work completed. There were also those who were not so busy, and had reached the four o'clock coasting hour, where they pretended to work. So, for various reasons, every city worker's eye was on the clock. At five, when the first wave sallied forth, all hell would break loose. The imprisoned mass of clerical working humanity arose as one and with but a single thought in mind — I want to go home — made for the exit. When one's train is the 5:06 at Cannon Street, and there is half a mile to be covered, including crossing busy streets, no one had better get in the way; much like the Golden Horde sweeping across Eurasia, the mass of office workers sweeps away all in its path and is quite a terrifying sight. The look of determination upon the hundreds of thousands of faces is identical to that of the lemming just before it hurls itself into the sea. It is the grim I-shall-make-it-or-die-trying type of look.

As it was, at that moment, safe to wander, Flora and Sophie did a circuit of the Bank, checked the window at the top of the office, dismissed several sites that had looked promising in the darkness, and generally peered into things. They made their way to Basinghall Street and explored Mason's Avenue, which proved to be a narrow alley. Here they became highly suspicious of a public house called Old Doctor Butler's Head.

"Public houses frequently have tunnels," said Flora. "Those iron covers lead to the cellars." She pointed to a covered opening in front of a shuttered section. "They could lift the covers and simply drop the wood they needed for the supports down the hole."

"They might. But I think the public houses with tunnels are those on the coast used for smuggling. I can't imagine they did that here. The place looks too respectable anyway."

"Calling a place Old Doctor Butler's Head doesn't sound very respectable to me. In fact, it sounds ghoulish. What should we do? Just go in and ask?"

"We must have a cover story," said Sophie.

"How about... we're archaeologists, and we're looking for Roman thingummybobs, and do they know where we can find any?"

"Really, Flora, I mean Gladys, we can't put it like that."

"I know, but that's the principle we shall operate under. Come on."

They entered and found the saloon. Behind the bar, a man was cleaning glasses with a cloth. Several patrons were already seated. Two more entered immediately after Sophie and Flora and ordered drinks from the barmaid. The agents approached the man.

"Good afternoon, ladies. What'll you have?"

"Two ports and lemon, please," said Flora.

"Coming right up."

"You ordered drinks?" hissed Sophie.

"We have to," whispered Flora. "Now, shh." She addressed the barman. "It's a beautiful day."

"So it is. Doesn't make the farmers happy, though. Crying out for rain they are... I've been told, so I suppose it's true, that the hops aren't doing too badly despite everything."

"You would be concerned for the hops, of course," said Sophie.

"No hops, no beer. We can't have that now, can we?" He brought the two glasses over. "Visiting London, are you?"

"I live here," said Flora, "but my friend is up from the country. She's an archeologist and her specialism is in Roman ruins and all that sort of thing."

"Is that right? Archeologist, eh?" He put the drinks in front of them and took Flora's money to put in the till.

"Yes," said Sophie, very much put on the spot. "It crossed my mind that this area was within the old Roman city, so there must be many relics right beneath us."

"I'm sure there are."

"What about Roman walls?" asked Flora. "Surely you have some in your cellar. It would cheer up my friend no end if she could only see a bit of ancient masonry."

"I wish I could oblige, but there's only old brick and stone down there, and they're no more than a century old."

"No tunnels?" asked Flora.

"Nothing like that. Now, if you want to see some old stuff, you should try Guildhall or the church next to it. But I don't think even they go back to Roman times."

"That is such a pity," said Sophie, who cautiously sipped her drink and found it surprisingly pleasant. "I was so hoping to find a tunnel."

"Can't help you there, but it's funny, you know. You're not the first person who's asked about such things."

"Why don't you have a drink with us?" asked Flora.

"That's very kind of you. I'll have a light ale, but later, if you don't mind. It's a bit too early for me."

"I understand perfectly." Flora gave him a coin. He took the price of the beer from it and returned her change.

"You know, I wonder if that was Professor Drysdale," said Sophie.

"Who was...? Oh, you mean the chap who was in here asking about the river? He didn't give his name. What did your professor look like?"

"Very tall, very thin with a stoop, an enormous nose, and scant grey hair."

"Not the same chap at all. I'd say he was forty, maybe fifty, at the outside. Shorter than me, a city gent with grey hair... I tell you what I do remember. He had one of the most beautiful pocket watches I've ever seen... All gold. A hunter, they call them. Kept looking at it, he did, as though he had to be somewhere."

"Why was he interested in the Thames?" asked Flora.

"No, it was the River Walbrook. He wanted to know all about our cellars as well. Did they flood? How damp did they get? I thought he was a bit soft in the head at first, but then he explained he's trying to find the Walbrook because it's moved. Well, we've all heard of it, but I can't say I've ever seen it, and as for moving about...?" He laughed. "Then he told me about how it comes out in the Thames after starting around Islington, and that London's been built over it. Said there were another six rivers like it. There was the Fleet, the Wandle... ahh, I can't remember the rest, but it was all very interesting."

"I should think it was," said Flora.

"And *do* the cellars get flooded?" asked Sophie.

"No, they're dry year-round. The air gets a bit moist, but only if it's been raining heavy. Now I told him to try the big office building in King's Arms Yard because the road subsided a few years back, and they said at the time it was because of underground water movement. They had the road up for weeks, they did."

"That may have been caused by the Walbrook," said Flora.

"It seems likely," said Sophie. 'What did your gentleman think?"

"I can't really remember."

"Was it a long time ago?"

"Not that long... Last year, October, I believe."

Some more customers entered the saloon bar.

"We're getting busy now," said the man.

"Don't let us keep you," said Flora.

"That was most interesting," said Sophie. "Thank you very much."

He smiled and moved away. The agents finished their drinks quickly and waved goodbye to the barman as they left. Once outside, they marched off to find King's Arms Yard.

"Poor Professor Archie," said Flora. "What made you say Drysdale?"

"It was the first name that came to mind. Please don't tell him how I described him. He'd never forgive me."

"Very tempting, but I won't... The enquiring gentleman was a Lud agent," said Flora.

"Yes, or Lud himself!"

"Underground rivers? I've never given them a moment's thought. I mean, who would?"

"Not I," said Sophie. "Who do you think would know about such things?"

"Haven't a clue. I bet Elizabeth could find out, though. That's just the sort of thing she likes."

"I'll ask her this evening to look into it."

They were only a hundred yards from King's Arms Yard, but the church bells tolled five and set the living avalanche in motion. A minute earlier, the streets had been easy to navigate, now they were impassable when going against the tide.

"Stand against the wall," said Flora. "It's the only safe place."

"How long does this pandemonium last?" asked Sophie.

"It's not infinite and should slacken off in a few minutes."

They paused next to a doorway from which issued dozens of clerks and typists. Some immediately broke into a run and dodged traffic in the road, while the slowest hurried at a brisk pace along the pavement. People brushed past Sophie at least twenty times. By 5:10, the pace had abated, yet the volume of people had increased. There was little room on the pavement and none for them to go in the opposite direction. The traffic in the road was at a standstill.

"No wonder Nick insists deliveries should be finished by a quarter to five."

"The cyclists can just about get through," said Flora. "Everyone looks so demented."

A passerby, moustache bristling, turned at hearing her comment and glared.

"Whoops," said Flora.

They pushed on and reached the imposing office building. The doors were wide open. In the vestibule, an old doorman sat in a comfortable snug chair in a corner. The employees were trickling past on their way home.

"Hello," said Sophie. "Could you spare a moment to answer a couple of questions?"

"Yarss," he said slowly, in a deep, hoarse voice. "What you wanna know, miss?" He stood up.

"Were you here when there was a hole in the road?"

"Yarss."

"Was it caused by the River Walbrook?"

"Yarss."

"Did anyone make unusual enquiries about it afterwards?"

He paused for a long time, then raised a hand to his mouth in a loose fist and coughed softly.

"A shilling if you don't know anything, and half-a-crown if you do."

"Five shillin'."

"Three."

He put his hand out.

"There you are, three and six, because I don't have the change. You must tell me everything you know."

"God bless you." The man put the money in his pocket. "A gen'lman stopped by October last lookin' for a river, can you believe it? He gave me five shillin', but that's beside the point now we've come to terms. Excitable fella, carried on abaht the river, the 'ole, and did we get water in our basement? I told him, the Walbrook is right under our very feet and the basement has a damp corner, but it never floods. Now the 'ole was more 'an three year ago. At first, there wor' water flowin' in the bottom. Then the sides fell in, and it got choked, but the 'ole grew 'alfway cross the road. The City took their time repairin' it, 'cause they had to pour concrete so it didn't 'appen again. They made an 'orrible mess while they were abaht it. Dust and muck everywhere an' it didn't smell too good sometimes. I reckon there's corpuses down there. The rot, that's what it smelled like to me. I'm an old soldier, an' went through the Boer War, so I know abaht all that."

"We commend you for your service," said Sophie, disturbed by what he had just said. "What was the gentleman like?"

"City man and well-to-do. Middle-aged, no more'n fifty. Wore a top hat and a beautiful coat, with the fur collar, you know. He had no, whatd'ya call it, facial hair. He had a nice walking stick with silver. Yarss, he was turned out very nice, right down to his spats. You could see straight off he was wurff a packet."

"Where was he from?" asked Flora.

"Being a gen'leman he could be from anywhere — it's hard to tell with the upper crust except for the Scotsmen and northerners."

"How is it you remember him so well?" asked Sophie.

"I was 'ere, the 'ole was 'ere, and he wanted to know abaht it, so I couldn't miss him, could I? He had me out in the street findin' the exact spot and showin' him the direction the water flowed. He made a drawin' of all that. And then, 'though we only spoke the once, he come back a few times, didn't he? So, there you go. That's why I remember him, and I think that's everythin' I can remember."

"I see," said Sophie.

"You're arter him, aren't you? He's either up to no good or he's done you wrong."

"Possibly no good, but it's nothing personal."

"What are *you* up to, then? You're not the police."

"No, we're not from the police."

"If I give your money back, would you tell me?"

"No." Sophie laughed.

The doorman smiled. "I wouldn't do that anyway, miss, but this is gonna make me think abaht it all over again… Don't mean to be rude, but the gen'leman what pays me wages will be down soon, and I've to shut the doors and look alert, and not be talking to two very nice young ladies."

"We will take your lovely hint and shove off," said Flora.

The doorman laughed. "Good luck to you."

Twenty minutes had made all the difference to the pavements. No longer packed, they were still congested, but the roads remained a lost cause. Sophie and Flora gave up all hope of finding Philpott. They went to the office building and climbed the stairs. There was no evidence that the watcher had returned, so they left for White Lyon Yard.

Chapter 21

Dinners and drains

Only the five women members of the anti-Lud campaign were present for dinner at White Lyon Yard. Afterwards, in the drawing room, Flora and Sophie gave their report, while Ada had little to contribute because she had gone home earlier to fetch more clothes. Aunt Bessie explained what had happened to her and Elizabeth.

"I've never been to Soane's Museum before. It is a most extraordinary place — eccentric, I should say. Soane was obviously a very decided man with excellent taste. The way he crammed so many fine pieces into such a small, rather bizarre space, created by three houses knocked into one, displays his unique mind. I think he may have been a little crazed. The museum is cunningly arranged and initially a little overwhelming. It gave me the distinct feeling that I was walking though his brain, so to speak. He was a good organizer, but there is so much to see, in the design of the building as much as the objects, that I felt I was going from one compartment in his mind to another. You felt that, too, didn't you, Elizabeth?"

"Yes, Lady Shelling. I remember you remarking that he had built a shrine to his own intellect... among other things." Elizabeth flushed because she recalled so vividly how Aunt Bessie had delivered her opinion to the tour guide who led the small group of strangers through the museum.

"It's free to get in," said Aunt Bessie, "but few exhibits are labelled or described, so they get you to pay for a rather poor catalogue. As that was unsatisfactory, we paid for the tour. The fellow was knowledgeable, but painfully slow. That was not his fault, but he would keep answering the most inane questions posed by a dreadful man who had not the decency to keep his lack of intelligence to himself."

"He was rather repetitive," said Elizabeth.

"Obviously, the man was trying to broaden his mind, but he has a long way to go. He sounded like a six-year-old. However, I suppose such is to be expected when one mixes with the general public. I enjoyed the museum, nevertheless. Until, that is, we met the Inspectress. What was the creature's name?"

"Miss Daniell," said Elizabeth.

"Yes. An obstinate person who refused us access to the Bank of England drawings. There are over six hundred of them, and we only saw two or three framed examples. All the rest are locked away and you must be on an approved list to access them. I remonstrated with her as best I could, which was difficult because I couldn't say the Bank of England was about to be raided. She said she was only abiding by the rules established by the museum's trustees. I offered her money for us to be shown the drawings, but she stood firm. It is rare for me to be defeated in my purpose, but I was, in this instance."

"Oh," said Sophie. "I'm sorry to hear that."

"I shall get over it... I already have."

"That's good," said Sophie, who was thinking more of finding out the thickness of the vault's walls rather than her aunt being rebuffed. "How does one get on the list?"

"You have to be proposed by two people already listed," said Elizabeth.

"I suppose they're all architects or engineers," said Flora.

"I know an architect," said Aunt Bessie, "but he's in a convalescent home."

"I don't know any," said Sophie.

"Neither do I, Miss King," said Elizabeth.

"Is it so important to find out about the vault?" asked Aunt Bessie.

"I thought so, Auntie. You see, if it is just a brick wall, then they could demolish it with pickaxes, but if it is much thicker, they might use dynamite."

"Ah, yes, of course. But the explosion would alert the guards."

"Lud may have a way of dealing with the guards. We just don't know."

"I still don't understand," began Ada, "why Lud's in such a rush. You said the scaffolding in the Bank was only for taking casts of stonework. They haven't dug the new vault yet, and probably won't for a while. So, why's he hurrying?"

"There's no apparent reason," answered Sophie. "Which must mean he knows something we don't."

"Perhaps the city has work to do around the Bank which might interfere with his tunnelling operation," said Flora.

"A new water main, perhaps," suggested Elizabeth.

"That's entirely possible," said Sophie. "We can't find out the information fast enough, though. It might take weeks to contact the right person and get an answer. We're being stopped at every turn, and only the police can expedite such matters."

"Will they help now?" asked Ada. "We have the fruit fella who owns the nightclub and is watching the Bank, the river fella who's right suspicious and might be tunnelling, the fellas with the cart in Basinghall Street, and someone like a director who knows the Bank is rebuilding the vaults. Ain't that enough for the police to get involved, miss?"

"One would think it were... Superintendent Penrose knows of some of this, yet he hasn't referred it. Perhaps he will now."

Hawkins entered to announce that Mr Philpott had arrived. A few moments later, he was in the drawing room.

"Mr Philpott," said Aunt Bessie, "we kept a dinner for you. Have you dined?"

"That is most gracious of you, Lady Shelling. I ate much earlier, and confess to being quite famished. May I deliver my report first?"

"Yes, you may."

"Excuse me for interrupting your gathering, but I have discovered something I believe to be of importance."

"Would you care for a sherry? asked Aunt Bessie.

"If it is no trouble, that would be most welcome."

"It's no trouble. Ring the bell, someone."

"I'll pour it, Auntie," said Sophie, getting up and going to where the sherry stood on a small table.

"You're becoming quite domesticated, Sophie. Now please, Mr Philpott, get on with it."

"Yes, Lady Shelling." He took out his notebook, found the right place, and then cleared his throat. "The area surrounding the Bank of England is heavily built-up and there are no open spaces such as parks, plazas, wide avenues, or anything else constituting a break in the conurbation that begins at the Bank's walls and extends for some hundreds of yards. Every building within a certain radius is devoted to commercial purposes and, even outside of that radius, there are very few residences..."

"Mr Philpott, do you intend being brief?" asked Aunt Bessie.

"Yes, Lady Shelling."

"Good. Then be so now, for all our sakes."

"Indeed, I will. What I was driving at was the population density. Overnight, it is minimal, due to there being so few residences. During a working day, a building big enough to house a dozen residents, as offices may contain upwards of fifty or even a hundred workers. The structures themselves are quite old, and not designed for such wear and tear. Add the vibrations from the Underground, trains, and traffic, and the older foundations of some buildings require additional support to preserve the superstructure from collapse. Such is the case for St. Margaret's on Lothbury — a church designed by Sir Christopher Wren. I happened to be outside when an engineer was finishing a conversation with a lady connected with the church. He had put chalk marks on the pavement to demonstrate a point. He left shortly afterwards. I entered the church and spoke to the very informative lady named..."

"Yes, yes," said Aunt Bessie.

"... She explained that the Church of England has approved a project to buttress the church's original foundation. The project commences in two weeks and will take several months to complete. I asked her how deep the required trench might be, and she said at least twenty feet, and probably more, and that the pavement immediately in front of the church will be unusable for pedestrians for the entire time."

"Well done, Mr Philpott!" said Sophie. "Lud's tunnel surely runs near or under the church. He must be aware of the impending work, so *that's* why there is such urgency."

They discussed this information for some minutes. Philpott learned of the gentleman interested in the River Walbrook and thought it significant. He added that he, too, had investigated Basinghall Street but, when the rush hour came, had switched to the open space of Guildhall. Philpott had gone inside and had been allowed to examine the enormous vault beneath the Hall, but found no signs of recent work.

"We know where the tunnel will terminate," said Sophie, "but how can we find the entrance?"

"I don't think we can," said Flora. "We've done the easier part and come up with nothing. The entrance has to be inside a building."

"Then our only chance to find it is through the men with the cart. Of course, they may have nothing whatever to do with it, but we'll go there shortly to investigate."

While they were thus talking and planning, Lord Laneford arrived.

"Have you had your dinner?" asked Aunt Bessie.

"That's very kind, but I had something earlier, thank you."

"Will you have a sherry, then? Or would you prefer something stronger?"

"A small sherry, if I may."

This time, Flora got up to get it. When she handed it to him, she said,

"There you are, Sidney," and smiled.

"You're too kind," he said, and smiled back.

"Perhaps, Sophie will also be so kind and bring you up to date," said Aunt Bessie.

"Of course, Auntie."

Sophie explained what they had learned and also summarized Philpott's report.

"We progress," said Laneford. He took out his pen. "I could get hold of only one Bank of England director. I don't know him well and he was circumspect and disinclined to tell me anything. He was more interested in finding out why I was interested in the Bank's security arrangements. I said there was a rumour that something might be tried, and he could not have been less interested. His reaction was not unexpected. The Bank has been secure for so long that it never occurred to him that the defenses could be breached. I'll have to lay all our cards on the table at some point but, not only am I not sanguine about how the directors will respond, but also I don't want to alert the director who might be Lud." He turned to Sophie. "Could you give the description of the Walbrook gentleman again?"

Sophie obliged him and he took notes.

"Excitable?" he asked. "I wonder what the doorman meant?"

"I took it to mean the man was pleased at finding out that the Walbrook was where it was."

"Yes. If so, then it must have agreed with his prior understanding of where the river would be. What do you think, Philpott?"

"I visualize the gentleman as being an antiquarian, my Lord. If he is indeed the person we are referring to as Lud, then he must be a historian, perhaps amateur, but very knowledgeable."

Laneford nodded his approval.

"May I make an observation?" said Elizabeth, clearly nervous about speaking.

"Of course," said Laneford.

She swallowed. "It appears to me, Lud is intelligent enough *not* to believe he is the King of London. I can't say, of course, what is in his mind, but his planning has been meticulous, and his timing excellent. He has hidden a complicated operation from everyone's view and has used historical documents as aids. I don't doubt that he somehow has access to Sir John Soane's plans of the Bank of England. He must be conversant with old King Lud's history and his own genealogy. Lud has used ancient maps to find the river. He employs criminals and is quite ruthless in his dealings, so he is aware of how people behave. The criminal element points to a large reward for all, otherwise they would not attempt as much as they have. So large is the reward that when one of the foreign gentlemen or criminals asks too many questions or is no longer useful to the plan, he is killed, and yet others continue on the project and say nothing. You believe Lud might be a director at the Bank… I don't know if that part is true, but he must at least know a director to obtain the information… Excuse me for speaking at such length, but I cannot imagine the man I've just described can believe himself to be King Lud, and he couldn't or wouldn't convince others of it. Therefore, it is an artifice or a conceit on his part." She stopped abruptly, having delivered her opinion.

"That was marvellous, Elizabeth," said Sophie.

"Thank you." Elizabeth had become shy again.

"Would you like another sherry, my dear?" said Aunt Bessie.

"Oh, yes, please," replied Elizabeth, more ardently than was usual. Ada got it for her.

A little later, Flora said,

"We should get going… I had wanted to get my things from my flat tonight."

"What about Basinghall?" asked Sophie.

"Well, if Mr Philpott would be so kind as to drive me home, we could meet in the area."

"I'll drive you," said Laneford, launching himself from his chair.

"Will you, Sidney?" said Flora.

Within seconds, the pair were out of the room. Philpott followed because he had to retrieve something from the car.

"Sometimes," said Aunt Bessie, "a small thing is denotative of a much larger thing. I have observed two such small things tonight. Would my wild guess at the larger be correct?"

"Yes, it would, Auntie. They are getting married but won't decide anything until after this case has finished. We were sworn to secrecy, so are you, even though you've guessed."

"Naturally, I shall keep the faith. I am heartily pleased for her and believe they will do well together. Now there's just you to be settled.

"Auntie," said Sophie sternly. "Not now."

"Later, then. I don't think I shall go to Basinghall, so you had better make a start if you hope to accomplish anything. Take Marsden with you."

Superintendent Penrose was announced and then entered the drawing room.

"Good evening, Lady Shelling. It's a pleasure to meet you at last. ."

"Good evening, Superintendent Penrose. Or should I call you Inspector?"

"That's only a little foible o' mine so as not to make the lads at the Yard too uncomfortable. 'Sides, I got accustomed to it. Call me Superintendent Penrose, if you'd rather, your ladyship. I hear you're a vital part of the network now."

"Just a minor consulting role and supplier of sherry and dinners. Have you had your dinner? I'm asking everyone that question tonight, it seems."

"That's thoughtful. I had something, but it was at the Yard, and it was not what anyone would call satisfyin'. I'll be going home late, so I'll say yes to dinner, thank you. If it's no trouble to you."

"None at all." She rang the bell for Hawkins. "Please be seated, and Sophie will explain where we have made progress."

Once more, Sophie recapped the day's events, adding the observations made. Penrose took notes and asked questions. When she finished, he was silent for a moment.

"Our man's clever. Usually, by this point, it would become a police matter. There's enough that bears looking into for us to take an interest. The problem is getting the Assistant

Commissioner to agree to it because we're short-staffed." He turned to Aunt Bessie. "It's like this, your ladyship. We have a few men on their holidays, and we've sent everyone we can to different royal residences. Lud has us tied up in knots, so he has."

Penrose turned back to the others. "Now I'm not directly in charge of any detectives, save for a sergeant who's my assistant. I must request officers from other departments. The two I normally use are already assigned. Inspector Morton's busy with summat he can't leave. Then there's Sergeant Gowers, who I might pull from Buckingham Palace, although he's helping to keep a tight lid on Handley's movements. Other than that, there's no one I can get for such a large operation. Having said that, I can take the matter upstairs and maybe they'll reassign some officers."

"How likely is it that they would?" asked Sophie.

"I can't say either way. My problem is, I'd have to convince them there's no threat against the Royal Family when they're convinced there is, but that there *is* one against the Bank of England... I doubt they'll believe me straight off, but I'll try. Now, if we had a name, that would be different. Names can be checked and then visited."

"What about the bloke in the car at the London Docks?" asked Ada.

Penrose smiled. "You got his number plate, Miss Carmichael, didn't you? When we spoke to him, he'd already reported his car stolen. Barrett is known to us and has a record, so we set a watch on him, but the men were called off because, as I said, we're short-staffed."

Aunt Bessie was about to speak, but Sophie shook her head and stopped her, certain her aunt would talk about raising a militia. Aunt Bessie initially glared back, then nodded, and said,

"Don't forget your dinner, Superintendent. It is probably ready in the kitchen by now."

"Thank you for reminding me, Lady Shelling."

"We're off to Basinghall Street," said Sophie.

"If there are any problems," said Penrose, "summon a constable. Perhaps we can force the issue that way... I don't like the idea of you young ladies tackling these people on your own."

"Several gentlemen will accompany us, including Lord Laneford, and I have my police whistle."

"That's all right, then, but I'll pretend I didn't hear that last part, Miss King."

The City that had been thronged was now deserted. The sky was still bright in the west where the sun had gone down, but it was practically night in the narrow streets. From empty Basinghall Street, the sound of single vehicles driving along London Wall to the north or Gresham Street to the south made itself apparent. The engines of bus, lorry, or car could be distinguished. Occasionally, a car traversed Basinghall and they could all hear its entry, burgeoning progress as it approached, diminishing sound of departure until it exited, and then, as a separate sound, it was lost.

A horse-drawn laundry cart entered the street, and Sophie listened to it intently. The unhurried horse clopped along, and the metallic ring of its shoes bounced off the buildings in short echoes, the night amplifying the singular sound, which would have been unremarkable during the day. The noise of horse and cart marked the slowness of the journey, imbuing it with an inevitable quality, as if the animal and contraption must forever plod the earth. After it had gone and it was quiet again, Sophie felt as though there had been a profound yet unidentifiable change, as if she had lost a valuable thing and did not know what it was.

"It's so still now," said Sophie.

"The motor car is taking over everything," said Elizabeth.

Their own steps were the only sounds being made.

"You felt it, too, then. It's quite sad, really, but there's no going back. When that horse had passed us, I felt as though a friend had bid a final goodbye."

"Yes."

They entered the short street leading to Guildhall Yard. A solitary pedestrian passed them on his way out.

"I doubt there's anything for us to see," said Sophie.

They toured the open space and then stopped in front of the entrance to view the building.

"It's quite sinister," said Sophie. The lamps below threw the top part of the entrance into deeper shadow.

"Why on earth do they have great big, ugly statues of Gog and Magog? In the Bible, they represent great evil and the gathering of enemies."

"They are Gogmagog and Corineus, Miss King. When a child, I had a picture book and, beneath one view of London, they called them the gods of London. That very much surprised me, seeing as we are a Christian nation. Later, I learned the statues are representative of the founding of Britain. Corineus killed the giant Gogmagog. Due to their hideousness, they may have come to be called Gog and Magog, or simply because most people were unaware of the myths the statues represent and they had to call them something. That is only my unscholarly opinion, Miss King."

"It sounds quite scholarly to me." Sophie laughed. "How is Miss Jones coping at the office?"

"Very well, overall, but she's rather anxious. It's a strain for her, especially if I'm working outside."

"Then I'll see her tomorrow. She probably feels put upon or abandoned, and I don't want to treat her unfairly. The problem is that, when these operations arise, they take up all my time."

"She understands," said Elizabeth, "but I believe she would appreciate an interview."

"Then that's settled. Let's continue exploring around Guildhall."

They came to the back of Guildhall and found an opening. There were no lights in the abandoned, dead-end alley.

Sophie switched on her torch. They saw dirty flagstones covered with a dust thick enough in the corners that weeds sprang from it and which was fast becoming soil. A narrow track kept clean by usage ran the length of the alley. Her light followed this path until it dimly revealed the door to a cottage or shack at the end where the alley widened.

"It's quite disgusting back here."

"There's smoke coming out of the chimney," said Elizabeth.

Sophie pointed her torch above the roof and there picked out a thin, grey stream of smoke against an inky sky.

"As someone's living there, we'd best be quiet… They must be cooking, because it's too warm for a fire."

"But it's strange the windows aren't open and there isn't a single light showing."

"We can hardly knock on the door and ask them what they're doing."

Elizabeth laughed. "Indeed, no, we mustn't do that, Miss King."

They left the alley. They observed Marsden sitting in the car, watching for the van of the previous night and, after getting his report, left him to it. Marsden, being bored, smoked. He had no real idea what was going on or what he was supposed to be doing and did not much care as long as he was being paid. No van had appeared so far. There was traffic, but no vehicles had stopped nearby. There were a few pedestrians — mostly men by themselves returning from work, or so he assumed. He had kept a tally as instructed, but he did not see the point of it.

Elsewhere, Mr Philpott was for examining and documenting anything and everything. Ada could see his work might have value, but thought he was being excessive. They entered a tiny court.

"Ah, here is the drain of which I spoke."

"So, you did," said Ada as they approached the cover.

"The vertical pipe below is of a much larger diameter than is warranted for the collection of wastewater from its catchment area."

"And what does that mean, Mr Philpott?"

"I'll show you." He produced a bicycle lamp and shone it through the grating.

"It's got water in the bottom," said Ada. "Who'd go down into that lot?"

"If you observe to your left, you will notice the large diameter pipe that a man could enter upon hands and knees."

"I can see that. But supposin' he's in it when it rains? He'd drown, and what a way to go that would be!"

"I concur with your assessment. But this pipe is short and must connect to a much larger pipe under Basinghall Street. The risk is negligible."

"I wouldn't say that, Mr Philpott. You'd never get me down there in that filthy muck. Anyway, there's moss around the cover, so it ain't been pulled up for a while. How'd they get in there, then?"

"I, too, noticed that. My current thinking is that they have tunnelled from one of the surrounding basements and broken into the pipe — from the top half, of course, so as not to flood their own works."

"You really think they've done that?"

"It is a possibility, Miss Carmichael, and should be explored. I shall return here tomorrow and try to gain admittance where possible."

"Basements, you mean? You can't just ask an' they'll let you in."

"I have planned a subterfuge. I will pass myself off as an inspector for the City of London and show them a letter of authorization. Of course, I require Lord Laneford's permission before I can undertake such an enterprise."

"Oh," said Ada. They began counting basements and Philpott drew diagrams.

Flora put her arm through Lord Laneford's and smiled dreamily while floating towards Lothbury to examine things.

There they discussed foundations and Lilypot Lane, the Bank's walls and colours of curtains, as well as the amount of gold to be stolen and the potential of Greece for their honeymoon. Then they wandered back to find the others.

It was just then that six men entered Basinghall from the southern end. They were not together as such — one of them was far in advance and acted as a scout. They passed the entrance to Guildhall Yard and quickly entered the alley at the rear. Without hesitation, they entered the cottage.

Ten minutes later, two of them left. They were cautious and, when the coast proved to be clear, they walked along, maintaining a twenty-yard distance between them. Flora and Laneford passed by each man and, although they noticed them, they saw them as nothing more significant than passersby.

At the junction with London Wall, Sophie and Elizabeth stopped.

"I don't know what else we can do here… We seem now to be looking for the sake of looking." Sophie was quiet for a moment. "I've been wondering if Auntie made a bit of a muck of it at Soane's Museum."

"Lady Shelling may have set about it the wrong way. However, I believe the answer the Inspectress gave would have been the same no matter how diplomatic her ladyship had been."

"Ah, I thought as much. Gladys and I will try again tomorrow and take a different tack. I believe it's probable that someone used Sir John Soane's drawings to plan the raid. Also, it's important we find out the thickness of the vault walls. If Lud uses dynamite to make a breech, it could kill someone."

"I'm not sure he would use explosives in a tunnel, Miss King. It might collapse on top of the gang."

"Oh, I suppose it would. Then why has he such an interest in explosives? He didn't use them against the King."

"It is most inexplicable." They waited in silence until Elizabeth spoke again. "Miss King, may I ask what it was like to meet the Royal Family?"

"The experience was as rewarding as one would expect. The first thing that struck me was that they were quite ordinary in so many ways, but that was only an adjustment to my expectations. What I noticed most of all is how trapped they are. I said they were ordinary, but they aren't free to lead ordinary lives. For example, they can't simply go shopping without an extraordinary fuss being made." Sophie paused. "It's hard to express how insulated and restricted they are, except to say I wouldn't want to trade places with any of them, despite all the trappings and their great wealth."

"Oh, that *is* interesting. One doesn't consider their personal costs, but only views them through their public lives."

"I have a few anecdotes about Queen Mary and Queen Alexandra."

"Do you, Miss King?" said Elizabeth eagerly. Sophie satisfied her curiosity.

They all stayed in the area keeping watch until gone midnight. The van never appeared and so they left, deflated, except for Marsden, who thought of the extra pay coming to him.

Chapter 22

Sir John's old place

At a minute past the opening hour of ten on Wednesday, Sophie and Flora entered Sir John Soane's Museum. They would have loved to explore the cramped place where treasures awaited unseen around every corner and rich artwork hung in cunning cupboards. But they were not there to look at those. Instead, they opened a door in the administrative area to discover Miss Elinor Daniell, Inspectress.

"Excuse us for disturbing you," said Sophie, entering the office with Flora at her heels.

The woman, about forty and quietly dressed, turned her intelligent face towards them. She stared, enquiringly and mildly hostile.

"Yes? This is a private area, and the guide can answer your questions."

"Miss Daniell, my name is Miss Phoebe King, and this is my associate, Miss Gladys Walton. We came to see you because we need your assistance concerning a matter of great urgency." Sophie paused.

"Really? I am at a loss."

"The two things I'm about to relate, you will find upsetting. The first is difficult to credit and you may not even believe us once we explain it, but the second you will believe and find distressing in the extreme."

"You have my attention."

"The first is this. We work for the police and the Home Office, and I can provide you with verifiable references, if you so desire. There is almost certainly going to be a raid on the Bank of England. We have no direct evidence, yet possess a growing body of circumstantial evidence. At present, we are in the invidious position of being unable to convince the authorities that the threat is real because they are entirely taken up with another threat. Did you read in the papers that someone threw a grenade into the grounds of Buckingham Palace?"

"Everyone has, but what has that to do with your outlandish statement?"

"Because the grenade attack was a blind, part of a campaign of threats against the King's life, which threats are also spurious. The campaign has been mounted to conceal the true plan of the persons behind the deceit, which is to steal gold or cash and bonds — gold, we believe — from the Bank of England."

"This is all utterly beyond me. I think you should leave."

"I would react the same way if I were in your position," said Flora. "We sound like cranks; we know we do. But how ridiculous we sound doesn't alter the truthfulness of what we're trying to convey."

Miss Daniell paused and considered. "How does any of what you've said involve the museum?"

"Because somebody has used Sir John Soane's drawings to plan the attack," said Sophie. "The only logical possibility is that an agent of these criminals came in and copied or stole the plans of the Bank that they needed. Should the raid go ahead, the police will be involved and will require some of the museum's drawings for evidence."

The Inspectress could now see the danger which had thrust itself into her ordinary day. These women may be mad, mistaken, or confidence tricksters, or they might be telling the truth, and she foresaw the potential risks to the valuable collection if the latter were true.

"Mr Spiers, the Curator, isn't here today, but Mr Scott, he's one of our trustees, is upstairs working with drawings. He's an architect, you see." She stood up, indecisive about what to do with her visitors, and did not want to leave them alone in her office. "You had better follow me."

They climbed the winding stairs, passing a wide variety of interesting curios that Flora and Sophie wanted to examine but could not. Miss Daniell was silent, absorbed by the perplexing and unwelcome situation that was developing. They reached a series of interconnected attics and there found Mr Giles Scott. He was in his twenties and much younger than either Flora or Sophie had expected. A thin man, they found him bending over and studying diagrams spread out on the work surface of a cabinet of drawers for architectural drawings. The room, made narrow by several cabinets, was bright, being directly under the skylights.

"Excuse the interruption, Mr Scott, but something urgent has arisen."

He looked up and for a moment strove to remember where he was.

"Urgent, Miss Daniell?" He glanced at Sophie and Flora.

"And unusual. This is Miss King and Miss Walton, and I believe you should hear what they have to say."

"Yes, of course. Pleased to meet you."

The agents responded, and then jointly explained the situation to him. The longer they spoke, the more permanent seemed the furrow in his brow and he did not interrupt them.

"Yes, he said... There has been a strange occurrence I should mention. Mr Spiers mentioned it to me, and several other trustees, that some of Soane's drawings were now creased, as if they had been rolled up and then inadvertently crushed, or so we surmised at the time he reported the damage."

"Which drawings were those?" asked Sophie.

"One was the final version of the plan for the entire Bank complex. Most were elevations and floor plans for the buildings surrounding Lothbury Court and Bullion Court."

"Did they include the vaults?"

"Naturally, Miss King... The odd thing about the incident was that we keep those drawings in different drawers. It was as if someone had collected them into one roll, bent them, then returned the drawings to their proper places."

"That's interesting. May we see a sample that includes the main vault?"

Scott hesitated, glanced at Miss Daniell, then back again. "I don't see why not." He went to a drawer behind him, carefully extracted a small sheet, and placed it on the work surface. They all looked at the meticulously executed working drawing filled in with mellow pink and yellow washes. They could see a crumpled edge along its top. "I'll bring another sheet to demonstrate where the crease corresponds across the drawings." As he took it from the drawer, he observed, "The selected drawings were all of a piece, and covered the area from the wall to the vault."

The second sheet was much larger and had a definite crease in the middle. "Do you see the small tear on the edge? We repaired that." He then put the smaller sheet on top of the larger one and it was immediately apparent by the orientation of the creases that the damage on both had occurred at the same time. "We considered calling in a conservator, but we're hopeful the creases will eventually flatten out."

"How could it have occurred?" asked Flora.

"We don't know. This is the only incident of its kind as far as anyone remembers."

"Would you point out the vault, please?" asked Sophie. "I'm unfamiliar with such diagrams."

"This is it here."

Sophie and Flora leaned in to see where he pointed.

"How thick are the walls?" asked Sophie.

"If you observe here, you can see the building rests on piers for its main support." He tapped a finger on one of the piers. "The curtain walls between are double-brick but weren't designed to bear any great load."

"So, in between this pier and that one, for a distance of approximately..." she looked at the scale to calculate it "...eight feet, there is no reinforcement of the wall?"

"That is correct. There may be a rubble wall, or something to permit drainage, but it isn't specified or marked in.

Certainly, there is no provision for reinforcement... Why is that important? Are these suspected raiders believed to be tunnelling their way in?"

"We think so," said Sophie.

He nodded. "Then, in light of what you know, can you interpret the riddle of the damaged drawings?"

"I'm not altogether sure I can. The important feature is that someone knew where to find the associated drawings and gathered them together in one bundle, but why they did that, I can't say, other than they were carrying them somewhere. Who has access to the drawings and could know where they're kept?"

"Quite a number, but only the staff or those persons on our Approved List," said Miss Daniell.

"How long is this list?" asked Flora.

"There are about five hundred names," she replied, "but they're not all active."

"Many are architects such as myself," said Mr Scott. "I'm here solely for research because a client in Cambridge is requesting a feature similar to something Soane did. Most of the others who have access consult the library of drawings for academic purposes. And they're all extremely careful how they handle them."

"Someone wasn't," said Sophie. "Could a person have stolen the drawings and then returned them?"

The question troubled both Scott and Daniell, as if a strange, brightly coloured giant beetle had dropped heavily from the ceiling and now scurried across the papers. They were both appalled and fascinated.

"I find it unthinkable, let alone possible," said Miss Daniell. "No one on our list would ever steal anything."

"Where did the damage come from, then?" asked Flora.

"I can't say," she replied, very much on the defensive.

"How certain are you about this raid on the Bank?" asked Scott.

"Ninety-nine percent sure," said Flora.

"Do you see, Miss Daniell?" said Scott. "The police will be involved if it is true. They will take the drawings... Now, if we assist these ladies, they may prevent the raid."

"What do you mean, Mr Scott?"

"A name on the Approved List is most likely to have done this. They had sufficient knowledge to collect all the drawings useful for tunnelling under the wall at Lothbury to reach the vault wall, which is not reinforced. It's a clever plan, if an expensive one."

"The person has money," said Sophie.

"Are you saying that I must give them the list?" asked Miss Daniell.

"Possibly." He turned to Sophie and Flora. "Is that what you want?"

"Yes," said Sophie. "Although we must narrow it down if we are to be in time. When did the damage occur?"

"That's difficult to say," replied Scott. "Mr. Spiers noticed the condition of the drawings in early January, and he believed the damage occurred in December, but he can't be more specific than that."

"I wish I'd known about this," said Miss Daniell. "Anyone accessing the drawings must sign the Register." Her attitude towards the problem was rapidly changing, because in comprehending the problem, she could see a part to play in solving it.

"The Register!" exclaimed Scott. "How stupid of me. I signed it this morning before getting the keys."

"Ah!" began Flora. "So, by examining the entries for December, we can get a short list of names?"

"Yes," said Miss Daniell. "I can cross-reference the entries with the cards and provide full names and addresses."

"That's excellent," said Sophie. The three women were on the verge of leaving the room. "Before we go, there is another matter I should mention."

Neither Miss Daniell nor Mr Scott spoke.

"During our investigations, a person revealed a secret to us. We vowed not to repeat it, and we cannot do so now.

But Mr Scott, you are an architect. What happens when a business outgrows the building housing it?"

"Well, it moves or adds an extension."

"Or rebuilds?" asked Sophie.

"That, too."

"I hear the Bank of England is very busy these days," said Flora.

"Some say it will get much busier," said Sophie.

"They're going to rebuild?" He looked stricken. Miss Daniell put a hand to her mouth.

"I'm sorry, but I thought you should know," said Sophie. "We can't discuss it further and we are in rather a hurry."

Miss Daniell squeaked something and bolted from the room. The agents thanked Mr Scott and said goodbye, while he could only smile awkwardly in return.

When they left the Soane Museum, Sophie and Flora possessed two strong candidates from a short list of thirty names, having dismissed the rest for a variety of reasons. These two were men who had studied the Bank of England drawings in December, according to the museum guide who had been brought into the agents' and Miss Daniell's discussion. They learned both men had spent many hours of research at the museum on successive days.

Within an hour of leaving the Museum, they could dismiss the first name, Robinson, as a candidate for anything evil. The offices where he worked were small, busy, and appeared so ordinary and blameless that the agents were prompted to enter immediately to begin their enquiry. Robinson proved to be a middle-aged and loquacious architect in partnership with several others. He was so delighted to see two young ladies cross his threshold that he was quite unconcerned about the reason for their visit. He offered them coffee, which they declined; then a drink, taking a small one himself after their refusal. He was talkative and completely open. When Flora and Sophie finally got him speaking about his examination of the Bank of England drawings, he explained he had always wanted to write a book on the subject but was now in two minds about the project. "It's the expense of including photographs and drawings," he told them, entirely negligent in asking why his visitors should want to know his business. They said goodbye, with him adding that, anytime they were in the area, they should drop in.

This left Sophie and Flora, with one name: Mr Cassius Bell, 12 Crescent, City of London. He had been on the Approved List for many years and, although the tour guide and Miss Daniell had tried to describe him, it became apparent that he was unremarkable, above the middle age, and had kept to himself. The agents decided upon first seeing Miss Jones at the agency, then to have lunch, and afterwards to visit the address.

Chapter 23

The residence of Mr Cassius Bell

Sophie and Flora got off at the Mark Lane Underground Station. They came out into sunlight and crossed Trinity Gardens where they halted to get their bearings. Across the road and sloping down to the water lay an open space of flagstones, which gave them an uninterrupted view of the busy, glittering river. Its south bank backdrop was of old wharves and tall warehouses — an unbroken line which stretched away to disappear into the eastern haze, but which terminated abruptly to the west at the massive structure of Tower Bridge. Next to the open space on the north bank was the Tower of London, its Union Jack barely lifted by the gentle, warm afternoon breeze. It felt more like August than the beginning of June.

Sophie consulted a street map, then looked up. "It must be over there." She pointed north-east and, although she did not yet know it, could see the top of isolated number twelve Crescent. "It isn't far, but we must reach it via Hammett Street off the Minories. What sort of name is that?" They began walking.

"I've heard the name is connected with a convent that existed centuries ago... Miss Jones bucked up after you spoke to her. What did you say, or can't you tell?"

"I can. I've made Muriel her assistant. She's very steady and will take charge of the typists when Miss Jones has to take over Elizabeth's duties on the employment agency side of things, which has slacked off lately, but we're still quite busy. Everything's now ticking over nicely."

They walked along The Minories, a typical London street both prosperous and worn, and came to Hammett Street. After entering the short thoroughfare, they came almost immediately upon the cobblestones of Crescent. Sophie had not realized it was so close, and the transition from bustling Minories to neglected Crescent was abrupt. Number twelve was a depressing sight.

"I don't like this," said Sophie. "This place is not at all how I visualized."

"It is rather run down. What do we do? Knock?"

"We must. Even though the houses are good, and it's not exactly a poverty-stricken area, I would say it is a dangerous one, especially after dark."

"I see what you mean," said Flora. "There's only a single lamppost, so it must be very dingy here at night. And thieves might lurk in the passageway."

"Yes, thank you very much, Gladys. I hadn't thought of that yet."

"Just simply pointing out the potential dangers. Now here's another. If we knock, and no one's in, all well and good. But if we ask for Mr Cassius Bell and he comes to the door and we believe he's Lud, then what?"

Sophie puffed her cheeks and blew. "We can say we're... um... Oh, I don't know... Say we're from the Soane Museum?"

"Phoebe! He'd know we're on to him, and we'd end up in the Thames!"

"Yes, even if we didn't mention the museum, we could let something slip out by mistake."

"I wouldn't, but *you* might," said Flora. "Anyway, there's an easy way around this. Just leave it to Auntie Glad."

"What are you going to say?"

"You'll see. I think it's quite ingenious."

"Then it *must* work. This is our last chance. I don't know what we'll do if Bell isn't Lud."

"There's only one way to find out, and the place is very promising. It has criminal hideout written all over it."

"It really does. Are you ready, then?" asked Sophie.

"Let me see the Bartholomew's for a moment, please." Flora took the map book and leafed through it. "We're ready." She handed back the book. "Don't say anything unless asked."

"What on earth are you going to say?"

"You'll see."

They approached number twelve. Flora gave a smart rap using the brass knocker, then they waited. A man opened the door wearing a cardigan. He was so tall it surprised them.

"Good afternoon," said Flora. "We've come about the furniture. May we come in?"

Morrish did not move, but asked in a deep, rumbling voice, "What furniture?"

"The furniture that's for sale. Is the owner at home?"

"No, but that's neither here nor there. There's no furniture for sale." He made movements preparatory to shutting the door. Flora put her hand on it so that he could not.

"I insist upon speaking to Mr Duncan. We've come quite a distance to view the furniture."

"There's no one named Duncan living here and no furniture for sale," said Morrish.

"Then who is the owner of this house?"

Morrish pointed to the brass plaque. "Gentleman by the name of Godfrey owns the property."

"Oh, I can't imagine how this can be. When my friend told me, I distinctly heard him say that Mr Duncan of number 12 Park Crescent was selling all his furniture. How can there be such a mistake?"

"I get it. You've got the wrong house. This is 12 Crescent, not 12 Park Crescent."

"Crescent?" Flora turned to Sophie. "Really, Agnes, I remember saying on the Tube that I thought we were heading in the wrong direction. Please find Park Crescent at once, or the entire afternoon will be wasted." Flora removed her hand from the door, turned back, and smiled. "I'm extremely sorry to have disturbed you Mr...?"

"Morrish."

"Mr Morrish. It seems we have made a silly mistake. Good afternoon."

"Good afternoon."

As the agents walked away and Morrish was closing the door, Flora exclaimed,

"Really, Agnes! How could you embarrass me like that? Give me the map. I'll look it up for myself." Sophie proffered the book, and Flora snatched it from her.

When they were out of sight, Sophie said,

"You laid that on a bit thick. I didn't enjoy being the unwitting sacrificial lamb."

"Had to do it but, you must admit, it was effective."

"Yes, it was. What did you make of Mr Morrish?"

Inside number twelve, Morrish turned away from the door. Mrs Morrish was standing silently at the other end of the hall.

"Who was that, Arthur?"

"A couple of ladies."

"What'd they want?"

"They wanted to buy furniture, but they'd got the wrong address."

Mrs Morrish was about to speak again when they heard footsteps on the stairs.

"Who were those two women?" asked Lefty Watts, who had peered through a narrow gap in the curtains to watch Flora and Sophie leave.

"They wanted to buy furniture but had the wrong address."

"All right, do you think?"

"I don't know," said Morrish slowly.

"What d'ya mean, you don't know? Were they or weren't they?"

Morrish hesitated.

"Ugh, you're too thick for words," said Lefty. He went out after them.

Morrish muttered under his breath.

Sophie and Flora were in an underground train on their way to Scotland Yard. They sat at one end of a carriage, which was only a quarter full.

"Don't look," said Flora. "There's a suspicious man standing down the other end." She had espied Lefty Watts, who had caught up with them.

"Hmm. In what way is he suspicious?"

"I happened to look in his direction, and he turned away suddenly, as though not wanting me to notice him, but he wasn't fast enough. He had been staring at us."

"What does he look like?"

"Big, reasonably well-dressed — a criminal type if ever I saw one. His ears in profile give him away."

Sophie laughed. "How can his ears be criminal? Now I want to look even more."

"Because, if I were to draw a hypothetical criminal, I would draw his type of ear."

"I thought it was foreheads that denoted criminality. That's what they used to say."

"Who? Criminologists?"

"I suppose so... Assuming you're correct, then is he a purse-snatcher looking for an opportunity or has he followed us from Crescent?"

"The shape of an ear *might* allow for such precision, but I'm not expert enough to answer you. Shouldn't we expect a reaction from number twelve, though? Our story was believable — at least I thought it was, but they must be on high alert and are verifying our story."

"I hadn't really thought of that. I suppose we should be extremely careful here. We can't go to Scotland Yard or the Agency. And we can't can't really go to Park Crescent in case he follows us all the way there."

"Let's go shopping, instead. Selfridges will do. I know the layout very well."

"A good idea," said Sophie.

With the change in plan, they both naturally gazed up at the Underground map above the windows opposite.

"We have to change at Bank for Oxford Circus."

"Bond Street's closer," said Flora.

The train rattled rhythmically through the tunnel and then slowed as it approached the next station. They stood up before it had stopped. When it had, they got out. The man got out, too.

"We can't accost him and give ourselves away," said Sophie, as they climbed the stairs to the Central line.

"No... Do you think we can lose him, then reacquire him with *us* following *him* instead?"

"No, we mustn't. He might see us. We must make him believe our cover story is true, but we can't continue with the furniture-buying part while he's watching."

"Then we shall lose him in Selfridges," said Flora. "Everyone gets lost in Selfridges."

In the vast department store, Flora enjoyed playing the part of the know-it-all friend guiding her quieter companion. Sophie grudgingly endured her part of meek simpleton — grudgingly because Flora was quite loud with her comments on occasion.

"You can't possibly think of wearing that colour of scarf!" Flora, at a counter, brayed for the benefit of Sophie, the shop assistant, and Lefty Watts who stood twenty feet away and was very much interested in ladies' raincoats just at that moment.

Sophie whispered, "Don't push your luck."

"What did you say, dear? You're muttering again," said Flora at the same volume. "You admire the colour? That's immaterial, because it makes you look bilious, and I can't have that! I'm the one who has to look at you."

"I'll repay you more than double for this embarrassment," whispered Sophie.

"You really should put yourself completely in my hands." Flora looked at her watch. "Come along. We can't dawdle here all day while you make up your mind. There's still the furniture to enquire about and it's getting late."

Flora sailed off towards the lifts. Sophie thanked the shop assistant and then hurried after her. Watts, no longer interested in raincoats, followed them. They lost him in front of the lifts. He thought they were waiting for one to go down and, in trying to be inconspicuous, failed to notice them go up the staircase. They shot through the store to descend by other stairs and so got out. Lefty Watts was still searching for them even after they entered a taxi to go to Scotland Yard.

When Watts returned to Crescent, he informed Morrish the women had indeed been looking to buy furniture and were not from the police, so they had nothing to worry about.

"Morrish... Twelve Crescent," repeated Superintendent Penrose as he reread his note in a ruminative tone. He picked up the telephone and dialled an extension. "Daniels, hop in here for a moment." He replaced the receiver. "You lost the fella who followed you... How good at his job was he?"

"Terrible," said Sophie. "He was often far too close."

"We spotted him early and couldn't miss him after that," added Flora.

"Did he catch you looking at him?" asked Penrose.

Sophie and Flora exchanged glances. "We don't believe so," replied Sophie.

"An amateur, then." Penrose leaned back in his chair. "Now, if he were a pickpocket, you wouldn't have noticed him. That he followed you all that way into Selfridges can only mean he came from Crescent... Why's there no definite article in front o' that there word? I find it annoying." Detective Sergeant Daniels entered and waited. "Summat's going on at Crescent's number twelve, so Morrish and the other fella are up to no good." He leaned forward. "We all reckon so, but that won't convince a justice to issue a search warrant. Owner's name is Godfrey and he might be involved, too. And all that lot is tied in with Mr Cassius Bell and the damaged drawings at the Soane Museum." He turned to the sergeant. "Daniels, get on to the Soane Museum, Lincoln's Inn Fields. Tell them we'll be arriving soon so no one's leaving before we get there. Don't take no for an answer."

"Yes, sir." Sergeant Daniels left the room.

"Did you speak to your superiors about the Bank of England?" asked Sophie.

"I did, and they immediately took it out of my hands. Instead, the chief constable is going to have a quiet chat tonight with the Bank's governor, Mr Montagu Norman."

"But suppose the director who's involved gets to hear of this," said Sophie.

"It's a risk, but he says he knows the governor and it couldn't possibly be him. Of course, the Chief Constable *would* say that because he knows the chap. However, I'm forbidden to do anything until he's spoken to him. That means I can't send any detectives to the Bank or otherwise help you. I'd send someone from the network, but they're all assigned to royal residences, so it would take them a day to get here. But here's another problem…"

"Another one?"

"Yes. If you're seen, there might be trouble, and I wouldn't like either of you to come to harm. The fella who followed you is big, and you described him as a thug. Morrish is tall. Both are likely to be violent and can recognize you. There may be more of them inside or who come visiting the house. You said the place is hemmed in by other buildings yet isolated and the area is not very busy during the day. Well, you'll have to be in the street to watch. Where are you going to hide so that you're not seen?"

"In a car?" suggested Sophie.

"There's a short road where we could hide," said Flora, "but anyone could unexpectedly walk past coming from Minories and see us before we see them."

"Then, that's no good."

"There's Vine Street, which runs into Crescent," said Sophie. "It's much longer, so we would have ample opportunity to see someone approach."

"Vine Street sounds better. Park the car facing away from the house and use the back window to keep it under surveillance. Should anyone walk along Vine Street, he'll see the driver, but won't think you have an interest in the place."

"That's a good suggestion," said Sophie.

Daniels opened the door.

"They've agreed to see us, Inspector. I've got a Mr Giles Scott on the line. He says the trustees are having an emergency meeting, and could we come over at once?"

"Yes," said Penrose. "You'll have to leave now ladies, because I can't give this job to anyone else, and I have one or two calls to make first. All I can say is, be careful. Don't take any risks."

"We won't," said Sophie.

Chapter 24

A near miss

After dinner at White Lyon Yard, and once Lord Laneford and Philpott had arrived, the agents set off in their different directions. Flora and Marsden accompanied Laneford and Philpott to the Bank, while Sophie and Ada took Rabbit to camp in the vicinity of number twelve. In Vine Street, they found a safe place to park from which the front door was visible. Although it was safe, it was not the best of vantage points. By nine, the shuttered house was just a grey shape, weakly illuminated by the single street lamp in the middle of Crescent.

"We shan't be able to identify anyone at this distance," said Sophie from the back, using binoculars to peer through the small oval window.

"Then, miss, what's the point of us being 'ere?"

"To see how many people use the place." Sophie continued observing for a moment longer. "Do you want to have a go?"

"Yes, miss." She got in the back and took over the surveillance. They were quiet until Ada spoke again. "Do you think the house is haunted?"

"That hadn't occurred to me… It looks like it should be."

"Yes. It could be a nice house, but it ain't, an' never will be… Why've they bricked up the windows?"

"I don't know."

"I bet somethin' horrible goes on inside. No one who's normal would brick up a window… And they're murderers, miss. A house full of bloomin' murderers, and here we are watching for them."

"We're doing it because we're going to put a stop to their wickedness."

"That's right an' all, miss… 'Allo. There's a tall bloke coming out."

"Where?"

Ada handed the binoculars to Sophie.

"That's Morrish… He's going toward Minories."

"What do we do, miss?"

"Follow him on foot."

They got out, then hurried past number twelve and into short Hammett Street.

"There he is," said Ada.

They watched as he entered a public house on the other side of Minories. They found a doorway and waited. Traffic was light and there were few pedestrians about. A courting couple, coming from the direction of the Tower of London, passed them.

"I find it strange," began Sophie, "if he is involved in a plan to rob the Bank of England so soon, how he is now casually going to a public house?"

"Well, they're not doing it tonight, miss." Ada looked towards number twelve, then back again. "I can't understand why the police don't go into the Bank an' tell 'em straight what's goin' on. I mean, s'posin' the gold gets lifted an' they're still fiddling about… What happens then?"

"The country will be in serious financial trouble. I don't know what the ramifications would be… Dire, I should imagine. To answer your question, I think the police have no hard evidence and, like everyone else, seemingly, can't quite believe it will happen. Other than that, I think they're reluctant to approach the Bank in case it's all a false alarm… We discussed this."

"I know, miss. But we keep findin' bits and bobs and it don't seem to make no difference to 'em."

"Yes, and it's very wearing. I don't know if it's a failure of the organization or of individuals, but the slow, reluctant pace they're taking is extremely disappointing. I'm excluding Lord Laneford and Superintendent Penrose, of course, but even their actions are anything but dynamic."

"Yes, but they believe it's possible, so they're doin' what they can. Perhaps they want to catch Lud more than save the gold."

"That may well be the case." Morrish came out carrying a heavy bag. "He's bought some beer."

"We should scarper, miss."

Scarper they did, reaching the safety of the car only just before Morrish could have seen them. There, they resumed their watch and, a quarter of an hour later, a car pulled up outside the house. A man got out and, before he could knock on the front door, it opened. The agents could see Morrish by the hall light. He came out, and they saw a woman shut the door behind him. Sophie climbed over the seats with difficulty, while Ada used the binoculars.

"They're just sittin' in the car with the lights off... Now they're on."

"I can hear their engine." Sophie started Rabbit.

"They're driving off!" announced Ada.

Sophie quickly executed a three-point turn, which threw Ada all over the place, and they followed with the headlights off.

"Can you warn me next time please, miss? I wasn't ready."

"Sorry. Are you hurt?"

"Oh, no. It was a bit sudden, that's all."

Under acceleration, Rabbit was noisy. The tyres squealed when they turned the corner into Hammett Street and the brakes squealed when Rabbit stopped at Minories.

"There they are," said Sophie, switching the headlights on.

"They might be going to the docks, miss," said Ada ominously.

"Yes," said Sophie, "they might."

They followed the car and, where possible on quieter streets, Rabbit ran without lights.

"We're very close to London Docks," said Sophie.

She and Ada had parked Rabbit and were hiding around a corner, observing the car which was now outside a small tenement building on a dark, rundown street. They could just perceive the outline of the driver waiting in the vehicle.

"I've got a bad feelin' about this, miss."

"So, have I."

The street was not exactly quiet. It was a warm night and many doors and windows were open, allowing the noises of domesticity to escape. Nearby and high up, a man was talking interminably, and they could hear the burble of his voice, but not what he said. Further away, several people were singing a popular song.

"I know that one," said Ada. She began humming the tune.

A few moments later, the sound of raised, angry voices erupted inside the tenement. The noise stopped suddenly. Then, two men came lurching out of the building. Between them was a violently struggling third and much shorter man. The agents could not make out what was happening. Sophie stepped towards them, reaching for the torch in her pocket.

"What are you doing!?" she shouted, as she switched on her torch and pointed it at them.

The contest between the three men did not stop, and the beam of light revealed a hand trying to clamp the short man's mouth. Sophie saw him bite the hand, and then heard him scream, "Meurtre!" The next instant, there was a whirl of events. Sophie saw a muzzle flash from the car and heard a bullet whizz past her cheek to hit a wall behind her. The short man struck out and broke free. One of his captors slumped over, clutching himself. The other captor yelled and cursed, shaking his bitten hand. Sophie dodged behind a car but kept the torch on them. The men piled into the vehicle, and she glimpsed Morrish getting out of the back to drag the slumped man inside with him. The car drove off and Sophie was still there, holding the torch.

"Miss! Are you all right?" Ada rushed up and started looking for a wound.

"Ah, yes, I think so... They shot at me." She sounded bemused.

"My 'eart stopped, that it did. I thought they killed you. C'mon, let's get out of here before the rozzers show up. Now, miss." Ada took her by the hand and dragged her away.

"Yes, of course. I'm sorry... They shot at me, and I wasn't ready... I didn't think..."

"Can you drive?"

"What? Of course, I can. I just feel so stupid at being taken unawares... Blasted cheek! Who do they think they are? They're lucky I didn't shoot back... Only Freda was in my handbag, which I left in the car."

They got into Rabbit and set off.

"Would you have shot back?"

"Why wouldn't I? They started it."

"Oh, I don't know about that. Guns are horrible. They shouldn't be allowed... Have you been for target practise yet?"

"No, I've been much too busy, but I shall certainly go next week... The unmitigated gall of that wretched, hideous creature — shooting at an unarmed person, because believe you me, he didn't know otherwise! Just wait until I get my hands on him, and all of them."

"What did that man shout? It was foreign, wasn't it?"

"Meurtre is French for murder. Thank goodness he got away."

"Murder." Ada tutted. "Godfathers, I reckon he was headed for a dip in the Thames, I do an' all. Do you know you saved a soul tonight? I'm right proud of you, miss, and I'm so glad that you're still alive... Blimey, it don't bear thinkin' about."

"Thank you for your concern."

"Weren't you at all scared?"

"It all happened so suddenly I hadn't the time to be frightened. Stupefied and dim-witted — absolutely."

"What do we do now?"

"Tell Superintendent Penrose, I suppose, except he must be at home."

"How about Lord Laneford?"

"Yes, he'll do, only we mustn't make a fuss of the gunshot. You know what men are like — they get all protective."

"I don't mind if they do, miss."

"Oh, I agree, but if we make a thing of it, they'll take us off the case. You know they will."

"Yes, that's right, miss."

At a quarter past ten, they found the others patrolling Basinghall. Near the Bank, they came first upon Lord Laneford, and when he heard a shot had been fired, he was most concerned.

"Did he shoot *at* you, Miss King?"

"Um… I wouldn't say that, exactly. It was more like a warning shot."

"I don't like the sound of this. And are you all right?" He asked tenderly.

"Yes, thank you, and we weren't scared."

"It made us jump, my Lord," said Ada, "but only that."

"Are you sure?"

Sophie and Ada nodded.

"Right. I'm calling a halt to the proceedings. If these people resort to gunplay so readily, everyone here is in jeopardy. In all good conscience, I cannot permit the continuation of our efforts."

"Can't we just observe?" asked Sophie.

"The risk is too great. The kidnapping you witnessed will galvanize the police and might force the Bank of England to take the threat seriously."

"But what will they do?" asked Sophie.

"Their most obvious task is to find the tunnel. The police will search the surrounding buildings looking for the entrance, while the Bank sets an around-the-clock guard in the vault."

"And what about Lud?"

"It's Thursday tomorrow, and the directors will hold the weekly Court of the Bank of England. All of them will be there, apart from those indisposed or abroad. I believe, or at least hope, our man will be present among them. They will certainly discuss the police action and, if that doesn't produce a guilty reaction in the director we want, I don't know what will."

"That sounds promising," said Sophie.

"There's Gladys and Mr Philpott," said Ada, as they came out from Basinghall. "I'll get them." Ada walked quickly in their direction.

"In a way, it's a welcome relief that this situation will be finally resolved," said Sophie. "It has been very nerve-wracking, Lord Laneford."

"Sidney, if you please, as we're to be friends. Flora — dear me, I should really say Gladys — has confessed that she mentioned our engagement to you." He smiled. "I rather thought she would, even though we're not making the announcement until after the case is closed."

"Ah, as that is so, allow me to offer you my most heartfelt congratulations."

"Many thanks, Miss King. Your approbation is most welcome and comes as a relief, actually."

"It does?"

"Yes, because I value your opinion. Not that you've demonstrated any antipathy towards me. It's just that one never knows, does one?"

"No, I suppose not," said Sophie, surprised by his diffidence and thoughtfulness.

"Let me hasten to add that Flora and I have agreed that she shall continue working for you as she does currently."

"You don't mind her working as a spy?"

"No. She enjoys the work, but it's best I say no more at present. It is for her to have this conversation with you." They watched the others coming towards them. "I'll tell Marsden he may go. I'm sure you're glad the day is over."

"Yes, it has been hectic."

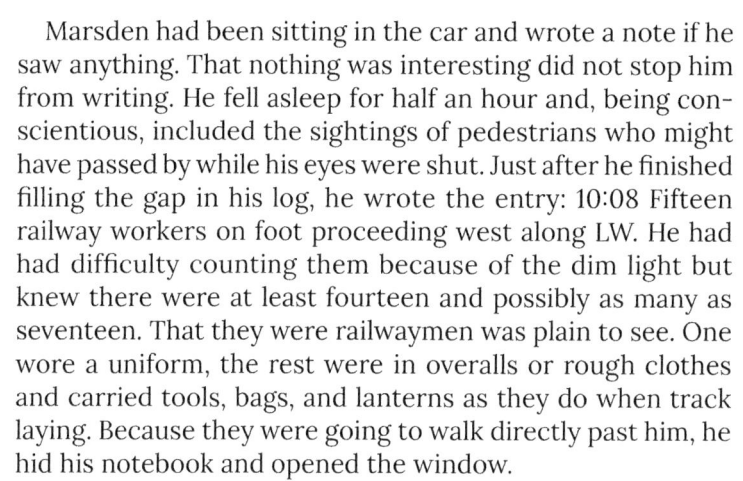

Marsden had been sitting in the car and wrote a note if he saw anything. That nothing was interesting did not stop him from writing. He fell asleep for half an hour and, being conscientious, included the sightings of pedestrians who might have passed by while his eyes were shut. Just after he finished filling the gap in his log, he wrote the entry: 10:08 Fifteen railway workers on foot proceeding west along LW. He had had difficulty counting them because of the dim light but knew there were at least fourteen and possibly as many as seventeen. That they were railwaymen was plain to see. One wore a uniform, the rest were in overalls or rough clothes and carried tools, bags, and lanterns as they do when track laying. Because they were going to walk directly past him, he hid his notebook and opened the window.

"Working late, eh? Have you just finished?"

One of them stopped to talk.

"Nah, mate, we'll be up all night. A broken rail at Bank Underground has got a train stuck, so we gotta walk there, ain't we? But that's all right, we stopped at a pub for a quick one and no one's the wiser, you know what I mean?"

"I do, indeed. There's a silver lining to every cloud."

"You got that right. Be seein' you."

"Good night."

The man caught up with the others, and Marsden wrote his entry.

Among the railwaymen, Lefty Watts walked next to Jimmy.

"I bet you've guessed what's going on."

"All I know is to dig the tunnel and get this over and done with," said Jimmy.

"No, you're smarter than that. You've put two and two together, haven't you?"

"What do you want me to say?"

"Nothing. Mr Godfrey gave me a message for you. He's lettin' you off the hook. You'll get extra money because you've done well on the tunnel and kept your mouth shut. Same for your two mates."

"That's thoughtful of him. I don't see André anywhere."

"Frenchie got homesick and left. Anyway, he's not needed anymore."

"And these other gentlemen? I take it we're to break through the wall tonight. I understood we would do that Saturday into Sunday."

"There's been a change of plan. Mr Healy and Mr Godfrey want it done tonight, and that's all you need to know."

As far as Jimmy could recall, Lefty had only ever mentioned Healy once before, and that had also been by accident. Lefty evidently assumed Jimmy knew of Healy, but Jimmy had never met him. Jimmy only hazily understood the organization that controlled his life. Healy was at the top, Godfrey was the operations manager, Barrett was the man blackmailing his family, and Lefty Watts was the thug enforcing his slavery. Jimmy had known Godfrey at school and they had fought once, with Jimmy winning the contest. They had met at a party nearly two years ago and avoided each other. But, by the end of the night, Jimmy had been drugged, supposedly gone deeply in debt after losing at cards to Godfrey, which game he never played, and had been photographed in a sitting room full of stolen paintings — posed in an armchair as if he were the owner. From that moment on, they blackmailed Jimmy and coerced him with the photographs and by direct threats against his family, particularly his sister. Soon, he was forced to rob a wealthy house in the company of others, thus making him dirty, as they were dirty. Because of Godfrey's vindictiveness, Jimmy had no choice but to go along with whatever they had planned until the gambling debt was paid off. Within a few months of being in Godfrey's power, Jimmy found himself in the tunnel.

The rest of the gang treated Jimmy unlike anyone else because he was plainly of a different class and was the subject of Godfrey's personal revenge. Jimmy himself was certain Godfrey would never let him off.

In the months of tunnelling, eight foreign men had worked for varying periods and then disappeared without warning. Now André — Frenchie, as Watts called him — had gone, too. André was a thief and former convict who spoke no English, but he did at least know what to expect at the end of the tunnel, because all of the current crew knew what was coming. The end of the tunnel. It was supposed to be Saturday night and here it was, Wednesday night, and they were supposed to escape Thursday morning after the night's work. Mateo would get his family away because they were under violent threat from the gang, André and Gustav would get their things, while Jimmy would retrieve his sister to remove her to safety. Then he was to go to the police. They had a plan of escape, but it was now ruined because Healy and Godfrey had brought the date forward.

They passed a man sitting in a car. Someone Jimmy did not know spoke to the driver and gave a reason for them all being in the street so late. Jimmy wanted to scream as this fleeting opportunity dangled in front of him. But what could he possibly say to a chauffeur in a matter of a few seconds that would make any sense at all? The chauffeur would die, he would, too, and the Bank of England would still be robbed because everything was in place and the gold would be gone tonight.

Chapter 25

Up late at White Lyon Yard

It was just before eleven at night according to the clock in the detectives' office at Buckingham Palace. Detective Sergeant Gowers was reading through daily reports submitted by police officers stationed throughout the Palace. In a chair and reading a book was Maxwell Handley. In another chair was a very bored Broadbent-Wicks.

"I say, what's *in* all those reports?"

"Nothing," said Gowers.

"Then why are you reading them?"

"Because they pay me to read them."

"Why do they pay you to read reports containing nothing?"

"Because one day they hope I'll find something. Give it a rest, BW. I said earlier, as soon as I've finished, we'll go for a drink. Read a book. I'll only be another ten minutes."

"I can't read a book in ten minutes, so there's no point in even starting." BW stared at Handley. "What are *you* reading?"

Handley looked up. He was no longer restrained, but neither was he permitted to be on his own. "A history book. Now, if you don't mind." He returned to his reading in what BW considered a pointedly rude and unfriendly fashion.

A full minute later, BW said to Handley,

"What's it like being a traitor?"

"I'm not a traitor. I'm a victim of circumstances."

"Come off it, old man. You're a traitor, good and proper... Victim of circumstances... Funny old phrase that. When one studies it, one finds we're all victims of circumstances."

"What are you talking about?" asked Handley.

"Don't you see? None of us chooses when and where we're born. We don't get to choose our name even. As a baby, one wakes up one fine sunny morning and there are the parents staring down and you can't do a thing about them. You're stuck with them. Same goes for relations and, let me tell you, some of mine have very peculiar habits. So, there you are: every baby a victim of circumstances."

"Did you have a rough childhood?" asked the astonished Gowers, distracted from his reports.

"I don't think so. In fact, on balance, I believe I did all right in the lucky dip of life. How about you?"

"No complaints, but I would like to finish these reports."

"Carry on, Sergeant Gowers. Don't let me stop you. What about you, Handley? You must have had a rough childhood to turn traitor. I mean to say, at school, they usually encourage loyalty and honesty. Did you miss those lessons?"

"Shut up."

"Sorry if you're offended, but you have behaved rather rottenly, so you have no real cause to be in a huff. I simply would like to know how your mind works."

Handley snapped the book shut and stood up. "This is intolerable!"

"You, sit down," demanded Gowers, pointing at Handley. "For goodness' sake, BW, stop winding him up."

"Righty-ho. Putting the old lid firmly on it. Although, I didn't intend on upsetting anyone."

The door opened, and Baron Stamfordham entered.

"Ah-ha! I thought I'd find you here." He stared fixedly at BW.

"Hello, Lord Stamfordham. Are their majesties sleeping peacefully?"

"Never mind about that. The committee has terminated your services immediately."

"Oh, that's a pity. Do you have it in writing?"

"It so happens that I do."

"May I see it?"

"Do you doubt my word?"

"Naturally, I completely believe, unreservedly I might add, anything and everything you have to say. You're a gentleman, after all. However, Miss King said that unless the King himself asked me to leave, anyone else must give me a written notice to quit."

"Unbelievable. Miss King said that?"

"Oh, yes. And, with me, her word is law. Therefore, you must produce a paper of some kind."

"Very well." Stamfordham struggled to control his temper. He took from his pocket a memo requesting that Broadbent-Wicks no longer be in attendance upon the King. At the bottom, written in a different hand, it said, 'Approved by the Committee,' which directive was initialled.

"Who is Horwood?" asked BW, reading a name amongst the initials.

"The Commissioner of the Metropolitan Police. Do you dare..."

"Excuse me," said BW. He arose and took the note to Gowers. "Is that his writing?"

Gowers looked at BW and then at the note.

"I should imagine it's his, so I think you'd better go, son."

"Thank you, Sergeant Gowers. I'll be on my way, then."

He returned the note.

"One more thing," said Stamfordham. "Please return the warrant that was issued to you. It has been cancelled anyway."

"Sorry, I can't do that."

"What do you mean, can't?" he asked in a shocked voice.

"Because I threw it away."

"You threw it away?" Now he was horrified. "No matter. A footman is waiting outside to escort you while you get your things and to see you off the premises."

"If their Majesties are still up, may I say goodbye to them?"

"Absolutely not!"

"What about Charlotte?"

"You are to leave at once."

"Oh, very well. Goodnight, Lord Stamfordham, Sergeant Gowers, and you, too, Handley, though you don't deserve to have a good night."

With that, BW left Buckingham Palace. He found a taxi outside, which took him to White Lyon Yard. There he alighted and paid the driver, then with suitcase in hand, he rang the bell and waited. Hawkins, Lady Shelling's butler, opened the door. He looked forbiddingly at the late-night caller.

"Sir?" he enquired, aided by his eyebrows.

"Hello. Dreadfully sorry to bother you at this late hour, but would Miss King be up and about?"

"Miss King?"

"Miss Burgoyne, then."

"Ah, Miss Burgoyne... No."

"How about Auntie Bessie, if she hasn't toddled off to bed?"

"Auntie Bessie? Surely, you mean Lady Shelling. This is her residence."

"Yes, that's probably who I mean. I had no idea Miss King's aunt had a title."

"What is it you want, sir?" Hawkins eyed the suitcase.

"Actually, what I want is a bed for the night. I've just been chucked out of Buckingham Palace and I daren't go back to Dalston or my landlady will flay me alive. She's a real Tartar about people coming in late and I've only just got back in her good books. You see, her lumbago keeps her up at night. The slightest noise disturbs her and the front door hinges creak."

"Why doesn't she oil them?"

"Exactly! That's what I said to her. Then she changed the subject — rather suspiciously, I thought. My belief is that she *wants* the door to creak, so she knows who's coming and who's going. She spies on us lodgers through the old net curtains, don't you know? But she doesn't stop there because she loathes Mrs Hutchins across the road, and... You're not interested in all of this, are you?"

"I might take an interest if I were acquainted with the parties, sir. The situation as it stands is as follows: should it be convenient, I shall inform her ladyship that there is a gentleman on the doorstep desirous of lodgings for the night. If you are known to her, all well and good, and it is conceivable a favourable conclusion to this matter may be found. However, should you be unknown to her ladyship, I will ask you to vacate her front doorstep at once. Your name, sir?"

"Douglas Broadbent-Wicks."

"Thank you. I must shut the door momentarily."

The door closed. Two minutes later it reopened.

"If you will enter, Mr Broadbent-Wicks, Lady Shelling will see you."

"How spiffing of her ladyship. And thanks for putting in a good word for me."

"The word I put in, as it were, sir, was factual and entirely neutral. You may leave your luggage in the hall for the present while I announce you."

Hawkins opened the door.

"Mr Broadbent-Wicks, your ladyship."

Hawkins retired as they greeted each other.

"Do sit down," said Aunt Bessie, who was wearing a lavender evening dress and a white cardigan.

"Thank you, Lady Shelling. Apologies for intruding at this late hour."

"Do I understand correctly that they asked you to leave Buckingham Palace?"

"It's rather involved, your ladyship, but yes. There's a committee in charge of the King's safety and it hasn't quite got the hang of things. They wanted us all to leave, but I managed to evade them for a while because I was in charge of the parrot, and I was getting on quite well with the King. I don't think Queen Mary cared much for me, but there you go. Can't win 'em all."

"Indeed, you can't, Mr Broadbent-Wicks. Am I further to understand that your landlady would be troublesome should you arrive home late?"

"She is subject to moods, particularly when rules are broken. I don't blame her, but it makes it awkward for a chap."

"Don't expect me to sympathize, Mr Broadbent-Wicks. If your landlady has gentlemen guests, it is also most necessary for her to enforce a strict code of conduct."

"Oh, I totally agree, but it makes it dashed tricky for me under the current circs."

"I see... My niece has mentioned your name in the past. What exactly is it that you do? I know of the spying aspect."

"Well, then, that makes it much easier. I'm a footman, or a spy, and often both. I also clean windows, but Miss Burgoyne has nothing to do with that."

"Now, how is it, Mr Broadbent-Wicks, that you only know me as Auntie Bessie?"

"Ah, you see, Miss King often refers to you and always calls you Auntie or Auntie Bessie. That's what I admire about Miss King. She never puts on airs and graces. She never let on that her aunt had a title. Now, if you were my aunt, Lady Shelling, I'd probably be dropping your name all over the place. I'd say to the chaps, you ought to meet my wonderful aunt, Lady Shelling. She's charming, graceful, and oh, so very elegant. That's what I'd say to anyone who would stop and listen."

Lady Shelling was speechless.

"I have two aunts and they're all right, but I don't think I'd tell the chaps about either of them. One of them was an inveterate head-patter when I was small, and several times my hair got caught in her rings and she pulled it out — literally pulled out my hair. Did my shriek stop her the next time? No, it did not. So, as I got older, I avoided her like the plague. One doesn't like to mention one's aunts when they do that sort of thing. I'm sure you were never a head-patter."

"I can safely say, Mr Broadbent-Wicks, that I have never patted anyone's head, and I fail to understand why anyone would want to do so."

"I'm with you there, Lady Shelling."

"Do you wish for something to drink, or have you had plenty already?"

"No. Honestly, I haven't touched a drop."

"A sherry, perhaps?"

"I'll decline, if I may. Not exactly my favourite."

"Something else?"

"Do you have beer?"

"Milk stout?"

"Oh, I love milk stout," said BW.

"I'm partial to it myself."

BW got up.

"Where are you going?" asked Aunt Bessie.

"To find the milk stout."

"No. Press that button," she pointed to it, "and sit down. You're my guest, not a footman."

"Sorry, my ladyship. Force of habit and all that." He rang for the footman.

"I understand. Tell me, what else does Sophie say about me?"

"She's always singing your praises. And I know this part is true. She very much appreciates your companionship and support."

"Does she, indeed?" Aunt Bessie was smiling. "You'll stay the night, of course."

"Thank you so very much, Lady Shelling. What a lifesaver you are."

Marsden appeared.

"Bring us milk stout, and inform Hawkins that Mr Broadbent-Wicks will stay the night."

"Yes, m'lady."

"He will be going out shortly but, when he returns, please be sure to let him in... Oh, and make a roast beef sandwich for him to take. Do you care for horseradish, Mr Broadbent-Wicks?"

"Uh... yes, I do."

"With horseradish."

"Yes, m'lady." Marsden left the room.

"Where am I going?"

"My niece left standing instructions with me, should you turn up. All week she and the others have been loitering around the Bank of England and have discovered some quite interesting things. I'm sure you would have asked where she was eventually and, when you did, I would explain the specific situation that had arisen tonight. But there's no rush. I'm sure you'll be in time before anything exciting happens."

"I don't understand."

"I barely do myself, but it seems to go like this. Sophie and Miss Carmichael were somewhere near the docks where Lud's gang was trying to murder a Frenchman. He got away after someone fired a shot. They returned to the Bank where Lord Laneford more or less said, 'That's it. Everyone's going home because it's too dangerous.' Are you keeping up?"

"Yes, Lady Shelling."

"They returned here and explained everything to me. They then went through Marsden's report. He had been watching London Wall."

"Why was he watching a wall?"

"It is a street, Mr Broadbent-Wicks."

"Ah, I get it. Sorry — Oh, and by the way, Lady Shelling, you can call me BW if you like."

"I shall do no such thing. At 10:08 precisely, a gang of platelayers…"

"Platelayers? You mean from the railway?"

"Mr Broadbent-Wicks, I am unaccustomed to being interrupted when I am speaking. You will kindly refrain from doing so immediately."

"Oh, absolutely, Lady Shelling. Sincerest apologies, and all that. I shan't say boo."

"Why would you even think to say boo? It is a child's word." BW was about to say something more about a goose, but she put up a hand. "Please desist from commenting or you can go to your room." After a few seconds of silence, she began again. "There were approximately fifteen platelayers carrying tools, etcetera. Marsden, surprisingly quick-witted in this instance, engaged them in light conversation. The story was that they were proceeding to the Bank Underground Station to repair a broken rail and couldn't get there by train, so they had to walk. A plausible reason for their presence in the street. They turned onto Basinghall Street."

Marsden brought in the milk stout, then left.

"Your good health, Mr Broadbent-Wicks." She raised her small glass of beer.

"And yours, too, Lady Shelling." BW raised his pewter tankard.

They drank, and if there were a line of froth on Aunt Bessie's upper lip, it was imperceptible, and her quick and dainty use of a handkerchief dealt with it, anyway.

"It is such a strengthening drink," she declared, having succumbed to the advertising slogans.

"That's what I say," said BW.

"I shall continue the narrative. Marsden recorded the sighting of these men. He was unable to communicate his findings until everyone returned here — all, that is, except for Lord Laneford and his man, who had gone home. When Sophie reviewed Marsden's notes, the fifteen platelayers were an obvious item. You see, and there was much confusion before the truth was established, it became evident that the fifteen platelayers had vanished because they never reached Bank Underground Station. Gladys and Mr Philpott were in the vicinity of Guildhall and the lower part of Basinghall at the time, and they never saw hide nor hair of the platelayers."

"I say, that's utterly amazing. You mean they just disappeared into thin air?"

"Perhaps you don't know," said Aunt Bessie, "having been immured in the Palace all week. I have heard the word so frequently now, it seems we have been discussing this irritatin' tunnel for the entire span of my natural life."

"They went into a tunnel!?"

"Excellent, Mr Broadbent-Wicks. It's the one through which they will steal the gold from the Bank of England."

"I say! They can't do that. Who do these platelayers think they are!?"

"I think you are missing several points. The platelayers are Lud's gang in disguise. The entrance to the tunnel is somewhere off Basinghall Street, and they used it tonight. Sophie thought Basinghall was a possibility, and that is now confirmed. That fifteen men are involved strongly suggests they intend imminently to steal the gold. Sophie and the others have gone to stop them, and she has left messages, where possible, for help to be sent at once. No one answered their telephones, but I am staying up to try their numbers into the wee hours until I find someone."

"Thank you, Lady Shelling, for putting me straight. I must go at once."

"No. You shall finish your drink and wait for your sandwich, then you shall leave."

"But they might need me."

"I'm sure they will find your presence most encouraging, but it is my opinion they will not find the entrance. They've been looking for it all week, so why would they suddenly find it tonight? They were very excited and, of course, rushed off just a few minutes before you arrived. At least they took sandwiches and coffee with them."

"But they are three women on their own at night!"

"And woe betide anyone who goes near them because they are armed to the teeth. Miss Carmichael is openly carrying a hatchet, which I sincerely hope she returns."

"Good heavens. What can I use?"

"Marsden will have found something suitable for your use among the tools. So please dismiss all that from your mind." She took a sip of beer and patted her lips. "Mr Broadbent-Wicks, tell me about your people. Where do they live, for example?"

Chapter 26

Different directions

The three remaining tunnellers — Jimmy, Mateo, and Gustav — were at a loss as to what to do next. They were in the tunnel with eleven other men, including Lefty Watts, and had no way of escape. Together, in whispers, they agreed that, once the gang had the gold, there was no chance they would be allowed to live. For as they now knew, although Jimmy had suspected all along, it was the Bank of England's vault that they were smashing their way into. The otherwise all-British gang openly spoke of the gold and even what they would do with their share afterwards. Many of them were armed, and Lefty Watts, acting as overseer, carried a shotgun.

They all worked hard. The tunnel had been finished and widened at the vault wall two days earlier. A plank floor had been laid over which a wheeled trolley would run carrying thirty bars, or 870lbs of gold, at a time. Four men were to pull the trolley by ropes while one man pushed it in a combined effort to get the valuable commodity up the inclines. Two others would hold ropes on the other end to control the short descents. Once the trolley reached the high point of the tunnel, it would be unloaded. Carrying two bars at a time, each man would then set the gold down on the bank of the Walbrook beneath the place where the skull was perched.

From there, four bars were to be transferred to a small raft. The raft, controlled by ropes, would float for some forty yards along the culverted Walbrook. At the other end, two men would stand in the water of the main sewer, waiting to place the gold in a heavy skiff. When the skiff was full, those men would walk it down to the grating if the tide was out or paddle it down if the tide was high. Beyond the grating, which was already sawn through, a waiting tug boat on the dark Thames, almost invisible to anyone on the embankment above, was moored close by to receive the shipments.

The three agents were at the entrance of St. Margaret church on Lothbury. Opposite stood the formidable wall of the Bank of England. Directly beneath their feet, had they but known it, lay the tunnel. At that moment, five grunting, straining men toiled over the trolley in the close atmosphere to bring up the first thirty bars from the vault. Mateo had breeched the wall with his pick and once the first few bricks had been shattered, the others came out readily with a crowbar. Soon, the hole was large enough for a man to enter. Three men had gone inside and began removing the wealth of the nation. By six o'clock, the gang was to be gone, leaving behind a time bomb of sufficient size to destroy the vault and the building above it. The timer, a simple Big Ben alarm clock, was set for seven and was already ticking, although one simple connection had yet to be made for the blast to occur. Where the agents now stood, debris would rain down in the early morning and smash the church's windows and doors.

"Lady Shelling might be right," said Flora. "If they're all tunnelling away still, then they won't use the entrance again until morning when they come out — with the gold or not, who can say?"

"Perhaps." Sophie spoke with some reluctance. "What do *you* think?" she asked Ada.

"I don't know what to say, except this. If there'd been fifteen platelayers wandering about every night, we would have seen them, or somebody would have. So, they're doing something special — as we all believe — an' I reckon they're turning over the Bank tonight, an' I don't want to go home because I shan't sleep, not a single, bloomin' wink."

"I'm exactly the same."

"I'm not," said Flora. "Once my head touches the pillow, I'm gone. You could set off the biggest of Big Ben alarm clocks right next to me and I wouldn't hear it; not even stir, probably."

"I know you're a deep sleeper," said Sophie, "but are you saying you could go to sleep right at this moment?"

"I believe so. Why don't we test the theory? I'll go back to White Lyon Yard and try. If I don't return in two hours, you will know I've dropped off."

"You're trying to oil out of it."

"Absolutely. I'm finding this area rather boring, and boredom makes my thinking go stale. If we could do something productive, then that would be different."

"I know what you mean," said Sophie.

"I'm the same, miss," said Ada.

"What ho!" cried Broadbent-Wicks, who had just rounded the corner. He continued calling out as he approached. "I thought I'd be spending half the night looking for you! Fortune smiles on the righteous, don't you know!? I'm not sure if anyone has ever actually said that, but they should have, don't you think!?"

"Be quiet!" Sophie said in a shouted whisper as he came up to them. "Whatever possessed you to start bellowing?"

"Didn't you hear the echoes? My first shout escaped due to the pure joy of seeing you all. The rest was because of the echoes. Surely you heard them?"

Sophie breathed out a deep sigh. "I may have, but we're on a mission, and should be silent for the obvious reason of not drawing attention to ourselves."

"I suppose it's blatantly obvious now that you mention it, and I'm very sorry and shan't do it again."

"What on earth goes through your mind?"

"Oh, lots, Miss King. For example, I had a very nice chat with Lady Shelling. She's now my favourite aunt and we're not even related." He laughed. "Well, anyway, she and I got talking, and once we got past the 'how's your family' business, she launched into a tirade about the directors at the Bank of England and the deficiencies of their brains. My goodness, she was hot on that subject. She was all set to continue for some time but, lovely woman and ladyship that she is, I thought I should slope off to earn my keep by protecting all of you. So, as she had some telephone calls to make, I took the opportunity to say toodly-pip and skipped lightly out of the house. I say, I really like White Lyon Yard. It's much better than my place in Dalston."

"When you started speaking," said Sophie, "I felt certain you were going to arrive at a particular point. However, do you mean to tell me that you uttered the words 'toodly-pip' to my aunt?"

"Ooh, no. Absolutely not. I was speaking metaphorically in so far as we parted like a pair of old chums, who look forward to seeing each other again. However, I was careful in what I said in front of Lady Shelling because I believe that, if I said something wrong, she would slay me on the spot. And Hawkins is a bit of a rum fellow. When he first clapped eyes on me, I got the distinct impression he would like nothing better than to hurl me into the street. As I was already in it at the time, I don't know quite what he would have done if he had let loose."

Sophie tried to suppress a laugh. "Why are we talking about my aunt, anyway?"

"Ummm... Ah! Yes. Because she said she couldn't imagine how Lud's gang thought they could get away with so many tons of gold in broad daylight or even at night. I said they must have something planned. She said, 'What?' and I could tell she was on the cusp of being annoyed with me. I couldn't be vague, so I said the first thing that came into my head."

After several expectant seconds of silence, Sophie asked,

"Could you enlighten us further, please, BW?"

"About what? My answer? If you insist, Miss King. I simply said that if Lud had gone into the tunnel-building business, he must have done it in a big way. He has a secret entrance, but perhaps he also has a secret exit. What about that for a good one, eh!? My idea gave Lady Shelling pause for thought... Do you know I inadvertently called her Auntie Bessie? She tore a strip off me, don't you know? Anyway, that's the type of thing that goes through my mind."

"I don't know if that makes it worse for us, or better," said Ada.

"Are you saying," began Flora, "that Lud might have dug a tunnel to the vault and then continued it on to a safe place to bring the gold out?"

"Yes, more or less," said BW. "Lady Shelling pointed out the difficulties of carting off all those heavy gold bars. How many lorries they would need, for example. Then, I thought it over on the way here. Suppose there were half a dozen vehicles all lined up in the street. I'm certain the spectacle of droves of furtive platelayers and foreign seamen thumping down hundreds of bars of the shiny stuff on the old floorboards would draw someone's attention. I know I would consider it odd if I saw them."

"You've gone quiet," said Flora to Sophie.

"We've searched this area thoroughly and there just isn't anywhere suitable to load lorries without their being noticed, except for the area in front of Guildhall, but people walk through there all the time. Let's face it, with all that activity going on, one telephone call to the police would ruin Lud's plan."

"What about the sewers, miss? asked Ada. "Mr Philpott likes 'em very much, an' he said there's a big one hereabouts. I didn't really want to listen to him explainin', 'cause it's not nice, but he said it comes out in the Thames."

"Sewers!" exclaimed Sophie. "What an appalling idea... I mean, your suggestion has merit, but it's the sewers themselves I find difficult to accept. I know we've discussed them before, but I've put them out of my mind since."

"Then that's just why he would use them," said Flora. "We've dismissed the sewage system for no other reason than it is loathsome. We like our criminals clean as a rule, and not to come at us wallowing in filth, which would then force us to wallow with them."

"Please, Gladys, don't."

"I'm not going down no sewers, miss," said Ada. "I just won't."

"None of us will," said Sophie.

"That comes as a gigantic relief," said BW. "But what do we do now?"

"We'll split up to try a couple of things. Nancy, you and BW go to the Thames to see if anything is going on there. Take a taxi if you see one, although it isn't far. Gladys and I shall go in Rabbit to visit twelve Crescent. If nothing is happening, we'll meet you in front of Cannon Street Station in an hour's time. If we aren't there, then come back here."

"Right you are, Miss King," said BW. "But what happens if there are things going on at both places simultaneously? Then what do we do?"

"Then we shall all use our initiative as the circumstances demand."

"What an excellent solution, Miss King... Taxi!"

Chapter 27

Early morning rain

Small clouds were rolling in on a breeze, hinting at rain later. The moon played hide and seek, making Crescent even more profoundly sombre while hidden. Sophie and Flora had spent five minutes watching the front of number twelve from the car.

"Why don't we knock?" said Flora.

"Knock, indeed! They were shooting at me earlier! We can take a closer look, though. We might overhear something if we get up close."

"No, we won't. They're all out burrowing like moles or swimming about like water rats."

"What a ghastly business."

There were no lights on in any of the houses, and it was as quiet as London could be. Distant noises blended to form a subtle rustling hum — the steady respiration of the sleeping city. Within Crescent, there was no life and no noise except for the agents stepping awkwardly on the cobblestones. The moon emerged and picked out the disfigured side of number twelve with an unflattering and bleak clarity.

"Don't you dare knock," whispered Sophie.

"Of course, I shan't, but I'll listen through the letterbox."

"What a marvellous idea. It never even occurred to me."

"It's useful when trying to locate one's landlady while trying to reach one's room safely and avoid the subject of back rent."

"Are you hard up?"

They stopped a few yards away.

"No, but I'm not exactly flush with the readies, either. Seeing Sidney so often is a drain on the exchequer, despite his paying for everything. All the subsidiary expenses add up, living expenses are going up, and acting jobs have *dried* up — for me, anyway. That's why I had hoped this mission would last as long as possible."

"That will all change when you marry."

"Yes... My poor parents, though. They're not very well-off, and the financial strain of a wedding will be a real burden on them, but they'll bear it without complaint."

"May I help? I have some money saved."

"I can't possibly impose upon you."

"Of course, you can. In fact, I insist, but we'll discuss it at another time."

"That's awfully kind of you."

"Oh, pish, tosh, and fiddle-dee-dee. Let's be quiet, though. This is a mission, after all."

They reached the doorstep of number twelve, and they both listened at the door. Flora shook her head and then bent down. She carefully opened the flap and peered into the dark hall. "Nothing," she mouthed to Sophie. She put her ear to the opening and listened for a full minute. "Silence has a very subtle but definite sound," she whispered as she stood up.

"No, it doesn't."

"You listen, then."

Sophie put her ear to the letterbox, then stood up. "It's extraordinary, but you're correct. Very slight, though. Perhaps the enclosed space is amplifying small noises."

"That could be. No one's moving about and there aren't any lights on."

"It's a pity Nancy isn't with us to pick the lock." Sophie tried the doorknob, and the door opened. "Good grief."

"I suppose we're going in," said Flora.

"We really shouldn't, but I think we must."

They glanced about the silent houses of the street before slipping inside and softly closing the door.

"For the country's most important river," opined Broadbent-Wicks while gazing at the black water from the Cousin Lane stairs, "the Thames is rather smelly."

"They say it used to stink something shocking," said Ada. "Come on, BW, the hour's nearly up. Anyway, we can't see nothin' 'cause the shore's as black as a coal 'ole in the dark."

"Yes, but the sewer outlet must be there somewhere." He pointed along the shore.

"It's a pity Mr Philpott ain't with us. He'd sniff it out fast enough. Do you know, I've never heard anyone go so demented about such a thing? He knows sewers forwards, backwards, and inside out. I don't think he's been sleeping." They started walking back. "Instead, I reckon he went to the British Museum and studied up on it, because all he thinks about is sewers. He researches them all day, and searches for them all night."

"That's a clever way of putting it." BW looked to the east. The sky was overcast. There were many isolated specks of light along both shores. All the vessels in the river were showing warning lights, and the moving craft had their running lights. One large freighter was so brilliantly illuminated it looked festive, as if there were a carnival aboard ship. The different docks lining the river glowed brightly, like separate cities, but everywhere else was enveloped in the darkest of greys, or absolute black. "What's your opinion of the Thames?"

"I don't like it," replied Ada. "When I look down on that cold, dark, horrible looking water, 'specially from a bridge, I feel like I'm goin' to fall in, an' that makes me want to *heave*."

"I'm sorry to hear that."

"Drowning must be a dreadful way to go... They say that all your life flashes before your eyes, and when you go down for the third time, that's it, it's all over... Makes me shiver just thinking about it."

"Yes, most unpleasant… All of one's life, though? That sounds like a lot to cram in during one's last breath."
"Don't BW, it's not very nice."
"Sorry… I felt a raindrop."
"So, did I. Let's run."

Sophie and Flora had searched the ground-floor using their torches and everywhere were signs of a hurried departure. The furniture remained, but someone had removed all the drawers and dumped their contents on the dining room table. A carpet was pulled back and an empty floor safe lay open. It was the same riotous scene in the kitchen where every cupboard hung open. The place had been ransacked.

"They took all the pictures," whispered Flora, directing her torch at empty hooks on the wall and rectangles of fresher-looking paint.

"Then they must have been valuable, because some pieces of furniture they've left are very good… They've taken all the silver."

"And there are no papers or correspondence anywhere," added Flora.

"Getting rid of the evidence, no doubt… I don't think anyone's here."

"Neither do I… Although, it would be more fitting to continue whispering."

"Absolutely. Do you think they'll return?" asked Sophie.

"I don't believe so, but what do I know?"

"Then one of us must go upstairs while the other keeps watch down here."

"I don't like the sound of that, and what good would it do? The only way out is through the front door, unless we scale the backyard wall. Whoever goes upstairs will be trapped, unable to get out before they enter the house."

"I've brought Freda with me," said Sophie.

"That is not reassuring. You don't know how to shoot properly."

"With Elizabeth's guidance, I have disassembled and reassembled the pistol several times."

"Oh, well, then that's all right. You needn't fire it. Just show the maniacal, brutal killers how well you take your pistol apart, and that will stop them dead in their tracks."

"Very funny."

"We're wasting time. We could have searched all of upstairs by now."

"Oh, come on, then. We'll do it together."

They ascended the stairs. The well-built house and had so far creaked very little while they moved about. There was one creaky stair, however, that unexpectedly made several noises which, in the stillness, were reminiscent of a few explosive bars from the final moments of the 1812 overture. Sophie and Flora gaped at each other by torchlight.

"Did you break it?" whispered Flora.

"I barely touched it with my toe."

"Which one is it, so I can step over?"

Sophie pointed her torch at her right foot. As she lifted her foot, the stair squeaked loudly.

"No more puddings for you," whispered Flora.

"Pshaw. You step on it, then."

Flora slowly stepped on the offending tread, and it barely made a sound.

"I don't believe it," said Sophie.

"You must take yourself in hand at once."

"That's enough of the ridiculous insinuations, thank you. One thing, though — after all that row, it's obvious we're alone."

They continued up and investigated the three top floors, noting that the gallery with the bricked-up windows contained no art, and that a safe and the filing cabinets were empty. They explored the cavernous space by torchlight.

"There must have been dozens of paintings on display," said Sophie, estimating by the number of spotlights she could see.

"If they did a bunk since you followed the car, then a veritable host of people must have cleared this place out."

"I suppose so, and they've left nothing for us to find. The people who did it must have been in addition to the platelayers — they couldn't be in two places at the same time."

"Gosh, Lud's gang must be huge," said Flora.

"We had better leave just in case they return."

"I don't think they will because there's an air of finality to this clear-out. Plus, they left the door unlocked."

The agents moved to the top of the stairs and stopped. Far below in the stairwell, the noisy stair tread creaked and someone had switched on the hall light. Flora and Sophie quickly switched off their torches after seeing each other's anxious face. Someone was down there but made no further sounds. The rain began — gently at first, but soon falling hard on the slate roof. Sophie put a hand on the pistol in her pocket.

To escape the rain, Ada and BW rushed to get under the entrance overhang of desolate Cannon Street Station.

"We're lucky to have missed that lot," said Ada, staring back out into the sheets of rain hammering the road, puddling everywhere, and transforming the dry gutters into streams. Several other people had joined them in their place of refuge.

"It will blow over soon," said BW confidently.

"We 'ope."

The station was still open but there would be no trains leaving for several hours, and all the kiosks were shuttered. A railway police constable patrolled inside. Under the overhang, a Metropolitan constable in his cape also waited out the sudden deluge. Ada glanced around and noticed three others — single men — all standing separately and all noticeably alert and avoiding anyone else's attention.

"BW," whispered Ada, who moved closer to him. "Don't say a bloomin' word. Just put your arm round me and don't say nothin' and look straight ahead."

BW stared and gaped. He looked questioningly into the rain, but it did not return him an answer.

"'urry up," insisted Ada, not daring to speak louder.

He put his arm around Ada's shoulders in the manner of all who, while desperately trying to go to sleep, discover they possess an awkward spare arm and lack a comfortable place to put it. It was impossible for him to remain silent.

"What does this mean?" he said in an awestruck voice.

"It don't bloody well mean a thing, so don't you go thinkin' it does. And don't look round. There are two or three blokes nearby who might be Lud's men, and they keep giving us funny looks."

"Including the policeman?"

"Not him, the others."

"Ah... Oh, what a disappointment."

"What do you mean?"

"I thought you had feelings for me, and it came as such a pleasant surprise."

"You can forget all about that."

"Then you're not going to ask me to kiss you?" He sounded deflated.

"If we weren't in a spot, BW, I'd box your bloomin' ears."

"Sorry. I'll behave myself... Trouble is, all this closeness has got me thinking."

"Well, stop that right now... And don't you dare tell anyone."

"Not even Miss King?"

"No."

"Why not? It's all part of the spying operation."

"Because... Just don't."

"Go on. What were you going to say?" He gave her shoulder an affectionate squeeze.

"What do you think you're doing? Did I say you could do that?"

"No."

"Then don't do it again... The reason is... I have a gentleman friend."

"Do you? Who is it?"

"I'm not saying."

"What are his initials?"

Ada laughed.

"The rain's slowing," said BW. "Five more minutes and it will stop altogether."

Ada glanced at the station clock. It was 2:11. The constable resumed his beat. They talked for a while and at 2:16 the rain ceased.

"You were exactly right about the rain," said Ada as two of the single men left the station. "We'll have to walk slow while we see where those blokes are going. BW, remove your arm, if you please."

They set off. The two men were heading down Cousins Lane towards the very section of embankment that Ada and BW were interested in. The third was somewhere behind them, but they dared not turn to look.

"I think they're Lud's men," said BW. "We should cross the road and go back to the Bank."

"We should an' all. So, do we reckon the sewer exit is right there and them blokes are sort of guarding it?"

"They must be. Should we alert that constable?"

"Use your noggin, BW. They'll be armed and we'll all be dead if we do. Reinforcements are needed — dozens of 'em — 'cause there's all the platelayers to be caught an' all."

"Then they might shift the gold to one of the boats we saw," said BW. "That's what it looks like to me."

"That must be it, otherwise those blokes, who ain't dockers, let me tell you, wouldn't be hanging about." Ada looked back across the road. "The third one's joined 'em now." Ada and BW quickly walked away and soon reached the rendezvous.

"It's been over an hour now," said Ada. "I wonder what's happened for the others not to be here to meet us."

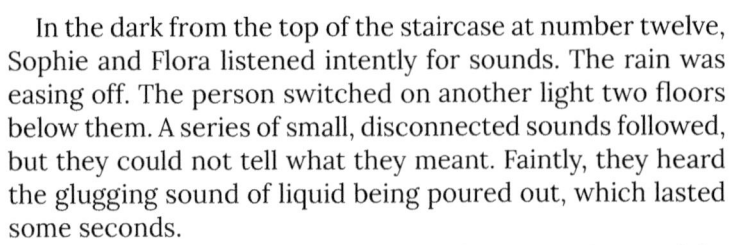

In the dark from the top of the staircase at number twelve, Sophie and Flora listened intently for sounds. The rain was easing off. The person switched on another light two floors below them. A series of small, disconnected sounds followed, but they could not tell what they meant. Faintly, they heard the glugging sound of liquid being poured out, which lasted some seconds.

"I can smell petrol," whispered Sophie in a quiet, panicky whisper.

"They're going to set fire to the house." Flora stared open-mouthed at her friend.

"Come on," said Sophie and, with her pistol in hand, quietly descended the stairs. Flora followed.

"Who's up there!?" boomed a man's voice from below.

"It's only us," said Flora unexpectedly, astonishing Sophie enough to make her stop. "Keep going," she whispered.

"Who!?" He was puzzled.

"We came back about the furniture."

"Oh, it's you... There's no furniture for sale, I told you that." Only a single flight separated them now.

"The people at the other place said for us to come back here, and that you had the furniture."

"How would they know...? They're wrong, anyway... Still, you can take some if you want, but I'm not helping you, because I'm busy."

The smell of petrol was stronger than ever. Sophie saw Morrish first, and it made her start. The tall man was holding a large petrol can. She stopped and pointed her pistol at him.

"Don't set the house alight."

"I have to." The tall man seemed unconcerned that she was pointing a gun at him.

"Why must you?" asked Flora.

"Orders."

"Who gave you the orders?" asked Sophie.

"Mr Healy... But it was Lefty's idea. He's to blame, not Mr Healy."

"Perhaps if you ask Mr Healy to reconsider?" suggested Sophie.

"He won't come back here now. It's all gone wrong, ain't it? We could have cleaned up proper... And now my wife... That's down to Lefty, and he must pay."

"What happened to your wife?"

"She didn't want to leave her home, did she? Then she fell over... I didn't touch her. I wouldn't do that. I shook her a bit and when she pulled away, she hit her head... Wouldn't see reason no matter what I said to her, so it's her own fault, really."

"Where is she now?"

"In the bedroom downstairs. She ain't moved for an hour... There was a lot of blood, so I knew straight off she was gone."

"Are you going to burn the place down with her lying there?" Sophie was appalled.

"Can't do otherwise."

"Would you mind terribly if we just squeezed past you?" asked Flora, gripping her blackjack but keeping it out of sight.

"Course... Help yourself if you want anything." He stood to one side. "You're lucky I heard you."

"Yes," said Sophie. "Thank you for warning us."

Carefully and cautiously edging down the stairs, they kept their eyes fixed on Morrish. The petrol sodden carpet squelched underfoot. Not daring to breathe, they passed him on the landing and got a few steps down the next flight before Sophie stopped to ask,

"Where will you go afterwards?"

"I'm going to get Lefty and break his filthy neck."

"Oh... Where is he?"

"At the Guildhall with the others... Anyway, like I said, help yourself, but you'd better be quick about it and get out of here."

"We're on our way," said Flora.

The agents hurried downstairs and out of the front door.

"What on earth can we do to stop this?" asked Sophie.

"Nothing. He's obviously deranged and, if he's the fellow who snaps people's necks, he'd snap ours soon enough if we tried to restrain him."

"I just couldn't bring myself to shoot him in cold blood." There was a tremor in her voice.

"I know," said Flora. "I think we should clear out at once."

They hurried back to Rabbit.

Chapter 28

Put the fire out

Lefty Watts was hoarse with shouting over the delays. According to the plan, three hundred and sixty bars of gold were to be taken. Early on, a wheel broke on the trolley and, after it was repaired, they could only risk the weight of ten bars being loaded on it at a time. When an axle broke, they dispensed with the contraption altogether, and ran the gold out by hand — bar by bar. The problem with the trolley, however, was not the worst delay. The gold piled up faster on the bank than could be floated by the raft down the Walbrook. Something unexpected and solid blocked the raft's progress, and it was not until someone acquired the knack of handling the ropes in steering it past the constriction that progress resumed, albeit at a slower pace.

A consequence of this holdup was that the first skiff did not reach the barge until 2:00 a.m. Watts desperately wanted the rope-handler to go faster, but even he could see the operation required patience and dexterity. Instead, he took out his frustration on others by cuffing, threatening with his shotgun, and roundly cursing. The only part of the original plan that was smoothly completed was that the dozen boxes of dynamite had been stacked open and connected as a single bomb in the vaults. All that remained to arm the bomb was for the last wire to be attached to the already ticking Big Ben alarm clock. They had set the alarm for seven.

By carrying the gold, Jimmy, Mateo, and Gustav kept clear of Watts. In an idle moment, they whispered to each other. It was warm, almost stifling, in the airless tunnel, despite the bellows being worked continuously.

"We have to jump Watts and get his shotgun," said Jimmy.

"Some of them have revolvers," said Gustav.

"I know, but if we take his shotgun in a surprise attack, we can disarm the others and then get out."

"How we get out?" asked Mateo. "The stove sits over the entrance. We can smash the floor — yes, that's easy. But they keep the stove alight. If it falls over, the cottage burns, and then we are caught like rats in a trap."

"That won't happen, because I have a better idea," said Jimmy. "We can break through the grating into the basement we've been creeping past all these months."

"Ah, then we must build a ladder," said Gustav.

"There's plenty of wood for that," said Jimmy.

"That's good," said Mateo. "What about the rest of the gang? They will fight us."

"They might," said Jimmy. "But if we say we only want to leave and they can keep our share of the gold — not that we're getting any, as we well know — it's possible they'll leave us be."

"No," said Gustav. "If we kill Lefty, they won't let us escape. You're not a criminal and have never been in a gang, so you don't know how we think. If he dies, there are two or three more who will want to take his place; to become the new Lefty. They will fight, that is certain."

"What do you suggest, then?"

"Take him hostage. Rough him up good — I'll take care of that." Gustav grinned. "Then threaten to kill him if they don't carry on working, just as you said. One of us guards him with the shotgun, while two of us build the ladder to break out. That is a plan that *might* work, because criminals need a leader, and you will be the leader after we take Lefty prisoner."

"I see. What do you say, Mateo?"

"We gotta try something, my friend. We must get out before they finish. They're going to blow up the Bank. If they don't kill us, we will hang." He shrugged.

"We have little choice," said Jimmy. "Are we in agreement, then?" The others nodded.

They heard Lefty shouting angrily by the Walbrook.

"Well, let's get ready to put the plan into action." Jimmy grinned a fatalist's grin.

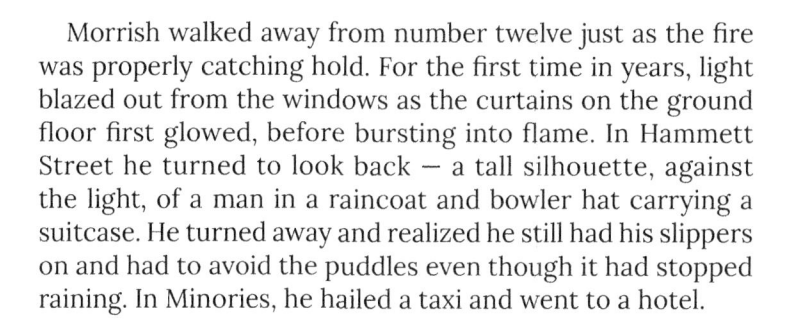

Morrish walked away from number twelve just as the fire was properly catching hold. For the first time in years, light blazed out from the windows as the curtains on the ground floor first glowed, before bursting into flame. In Hammett Street he turned to look back — a tall silhouette, against the light, of a man in a raincoat and bowler hat carrying a suitcase. He turned away and realized he still had his slippers on and had to avoid the puddles even though it had stopped raining. In Minories, he hailed a taxi and went to a hotel.

The agents reunited outside St. Margaret's in Lothbury. They excitedly exchanged their stories while sitting in Rabbit. Ada and BW were sure Lud's gang was transferring gold to a boat or a barge near Southwark Bridge. They could not be positive about this because they had not witnessed the event, but the proximity of the suspicious men to the embankment gave credence to their theory. Then Flora dramatically recounted the experiences she and Sophie had undergone at number twelve, as though they had endured a horrific night of torment in a ghost-ridden house. With everyone up to date, they discussed what they would do next.

"We should tell a policeman," said Flora.

"No," said Ada. "If we did that, we'd all be down the nick straightaway and spend hours gettin' nowhere."

"I think Ada's right," said Sophie. "Even if we convince the local police to act, they'd have to contact Scotland Yard. It would take so much time, and we still have two important things to do — wait for Morrish to show us where the entrance is, because he said he was going to Guildhall after someone called Lefty, and follow the boat with the gold."

"We still have to report all of this," said Flora. "How much more absurd can it be? We're in the middle of London while the greatest robbery of all time is underway, and nobody knows but us!"

"It is ridiculous, and it's all the fault of bureaucracy — all the petty games being played. However, I had hoped Auntie would have found someone by now. It's almost three, and no one has shown up. We can't just hang about doing nothing."

"They've all slacked off," said BW. "And do you know why...? I'll tell you. Everyone is nice and warm and in bed because the police are taking over in the morning, as Miss King explained earlier. Everyone thinks it's somebody else's problem now. I saw plenty of that type of thing when I worked for the Inland Revenue."

"Yes!" said Sophie. "And Lud has found out the police are taking charge and moved up the date of the robbery because of it... I can't believe we must continually plead our case to get anything done. Then, when they finally listen, they make a muck of it... They're all too, too tiresome for words."

"I'd like to know where Sidney has gone," said Flora. "I can't believe he's sleeping through all of this."

"And Archie and Superintendent Penrose," added Sophie. "Well, we won't worry about them. Ada, if you wouldn't mind, I'll take you to Canon Row Police Station next to Scotland Yard, where your job will be to convince the police that the robbery is taking place. Do you think you can do that?"

"I'll try me best, miss... I'd better leave the hatchet in the car."

Sophie started the engine.

"Flora and BW, I'll drop you off at Guildhall. Stay together and watch for Morrish's arrival, but for goodness' sake, stay hidden."

"We'll certainly do that," said BW.

"When I return from White Lyon Yard, I'll park in Gresham Street before joining you."

In the overheated cottage in the nameless alley behind Guildhall, Old Davey could not sleep. For the first time during the tunnelling operation, he had a companion sitting with him. A small, fleshy man in his shirtsleeves and wearing a shoulder holster sat in a chair, suffering. He used a handkerchief to mop himself almost incessantly.

"How d'ya stand this 'eat?" he asked, running the cloth around his neck.

"You get used to it," said Old Davey, who seemed untroubled by the temperature. He was suspicious of the newcomer for several reasons. The man had a revolver — that was reason enough to be concerned. Davey knew that whatever the operation was, it was soon ending. Recently, he had seen evidence of this in the faces of the men descending into the tunnel, as well as the change in Lefty Watts' demeanour. He had also observed the quantities of wood and other materials being taken down the ladder in recent days, and that had told him much. Tonight, so many men had gone down the hole beneath the stove that it had to be the last day of operation. Then there was Lefty's comment to him as he gave Davey his coins. He had said he would get him his bonus in the morning and Davey was to keep the fire going until six a.m.

"Put the fire out," said the man.

"Can't. Lefty said. It's burning much lower, anyway."

"It's hotter now than earlier... I'll open a window."

"If you do, there'll be trouble and Lefty will blame me as well as you," said Davey.

"Lefty." The man enunciated the name with some disdain, but he did not open the window. "I'll be back." He went out and lit a cigarette.

Davey reviewed the situation. He was in hopes of the unspecified bonus, but that prospect seemed less certain now. In the hours during which he and the man with the revolver had sat in the cottage, they had discussed a few things, but never the robbery itself. Old Davey knew it was something big and slowly it had dawned on him that, when it was over, they would no longer need him. With difficulty he came at the question of what would a man like Lefty Watts do with an old caretaker like himself who knew too much? Finally, and reluctantly, Old Davey concluded his 'bonus' would be a bullet, or a broken neck and a swim in the Thames. That payout could come as soon as the stove was cool enough for a man to lift by himself. Quietly, Old Davey opened the door of the firebox and put in more coal.

Davey was just closing the stove door when he heard voices outside, followed by a muted, strangulated gasp. There followed several quiet moments, and then the front door opened. Morrish, carrying a revolver, had to duck to avoid the lintel. "Give me a hand," he said in his deep, troubling voice while staring at Old Davey. Behind him, stretched out in the alley, Davey could see the other man and the still glowing tip of his fallen cigarette. It shook him and he did not know what to do, so he obeyed. Together, they dragged the dead man by his feet into the cottage.

"Small place, ain't it?" said Morrish, looking about the room.

"Yes, but it suits me." Old Davey anxiously wondered what would happen next.

"The hole's under the stove, right?"

"That's right."

"Put the fire out. It's too hot in here... what a stupid waste of coal."

"Lefty ordered me to keep the fire burning so that no one would ever think of looking for the hole beneath the stove. It was all right in the winter... but it's been so hot lately." As the man had just killed someone, Davey unquestioningly started saving the coal he had just put in the firebox.

"Down there with the others, is he?" asked Morrish.

"Yes."

Davey shovelled out the embers into a bucket, while Morrish, after putting the revolver in his pocket, took a boot off the dead man.

"Too small for me. Pity, they're nice... I lost all my shoes tonight... What size do you take?"

"About the same as him, by the looks of it."

"You take them, then. Can't have good boots going to waste." He handed them over.

"Thanks... You goin' down there?" He nodded towards the stove and began changing his boots.

"Yes."

"What do I do afterwards?"

Morrish stared at him. "If I was you, I'd clear out as soon as we've moved the stove."

"I won't go to the police." Davey was still worried.

"Course, you won't, because you're in as deep as any of us, and we'll all swing just the same."

"I had nothin' to do with it... Lefty made me look after things here. Said if I didn't, he'd kill me."

"No. He'd have had me kill you. That's what he meant. But I've had enough of him and his big mouth. He made me kill my wife, now I'm going to kill him. So, like I said, clear out... How'd you move the stove while it's still hot?"

"Like this."

With the quickness of long practise and anxious to get rid of Morrish, Old Davey detached the chimney and produced the two planks with which they could lift the stove. They moved it aside, and he then reattached the piece of chimney. Finally, he got out the keys and crowbars for lifting the tiles and slab beneath.

"That's clever, that," said Morrish. He stared down into the lighted tunnel.

"By the ladder is a switch for the lights, but it only works for the first eighty yards or so. There are other switches further on."

"Thanks." Morrish got on to the ladder. "You can go now."

"Yeah, I will... What is it they're stealing? I've always wondered, but didn't like to ask."

"The gold from the Bank of England."

"Well, I never... Is it, really? I knew it was something big, but that?"

Morrish smiled. "Leave everything and just go." He descended the ladder.

Old Davey hurriedly despoiled his own cottage, putting all his valuables and irreplaceable mementoes into a sack. He also took the dead man's jacket, watch, money, and ring. He hesitated over the gaping hole in the floor. It occurred to him that if he put the slab back, all his problems might go away. A slow thinker, he had finally comprehended how it all might end. All he knew was that either Lefty or Morrish would somehow come after him. Of the two, he preferred it to be Lefty, because he did not understand Morrish at all. He looked at his new watch — it was just past five — then he looked at the dead body. Davey took a coat down from its peg and hoisted his sack more comfortably over his shoulder. He opened the front door, only to discover a young woman bending down, listening at the keyhole.

Sophie jumped up, looked startled, then levelled her pistol at Old Davey.

"Make a wrong move and I'll shoot."

Chapter 29

Keep the Fire Burning

For the first time in months, the cottage windows and door were all open to let in the air. While Sophie got vital information from Old Davey, BW and Flora investigated the place.

"So, Lefty Watts and another bloke came in saying they were archeologists, and did I know where the old well was? I said, what old well? 'cause I'd never heard of it. Anyway, they had this bit of a map and gave me a quid to tap me floor. I said yes, 'cause they said if I didn't let 'em they'd break me arms and legs. I knew then they weren't archeologists, so I took the quid. They started tappin', found the well almost at once, and then tore me floor up, an' that hole has been there ever since."

"The vile wretches bullying you like that," said Sophie.

"Thank you for understanding my situation. It got worse, though. When Lefty shoved his revolver in my face, I decided I'd do whatever he said. Anyway, we come to terms an' I was to get two bob a day every day they was tunnelling, an' I was to keep me mouth shut an' not ask questions. Well, for an old un' like me, the money was welcome an' broken limbs or a bullet were not. You can see my difficult situation. There was nothing I could do but go along with 'em."

"I can sympathize if it's true... But it's so hot and smelly in here," said Sophie. "How can you live like this?"

"They made me," he said. "They didn't give me a moment to myself."

"So you say. I'm not entirely convinced. Are you sure you didn't have a part in the killing of this poor man?"

"I never touched him, honest. But he is a criminal like the rest. The tall bloke killed him outside and made me help bring the body in, an' I had to 'cause he had the gun. You would have done the same, anyone would."

"But you stole the dead man's boots," said Flora.

"The tall bloke made me take the boots 'cause they didn't fit him."

"A likely story. His name is Morrish for future reference," said Sophie.

"I didn't like to ask him that much. Are you police?"

"No," she replied.

"Then I'll just be on my way." He got up from the chair.

"You're not going anywhere, so just sit still."

"You have to let me go if you're not the police."

"Sit down and be quiet," said BW.

"Where does the tunnel lead?" asked Sophie.

"This end is the old well wot dried up years an' years ago, but I dunno where it comes out."

"Yes, you do."

"That's true, but I didn't before tonight, which is what I meant. Whatshisname Morrish said they was stealing the gold from the Bank of England, so they must have dug a tunnel to it. Can I go now?"

"How many are down there?"

"Oh, it's gettin' right crowded — twenty? But I never counted 'em proper."

"You could have done something about this frightful situation in all this time!" said BW.

"Have you ever met Lefty Watts?"

"No."

"Then don't. But I'll tell you this much. The tall bloke, Morrish, has gone after him. Says Lefty made him kill his wife. Is that true?"

"We believe she's dead, but are not sure how she died," said Sophie.

"Blimey. They're a-pilin' up a bit too quick for my liking."

"Can we put something over the corpse?" asked Flora.

"Righty-ho," said BW. "What does one do about the eyes?"

"BW," said Sophie tersely, "just deal with it without commentary, please."

"I shan't say another word." He then got on with things.

Ada came through the door.

"What the bloomin' heck is goin' on?" she said as BW draped a blanket over the corpse. "You never shot him, did you, miss?"

"No. Morrish broke his neck and then he went down that hole." Sophie pointed to the open tiles.

"Godfathers!" She peered cautiously over the side of the hole. "Blimey, is that the tunnel? There are lights on... For some reason, I never expected that." Ada looked at Old Davey. "Hello. Who are you?"

"Old Davey — the fella with no future wot lives here. Who are you?"

"You don't need to know. How about a pot o' tea?"

"Well, I could go for one, but Morrish told me to put the fire out, and he's already killed two people tonight and is workin' on a third."

"That's goin' it a bit for anyone. Is he one of the unfortunates?" She glanced towards the form under the blanket.

"That's right. Morrish took that bloke's revolver and is in the tunnel lookin' for Lefty Watts. There's a load of 'em down there robbin' the Bank of England."

"Oh, I know about the robbery. Shockin', ain't it? Where do you keep the tea?"

"In the can, on that shelf. I'll get the fire goin', shall I?"

"We won't have no tea if you don't," said Ada. She turned to Sophie. "I told 'em at the police station, miss. They believed me and got right busy. Contacted Scotland Yard, they did, and then they were all rushing about while I twiddled me thumbs so, when they weren't lookin', I come out. When I arrived, I saw the door of this cottage open and thought this had to be the place."

"Well done, Nancy!" said Sophie. "We haven't been here long ourselves and now I must find out what they're doing," said Sophie.

"You're goin' down the hole, miss? I don't think you should."

"My mind's made up. You can stay and have tea, if you like, but I must do something!"

"I say, Miss King," said BW. "I'm coming with you. It's far too dangerous for you to go alone."

"And don't think I'm staying here with a corpse," said Flora.

"I left the hatchet in the car," said Ada. "Hopefully, I won't need it."

"But I've just lit the fire," said Old Davey in a plaintive voice. "Are you stayin' for tea or not?"

"Keep the fire going," said Sophie. "We'll be back for tea shortly. And don't go anywhere."

"No, I won't do that."

One after another, the agents descended into the tunnel. Then Sophie popped her head back up to say,

"Should the police arrive, please tell them the following: Miss King requests they enter the tunnel at once and also to send men to apprehend the boat being loaded with gold at Walbrook Wharves by Cannon Street Bridge. Have you got that?"

"Er, down the hole and at Walbrook Wharves. I've got it, Miss King." He tapped the side of his head.

"Thank you." She disappeared.

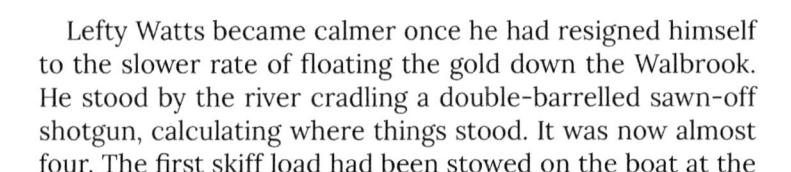

Lefty Watts became calmer once he had resigned himself to the slower rate of floating the gold down the Walbrook. He stood by the river cradling a double-barrelled sawn-off shotgun, calculating where things stood. It was now almost four. The first skiff load had been stowed on the boat at the wharf, and the second load was two-thirds complete. All but twenty of the remaining bars to be taken were stacked on the bank next to him. He judged the men at the other end would only have the skiff partially loaded for the final run. The last load had to leave before six or the ebbing tide would drop the water level too low for the skiff to reach the boat. Concerning the remaining forty to sixty bars, as he estimated the surplus, they would stay where they were stacked, and this surplus interested him.

Lost in meditation, Watts considered the gold they would leave behind. By weight, it would amount to between half and three-quarters of a ton, which was a fortune he could not spend in several lavish lifetimes. His eyes roved over the surroundings for a place to hide such a treasure. Watts also considered whom he might trust with this little side operation. The shortage in the gold bar count was easy to explain to Messrs Healy and Godfrey, although he did not doubt they would make an excessive, even punitive, deduction from his own share for having failed to reach the target. Where to hide the gold, though? He thought about burying it, and the only person whom he could trust, even if it were in a limited way, was Jimmy Mitchell. He looked along the vault tunnel. Gustav was coming towards him, carrying a gold bar.

"Where's Jimmy?" asked Lefty. "I want him."

"He's right behind me."

When he drew level, Gustav threw the bar on Lefty's foot, who howled, dropping the shotgun, and doubling over. Gustav started to pummel him. Jimmy ran forward and snatched up the shotgun. Cocking a hammer, he pointed the gun at the two men working in the river.

"I want your revolvers." The men put their hands up. "Stop hitting him," he said to Gustav over his shoulder.

"He's unconscious, anyway." Gustav went through Lefty's pockets and found an automatic pistol and some extra shotgun shells.

Mateo moved to disarm the men in the river while Jimmy covered him. One had a revolver, the other a large knife. In the other direction, Gustav aimed the automatic at a man in his early twenties who was carrying a bar. He ordered him to stop.

"Listen to me," said Jimmy. "We're not taking any gold, and all we want to do is to leave, so you can carry on working. What you're doing is none of our business. We're getting out and, as long as no one interferes with us, no one will get hurt. Make a move, though, and Lefty will die. So will many of you. What do you want? A needless fight or the gold?"

No one spoke.

"Give me an answer!"

"We're only here for the gold," said a man in the river.

"How about you?" asked Gustav of the young man holding the bar.

"We won't fight *if* you keep your word. What's the point when we only want to get paid?"

"Give me your gun."

The others are all armed," he said, "and I'm keeping my pistol in case the coppers show up. Taking mine won't make no difference to you now."

"Hmm." Gustav stared at the man. "Despite what he said," he nodded towards Jimmy, "we're taking three bars because we also want to be paid."

"That's interesting," said the man. "I've got no problem with you doing that 'cause we won't shift it all in time, anyway. But to show goodwill, take a fourth bar with you. They tried to do Frenchie last night, but he got away. It happens I know where he is. Lefty was going to do him, and the rest of you, because he has to get rid of loose ends. I didn't like any of that — it's all so unnecessary. Now, if all goes well, and you don't block the exit on us, I'll give you the address where Frenchie's hiding." He stared back with an unflinching gaze.

The younger man's self-possession and intelligence impressed Gustav. "And what about Lefty?"

"Do what you like. He's finished either way, ain't he?" He shifted the weight of the bar he held. "I'll put this down; it's heavy, like."

"Slowly." Gustav took a more careful aim.

The man smiled. "You'd have shot me already, if you were going to." He put the bar on the pile. "I'll tell the others about the new arrangements," he said. "They won't complain, but they'll be right anxious about gettin' out."

"They needn't worry," called Jimmy. "We're leaving a different way."

"Are you?" The answer surprised him. "That's wise, that is. I'll set a man to watch what you do, if it's all the same — just to make sure you don't have a change of heart. If you mess about, the deal's off and we'll shoot each other."

Jimmy laughed. "That's reasonable... Is that all right with you?" he asked Mateo and Gustav.

They all agreed to the proposition.

The man called to the two men in the river. "Right, you two get busy, and don't get the raft fouled. With Lefty out of it, there's more for the rest of us."

The gold started moving again. Jimmy and Mateo collected tools, the materials to build a ladder, and four bars, while Gustav crouched low on the opposite bank with the shotgun. Lefty Watts lay beside him with his wrists tied. Now conscious again, he glowered over the change in his fortunes.

The narrowest, lowest, and most challenging part of the tunnel for the secret agents came at the beginning. It was not until they had gone along the old bed of the Walbrook, mounted the six steps, and slithered through the gap into the old tunnel that they were relieved enough to complain.

"What a ridiculous excuse for a tunnel," whispered Sophie, straightening her hat. "They've had months to do it properly."

Flora was brushing her clothes. "They should have installed a full-length mirror... At least we can stand up straight in this older part."

"Let's hope it continues like this... These must be the Guildhall's foundations." Sophie pointed to the massive stones.

Soon, they were quietly passing the ancient Roman and old Saxon walls with their inscriptions from more recent eras.

"My word!" exclaimed BW. "We're walking through a jolly old slice of London history."

The others shushed him to silence.

They pressed on — rapidly at first, but afterwards much more slowly, because the expectation of meeting Morrish or Lud's gang increased with every step they took. When they arrived at the unlit cross tunnel, it was obvious which branch was in use from the foot-worn floor. The short, dark tunnel ran more or less straight, and Sophie could see a sliver of dim electric light at the end. As she watched, and as the thick, damp, mouldy air assailed her nostrils, a figure momentarily blocked the light. Someone was lurking in the darkness. She pulled back quickly and put her finger to her lips, warning the others to be silent. Then she peered around the corner again.

In the cottage, Old Davey had made tea and was just draining his cup. There was no point in him washing it up as he was leaving. He hoisted his sack and was about to go when the front door burst open and two armed men wearing khaki military tunics rushed in.

"Sit down and keep your hands in sight," said Sinjin Yardley, pointing a revolver at Davey who had raised his hands in horror.

"I'm an innocent civilian, I am." He sat down.

"Here's the entrance, right enough," said a big Yorkshireman named Len Feather who carried a rifle and a revolver. He then lifted the blanket. "And who's this poor beggar with a broken neck?"

"I don't know his name, but Morrish killed him."

"Morrish?" said Yardley. "And what is your name?"

"Harry Smith."

"Is this your domicile?" asked Yardley.

"Do you know Lefty Watts?" asked Old Davey.

"No. Who's he?"

"He's a crook and, no, I don't live here. Could you put your gun down, please? It's making me nervous."

Yardley nodded for Len to search Old Davey.

"You're up to summat," said Len to Davey when he had finished. "He's got a lot o' coin, but no weapon," he said to Yardley. Len picked up Davey's sack and examined the contents. "Nice little haul, you got yoursel'."

"Ahh," said Yardley. "So, you're a thief." Yardley returned his revolver to its holster.

"No, I'm not, guv'nor, I swear I'm not... It's like this, see. I live here, but I'm 'eartily sick of it now. I just want to go away somewhere quiet."

"You're not going anywhere. The corpse has no boots, but you are wearing a newish pair... First, put out the fire, it's stifling in here."

"Wouldn't you like some tea, guv?"

"Tea?"

"I just thought I'd ask." He got up slowly.

"Who's in the tunnel?"

"Well... There are the miners — there's three of 'em who go down the tunnel reg'lar. There's Lefty Watts and his gang, an' there's at least a dozen of 'em. Then there's Morrish who killed his wife and that bloke there, and who has gone after Lefty to do the same to him, an' I 'ope he gets him. Finally, there's Miss King and her friends who have gone to put a stop to everything."

"Miss King!?"

"And her friends — two ladies and a young bloke. She said I'm to tell the police to go down the tunnel and also to go to Walbrook Wharves, where they're loading the gold. How she knows that, don't ask me. But she said she was coming back for tea soon, and to keep the fire burnin' accordingly. Whereas Morrish wanted the fire put out and Lefty wanted it kept alight like he usually does. That's why I asked if you wanted tea. It would make my life so much easier if you had some."

"Stop right there... The police will be here soon," said Yardley.

"Oh, I see. I mean, I knew *they'd* come eventually, but I wasn't expectin' *you*, guv."

"Yes... Call the men in, Len."

Len went to the door and gave a low whistle. Five men with rifles crowded in and the cottage was full.

"Are you all from the army?" asked the bewildered Davey.

"Quiet," said Yardley. "Right, gentlemen. We're going in. Safeties on, so there are no accidents." Several safety catches clicked. "Three ladies and a gentleman whom you know from Sandringham are present in the tunnel. They are to be secured first before we tackle the gang. There are fifteen to twenty belligerents led by a man named Lefty Watts."

"Big, hefty bloke with a nasty look," added Davey.

"And there's another man in the tunnel named Morrish. He murdered that fellow there by breaking his neck." Yardley pointed at the blanket. "It seems he is intent upon giving the same treatment to Watts"

"Morrish is a really tall bloke with a deep voice, so you can't miss him."

"Thank you," said Yardley. "Do you know the layout of the tunnel?"

"Never been down there, guv, and never will."

"Is everyone ready, then?"

They all replied, 'Yes, sir.'

"He's going to bolt," said Len, nodding at Davey.

"I think he's on our side," said Yardley in a pleasant drawl. "Can you catch?" He tossed a half-crown to Davey, who caught it. "Stay and tell the police of the situation in the tunnel."

"I'll do that, guv'nor. Good luck and God bless all of you."

Yardley smiled, then led his men down the ladder. Old Davey stroked his beard abstractedly while waiting for the last man to descend. As soon as he was gone, Davey picked up his sack and got out of the cottage.

"What's he doing?" asked Flora in a whisper.

"Now he's not moving," replied Sophie. "He must be able to see something that we can't from here."

"Let me see." Flora looked for a moment. "The tunnel is larger where there are lights."

"Do you think it's the vault?"

"We haven't come far enough, miss," said Ada.

"What do we do?" whispered BW.

"I don't know," said Sophie. "Any suggestions?"

"Go home?" suggested Flora.

"Serious suggestions only, please."

"He's moving," said Flora. "Surely he's not coming this way!"

Sophie peered into the tunnel alongside her friend.

Morrish was waiting for Lefty Watts to drop his guard, but an opportune moment never seemed to present itself. Invisible within the dark tunnel, he watched the progress of the operation and heard Lefty shouting orders. His original plan was to kill Lefty straight off, but the gold being piled up by the river made Morrish hesitate. Knowing that Mr Healy and Mr Godfrey wanted Lefty to get the gold out, he, Morrish, could not intervene until it was all over. So, he brooded in the darkness over his loss and bided his time.

When Watts was beaten and taken prisoner, Morrish could make no sense of what had happened. He heard some of the conversation, especially Jimmy's, although he did not know who he was. Then he watched as Watts was bound and moved to sit within a dozen feet of the end of the tunnel where he was hiding. He quietly retreated so as not to be seen by the man with the shotgun. Morrish saw two others building a ladder and could not understand why they would do that. He became indecisive and swayed, shifting his weight from foot to foot. He took the revolver from his pocket.

Chapter 30

Negotiations

The ladder Jimmy and Mateo built was a rough, heavy affair made from short planks nailed together. They got it into a secure position. Mateo scrambled up and began attacking the stones around the grating with his short-handled pickaxe.

"The mortar is no good," he called down.

Jimmy shielded his eyes from falling dust and grit while steadying the ladder.

"Hey! Give some warning." A large piece had broken off, narrowly missing him.

"You got the easy job, so don't complain... It's moving." He attacked another section, and the grating came loose. Mateo shoved upwards, and the grating slid noisily across the basement floor. He put his head through the opening.

"What do you see?" asked Jimmy.

"It's dark, but there's a street lamp... Two small windows at ground level with iron bars... Boxes... A lot of boxes, and some cupboards... A door. Hold the ladder tight, I'm going to see." He stepped up a rung and, with a struggle, hoisted himself through the opening. Mateo was gone for two minutes. When he returned, he put his face to the opening. Jimmy could see his grin in the gloom.

"It's empty and we can get out the back — no lock, just two bolts. Jimmy! They have nice carpets on the floor." Mateo laughed. "Pass up the gold."

"I'm not happy about this part," said Jimmy, climbing the ladder a rung at a time and clutching a bar to his chest. Gustav steadied the ladder while still holding the shotgun.

"Guilty conscience, huh? You'll get over it." Mateo laughed.

"You're one of us now," said Gustav.

Watts spoke to them. "They'll catch you when you try to unload it."

"Why do you care?" asked Gustav.

"I don't, apart from you leading the police to the rest of us. That kid you did the deal with — he's all mouth. Fancies himself, but he's wet behind the ears. It's me you should talk to."

"Shut up or I'll beat you again."

"Jimmy! Listen to reason," continued Lefty. "You can still get your payout. Just untie me and we'll forget everything."

"You were going to kill us when this was all over." He carried the third bar up the ladder in a tool bag. "Don't bother denying it, when I know you've been killing off men all along. Once anyone asked a question too many, he signed his own death warrant. You were going to do the same to us."

"No, Jimmy, not you, I swear it. You've got it all wrong. And none of that killing off of the foreigners was my idea. I just followed orders. Anyway, it wasn't me who did the killin', was it? That was all Morrish."

"But you assisted him."

"I cleaned up afterwards, that's all. I had to, didn't I? But that man's a lunatic and should be put down, and will be, since Healy no longer needs him."

"Getting rid of the extra baggage, eh?" said Jimmy. "You're just as filthy as any of them."

"The man's sick in the head, so don't go sayin' I'm the same. He enjoys killing…"

Morrish, roaring, rushed forward, shooting repeatedly. Two bullets missed their mark, but two of them struck Watts. Gustav fired the shotgun, and the blast knocked Morrish down before he could fire again. The following silence in the confined, cordite-reeking space was awful after the deafening explosions.

"Are you all right?" Mateo called down.

"So far," said Jimmy. "Let's hope that's it." He carried the last bar up the ladder in a sack.

"Lefty's dead," said Gustav, who then inspected Morrish while loading a fresh shell. "This one won't last long." He now searched Lefty's body and Morrish's pockets for money.

"What's going on here?" called the young man from across the stream. He had a revolver in hand, while the rest of the armed gang crowded behind him.

Sophie peered cautiously into the dark tunnel, trying to gauge what was going on. "Stay here," she said to the others, and slipped into the darkness with her pistol in hand.

As he descended the ladder, Jimmy answered. "Presumably that's Morrish." He pointed to him. "He came out of nowhere shooting at Lefty."

"Oh, I see… Poor old Lefty." Moss crossed the plank to whisper Frenchie's address to Jimmy. He turned to the men in the river. "Oi! Don't stand there gaping. Get that gold moving. And don't stop 'til I tell ya."

"Who put *you* in charge?" asked a brawny man named Tom who was standing on the further bank.

"Me, Teddy Moss, because I'm the bloke who just wired the bomb, and it's going off in an hour. Also, my friend, I have ideas, which is probably something you struggle with."

"You want to watch yourself," said Tom.

Sophie was near enough now that she could hear what was being said.

"Yeah? How about this one, boys? It concerns all of us. We were gonna get a monkey each for this work. A ton tonight and four hundred when they sell the gold. Right?"

Several agreed with his statement.

"We'd never see that four hundred. Lefty would skim it, and you know that for a fact." The men were silent.

Jimmy disappeared through the hole, then Gustav followed. Sophie was now as near as she dared get.

"Each of these bars here is worth nigh on two thousand nicker," said Teddy. "None of us can sell it for that, 'cause it's Bank of England gold and will soon be too hot to the touch, you might say. But we'd get a thousand a bar, easy. All we do is go up the ladder like those gentlemen did, each of us carrying his bar. Then the vault can blow up and we'll be safely out of it. There you go, boys; I've just put a thousand in each of your pockets. You'll still get your ton and maybe, *maybe* the four hundred as well. And that is why I'm now in charge."

"What about Barrett and Mr Godfrey?" asked Tom.

"Barrett's too soft and neither of them are here, are they? So, I'm taking over."

"No, you're not."

Teddy shot Tom dead with a single bullet.

"Yes, I am." He spoke to the corpse. "You should learn to treat me with respect." He addressed the others. "Anyone else want to complain?" He waited. "No? It's like this, then. We'll send down one more raft and then get out. I don't like it that anyone can come down the tunnel when they want. So, start cleaning up, boys." He turned to two men about his own age whom he obviously knew. He whispered, "You two get up there first and take my bar with you. Hold hostage anyone who comes into the building, right?"

They nodded and set off.

"Why don't we take *two* bars each, Mr Moss?" a man asked.

"'Strewth! Do you know you must be a genius?" Teddy spoke in a wry, caustic tone. "How have I ever managed without you? But tell me something. What happens if one of these dopes I'm babysitting drops a twenty-nine-pound bar of gold in front of a copper? Would he help pick it up, I wonder, or would we all get nicked?" He lowered his voice. "I think we'd get nicked. Now, please, you can see I'm busy, so don't ask no more stupid questions or I'll put a bullet in your knee."

Sophie moved further back along the tunnel and reached the others. She blew her police whistle. That plaintive sound caused instant panic. The two men Moss had sent ahead were already up in the basement. Teddy grabbed another bar and immediately waded through the water to reach the ladder first. Following in his wake, every other man picked up a bar or two and made a dash. Being encumbered, Moss barely got off the ladder when the others reached it. Everyone wanted to be next up and so fear and greed destroyed what chance they had. With two men ascending, and the rest pushing and shoving, the ladder toppled over to break under the weight of the men on it.

"We'd better leave, miss," said Ada. "They're goin' mad."

"I think you're right."

The agents turned to go but could not retreat.

"Stay where you are!" shouted a man aiming a rifle not ten yards away. He pointed it at Broadbent-Wicks.

"I say, I'd rather you didn't shoot," said BW, "there are ladies present."

"Who are you?"

"My name's Broadbent-Wicks, but… Yes, we had better leave it at that for the present."

Yardley came forward and called,

"Broadbent-Wicks. Is everyone safe?"

"Oh, you're the gardener chappie, aren't you? Call me BW, and, yes, we're all safe, thank you. How are you?"

From the side tunnel, Sophie shouted, "Get a move on! They're advancing." She sent a shot down the dark passage and then hid. Two revolver shots rang out in reply.

Yardley pushed past everyone and reached Sophie's side.

"What do you think you're doing!?" He spoke angrily.

"My job! And don't you start shouting at me! Things are bad enough already." She fired another shot into the tunnel.

"Miss King," said Yardley as patiently as he could, "please retire to the rear and allow me to sort this out."

"Oh! Just when we've got everything under control, you arrive to take over. It's a pity you weren't here yesterday when you were actually needed. Excuse me." She squeezed past everyone. "Get that blasted rifle out of my way." The man, an old sergeant named Atkins, obeyed her order. She stopped to call back to Yardley. "It might interest you to know that they can get into a basement, but they just broke the ladder.

Also, there is a time bomb in the Bank's vault. I didn't catch the time it was set to go off. Soon, I believe."

"There's a bomb?" said Flora, interested.

"I'd like to go now, please, miss," said Ada. "I think this is enough excitement for one day, and it's been a very long one, it has an' all."

The other riflemen now came forward, passing the agents with difficulty in the narrow passage. Yardley asked BW to leave the tunnel and inform the police to search for the basement.

"Hello, Miss King," said Len Feather, as he moved up the line. "Sorry about the tight squeeze."

"Hello, Len. It can't be helped."

"Ay-up, BW."

"What-ho, Len," said BW. "Can't stop to chat. I'm on a mission, don't you know?" BW moved past Len and hurried off.

"Hello, Nancy," said Len with a certain warmth in his voice.

"Hello, Len."

"We just got back from Sandringham, and I found your letter waitin', like. Sorry, but I haven't had a chance to read it yet. Oh, but I will as soon as I can."

"That's nice," said Ada, awkwardly, because she could feel the weight of Sophie's and Flora's eyes on her.

"Hello, Miss Walton."

"Hello, Len. Be careful. There's a time bomb in the vault. I can disarm it if you don't have anyone with you."

"Can you? Now, that's right useful. What time's it set for?"

"We don't know."

"Be careful, Len," said Ada.

"I will that."

At that moment, Sophie heartily wished to tell Sinjin to be careful.

Yardley began negotiations with the gang while keeping under cover. Len joined him.

"You men! The police are on their way, so you can't escape."

"Who are *you*, then?" someone called back.

"Army... We have rifles and grenades and you're sitting on a time bomb, so I understand."

"That's right... Looks bad for us, don't it?"

"It does, indeed, so be a good fellow and tell everyone to put their weapons down."

"We must discuss it first. Don't go rushing us or we'll shoot."

"Of course, you will, but you'll lose nonetheless, and you know that."

"So, you reckon."

"By the way, how's the time bomb? Still ticking?" The other man made no reply. "What time did you set it for?"

"Never you mind."

"I don't mind. It won't touch us here, but we'll have to dig out your remains... Were you in the war?"

"Course."

"Ever seen the aftermath of an exploded mine...? I saw it at Messines. That was a very nasty bit of business."

"We all saw things."

"That's true... and they're hard to forget."

"Yeah."

Yardley whispered to Len. "I don't think they'll rush us, but get the men into position in case they do."

"Aye, sir — just like old times. It's a pity they're our own countrymen." He signalled the other soldiers to get ready.

In the quiet, they heard tapping.

"They're repairing the ladder," whispered Yardley. "The police won't arrive in time to stop them."

"Check your weapons," said Len to the rest, "and be sure of your target before you shoot."

"Miss King!" called Yardley. "If you would join me for a moment, please."

Sophie moved back up the line.

"How may I help?" she asked.

"Are you familiar with the layout beyond this section of tunnel?"

"Not completely. The roof is about twelve feet high, the open space is dome shaped, and is twenty-five or thirty feet wide, but I don't know how long it is — perhaps the same. The

River Walbrook runs through the middle between two banks. It isn't deep — one or two feet — because I saw the top half of a man wading in it. The banks are flat on both sides. The far bank is larger, and the nearer is quite narrow. I think the ladder was positioned to the left on the nearer bank. I could see some gold bars stacked on the far bank to the left of a tunnel entrance which I'm certain leads to the vault. It's the one they're all using, anyway."

"Thank you very much, Miss King."

"I'm sorry for how I spoke just now."

"No need." Sinjin smiled.

"Good luck."

He smiled again, then turned to the others.

"Best stand well back, miss," said Atkins.

"Yes." She moved away and her heart was in her mouth.

"We must clear the way to the bomb so it can be diffused. If we don't, civilians might be killed and injured. Also, we cannot be sure the Bank buildings have been cleared. Understood?"

There was a chorus of 'yes, sirs.'

"We'll advance to the end of this tunnel and use grenades to clear the open space. We cannot cross the river without risking being caught in a crossfire. Excuse me, a moment." He paused, then called out to the gang, "Have you come to a decision!?"

"We're evenly divided. Give us a few more minutes, will you?"

"Five minutes, that's all!"

"Fair enough."

"Right," whispered Yardley to his men. "Let's go." He plunged into the dark tunnel, crouching and keeping close to one side, while Len was on the other just behind him. Atkins was third, walking upright and aiming his rifle. They moved slowly and quietly. Water dripped and the noise of hammering, at first becoming louder as they closed, now suddenly stopped. Against the light, the silhouette of a man's head bobbed into view for a second. Atkins fired a shot.

"Missed the beggar," he said under his breath while working his rifle bolt.

"We surrender!" said the man, throwing a revolver down where Yardley could see it and then standing out in the open with his hands raised.

"Careful, lads," warned Len.

Yardley halted at the end of the tunnel and called out. "Every man shall drop his weapon and stand in the river with his hands up where I can see them. You have five seconds, or we'll use grenades. Five... four... three." He stopped counting because all the men rushed into the river as ordered. Yardley and his men advanced with their guns trained on the remnants of Lud's gang.

"You said five minutes," said the man who had parleyed with Yardley, "we'd have been gone in two."

"It just isn't your lucky day. Is this all of you?"

"Yes... Who nearly parted my hair?"

"Me," said Atkins.

"You missed me by a quarter of an inch — not even that."

"I'll do better next time."

Len first checked the dead bodies, then the ladder next to which he found an automatic, two revolvers, and some coshes lying where they had been dropped. "We'd better search the prisoners, sir."

While that was underway, Yardley asked what the captives knew of the bomb. He learned it was set to go off at seven, but no one knew how it operated.

"Excuse me," called Flora, who, with the other agents, had gathered in the tunnel's mouth. "I can probably see to it. May we come out? This tunnel is very smelly, as you know."

"You don't know how to disarm a bomb," said Sophie, "so stop telling everyone you do."

"I know more than you do, plus I have confidence."

"Is that what it's called?"

"I don't want the nation's bank blown to pieces, and neither do you. I'm volunteering. No one else is, so there's no argument."

"What's your name?" Yardley pointed at the man who had conducted the negotiations.

"Stevenson."

"My name's Yardley. All you men are in serious trouble. If you help to disarm the bomb, I'll put in a good word for you. First, the bomb. Then you'll tell me who it was who killed these three men."

"That's easily explained. Morrish killed Lefty Watts." Stevenson pointed out the different corpses. "A foreign bloke, don't know his name, but he's long gone now, killed Morrish... and then he killed that bloke over there." He had changed the story in case it got back to Teddy Moss.

"He used a shotgun and a revolver?" asked Len.

"That's right, isn't it, mates?"

Several others backed up his revised story.

"The police will sort all that out," said Yardley. "Who will step forward and lead us to the vault?"

"I'll go," said Stevenson.

"Good man. Len, look after things here... Miss Walton, would you be so kind as to accompany us?"

"I would usually answer 'with pleasure'. Could somebody possibly help me across the river, please?"

Without waiting for permission, two of the gang put an extra plank into place and helped Flora across.

Chapter 31

Time to Go

Old Davey had worked out a plan. He waited at the entrance to the alley and only had to retreat once when a constable on his beat passed by. After he had gone, Davey resumed his position.

It seemed like an age before anyone came. A car pulled up and two men in plainclothes got out. They blocked the street with their car. A big man approached.

"Who are you?" he demanded.

"Jeremiah Hoskins." Davey supplied the name of his long dead Sunday school teacher. "Are you the police?"

"That's right. I'm Superintendent Penrose, Special Duties, Scotland Yard. Why are you loitering?"

"Well, sir, I'm not loitering, as such. Miss King and then a gentleman from the army asked me to wait here and give messages to the police. I was passing by and they asked me to help."

Penrose fished in his pocket for his pipe. "If you'd be so kind as to deliver those messages, Mr Hoskins."

"It's like this..." He reeled off the litany of events, people, and circumstances that he now had by heart, although he had made some changes concerning himself.

Penrose lit his pipe and only interrupted once to say to his sergeant, "Daniels, there's a murder victim in that there cottage, as well as the tunnel's entrance. Take a look."

While Old Davey was still talking, a fleet of police vehicles arrived and filled the street. An inspector approached Penrose.

"Gould," said Penrose, "stay here with twenty men. The tunnel entrance is in the cottage and there's been a murder. Some of our people are down below. They are a Miss King, with three others in her party, and a Mr Yardley with half a dozen in his. When they appear, don't hold any of them. Got that?"

"Yes, sir. Where are you going?"

"Down to Walbrook Wharves by Cannon Street with the rest of the men. That's where they're loading the gold... And have someone ring the river police. They have two boats on the river standing by, so send them to the wharves."

Gould immediately gave instructions to his officers. "What about that man?" he asked.

"That's Mr Hoskins, who's been very helpful. Just take his name and address and let him go home. Poor chap has been up all night doing his civic duty."

Penrose departed. After Old Davey had given his fictitious name and address, he walked down to Billingsgate fish market where a public house was open all night. There, he drank a pint of bitter with a whisky chaser, and then entered the lavatory. He shaved off his beard and cut his hair, discovering in the process a pale, more youthful face than he remembered. "You're only as old as you feel," he said to his reflection. He washed, then dried himself on a disreputable-looking rag hanging from a hook. He left — in fact, he left London altogether. Davey walked to Liverpool Street Station to catch an early train to Southend-on-Sea. He dozed en route but, by the end of the day, had a temporary job at the Kursaal Amusement Park, which was made permanent later on. He found lodgings on Pleasant Road with a widowed Irish landlady roughly his own age who immediately took a liking to him and he to her. Under yet another assumed name, Davey lived in Southend pretty much happily ever after — fishing from the pier, and with the sea, which he had always loved, a mere hundred yards from his landlady's doorstep.

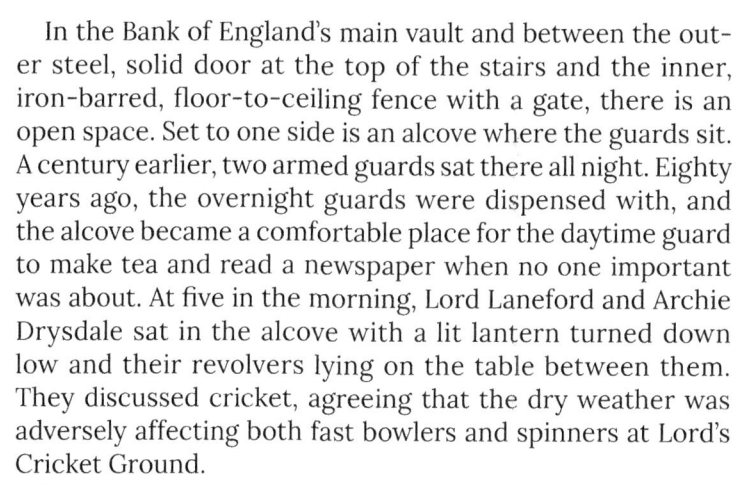

In the Bank of England's main vault and between the outer steel, solid door at the top of the stairs and the inner, iron-barred, floor-to-ceiling fence with a gate, there is an open space. Set to one side is an alcove where the guards sit. A century earlier, two armed guards sat there all night. Eighty years ago, the overnight guards were dispensed with, and the alcove became a comfortable place for the daytime guard to make tea and read a newspaper when no one important was about. At five in the morning, Lord Laneford and Archie Drysdale sat in the alcove with a lit lantern turned down low and their revolvers lying on the table between them. They discussed cricket, agreeing that the dry weather was adversely affecting both fast bowlers and spinners at Lord's Cricket Ground.

"They're coming back," whispered Archie, turning the lantern flame to its lowest glimmer.

Both men sat still, sipping their tea and listening. They were hidden in the alcove, and the hole in the vault's wall was around a corner and not visible from the fence. They could clearly hear Lud's men, though. The robbers had whispered and tip-toed about upon entering the vault at the start, but over time they had lost all caution.

Archie, who had now finished with the diplomatic row, and Laneford were there because they had held a late-night conference with Penrose at a restaurant on the Strand some hours earlier. Yardley and his men had been recalled from Sandringham even earlier and were on their way to report to Penrose at the Yard and receive further instructions.

After the meeting in the restaurant, Laneford returned to his hotel with Archie accompanying him. At gone three in the morning, Sophie returned briefly to White Lyon Yard and found Aunt Bessie still awake. She quickly told her that, thanks to Morrish the Murdering Maniac, they had discovered the whereabouts of the tunnel's entrance and it was at Guildhall. Aunt Bessie immediately, but unsuccessfully, tried Archie's number again, at which point they both made loud exclamations about defective thinking. The word pudding-head briefly became fashionable. Then Sophie left because she had to meet Flora and BW. Moments later, Lady Shelling was speaking to Lord Laneford, informing him that Guildhall was the place to be. This news ran quickly through the network, and a plan was hastily devised.

Laneford and Drysdale had arrived very late at the vault. It had taken two hours to awaken and convince various incredulous Bank officials, including the Governor, and to get the keys to the vault. Upon arrival, Laneford and Drysdale had gone into the guards' alcove to listen. After a quarter hour, they had heard enough, and reported to the Bank's Governor, Montagu Norman, who waited upstairs outside the vault.

An urbane and fashionably dressed man, Norman wanted to ascertain this for himself. At 4:47 a.m. his own ears provided the evidence to make him a believer that thieves were at work. Archie first heavily cautioned the man before quietly opening the steel door and ushering downstairs to the guards' area. The whole banking industry of Britain shook when Montagu Norman trembled. He saw the glow of lanterns in his vault and heard the thieves complaining the bars seemed to be heavier now than earlier while they were removing them through a hole in his wall. He blanched in the darkness and then became enraged. In the discussion that occurred when they were outside again, he roared when describing how the thieves should be slaughtered by the Bank's guards. This paroxysm of anger did not suit him. Naturally, his manner altered yet again when Laneford delivered the balance of the report. He and Drysdale had overheard the thieves referring to a large bomb that seemed to be somewhere in the vault, which ruled out a direct attack on the thieves as being too dangerous, especially since no explosives experts were present, although they had been requested. Upon hearing this, Norman became faint and removed himself to another building much further away to lie down for a while.

Drysdale and Laneford conversed quietly when they could. They noticed that the sounds in the vaults had become intermittent and now had ceased. The current silence had lasted over ten minutes.

"Do you think they've gone?" asked Laneford.

"I don't know," said Archie. "From the last conversation we heard, I understood they were taking twenty more bars."

"That's what I thought. Shall we look?"

"Why not?"

Archie picked up the keys from the table, and Laneford took the lantern. The vault was silent, and their soft footsteps sounded ominously loud on the way to the gate. Archie was about to put the key in the lock when they heard a noise from around the corner and saw a glow of light. Laneford extinguished the lantern. They stood stock still, not daring to move.

"All quiet."

"Get a bleedin' move on, then."

There were more noises and a faint sound of grit being ground underfoot as two men stepped through the hole.

"Ain't much left here… That rope might be useful."

"I got the tools, so let's go. It's all gonna blow up, anyway."

"Right… So the tall bloke was Morrish? I'd never seen him before."

"Yes, that's him. He still had his slippers on. Shows he was mad like they say."

"Funny that, wearing slippers. What'll 'appen now Lefty's gone?"

"Dunno, mate. C'mon, let's hop it, before something else goes wrong."

"Yeah, this place is getting' to me now."

"I didn't mean the place, you twerp. I meant that I've got a bad feelin' about this job. Once trouble starts…"

The glow of light disappeared, and the vault became silent again.

"That was close," said Archie.

"Yes... I've left the matches on the table."

They stumbled in complete darkness, feeling their way back to the alcove where Laneford relit the lantern. They sat down.

"It sounds as though they're leaving," said Laneford.

"Yes. I noticed they were unconcerned about the bomb. Makes we wonder if it's on a timer or if it's wired to a plunger."

"Hmm, yes... What difference does that make?"

"I'm not sure. If a timer, I might be concerned about it going off early. They weren't. If the gang is going to detonate it remotely, then from the conversation of those two, it hasn't been wired up yet."

"Ah, but those two might be the demolition experts."

"A good point," said Archie. "I think not, though. They made no reference to the bomb, which they would have done were they the ones responsible for it. They were just sent to clean up the equipment, nothing more."

"What shall we do?"

"As it appears they have finished robbing the bank, I think I'll examine the device."

"Are you familiar with explosives?" asked Laneford.

"Only as far as pulling pins from grenades and throwing them away as fast as possible. Although I had to replace a pin once, and that is much trickier to do than it appears. It definitely concentrates the mind."

"I'll come with you."

"No, I'd rather you didn't, sir."

"Don't go formal on me, Archie."

"Well, if you insist, Sidney."

A minute later, Laneford was listening at the hole in the wall, while Archie examined the clock and control mechanism sitting atop a pyramid of dynamite boxes. He traced the various wires.

"Can't hear anything," said Laneford, now joining Archie.

"It looks simple, but I have heard these things can be booby-trapped. There are no external wires, so all the important stuff is right before us, probably hidden in the top box of dynamite."

"There's rather a lot of it," said Laneford. "It goes off at seven... I have a Big Ben. It's very reliable."

"Never be late again. Big Ben, the leading choice of punctual workers and anarchists everywhere. Approved by the Bank of England... There, how's that for a new advertising slogan?"

"It is absurd to see such an ordinary household item put to such a use. Under the circumstances, your advertising copy is entirely appropriate, but you'll never get the Bank's endorsement."

They laughed.

"We'd best leave it to the experts," said Archie.

"And we should lock the gate, just in case they return."

"Yes. So, there's fifty minutes to run on the clock and the explosives team from Aldershot should arrive in about twenty or thirty minutes. Cutting it a little fine."

"Yes."

Laneford opened the steel door and informed his man Philpott, a City Police inspector, a Yard detective, and several bank officials that there was indeed a large time bomb planted within the building, and asked that the explosives team be rushed through as soon as they arrived. Laneford could see the fear his audience felt, which only increased when he told them the device was set to explode at seven. He added, almost unnecessarily, because they were all itching to be about their duties, that the surrounding area should be cleared immediately. Within ten minutes of their leaving, all the underground trains on the Central Line were at a standstill and Bank Station was closed off until further notice.

Laneford returned to the vault and resumed his seat in the alcove. He then asked Archie,

"Ever tried your hand at fly-fishing?"

Wherrymen, ferrymen, bargees and rowers, gondoliers, voyageurs, and lightermen, canoeists, punters and paddlers — to this list of freight-upon-the-water-movers can be added the skiffwalkers of Walbrook River. The two men — one older, one younger — were tired, hungry, thirsty, wet, smelly, and extremely depressed while standing about waiting and doing nothing in the pitch-black tunnel. The gold had stopped being floated down on rafts and they had run out of lamp oil for their lanterns, so they now had to do everything by touch. Worst of all, their cigarettes kept going out, and they only had two matches left between them. Like disembodied spirits, they conversed in total darkness.

"I told you to bring more paraffin," said the elder.

"No, you didn't," said the younger.

"I told you day before last, we wanted more paraffin."

"That's not true... Anyway, why didn't you bring it?"

"Strike me dead! Why would I, when I thought you were bringin' it!?"

"Don't get angry, but you never said a word abaht it."

"Yes, I did." They were silent for a while.

"Do you think that's it for the gold?" asked the younger man.

"How should I know?"

"I'm only askin'. I know you don't know, anymore than wot I do. But is that it for the gold?"

"Yes," replied the elder.

"How'd you reckon that?"

"Aw, shut it."

"You shut it."

"So, help me... I'm dyin' for a smoke."

"So am I... Do you know the skin on my feet has gone wrinkly an' I can't feel me toes no more?"

"That's trench foot," said the elder emphatically. "Your toes will drop off. But how abaht a nice smoke though, eh?"

"You dropped a match last time."

"'Cause you dithered abaht like the undertaker tryin' to get his bill paid outside the tomb of Jesus, which slowness made me burn me fingers. And your fingers... Now your fingers are no better than uncooked sausages at the best of times, an' are about as useful for delicate work. Also, you broke two matches earlier. How'd you manage that at your age?"

"All right, we'll give it another try. Let's go down the end, 'cause I think the sun should be up now."

"That's a good idea. Don't let Barrett see us, though, or he'll start shoutin'."

"You strike the match, an' I'll light me cigarette."

"No, you won't. I'll strike the match, light me own fag, an' you'll get a light off mine."

"All right... 'Ave you got the matches?"

"I gave 'em to you... No, tell a lie, I've just put me 'and on 'em in me pocket. Bein' in the dark for so long turns yer 'ead right round, don't it?"

"Yeah," agreed the younger. "But if yer 'ead goes right round, it's facin' the same way as when it started, so there's no difference."

"You do go on... Judgin' by the tide, we've got a quarter hour before we're finished. We'd better tell Barrett no more gold has come down for a while."

They left the half-loaded skiff where it was moored to wade knee-deep through foul water. They bowed their heads to avoid scraping the thick slime off the curved brick roof above them. After a few yards, they followed a curve in the tunnel, which brought into view the light of a dull dawn at the sewer's end.

"We should go right now," said the younger, a big, soft-looking fellow of eighteen or nineteen, as they reached the opening where they had sawn through the bars the night before.

"Smoke first, then talk to Barrett." The elder was an old ragged, bearded, disreputable-looking, little individual.

They stared up at the tug anchored fore and aft to their right. The boat seemed deserted and stood off a little way where the water was deeper to avoid being grounded when the tide was out. The two men successfully lit their cigarettes and allowed a few reflective silent moments to pass. Then the elder gave a low whistle.

A man emerged from under a tarpaulin and peered over the side of the tug, his face a pale and puffy blotch in the dreary light.

"What's doin?" he whispered hoarsely.

"You were asleep."

"Nah, not really. Freezin', ain't it?"

"Never mind that. Tell Mr Barrett the sun's up, the tide's goin' out, and no more gold's come down the pipe for the last half hour."

"I'll see what he says."

The man went to the wheelhouse and returned quickly.

"I had to wake him. He says he don't like none of that and to bring what gold you have at once."

"Right."

The skiffwalkers returned, complaining as they went.

"We could have gone half an hour ago," said the younger.

"Yes, but we didn't know we could go, then, did we?"

"What do you mean?"

The explanation was never made because at that moment, someone with a megaphone started bellowing and then two police launches raced into view.

"River Police!" exclaimed the elder. "That's flamin' cheatin', that is."

The skiffwalkers flattened themselves against the wall inside the tunnel. They heard shouts, several shots from somewhere around the warehouses, and the inevitable sound of police whistles — a mournful, tuneless flock of them.

"What do we do about the gold?"

"Gold!? 'Ow abaht savin' our skins!?"

"Yeah, s'pose. Can't we take some wiv' us, though, 'cause I don't think we're gettin' paid now."

"You know what? There's no way out of this for us an' they'll find us in here, so we'll chance it, eh? We'll push the skiff out an' see what 'appens."

"All right."

They untied the craft and walked it through the tunnel.

"Are you gonna do the talkin' if they stop us?"

"Yes, but I ain't yer muvver. You'll 'ave to speak for yourself when the time comes."

"I know that... Is us wiv this gold like us bein' 'anged for a lamb as for a sheep?"

"Uh, I think you've got that mixed up."

"No. That's what me dad used to say before he went inside."

"Why am I not surprised? A sheep is more valuable than a lamb, see. You're sayin' it the wrong way round."

"No, I ain't. A lamb is newer than a sheep. Everyone knows that."

"It's just not worth the effort."

"What ain't?"

"Never mind, I'll explain later. Let's get outta this first. Remember, if we have to bolt, we run in different directions."

"Why? I wanna go with you."

"So, help me, I might as well put a gold bar in each of me pockets, an' just walk out into the middle of the river."

"You shouldn't do that. You'd drown."

"What 'ave I done to deserve this? Shut it now. Just let me think."

When they came to the grating, the elder whispered,

"Stop for a moment, an' do everythin' I say. Chuck the 'acksaw as far as you can into the river, but don't let 'em see you."

"All right." The younger threw it about fifteen yards.

"That's the main bit of evidence against us gone."

"What about the gold?"

"Shut up, and 'old the skiff steady."

The elder began moving his feet about under the water in an odd fashion. He took out a bar from under the tarpaulin and dropped it in the water. He made some more curious movements with his feet to cover the bar in the hole he had made. "That's the best I can do."

"Are you takin' a leak?" whispered the younger man.

"'Course I ain't, you thickhead. Let's move on and follow me lead. Don't go speakin' up on your own."

"All right."

"Now we'll push the skiff clear but 'old it steady in the current just outside."

"All right."

Once through the grating, they halted where the Walbrook joined the Thames.

"Oi! Oi, oi!" the elder bellowed, waving vigorously at the nearest police launch. "Wave, you mug," he whispered to the young man.

An officer with a megaphone on the nearest launch boat saw them. "Stay where you are!"

"Yes, captain," said the elder. "We've found gold and put it in this 'ere skiff!"

"Did you say, gold!?"

"Yes, gold! We're mudlarks, we are, an' it's our'n by right of Treasure Trove."

"We'll see about that."

"No, it's our'n. I'd 'ave paid you for your time to give us an 'and, but I won't if you're gonna be all official."

"Stop talking rubbish, man. You're not entitled to stolen property."

"It ain't rubbish, an' we know nothin' about no stolen property. There's a fortune 'ere an' it's our'n."

"No, it isn't. And mudlarks can only operate when the tide's out."

"Usually that's true, but mudlarkin's a very competitive trade an' you must get in first before the tide's out or the good stuff's gone. Ain't that right?" he asked the younger man.

"It is very competitive, an' you 'ave to get in first!"

"See!" shouted the elder.

Policemen in waders had descended into the river by some nearby stairs. In a single file close to the foot of the wharves, they made their way towards the skiffwalkers.

"Hallo, Charlie!" shouted a sergeant among them. "You're under arrest! Just stay put and don't do anything stupid!"

"'Ello, Sergeant Priestly! How's the family!?"

"Tolerable, thank you!"

"Are we nicked?" whispered the younger.

"Oh, yes," whispered Charlie. "Now that Priestly's shown up, it's all over. No matter what the charges, they'll try for five years, but we'll only do two, you'll see."

"But we haven't been to court yet?" He frowned. "I'll miss the West Ham games."

"Yes, but at least there'll be somethin' waitin' for us when we get out."

"What's waitin' for us?"

"Never mind. Let me look after things. Now be a good lad and just say we were hired in the pub, knew nothing until we arrived here, and then we couldn't get out of it because they would 'ave killed us. Got all that?"

"I think so."

Chapter 32

A little change is needed

The sun shone through a break in the clouds just when Superintendent Penrose decided he would indulge himself in a leisurely pipe and contemplation of the river from the wharf. Nine prisoners were being herded into Black Marias and the tenth was being brought to him. The gold had been recovered and, more importantly, no one was injured beyond a few cuts and bruises. A constable marched a despondent, handcuffed man to where Penrose was standing.

"Mr Barrett," said Penrose without looking at the prisoner, "bank robbery is not in your usual line of work, is it…? What's a blackmailer like you doing here?" He expelled a puff of smoke. "They'll be wanting us out of the way so they can carry on their regular business." He pointed out a group of dockers and warehousemen. "Do you smoke?" He turned to face Barrett, who did not answer. "I want Healy and Godfrey. If I don't get them, everything falls on you. The whole lot… Off the record, and for the moment, that will mean all the murders will land in your lap. You'll be responsible for everything Morrish did… Just think of that. He's dead, and we've only got you. Still, if you're not inclined to help, neither am I… Between you and me, you're not capable of planning a job like this, and you probably never agreed to the murders, but you went along with them because you had no choice. Now, what can you tell me that I might find interesting?"

"I don't know who Healy is. He talks posh, has money, and he's clever... Huh, not clever enough, as I now know."

"Ruthless, would you say?"

"Yes, but he don't come across like that. He's a gentleman, right?"

"Superficially, it sounds like he is. What about Godfrey?"

"Look... I might have something, but I need something from you."

"Like what?"

"I don't get charged for the murders and..."

"There is no 'and.' We'll drop the murder charges in exchange for Godfrey, and we know about the Crescent house and his residence."

"Oh. Godfrey leased or rented Crescent to Healy, but he has another place. If I give you that, the one he thinks no one knows about, and you don't pick him up, then what happens?"

"We are bargaining in good faith, at least I am. We'll drop the murder charges if you give me his hideout. Take it or leave it, but I must have the address now if it's to be of any use."

Barrett looked up and down the wharf. "His hideout is in..."

Penrose took down the address. "Right, take him away," he said to the constable. "You lot! Come with me!" He called to a group of detectives and constables waiting by their vehicles. Penrose got in the first car, which tore away as soon as the doors were shut.

"Excuse me, Mr Stevenson," called Flora. "Did you dig this?"

She spoke to the gang member who was leading the little party through the final, meandering part of the tunnel and into the vault. Yardley was second in line, with his revolver drawn.

"No. They had foreigners do it," answered Stevenson.

"Oh... They were most industrious — quite mole-like, really."

"But they came to a sticky end," said Sophie, who had insisted on accompanying Flora. "This whole operation is founded on blood."

"I know that, but I'm only trying to be pleasant," said Flora.

"It will only be pleasant when this is all over."

"You're tired, aren't you? Try to buck up."

"There is a trail of bodies behind us. We're crawling through a filthy tunnel towards a time bomb, and it's six something in the blasted morning. How can you be so infernally chipper?"

"You're usually the one saying that sort of thing to me. Oh, how the tables have turned."

"Utter twaddle — you're tired, too."

"Yes. I'm like a sparkler nearing its end, but still heroically fizzing away. However, if my head is ever allowed to touch a pillow again, I must not be awakened for at least forty-eight hours."

"I feel like that, too, but before sleeping, I'm going to have the largest breakfast imaginable, and most definitely get cleaned up, of course."

"Ooh, breakfast — yes, please."

A rifleman remained behind to work the bellows. At that moment, the first police officers were emerging from the dark tunnel at the Walbrook to discover they had much work on their hands.

Stevenson entered the vault with a lantern, and Yardley followed. In the alcove beyond the iron bars, Archie and Laneford were instantly alert.

"Where's the light switch?" said Sophie.

"Here's the bomb," said Flora. "Gosh, it's massive... Look! A Big Ben alarm clock, just as I predicted!" The smile in her voice was evident to all.

Lord Laneford was at the gate. "Flora? Is that you?"

"Sidney!" She was overjoyed. "What are you doing here in the dark?"

"Primarily, waiting for an explosion. Explosives experts are on their way, and Drysdale and I are rather hoping they will arrive in time."

Archie switched on the lights.

"There are four of us here," said Yardley, "including Stevenson, a gang member who is now assisting us."

"Ah, do I understand you have been successful?" asked Archie.

"Yes," said Yardley. "The tunnel's clear and many of the gang captured."

"Excellent. You're locked in but, fortunately, I have a key."

"Hello, Archie," said Sophie. "We wondered where you had gone."

"The diplomatic headwinds abated." He opened the gate. "With that work at an end, and as I had nothing else to do, I came here."

Laneford and Archie joined the others.

"What do you think you're doing?" Laneford curtly asked Flora, who was studying the bomb's wiring.

"I'm about to diffuse the bomb. Can everyone stand back or go away, please?"

"You don't know anything about explosives," said Laneford.

"Not much, but I know my alarm clocks."

"May I interject with a proposal?" asked Archie. He had their attention. "I have suggestions based on three possible scenarios, which are as follows. We can leave the bomb, and it may explode. The army might arrive in time to disarm it. Miss Walton obviously feels sufficiently competent to deal with it now. Therefore, we have the options of a certain explosion, the possibility the army will arrive in time, and the risk that Miss Walton might make a mistake — a remote risk, I'm sure." He smiled at Flora.

"With trepidation, I vote for Miss Walton," said Sophie.

"And I vote for myself, without trepidation," said Flora.

"I'm staying, of course," said Sophie.

"Then, so am I," said Yardley.

"I'm not leaving, either," said Laneford.

"Well, doesn't that put me on the spot?" said Archie.

"You're all so utterly, utterly lovely but, please, buzz off, and I mean *all* of you."

"What about waiting for the explosives experts?" suggested Archie.

"The alarm is set for seven," began Flora, who looked at the alarm clock, "and Big Ben says 6:52. How much longer can we wait?"

"That clock has gained since we last looked at it," said Laneford.

Everyone consulted their watches.

"It's eight minutes fast," said Archie.

"Seven, old boy," said Yardley.

"Yes, seven minutes fast," said Sophie.

"I have nine," said Laneford.

"And I also have eight," said Flora. "Do you like my new watch, Sidney? I adore it." She showed it to him.

"Can we go, please?" asked Stevenson.

"Yes," said Archie. "Let's get out of the building, and there may still be some officials present who should also leave. As Miss Walton is the only one who even *feels* qualified, she must be given the chance. The rest of us shall leave."

As they went, Yardley said,

"Watch out for booby-traps."

"Yes, of course," said Flora, who immediately searched for extra wires.

"I love you," called Laneford.

"And I love you, too," said Flora.

"We're engaged," said Laneford, in answer to Yardley's quizzical look.

"Congratulations," said Yardley.

"We're going to a dining room!" shouted Sophie to Flora. "What do you want for breakfast!?"

"Everything they have!"

Left alone, Flora examined the wiring. She traced the wires by lifting the lid on the top box. It was half full of dynamite sticks and resting on top was an unfamiliar item beside the battery and the detonator.

"That must be the condenser thing Mr. Markowicz mentioned," she muttered while examining a cheap cigarette case unattached to anything. "But it's not attached?" She took it from the box and opened it. Inside was a note from King Lud which read, 'Well done!'

"Cheeky blighter." She set it aside.

Flora considered what she must do. First was to remove the back of the clock to see if it was booby-trapped or a second battery was inside, but then it hit her.

"I don't have a screwdriver!"

Flora tried her thumbnail in the screw slot, but it broke. She looked at the time and at her watch, her 'sixpence' watch, which gave her an idea. Flora took out the few coins in her pocket, but they were only pennies and half-crowns, too large for the slot. Now she was really frightened, because there were only three minutes remaining on the Big Ben alarm clock.

Broadbent-Wicks had rushed along the empty tunnel, through the empty cottage, and charged over to Moorgate to stand in the middle of the road, musing over why policemen always disappeared when you wanted one. Sent on a mission to recruit officers to find the grating in a basement of an unknown building smacked, he decided, of being on a fool's errand. Not that he blamed Mr Yardley, far from it, but he believed he had not thought the thing through because of his being busy at the time.

He wandered, staring at things around Moorgate near the Bank of England. He asked a pedestrian if he knew where to find the River Walbrook. It was a simple question, but the man just ignored him and continued on his way. BW sat down to rest on a sheltered doorstep. There were a few people about now, already on their way to work even at this early hour. The lights went on in a building further up Moorgate. The workday was beginning, and BW felt very dissatisfied with doing nothing. Just then, a door slowly opened in the darkened building across the street. A head popped out to peer up and down the road. *That's funny*, thought BW. Three men burdened with sacks came out quickly and BW leapt to his feet.

"What-ho!" he shouted. "I only want to ask a question!" and he hurried towards them.

They ignored him and walked away from the Bank.

"Please, I insist you stop... It's a very simple question... Where is the River Walbrook?" He was closing in on them. "I know it sounds barmy." He was walking right behind them now. "But I have a very good reason for asking. You see, you won't believe what's going on in a tunnel right underneath us... or, at least, it's definitely nearby somewhere... Please, I wish you'd stop."

"We shouldn't have stopped to clean up," said Gustav, who had the shotgun thrust in his belt under his jacket. "We must get rid of him,"

"That's right," said Mateo.

"He'll get tired," said Jimmy.

"I heard that. You know something, don't you? If there were a policeman about, I'd summon him."

Jimmy wheeled round. "For your own sake, go away at once."

Gustav pointed the shotgun at BW.

"If you put it like that, I shall. Are you Lud's men?"

"Lud?" queried Mateo.

"Lud is the ganef — pardon my Yiddish — who put the wind up King George and is emptying the gold out of the Bank of England."

"Who are you?" asked Jimmy.

"Ah, if you give me your names first, I'll give you mine... Is that shotgun loaded?"

"Yes," said Gustav.

"Then please point it somewhere else."

"We gotta go," said Mateo.

"You seem like a decent chap," said Jimmy. "How do you know so much?"

"I was in the tunnel... A-ha! I bet you were, too, and there's gold in your sacks. You came out through the grating, didn't you?"

The three men were surprised. "Lud, as you call him, although we've never met him, had us kidnapped and then blackmailed or otherwise forced us to work for him."

"He also threatened our families," said Mateo.

"Oh, I say, what an absolute rotter. And now you're escaping his evil clutches, what? Can't say I blame you."

"That's right, and we'd like to be on our way."

"I can see why. However, the gold belongs to the Bank of England. Why don't you give it to me, and then you can just toddle off? I'll make sure it's returned safely."

"We haven't been paid," said Mateo.

"That's awful," said BW, "and on top of everything else. Really, my heart goes out to you."

"The Bank has lots of gold," said Gustav. "They won't miss this."

"Oh, I know... But listen here. It looks like you're taking far too much for compensation. How many bars do you have?"

"Four," said Gustav.

"Don't you see? There are only three of you, so you must give one to me."

"But it's for a friend who was working with us," said Mateo.

"Ah, but he's not here, so he doesn't count."

There were more people passing by on their way to work.

"What do we do?" asked Gustav.

"Give him the bar, so we can go," said Jimmy.

"Really, Jimmy?" said Mateo.

"Is your name Jimmy? Mine's Broadbent-Wicks. Pleased to meet you." He extended his hand. Jimmy shook it and smiled.

"And you are?" BW asked Mateo, who declined to answer but shook hands, whereas Gustav did not.

With some reluctance, Mateo took a gold bar from his sack and gave it to BW.

"Thank you very much. My goodness, what a weight." The four men were attracting attention.

"My sack was getting heavy, anyway," said Mateo. "We have to go now."

"Well, cheerio, and all the best to you."

The others said goodbye and hurried off. BW thought for a moment about what to do with the bar. He decided he must return it to the Bank immediately. He marched away and unfortunately, or fortunately, missed three more men — Teddy Moss and his associates — also leaving by the same door of the same building, who were similarly burdened with sacks. BW cheerfully turned a corner, only to be brought up short by a large policeman standing in his way. They looked at each other. The constable noticed the gold bar and, despite all BW's entreaties and references to Miss King, arrested him on the spot.

"Hello, it's only me," called Lord Laneford, who had returned to the vault.

"Sixpence!" screamed Flora. "Give me a sixpence!"

"Good heavens," he said, hurrying through the gate while reaching for his change.

He had a single sixpence, which Flora nearly dropped when he gave it to her. She began unscrewing the back.

"Thank goodness you came back... Why did you?"

"I always meant to as soon as I had ensured the safe removal of all the others. Did you really think I would leave you to face this alone?"

"I wondered." She removed the back plate. "A-ha!"

"Good news, I take it?" He peered over her shoulder.

"No booby traps or second batteries... All I need do now is unscrew two wires... And then, most importantly, not let them touch each other or there'll be an extraordinarily big kaboom."

"Good grief!"

"Move away, please."

Laneford took a pace or two and began to survey the thousands of bars remaining in the vault. To keep his mind occupied, he started counting them, but quickly stopped. And, for the first time in a while, he prayed, finding it a much more profitable exercise under the circumstances.

"Ta-da! Ladies and gentlemen, for your consideration, delectation, and utter amazement, I hold here in my hand the one and only and completely original wicked device — now rendered harmless, I assure you — that was mere seconds away from blowing up the wealth of the nation." The alarm went off.

Laneford emitted an audible sigh of relief. "Well done, Flora, and I mean that sincerely. Should I shout for an encore?"

"Ha! Anyway, I never do encores — always leave them wanting more, that's my motto." She handed the alarm clock and battery to him. "And here is your sixpence back."

"Please, keep it as a memento. Never before in any field of human endeavour has a sixpence been so thoroughly well earned."

"Thank you. Actually, I'm starving and would like to eat, please."

"Allow me to escort you." He held out his arm.

She took his arm and, with her other hand, held up the coin. "There it is — the sixpence that saved the Bank of England."

"You can dine out on that story."

"No, I shan't do that."

"Just as well. They'll keep as much as possible of all this from the newspapers. They might even get away with a complete suppression of the story."

Laneford smiled and stood aside for her to ascend the stairs.

"It's a funny old business we're in," said Flora.

"Isn't that the truth?"

Chapter 33

Court Room

It was eleven o'clock Thursday morning and Sophie was back in the Bank of England, this time accompanied by Superintendent Penrose and Lord Laneford. Flora and Ada were asleep at White Lyon Yard and BW had gone missing. Sophie was not yet actually worried about him, because he apparently existed under some type of supernatural protection, but she was starting to be concerned.

In the grand, wood-panelled anteroom to the Court Room — where the Bank's directors routinely met — Sophie had an idea. She successfully made a telephone call by the instrument on the desk and then returned to her seat. Penrose sat in an adjacent chair with his eyes shut, although he was not asleep. Laneford looked out of a window.

"It's so quiet here," he said. "Pity."

"What is a pity?"

"That they're tearing it all down. Montagu Norman confirmed it as fact. The sad part is we shall never see the like of Soane's work again... He was a genius, you know. He fitted all the new buildings in with the old with such a degree of sympathy that... Sorry for being a bore."

"You're not at all boring," said Sophie.

"And you're being too kind." He returned to his seat.

A messenger flitted through the anteroom where they sat and approached the double-doors of the Court Room. He went in with a supreme show of quiet, efficient deference.

Through the doorway, Sophie glimpsed some directors sitting on either side of a long table.

"How many directors are there?"

"I'm not sure," said Laneford. "About twenty-five, I believe."

"I wonder what's taking them so long."

"As a group, they are slow and cautious. That hundreds of thousands of pounds in gold disappeared from their vault overnight is a shock hard for them to assimilate. Even though most of it has been recovered and the Bank's loss minimized, you can't blame them for being upset."

"No, of course not. How much was lost?"

"Nine bars were originally missing, but one was recovered and is now at Moor Lane Police Station. You won't believe this but, when they caught one of Lud's gang, he was walking along, without a care in the world, openly carrying a gold bar just outside the Bank. A constable saw the bar and took him in charge immediately."

"How on earth did the idiot think he would get away with it?"

"Who knows?"

They were quiet for a moment.

"Have you any suspicions as to which director is Lud?"

"None... Let me add that there are several directors whom it *cannot* be for different reasons... To be frank, I'm finding it hard to believe that any of them can be Lud, but one of them surely must be."

"There may be a way of telling — we shall see."

"Oh? What do you mean?"

"Just a very modest idea I've had. What we know about Lud is this: he is intelligent but with a mercurial mind, he is an excellent organizer, inventive, opportunistic, yet otherwise ordinary and unassuming. Added to that, he believes he could be the king of London. It's that last part that is so elusive. If he thoroughly considers himself to be a descendent of Lud, surely he would have told others. If not, how has he kept it to himself?"

"That is the question. When we go inside, we'll ask. Remember, though, none of the directors are yet aware we suspect one of their number. Be prepared for ruffled feathers and a bumpy ride as the insinuation becomes apparent to them."

The mood in the grand Court Room was as depressing as could be. No one smiled or quipped as they usually did. No director had sufficient energy to raise a point of order. The bankers were in the greyest and most solemn moment of their lives — almost wishing that the bomb had detonated. One would think they had lost all their valuables and families, and not just a measly matter of eight bars which loss the Bank's deep pockets could easily sustain — indeed, had already sustained in the manner of a gentleman of leisure flicking away a pesky fly from a tea table.

The gold was no longer of consequence. Now, it was all about the loss of reputation. That thieves had laid unwashed hands on the Bank's assets, sending them through sewers and rivers under tarpaulins to put them on a common tugboat, was horrendously shameful enough to the corporate mind of the directors, but that one orphaned bar should be carried through the streets and then lodged like a miscreant in a police station provided the curdled cream for the humble pie they were being forced to swallow. Yet there was an even worse calamity facing them that deepened the general gloom to a level which not even the Great War had achieved. This body of financial genius resolved the dilemma into a single, and as yet unanswerable, question: what would happen when everyone found out?

Stoically, they had approved the minutes of the last meeting. Mechanically, they had approved the list of promotions. Resignedly, they had signed off on the piffling shortages in the branch accounts. They had discussed, in a desultory way, the robbery which was the most extraordinary of items ever put to the board of directors, but they had got nowhere, except to agree that something must be done. Not mentioned were the warnings prior to the event, although several around the table were acutely aware they could have prevented this complete debacle had someone acted sooner.

That type of finger-pointing might come later, but not this morning. Today, they must stick together.

"We had better bring them in," said the Governor, Montagu Norman. A bell sounded in the anteroom to summon the visitors.

Many women work at the Bank of England. A few are supervisors, and some are secretaries to senior managers and department heads. However, never before had a woman attended a board of directors meeting in any capacity. When Laneford ushered Sophie into the room, some directors were so dumbstruck it was as if a heavy antlered moose had just wandered into their meeting. In a ragged fashion, a few rose out of curtesy, while one director was on the verge of savagely raising a point of order, certain everyone would back him in having Sophie removed.

"Gentlemen," said Norman, who stood up. "This is Lord Laneford, whom some of you know. Superintendent Penrose of Scotland Yard, and, um, Miss King..." He sensed the rising antipathy. "...She, along with her colleagues, helped thwart the robbery and was instrumental in preventing the detonation of the bomb. In fact, gentlemen, it should be noted and entered into the minutes that we are profoundly in her debt." He began clapping. The entire board followed suit, a few with evident reluctance. Sophie, flushed with embarrassment, was momentarily put off from surveying the men in her search for Lud. They all sat down, including the visitors. Sophie felt tiny in the glorious room. Another day its decoration would have fascinated her, but not today.

The meeting then entered a strange phase, so Sophie thought. The directors suddenly became animated and vociferous over what should and should not be recorded in the minutes. Then it occurred to her they were intent upon covering up the episode. Eventually, the directors voted, carrying the motion that the attack and robbery would henceforth be known in the Bank as The Shortage in the Gold Accounts, 1921 — thus it had been spoken, thus it was written, and thus it would be done.

Superintendent Penrose was invited to speak first to report on the current status of the police case. Until he had entered the room, he had seemed half asleep, but the moment he spoke, he was wide awake. He stated that a majority of the bank-robbers had been apprehended, although several remained at large. Penrose added that four had died because the criminals had fought among themselves. He mentioned Morrish and the string of murdered foreigners. While he spoke, Sophie studied the directors. Nineteen were present, and they were all attentive to what Penrose said, with none standing out as fearful, apprehensive, fidgety, or angry. Naturally, with such an array of individuals, Sophie found it easier to impute cunning and malice to some rather than to others. Well aware that looks could unfairly tell against a person, she tried to set her impressions aside. If Lud were present, and she was growing increasingly unsure of that, he blended in perfectly.

Penrose continued, relating that, although there was much work to be done, the criminal organization's hierarchy was now known to the police. He paused and looked around the room, as did Sophie. He then stated that there were four men at the top. Slowly, he brought out the names with explanations, often pausing.

He dealt with the two lieutenants first. He explained that a man named Morrish had murdered Lefty Watts, one of the leaders. Sophie's eyes darted quickly from face to face. Barrett was in custody and was helping the police with their enquiries. Again, he paused, and again, Sophie searched.

From information received, the police had gone to an address, a hideout, to apprehend the second in command, the man named Godfrey. He had narrowly escaped arrest by a matter of minutes and the police had instituted a nation-wide search while alerting the various port authorities and Croydon Aerodrome.

"Now we come to the man in charge," said Penrose, "the instigator who has troubled His Majesty and robbed the Bank of England. We know where to find him, but we don't know his real name." The longest pause occurred now. "May I put a question to the board, Mr. Norman?"

"Please," he said.

"Does anyone present know a Mr Healy?"

The directors looked indifferent, puzzled, or thoughtful. Several turned enquiringly to their colleagues, and finally one spoke.

"It appears not," said a director named Laidlaw. "Are you inferring something?"

"I don't believe I am."

"Oh."

Some directors understood only the face value of the exchange and dismissed it from their minds, but about half of them understood, at varying speeds of comprehension, that the police suspected a banker was behind the robbery, and possibly a director seated at the table.

"I should clarify the point," said Penrose. "Mr Healy is the brains behind the whole business. He also believes himself to be King Lud, whom you may have read about in the newspapers... Thank you, gentlemen."

Whispers ran around and across the table. There were head shakings and sour or apprehensive looks. Sophie tried to identify someone who was not engaged in the directors' process of rendering Penrose's inference of no consequence to themselves.

"Could the visitors be removed for a moment?" suggested a director to the Chair, Mr. Bonder. "We need to discuss a matter."

"May I speak?" said Laneford, also addressing the Chair.

"We'll hear Laneford first," said Bonder. "He is our guest, after all."

"Very well," said the director with reluctance.

Laneford started with a preamble that valued the significant importance of the Bank of England to the wellbeing of the nation and the Empire. He lauded bankers and, particularly, the directors present for their unfailing dedication to upholding the financial system to a level of integrity that was the envy of the world. His audience, even though accustomed to such platitudes, almost purred under these commendations which were being made despite the calamity that had beset them.

"What I have just stated," continued Laneford, "applies to every gentleman at this table. There is, however, growing evidence, which, I'm sure, will continue to accumulate over the coming days, that points to a person among us. Inside knowledge was obtained and used to facilitate the robbery. I am referring, of course, to the Bank's reconstruction plan."

"How do you know about that!?" exclaimed a director.

"Gentlemen," said Mr. Bonder, "I need not remind this august body of our rules of conduct. Please, allow Lord Laneford to finish... Pray continue, sir."

"I thank the Chair for the opportunity. I understand the vaults will be relocated and much improved, while Bullion Court is to be torn down to erect a larger building. You are upset that I should know this, and I agree with you. It should not have come to my knowledge. But bear this in mind, the only reason I know anything about your plans is because Healy or Lud, as we have been calling him, acted upon that same knowledge. How did he acquire it? Someone here told him. Either that, or a person present today is Healy. I believe Lud may be amongst us right now."

"This is outrageous!"

"Yes, it is," answered Laneford. "Someone has broken trust for personal gain. At best, it may have been an incautious word to the wrong individual, but I believe not. The level of inside knowledge demonstrated in the plan was far too precise to be attributed to a casual slip of the tongue. Lud or Healy acted on certain knowledge and developed his scheme based upon that foundation. I'll ask another question, if you'll allow it. When will work begin on the new vaults?"

He spoke into a profound silence.

"I propose we tell him," said the director named Laidlaw. "Does anyone second the motion?"

Two directors raised their hands.

"We'll put it to a vote, then," said the Chair. "Don't record this motion," he said to the Secretary.

They voted, the motion passed unanimously, and Governor Norman undertook the explanation.

"I shan't discuss anything of the plan beyond that which you have already asked, but I shall explain as fully as I can. All the preliminary work for the construction of the new vaults is complete. We are building them first before any of the more, um, obvious work commences. For such a large project, we invited His Majesty King George to a private, groundbreaking ceremony before we started. His unfortunate current troubles have delayed the ceremony, after which the builders were to begin their work the next day. I cannot say any more on the subject, other than this: as a precaution, because of the builders within the precincts, the bullion would have been removed from that vault very soon after the ceremony. That is all any of us..." he hesitated, reluctant to glance around the room, "...will say on the matter, and I'm sure you can appreciate why."

Several board members put up their hands and a squabble about procedure broke out, coupled with a renewed desire to clear the room.

"I'm sorry," said the Chair, "you'll have to leave."

"And I'm sorry, too," said Penrose. "I don't want to be heavy-handed," his Somerset accent was more pronounced than ever, "but there are detectives waitin' to interview all you good gentlemen, and I insist it's necessary you speak to them."

"I'm afraid, Superintendent Penrose, that isn't possible," said the Chair.

"Arrh, I see. Well, I can have a warrant here within half an hour, but I feel that is so un-necessary and avoidable really, when you could just agree to spare us a few minutes... That would be a wide-ranging warrant, by the way, and I can soon get the officers to execute it. Nothing personal, just standard police procedure, and I could have come with the warrant in my pocket."

"You're getting above your station," said a director.

"That just isn't true, sir. May I have your name, please?"

"Can you promise the interviews will be brief?" interrupted the Chair.

"No, I can't. We're after Healy and we've followed him here. Now, if we can, we must find him. Surely, you want him arrested?"

"Of course," said the Chair unenthusiastically. "There must be no fuss, though."

"Discretion is wanted — I understand that perfectly."

"Can we have a few minutes first, please?"

Penrose looked towards Laneford.

"I'll just point out that Miss King has yet to speak." Laneford beamed upon them. "I think you'll find her worthy of your attention."

"Thank you," said Sophie, before anyone interjected. Now standing, she swallowed hard and began. "Thank you, gentlemen, for this honour. What I'm about to say is directed at only one individual. I'm speaking, of course, to the man named Lud. You are clever, undeniably so. But you are loathsome, by any and every measure of human decency. You, Lud, are a degraded, detestable monster. You killed men as if they meant nothing, all but breaking their necks with your own hands. For that loss of life, you bear full responsibility."

While she spoke, Laneford and Penrose glanced around the group, even subtly repositioning themselves to get a better view of any individual who interested them.

"I cannot fathom how any *sane* person could be so obsessed with their forebears in this day and age. You are no king, that's for certain. That you are a descendent of the historical Lud is just your fancy. You have no proof, because there is no proof. If you possess documents, show them, and we will believe you. However, you know you don't have the necessary proofs. You live a lie of your own making, and the only wisdom you have ever demonstrated is not to have confided the product of your fevered imagination with any other person. You see, by now, a gentleman sitting here would have spoken up, declaring that you, Healy or Lud, had made a claim of descent from the ancient King Lud. So, then, it is a charade based on myth. All that stupid nonsense you perpetrated —

how you must have smiled to yourself when you threw the Royal Family into such a frightful panic. Did that please you?" Sophie smiled. "You aren't pleased now, of course, when all your labours have come to nothing. It has *all* come to nothing. By the way, the Royal Family conducted themselves superbly throughout everything. So, you failed there, too."

Sophie tried not to let her attention dwell on any particular individual, but there was one man who was so engrossed in what she said that she unwittingly looked at him more frequently than the rest.

"See this, Lud?" Sophie produced the sixpence Flora had used. "This is the sixpence that saved the Bank of England. A friend of mine, a woman with a sixpence, disarmed the time bomb with only a minute to spare." There were several comments made at this point. "An ordinary woman with an ordinary coin destroyed all your plans and dreams. The Bank of England is more indebted to her courage than to anyone else's. She is brave and you are a coward who now fears for his life. If you are present, Lud, and I think you are, redeem yourself. For once, be a gentleman and stand up."

No one moved. It is likely that if one person had applauded, all would have.

"Miss King, we have heard you," began Montagu Norman, "and I feel I speak for us all here when I say that you have forcefully and succinctly brought to our attention certain aspects of the situation that we may have overlooked. We will consider all these things in due course. May I say, in all sincerity, we thank you for speaking?" He turned to Penrose. "Superintendent, we must have our few minutes, and they will be all the more agonizing now."

"Ten minutes?" suggested Penrose.

"I think that will be sufficient."

On their way out, Sophie heard the man she had been staring at utter these words, "Thank goodness I'm Scottish. The way her eyes bored into me, even I was beginning to think I was the wretched Lud."

In the anteroom, all three of them compared notes. Laneford had a list of the directors' names, and he wrote their position at the table by the side of each one. They each gave their top two or three candidates for the personhood of Lud. Both Penrose and Laneford chose the same man as one of their choices.

"Lud's a smooth character," said Penrose.

"Do you still believe he's in there?" said Laneford

"I believe so. Evidence points that way. We'll know a little more after the interviews."

"I had such high hopes he'd give himself away," said Sophie.

"Bear this mind. He's 'uman, so he must have come close to it, but he also thinks differently. To have men murdered and be untroubled means he'll keep a straight face no matter what. But I'll tell you this, he's a name on my list, or I'll leave the force."

"How can you be so sure?" she asked.

Penrose laughed. "I've been a policeman for a very long time, and I'm seldom wrong when spotting a bad character... Do you think they'd mind if I smoked my pipe?"

"I think they would," said Sophie.

"I'll have to hold on then... How is Lady Shelling?"

"I thought you were asleep when I telephoned."

"Good, but watch out for people pretending to be asleep in future — not that I was altogether pretending." He put his pipe in his pocket. "I didn't quite catch *everything* you said, but you're up to something."

"Well, I had hoped..."

The doors suddenly opened, and a director requested they return to the Court Room.

It was obvious from the outset that the mood of the directors had changed completely. They were concerned with minutiae instead of the main issues. They wanted to know how soon the interviews could be finished. There clearly had been no reckoning amongst them, and so they, with the potential traitor included, turned a bland corporate face to the world — beginning with their visitors.

No one spoke at any length, but they all wanted to say something, and this took up time. Finally, Penrose was asked to bring in his detectives, and he was on the point of leaving when a messenger boy rushed in and waited to be recognized by the Chair.

"Yes?"

The boy approached, and in a high, clear, adenoidal voice announced his message. "Sir, Lady Shelling and her companion are desirous of being admitted to the Court Room at once, because Lady Shelling has information pertinent to the conclusion of the case... That's the first part, sir. The second part is as follows. If Lady Shelling and her companion are refused entry, they will go immediately to the editor of the Times to sell the story. Her ladyship said he will buy it because it's explosive, and he's been a delightful dinner guest at her house three times and is coming round again next week."

"Unbelievable," said the Chair.

"She said a bit more, sir, but I don't like to repeat it."

"Very judicious, and you have already said quite enough."

"I know of Lady Shelling," said a director. "We'd better let her in, or she'll keep her word."

"But how is she involved?" asked Montagu Norman.

"She's my aunt," said Sophie.

"Oh," said Norman.

"Tell Lady Shelling," said the Chair, "that it would be a pleasure to admit her to the Court Room, and would she be so kind as to join us?"

"Yes, sir." The messenger shot off.

They all waited — some silent, some whispering comments. Eventually, the messenger returned and opened the door. He smiled because Lady Shelling had just given him half a crown.

As soon as she entered, Sophie knew her aunt was going to do her little old lady routine. All the men stood up.

"How tiresome I must seem," began Lady Shelling, smiling and deliberately dithering, "disturbing all you busy gentlemen with my little petition." The directors made all the right responses. Her aunt then became, as Sophie considered it, revoltingly roguish. "I don't know what you must think of me." Sophie had a good idea what they thought.

"Here she is," said Aunt Bessie to Sophie, and she took Miss Daniell of the Soane Museum by the hand and pointed her towards Sophie. The rather alarmed and bemused lady approached.

"Hello, Miss Daniell," Sophie whispered to her. "Thank you for coming."

"Lady Shelling said it was imperative I came... She's rather forceful, isn't she?"

"Oh, yes. Just point him out when the time comes. We'll wait until they've settled down."

Everyone returned to their seats and waited for the Chair to restart the proceedings. Obviously, everyone was expecting something momentous from Aunt Bessie.

"Do you see him?" whispered Sophie.

"Yes," replied Miss Daniell.

Sophie spoke and the meeting resumed. "Mr. Norman, allow me to introduce Miss Daniell, Inspectress of the Soane Museum." Something like a shocked groan ran around the table because all the directors were suddenly conscious of the fact that they had secretly planned to demolish Soane's work. "She is not present in any connection with your plans... Although I'm sure that, as an important officer in the institution she represents, she would be happy to receive and exhibit any of the Bank's artefacts you may wish to bestow upon the museum," Sophie heard a muttered thank you from Miss Daniell, "she is, in fact, present here this morning to identify a person on the Soane Museum's Approved List. These are members who are permitted access to Sir John Soane's drawing collection. Within that collection are numerous architectural drawings, many of which were used during the construction of the current Bank of England complex. Lud accessed those drawings..."

Penrose coughed significantly.

"... but it is unnecessary to explain all of that now. The individual whom she can and will identify is Lud or Healy. Miss Daniell, however, knows him only as Mr Cassius Bell."

Sophie looked at Penrose, who smiled back. He ambled around the table.

"Miss Daniell, kindly point out the person you know as Cassius Bell."

She lifted her arm and pointed. "He is the one!"

Penrose put a hand on the man's shoulder. "John Laidlaw. I'm arresting you on the charges of robbery and conspiracy to murder. Do you wish to say anything in answer to the charges? You are not obliged to say anything unless you wish to do so, but whatever you say will be taken down in writing and may be given in evidence against you."

Chapter 34

King vs King

Every person in the Bank's Court Room believed John Laidlaw was guilty within seconds of his being arrested. He looked and acted the part of someone confronted with his crimes, in that his face became small and pinched and vitality left him as quickly as if he had been punched hard in the stomach. Laidlaw offered no defence, nor protested his innocence, and this confirmed his fellow directors in taking against him.

Superintendent Penrose requested a room to use, and the Governor directed him to a nearby office. On the way out with his prisoner, Penrose spoke to the messenger boy, who ran off at once on his errand.

"Miss King," said Miss Daniell. "I must leave now — the museum, you understand."

"Yes, of course. I can't express the gratitude I have for your coming so promptly."

"Oh, you know... It was unpleasant, but it had to be done. And thank you for sticking up for the museum." She glanced around the room. "Hopefully, your appeal didn't fall on deaf ears... Businessmen and financiers are always such decided persons."

"They are, and they are always busy. However, if you give them no rest, they'll be more inclined to help just so they can get some peace. You know, the squeaky wheel."

"Yes!" A light came into Miss Daniell's eyes.

They said goodbye. Aunt Bessie was about to leave, so Sophie went over to her.

"Walk with me a little way," said Aunt Bessie furtively looking about. They distanced themselves from the others who had broken up into small groups where they could express their feelings and state that they could never have believed it of old Laidlaw. "I am deeply troubled," said Aunt Bessie.

"What about? And thank you for acting so decisively upon my request to bring in Miss Daniell."

"Never mind all that, my gel. I've gone out on a perilous limb for you."

"Oh, dear, Auntie. Whatever have you done?"

"Well, I only met a Chief Editor of the Times once, and that was years ago. He's retired now. That is the perilous limb I'm dangling from for your sake."

"Auntie, don't tell me you fibbed?"

"This is not an occasion for levity. Will they find out?"

"Who, this lot?"

"Yes."

"No, absolutely they won't. They're afraid of the newspapers at present and will be careful what they say for months or even years to come."

"Is that right? Then I'm in the clear... How wonderful it turned out, then! What did you think of my performance?"

"It was rather marvellous, Auntie."

"Do you think so?" she was smiling. "I had to bully everyone, of course, and I so detest doing that. Still, overall, I found the exercise quite invigoratin'. I'm off to lunch now. You can join me if you wish."

"Thank you, but I want to stay here to find out about Laidlaw."

"I'm sure you do. Let me know what you discover... Sidney!"

She caught Lord Laneford's attention, and he came over. They greeted each other.

"I want a word while you escort me from this blessed bank. You'll save me from getting lost and poor old Sophie here from sending out the search parties." She took his arm, and they began walking. "I wish to discuss your engagement to Flora…"

"You know about it?"

Sophie heard her aunt's musical laugh.

Sophie waited for an hour and felt her weariness catching up with her. The Bank's board of directors and executives had all gone to lunch, so she sat alone in the Court Room. Two detectives and a constable had gone into the office, which Penrose and Laidlaw had entered earlier. So far, no one had emerged. She was thinking about leaving when the door opened. A detective approached to invite her into the office.

She sat in the seat Penrose offered her. Naturally, all her faculties concentrated upon Laidlaw. An average-looking man of ordinary stature, late forties, with a tanned complexion and greying hair which was very thin on top. He presented as the prosperous banker that he was in his formal, old-fashioned attire, but he was also healthy-looking, like someone who enjoyed long walks in all weathers. What initially surprised Sophie was that Laidlaw had regained his composure and even appeared to be enjoying the situation as though he relished his arrest.

"Forgive me for not rising, Miss King." He lifted an arm to show he was handcuffed to the chair. She did not answer.

Penrose signalled for the detectives and the constable to wait outside. When they had gone, he said quietly,

"You only have a few minutes."

"They're taking me to Scotland Yard," said Laidlaw. "The poor superintendent here knows exactly what charges to lay and would do so formally as soon as we entered the Yard, but several senior officials aren't quite so sure." He then grinned before whispering, "They don't know what to do with me. I present the authorities with a dilemma."

His behaviour puzzled Sophie, who glanced at Penrose, but he only gave an indifferent shrug.

"Penrose has very kindly allowed me to explain things. He must, in a way, because I'm to be handled with kid gloves for the time being... The authorities want me to plead guilty to certain charges to avoid a trial — mustn't air the dirty linen in public. With that being the case, I am accorded some latitude. Now I wanted to speak to you because I feel I must correct some of the erroneous ideas you hold concerning myself." While he spoke, he became increasingly smug.

"I'm prepared to hear you out," said Sophie, "but not if you're going to make a display of yourself. I'm not that interested in what you have to say."

Laidlaw stopped smiling and seemed at a loss for words, and this sudden change also puzzled Sophie, yet she asked,

"Why do you believe you're a descendent of King Lud?"

"But I don't!" he exclaimed as if reanimated.

"Then I don't understand..."

"I know you do not." He laughed, pleased.

Recognizing that Laidlaw was impatient to speak of himself, Sophie waited rather than answering him.

"I'm not the demented being you think I am, Miss King. Allow me to explain the matter to you."

"Please, do," she answered, humouring him.

"I come from Shropshire and was born into the senior branch of the Laidlaw family. On the family estate where I grew up, there is an old library containing many, many ancient texts relating to our family. Some are unique works of poetry in Welsh, Saxon, and Latin which the British Museum would consider itself fortunate to have." He paused as memories welled up.

"Although I have a younger sister, I grew up a lonely boy and, when I wasn't with my tutor, I was left to my own resources for entertainment... Long, solitary walks are and were my favourite exercise, while I simply detest sports, because they require no imagination. Now, Miss King, you will wonder what it is I contemplated on my walks over hills and by rivers from the age of twelve onwards."

Sophie found him irritating, but kept quiet.

"My other chief pursuit was reading the texts in the old library and struggling with ancient languages to extract the meanings." He stopped suddenly. "I could elaborate, but poor Penrose just consulted his watch as a reminder for me."

"You have five minutes," said the Superintendent.

"Five minutes..." Laidlaw consulted an impressive gold hunter watch. "Miss King, I was an impressionable, imaginative boy and inordinately proud of my family. Among the documents were many references to Lud or Lludd, as he should be called. Some histories were fanciful, but I read them as fact — inspiring facts for my juvenile mind... I see you have not guessed... The name Laidlaw means Lud's Law... Now, do you see?"

"I believe I see a glimmer."

"Of course, you do. Following the texts and my young fancy, I traced a lineage... It might even be true. By the time I went to university, I had set aside such a childish notion. But having once believed, and driven home such belief in my long walks, I have never really let go of them... Fond memories... But now, you wonder, where do the Saxe-Coburg and Gothas come in?" He moved his arm to gesture, but found it restrained. "I have no personal animosity against them, although I'm aggrieved that Germans and Danes sit on the throne. Romans, then Saxons, then Normans, and then descendants of Normans — when would a true Briton sit on the throne once more?" He laughed. "Never, of course." He glanced at Penrose and hurried his narrative.

"King Edward VII slighted me... Over what is immaterial."

Sophie perceived it was material to Laidlaw, but he was not about to explain what it was.

"After that, and despite an excellent career in banking, I became very frustrated with the status quo. My life looked too predictable. Too much of what happened last year would happen the next... I sought less than respectable people. I shall not mention them again because of the imminent legal proceedings. However, that I could be a respectable banker by day and a criminal by night was so exciting. It sounds lurid and pathetic, but that is because you have not lived in such a manner." He stopped, becoming aware for the first time that Sophie might have a story of her own. She was sitting there in front of him — the woman who had challenged him right where he thought he was safest, the person who had brought in the damning witness and evidence that would hang him, and the friend of another woman who had prevented the bomb from exploding. "Perhaps you do understand?"

"I can appreciate some of what you're saying, but I disagree with your motives."

"I see... Well, I organized a campaign of sorts against the Saxe-Coburg and Gothas — more in jest than anything — and was fortunate enough to be nearby when the suffragette bomb went off in Westminster Abbey. Then, when I wrote to the newspapers, my goodness how the dogs yapped and growled." He laughed briefly at his reminiscence.

"During the war, I was instrumental in bond issues and raising funds for the war effort. Last year, in the New Year's Honours List, they made Arthur Wheeler a baronet for his War Loans work. He was made a baronet!" Laidlaw became spiteful, "while I got *nothing!* I advised Wheeler frequently and raised four times the amount of money he did... And I got nothing?" With his free hand, he pointed savagely at Sophie. "I decided right then that I would exact my revenge." He pulled himself together enough to look bland again. "I decided I would scare the Saxe-Coburg and Gothas, to scare all of those flunkies who cluster around them. I never intended to harm George because the poor fool is at the mercy of his advisors. However, I wanted to scare the polluted system, though, oh, yes... Then the Bank reconstruction plans came up, and the work was approved by the board... Really, it was an opportunity too good to miss, and I knew just how to get the job done from beginning to end. Sadly, the plan went awry." His expression was one of only mild disappointment. "There was much more to the plan. After a robbery and an explosion, there would have been a loss of confidence in the Bank. I would have purchased city properties when the prices fell. When confidence in the Bank returned, as it was bound to, I would have made a greater fortune than the value of the gold." He looked hard at Sophie, as if expecting her to comment.

"Time's up," said Penrose.

"A few more minutes?" asked Laidlaw.

"No."

"I notice," said Sophie, "you have neglected to mention your part in murdering all those foreign gentlemen."

"They were the illiterate dregs of humanity, Miss King. It was necessary to my plan to remove them, and they aren't missed."

"I've never heard anything so vile or contemptible. You are a monster."

"W-what?" he stammered, shocked, as if she had slapped his face.

"Take him away," said Penrose to the other officers.

After Laidlaw had gone, Penrose and Sophie remained in the office for a moment.

"I don't understand," she said. "He seemed completely detached from reality."

"I've met his type before, that's why I short-listed him in the Court Room," said Penrose while packing his pipe. "As soon as you started your speech, I knew he was Lud. Did he upset you?"

"Yes... He made me angry more than anything. How could anyone be so wrapped up in himself and be so callous?"

"He explained that, you know. Solitary little lad with no one to correct his thinking. Nervy and sensitive to insults... A personal affront festers on the inside with that type, and they can't let go of it."

"But why did he tell all of that to me?"

"I'm no specialist in how a person's brain works, so take this as just my opinion." He opened a window, then lit his pipe. "I would say he wanted to impress you with how clever he is." He puffed out a cloud of smoke.

"Why on earth would he do that?"

"Because you're a very nice young lady, and he's an inveterate bachelor." He saw the horrified look on Sophie's face. "I don't doubt he finds it difficult to talk to a young lady. He wanted to impress you... Then you called him a monster." He sent another puff into the air. "You've upset him, you have." Penrose was almost smiling.

"What will happen to him now?"

Penrose's face darkened. "My guess is a deal will be worked out and he'll just do prison time."

"That doesn't seem right. You don't like that, do you?"

"No, I do not. There's one law for all, or should be. But there, people will want to save their reputations and sweep what they can under the carpet."

"Surely the newspapers..."

"No, Miss King. Not this time. In this instance, there's so much power and influence washing about that a body could drown in it. They'll feed the newspapers a story and that will be it. Laidlaw will get a heavy sentence for summat, but who knows what that'll be? The Bank of England might not even appear in the case. As for the rest of the gang, they'll be tried for robbing a bank, but again, it won't be this one... Probably one across the street."

"No!"

"I might be wrong, you know."

"When I give my testimony, I'll state exactly what happened."

"Who says you'll appear? And, if you do, you can only answer questions. They won't give you a soapbox to air your grievances."

"Huh... How often does this happen?"

"Not often. There were a few awkward things during the war that had to be hushed up."

"Do you agree with this behaviour?"

"No, it's unfair, as I said, but it shouldn't come as a surprise. Name me a civilization or empire in history where this type o' thing didn't happen and... I'll give up my pipe." He smiled now. "It's just 'uman nature."

"I knew you were going to say that."

Chapter 35

The Closing of the Book

"I've closed the betting for the Princess Mary Matrimonial Sweepstakes," said Aunt Bessie.

Sitting with her in her drawing room were Sophie, Flora, Ada, and BW.

"Have you? And why is that? asked Sophie.

"Because it is a dead certainty that she and Harry Lascelles shall marry. It was your evidence that helped inform my decision, but I also received confirmation from Harry's family. I suppose it's for the best — there was never much interest, anyway."

"I'm sure you'll find something else."

"I am toying with the idea of opening a book on which one of you, and perhaps Archibald, will marry first."

"Don't you dare," said Sophie.

"It was only something that crossed my mind."

"I'm not getting married," said BW, extremely concerned. "I don't know anyone to marry."

"One day you shall," said Aunt Bessie, "but I hadn't considered you for the...," she glanced at Sophie, "hypothetical running."

"That's a relief."

"I trust your spell in jail was not too frightful," said Aunt Bessie.

"Not really. They were rather rude at first, and I had to tell them to mind their manners. Then things got worse, and they turned belligerent. And they wouldn't believe me when I said the friend of a man named Jimmy had given me the gold bar because they had too much. But after Superintendent Penrose telephoned to find out how the gold bar came to be at the station, I got on marvellously with the police chappies. Do you know they were the team who won the gold medal for tug-of-war at the Olympics last year? From the size of them, I can see why. Anyway, they were most apologetic and then we had tea with rum in it. I felt quite woozy afterwards, but they were obviously hardened to it."

"Do you mean to say our policemen are drunk on duty?" asked Aunt Bessie.

"I doubt it's all of them, your ladyship. They said it keeps out the cold."

"But it's been warm for months," said Ada.

"I never thought of that," said BW. "Perhaps they were joking."

"This person Jimmy intrigues me," said Sophie. "Do you think he was only a tunneller rather than one of the gang?"

"That is entirely possible, Miss King. His companions were foreign, but Jimmy was a gentleman, yet they were all dressed like workmen."

"Does it matter?" asked Flora. "We've probably seen the last of them."

"I suppose not," said Sophie. "Superintendent Penrose mentioned that half a dozen men escaped with gold bars and, although they haven't been named, he believes that one of them is being protected by the men who were captured. He believes they are doing it out of fear. So, there is a violent criminal on the loose, but he doesn't sound like the man you met."

"No, Jimmy seemed like a decent fellow. The chap with the shotgun — he was thoroughly unpleasant and threatened me with it."

"You poor thing," said Sophie.

"Then who is Godfrey?" asked Aunt Bessie.

"A ringleader, Auntie. He's escaped, too. Oh, and by the way, they arrested a builder working on the scaffolding —

he was the lookout signalling to the man we now know as Barrett."

"Ah, that's the orange peel man," said Aunt Bessie.

"Do you think Lud is mad?" asked Flora.

"It's hard to say. He looks quite ordinary, but his thinking is all wrong. It's as if... It's as though there's nothing in his mind to stop him from doing what he wants once he's decided upon it. If he had decided to blow up the Royal Family, he would have carried out the attack with no compunction and no more justification than his own warped view of things... I hope there aren't too many of his type knocking about."

"There are probably more than we realize," said Flora.

"Yes," said Aunt Bessie. "With even a modicum of power or authority, a man, or a woman, can become tyrannical because they are only thinking of themselves. Pride and selfishness make some people cruel, which truism applies to domestic tyrants who abuse the others in a household up to a Laidlaw who will kill foreigners when they are no longer of use to him."

"And he had his man Morrish kill 'em, your ladyship," said Ada. "He was a bad'un an' all."

"Yes," said Aunt Bessie. "Do we know anything about Morrish?"

"They're looking into his past," said Sophie. "All they know at present is that he and his wife served Laidlaw for many years, and Morrish was in the army in 1914, but was invalided out with a head wound. I think this is where we will have to invent our own story because I'm given to understand Laidlaw will say nothing beyond the narrative the authorities are concocting for him. The peculiar man seems to relish the attention."

"He has an inferiority complex," said Flora. "They were quite fashionable before the war, but are passé now. The next big thing is we're all going to have egos. Professor Freud says so."

"What on earth is an ego?" asked Sophie.

"I've no idea," answered Flora, "but it will be immense when we find out. At a recent party, Sidney and I met the man who is translating Freud's latest work into English. He must have used the word ego twenty times and lost us completely. However, I've never seen anyone get so excited about something so incomprehensible. Therefore, it must be the next big thing in the intellectual line."

"It was tedious enough listening to politicians," said Aunt Bessie. "Are we now to be buttonholed by effervescent brain specialists also pretending to be intelligent? Such a change marks the end of genteel conversation. You'll see I'm right."

"Hopefully it won't be as bad as that," said Sophie, laughing.

"Ah! That's because you have hope of the future, whereas I have seen the past. Despite its shortcomings, which everyone is at pains to point out, the past was more beautiful and more romantic and more peacefully settled than the present. For every innovation, there is a loss of something old, and interesting, and we often lose by the exchange while convincin' ourselves we've never had it so good... I could go on, but I think I've made my point."

Hawkins entered to announce Archie Drysdale. After the initial greetings and a few moments of polite conversation, Archie congratulated the agents for a job well done. He then asked to see Sophie privately in the study.

"What's happened?" she asked once they were alone.

"I'll come to that. First, allow me to congratulate you personally. Had you not tenaciously stuck to your post, the Bank of England would have been prematurely demolished and people would have been badly injured or killed."

"Thank you, Archie. It was a most frustrating experience."

"I quite understand. As for Flora, she deserves more than a medal. She really has nerves of steel, don't you know?"

"In some situations. Now, had she seen a mouse in the vault, she would have run away screaming."

"Then we were most fortunate and I shall speak to her privately... Um, Sophie. How are you feeling?"

"All right. Tired, of course. I slept for an hour earlier, and will sleep well tonight, I'm sure. Why do you ask?"

"A job's come up..."

"Already! Don't they ever stop!?"

"No, and, while they are many, we are few. So, it's no rest for the wicked."

"That sentiment is entirely inappropriate. It should be no rest for the conscientious, thank you. What is this job?"

"A wealthy chap in South London is doing things he shouldn't. At least, we suspect him. Penrose can get you all in there next week. Will Monday be suitable?"

"If you could make it Tuesday or Wednesday, please. I must be in the office Monday or it will all go to pot, and I shall never be able to face Miss Jones again."

"We mustn't upset Miss Jones. I'm sure Wednesday will do."

"Can you give me some specifics? The others will ask questions."

"Industrial espionage, foreign powers, and a murder in the wooded part of Streatham Common. Penrose has all the details."

"I would have liked a week off from spying, just to catch my breath."

"Wouldn't we all, my dear old Soap? And it's espionage, if you please."

Epilogue

Within a week, a large envelope was delivered to the hotel where Lord Laneford was staying. He opened it and, as he had expected, found it contained a brief note to himself and four plain, sealed envelopes. The note politely requested he distribute the envelopes, each marked with a set of initials, at his earliest convenience. He hastened to comply, and so PK, NC, and BW each soon received an envelope containing a hundred-pound banknote with an accompanying typed message on plain paper simply stating, 'For services rendered.' GW also received the same envelope, the same typewritten message, but her banknote was a rare bird, indeed — a thousand-pound note — and Flora did not know whether to frame it, spend it, or save it for her marriage.

Another letter of interest arrived, only this time the addressee was in Brick Lane. Morrie opened the elegant, embossed envelope and almost fainted. Telling his assistant to mind the shop, he rushed down Brick Lane in his shirtsleeves, clutching the missive. He rushed up the stairs of Mrs Green's establishment shouting "Evie!"

She opened the door at the top of the stairs.

"Whatever's the matter?" she asked, then noticed the letter. "Are you bankrupt?"

"Meshuggenah! 'Course I'm not bankrupt. Look, look!" He thrust the letter into her hands for her to read, but then explained the contents while she read. He spoke with a growing note of satisfaction.

"Prince Edward wants a fitting. And at Buckingham Palace, no less. He wants me to make him suits... Three suits, Evie! Think of it!

"I'm trying to, but you're so noisy."

"Do I get to put 'By Royal Appointment' on, er, everything?"

"Does it say, 'By Royal Appointment?'" she waved the letter.

"No."

"Then you can't use it. It's a special warrant, but he can't give it because he's not the King."

"Ah, but he will be."

"Morrie — you don't have the warrant! When you have the warrant — then you have the warrant — but not until."

"What else does he say — I can't take it all in."

Evie Green muttered as she read the letter. "He says BW recommended you to him."

"BW? I don't know no... Wait a minute. That young man you sent me for a special price suit, he's a BW."

"There you are."

A young boy ran up the stairs.

"Zeyde, you're wanted in the shop. Two customers."

"Oh?" said Morrie, agreeably surprised. "I come."

"One of them," said the boy importantly, "is a Scotland Yard detective. He told me so."

"Benjamin, that's a terrible joke to play on your grandfather."

"I wouldn't joke like that, zeyde. He's a customer who's a policeman. What can I tell you? All I know is he wants a suit and says BW sent him."

"What!" Morrie hurried down the stairs.

"Mazel tov!" Mrs Green called after him.

In a small but well-decorated flat in the Bayswater Road area, a man and a woman sat at a small kitchen table drinking tea. It was late morning.

"What will you do now?" asked Godfrey.

"Back to the stage, I suppose." Lottie drew on her cigarette. "All my little dreams have come crashing down... He loved me, you know?"

"I know."

"Yes... I never had the faintest idea he was anything to do with the Bank of England... Are you sure it's him they've arrested?"

"It can't be anyone else. I got the one tip, but..." Godfrey laughed mirthlessly. "I can't help you anymore now. I can't even help myself."

"And what will you do?"

"I just don't know."

"Look," said Lottie. "You must face facts. It's all over. I've done it, you must, too. You can stay a little longer, but that's it. I don't have money coming in... Then there are the neighbours."

"They don't know I'm here."

"They will. You can be sure of that. Eventually, they'll find out and I can't take the risk. For a while, you can be my brother, after that they'll talk among themselves. Mr Godfrey, I'm in the clear. My hopes are dashed, but I can go on. Whereas you're wanted for murder and everything else. The longer you stay, the greater the chance I have of being caught and charged with those things I had nothing to do with."

"You were aware of them."

"But I had nothing to do with them. As far as knowing — I guessed some, but he never mentioned murders... Makes me feel sick thinking about them."

"I have no money, all my possessions are gone, and there are now no friends I can turn to."

"Stop it, will you? Don't take advantage of my good nature. You can stay two more days, but then you'll have to leave."

Godfrey turned his tired eyes towards her. She did not like to consider what he might be thinking and wished he would go immediately.

"Thank you," he said.

"More tea?"

"Yes."

Someone knocked on the door and they both stiffened, staring at each other with frightened eyes.

"See who it is," said Godfrey.

Lottie got up and, with dread, took the half-dozen steps to the door.

"Who is it?" she called before opening.

"Friend," said a man quietly. He dropped his voice even lower. "And not a copper. I have a proposition to make to you and your guest."

She cracked open the door and eyed the young man suspiciously.

"Neither of you know me," whispered Teddy Moss, "but you'll be glad to make my acquaintance."

"What's this about?"

"Open the door, and you'll find out."

She did so, and admitted the broad-shouldered, youthful man. Early twenties, she thought to herself.

"Nice little place you've got yourself, Miss Bradley. Done up very nice."

She shut the door. "How do you know who I am?"

"I make it my business to know everything that's important to me." He looked at her frankly. "Oh, I can see why he went for you. But they've tucked him away now, and I'm sorry for your upset. Did you care for him?"

"I did."

"Yeah, I like that. But it's time to move on, eh? Only you can't, because of your lodger. How are you, Mr Godfrey?"

He came out of the tiny kitchen.

"Who are you?"

"It's going to pay you to be polite to me... You see, you're a bit of a problem, and I have two ways of solving it. One, oh, you definitely don't want to hear about, but the other you do."

"I'm at a disadvantage..."

"Disadvantage, eh?" Moss laughed. "You've got to love the public school system. Your world's just fallen apart, and here you are at a disadvantage. Can't have that, can we?" He turned to Lottie. "Where do we sit, love?"

"The sitting room," said Lottie.

"Well, that makes sense."

Moss entered and seated himself. He looked around the boxy room at the pretty little things with which Lottie had adorned the place. The others also sat down.

"The feminine touch," said Moss appreciatively. "It's a beautiful thing."

"If you have something to say," said Godfrey, "I wish you'd get on with it."

"I'm sure you do. But I'm enjoying myself and I won't be hurried. You'll remember that, because I've got most of your artwork." He smiled.

"Where is it?"

"Whoa, Godfrey! Hold your horses!" He smiled. "We left the tunnel to get the van, and then went round to your lockup and got a vanload — had to leave some, though. We'd just loaded up and driven off when the police arrived. Lucky they didn't catch us, 'cause we had the gold with us as well." He laughed.

"But that's my property."

"*Was* your property. You can't sell the paintings, and can't even show your face. I'm looking after it now because without me you'd have nothing… You had a narrow escape — who d'ya think it was who tipped you off?"

"You?"

"I sent the kid round to your hideout with the note that got you out in time. What you don't know is that someone grassed — Barrett, probably."

"How did you know to do all of that?"

"I was down in the tunnel when it all started goin' wrong. I could see it was a flop, so I got out with what I could… It was Barrett who hired me, but I know Lefty… knew Lefty. Anyway, it was my boys who shifted the stuff out of number twelve. And it was me and a couple of others who were down in the tunnel, like I said. As soon as Morrish killed Lefty, I knew a lot more bad stuff was comin' — could feel it in me bones. So, I looked after number one. I'm smart, you see. I'd never bring in personal stuff like you did with that bloke, Jimmy Mitchell, or get all fancy with foreign criminals like Healy did. What's his real name, anyhow?"

"Laidlaw, or so we think."

"The Bank of England director they've just nicked? Well, well... "

"What happened to Mitchell?"

"Never you mind. That's all over and done with. You work for me now, and here's what you're goin' to do — shift the artwork abroad. You've got the contacts and will sell it for me. That way, you'll get half of what it sells for. Plus, there are a few situations where a bloke like you could be useful. Cheat me once, though, and you're dead. Take it or leave it."

"I'm to decide my fate now?"

"I'll give you ten minutes, so go sit in the kitchen and think it over, 'cause I want to talk to Miss Bradley in private. Oh, yes, I can put you in a safe house until we get your new identity sorted out. Go on, then, and shut the door after you."

Godfrey left the room.

"You seem to think of everything," said Lottie.

"If I don't, nobody else will." He stared at her for a moment. "Seems to me you've been left high and dry. Am I right?"

"Very high and very dry."

"A little birdie told me a woman pulled a very clever stunt for Healy in Buckingham Palace. Was that you?"

"There's no use in my denying it, I suppose."

"Actress, were you?"

"That's right."

"Going back to it?"

"I must."

"What if I told you I picked up a few other interesting things from number twelve?"

"I'm sure you did, but I wouldn't know what they were."

"I'll give Healy his due. He was a clever fella." Moss leaned forward and came quite close to her. He whispered, "You and him," he nodded towards the kitchen. "Anythin' goin' on there?"

"No, and there isn't likely to be, either," she whispered back.

"Keep it that way... Like I say, Healy was a great planner and real thinker. He left lots of drawings and notes, which are also in my possession. He's given me ideas... This is just for your ears only. I've taken over Lefty Watts' business, and some of Barrett's, as well. I also have my own business. And," his eyes glittered, "I was the only one who made anythin' out of the Bank job. I've taken over. It's all a shambles, but I'll make things work. You've got talents I can use and will pay for handsomely. If you want to be an actress, you can be one, but if you stick with me, you'll go places."

"It's all talk."

He leaned back in the chair and stared at her steadily. "Now, it is, yes. But the time for action will come soon enough. I don't have to boast or build myself up, but I'll make things happen all right."

"You're so sure."

"I have to be." Moss nodded towards the kitchen again. "He's goin' to say yes to my little proposition, because I'm his only hope, and that fact only has to sink in. Now, with you, it's different. You're free to do as you please. So how about we go to a classy restaurant? You look like you need cheering up and we can talk things over. Say yes, and you won't regret it. Say no, and I'll wish you good luck in your career."

"We're just going to talk business?" asked Lottie.

"I can't promise that," said Moss, "because I've taken a liking to you."

Godfrey returned to the sitting room.

"Very well, I agree to your proposal," he said.

"You're a wise man. Collect your things and go to the car parked outside. Andy will take you to the safe house." He paused for a moment. "You got any money?"

"Hardly anything," said Godfrey.

Moss took out his notecase and withdrew four five-pound notes. "This is an advance."

Godfrey struggled for a moment. He had been the one to give out money until recently, and now he, an unwilling mendicant, depended on the largesse of such a low man.

"Thank you," he said as he took the banknotes.

Lottie and Moss chatted until Godfrey was gone.

"Now, then," said Moss, "where were we?"

"You said we would talk things over in the restaurant," replied Lottie. "It sounded like it was only business. Give me some idea what it is you want me to do or I shan't go."

"I didn't quite say it was only business... Why not? You need to trust me, I can see that. Someone grassed, and that's why Laidlaw's plan went wrong. I keep wondering how the police found the tunnel, because everyone I could find who was watching for them said they never moved until the last minute. But someone had worked out that all the stuff with the Royal Family was a blind and that the real job was the Bank. I want to find out who it was. Was it the Yard, the Secret Service, the Palace, or was it someone else we don't know about? Because of what I mean to do, I have to know so that they don't cause trouble in the future."

"If the Palace was involved, then it could be Maxwell Handley."

"I don't know him... Can you talk to him?"

"Yes... It won't be easy."

"I'll pay you."

"How much?"

"We'll discuss that over dinner."

Lottie sat quietly for a moment, then arose with a smile. "I'll get changed"

The authorities limited the fallout from the whole affair. By keeping any mention of the Bank of England, the Royal Family, tunnelling operations, and murdered foreign seamen from the charges laid, they achieved two things. The first was the press was successfully kept in the dark. The second was that all those who were captured pleaded guilty to lesser charges in exchange for their silence in court. All of them got two years' imprisonment on explosive substance charges or for causing an affray or obstructing peace officers. The court appearances came up on different dates, and so they escaped undesirable Fleet Street attention.

A deal was reached with John Laidlaw, alias Healy, alias Cassius Bell. He was charged under the Larceny Act for operating an art theft ring, the evidence for which was a recovered Rembrandt and several other paintings. Laidlaw pled guilty to the charges and was sentenced to fourteen years' imprisonment, with the recommendation that a license for parole be issued after his having served seven years. Barrett was similarly sentenced. Maxwell Handley received two years for the part he played. Thus, the authorities suppressed the episode and avoided a sterling crisis.

Only two men escaped any charges, as it was deemed expedient to keep them out of the courtroom because they were too unintelligent and unpredictable to be controlled. One moonless night, those two men returned to Walbrook Wharves carrying tools. They trudged along the strand at low tide and stopped at the gaping hole where the Walbrook came out. The iron bars had not yet been repaired.

"Shall I light the lantern?" asked the younger.

"All right, but keep it turned down low," said Charlie, the elder.

"Oh, no... I dropped me matches in the water."

"You're not gettin' mine. Give it to me."

"Don't break the lantern, it's me ma's."

The elder lit it and stepped inside the tunnel.

"Really," said the younger, now holding the lantern, "we should light a fire."

"And tell every copper for miles we're down 'ere? What's the *matter* with you?"

"Nothin'. I like fires that's all, 'cause they're cheerful. What's the matter with *you*?"

"You." The elder stepped into the water in the tunnel.

"What? That don't make no sense."

"It does to me," said the elder. "Now shut up." He began probing beneath the muddy bottom with a steel rod.

"*You* shut up."

"Only if you shut up first."

"All right."

The elder probed systematically in the mud along the wall where he believed the gold bar to be.

"I don't get it," said the elder.

"What?" The young man turned a puzzled face to the elder. "What we lookin' for, anyway?"

"Just something I dropped... Ooh... P'rhaps, just p'rhaps, it's settled deeper in the mud and slid a bit." He started probing again.

"I dunno what you're talkin' abaht. Why don't you never tell me nothin'?"

"Quiet a moment... There's no sayin' how far it's gone."

"You're mad, you are."

"Hello..." The elder used a spade to dig down through the ooze and gravel. "Hello-a-lo, and what do we have here?"

"What?" The younger man leaned closer. "Oh, it's a gold bar."

Charlie washed the bar in the filthy water, then quickly scanned the surroundings.

"Give me the sack."

"I couldn't find one, so I brought a tea towel. It's all right to use, 'cause it's got a big 'ole in it."

"So, help me... A tea towel?" He sighed. "We have to hide this, so take off your jacket."

"Use your own. Why would I give you me jacket when I don't have a bar?"

"How thick can you be?" He paused a moment. "I'll give you a quid for your jacket, but I'll owe it to you."

"All right." He removed his jacket and handed it over. "How much is that bar worth, then?"

The elder wrapped it in the jacket.

"I dunno exactly... How much do you think it's worth?"

"Well, I don't want one, so I wouldn't give you nothin' for it, but them blokes who got done wanted 'em bad... I dunno — a tenner?"

The elder shook with laughter while struggling to say, "So help me... I'm sorely tempted."

OTHER BOOKS BY G J BELLAMY

SOPHIE BURGOYNE SERIES
Secret Agency
Lady Holme
Dredemere Castle
Chertsey Park
Primrose Hill
An Old Affair
Royal Fright

BRENT UMBER SERIES
Death between the Vines
Death in a Restaurant
Death of a Detective
Death at Hill Hall
Death on the Slopes
Death of a Narcissist